MYSTERY WRITERS OF AMERICA PRESENTS

In the Shadow of the Master

Also by Michael Connelly

FICTION

The Brass Verdict

The Overlook

Echo Park

The Lincoln Lawyer

The Closers

The Narrows

Lost Light

Chasing the Dime

City of Bones

A Darkness More Than Night

Void Moon

Angels Flight

Blood Work

Trunk Music

The Poet

The Last Coyote

The Concrete Blonde

The Black Ice

The Black Echo

NONFICTION

Crime Beat: A Decade of Covering Cops and Killers

AS GUEST EDITOR

The Blue Religion

Murder in Vegas

The Best American Mystery Stories 2003

✦ *Mystery Writers of America Presents* ✦

IN THE SHADOW OF THE

Master

Classic Tales by Edgar Allan Poe and Essays by

Jeffery Deaver, Nelson DeMille,

Tess Gerritsen, Sue Grafton, Stephen King,

Laura Lippman, Lisa Scottoline,

and Thirteen Others

EDITED BY

Michael Connelly

ILLUSTRATIONS BY

Harry Clarke

wm

WILLIAM MORROW

An Imprint of HarperCollinsPublishers

FIRST EDITION

Designed by Jennifer Ann Daddio / Bookmark Design & Media Inc.

Library of Congress Cataloging-in-Publication Data

Poe, Edgar Allan, 1809–1849.
   In the shadow of the master : classic tales / by Edgar Allan Poe ; and essays by Jeffery Deaver . . . [et al.] ; edited by Michael Connelly ; illustrations by Harry Clarke. — 1st ed.
      p. cm.
   Title appears on item as: Mystery Writers of America presents In the shadow of the master
      ISBN 978-0-06-169039-6
   1. Horror tales, American. 2. Poe, Edgar Allan, 1809–1849. I. Deaver, Jeffery. II. Connelly, Michael, 1956–. III. Mystery Writers of America. IV. Title. V. Title: Mystery Writers of America presents In the shadow of the master.

PS2602.C66 2008
813'.3—dc22   2008025031

09 10 11 12 13 ov/qw 10 9 8 7 6 5 4 3 2 1

Contents

......

Contents

Contents

About Edgar Allan Poe

. . . . . .

Edgar Allan Poe (1809–49), while a mainstay of literature today and the recognized creator of the modern genres of horror and mystery fiction, spent much of his life chasing the public and literary acclaim he craved.

Born to David and Elizabeth Poe, young Edgar knew hardship from an early age. His father abandoned the family a year after Edgar's birth, and his mother died of consumption one year later. Taken in, but never legally adopted, by John and Frances Allan, Edgar traveled with his new family to England in 1815, then continued on alone to study in Irvine, Scotland, for a short time. Afterward he studied in Chelsea, then a suburb of London until 1817. He returned to Virginia in 1820, and in 1826 he enrolled in the newly founded University of Virginia to study languages. During his college years, he became estranged from his foster father, claiming that John Allan didn't send him enough money to live on, but the reality was that Poe was losing the money on gambling.

In 1827 Edgar enlisted in the U.S. Army at age eighteen, claiming he was twenty-two years old. It was during this time that he began publishing his poems, including an early collection, *Tamerlane and Other Poems*, printed under the byline "A Bostonian." He attained the rank of sergeant major of artillery and expressed a desire to attend West Point for officer training. Once accepted to the academy, however, he was dismissed for not attending classes and formations.

After the death of his brother, Henry, in 1831, Edgar decided to try making a living as an author. He was the first well-known American to make such an attempt, but because of the lack of an international copyright law and the economic effects of the Panic of 1837, he was often forced to ask for the monies owed him and compelled to seek other assistance. After winning a literary prize for his story "Manuscript Found in a Bottle," he was hired as the assistant editor of the *Southern Literary Messenger*, but he was fired several weeks later for repeated drunkenness. This pattern of dissipation would haunt Poe for the rest of his life.

After marrying his cousin, Virginia Clemm, in 1835, Poe returned to the *Messenger*, where he worked for the next two years, seeing its circulation rise to 3,500 copies, from 700. His only full-length novel, *The Narrative of Arthur Gordon Pym of Nantucket*, was published in 1838 to wide review and acclaim, although once again Poe received little profit from his work. The year after saw the publication of his first short story collection, *Tales of the Grotesque and Arabesque*, which received mixed reviews and sold poorly. He left the *Messenger* and worked at *Burton's Gentleman's Magazine* and *Graham's Magazine* before announcing that he would start his own literary publication, *The Penn*, later to be titled *The Stylus*. Tragically, it never came to print.

Virginia first showed signs of tuberculosis in 1842, and her gradual decline over the next five years caused Edgar to drink even more heavily. The one bright spot in this time was the publication in 1845 of one of his most famous works, "The Raven," which brought him widespread acclaim; unfortunately, he was paid only nine dollars for the poem itself.

Shortly afterward, the Poes moved to a cottage in the Fordham section of the Bronx, New York, where Virginia died in 1847. Increasingly unstable, Edgar tried to secure a position in government, unsuccessfully courted the poet Sarah Helen Whitman, and eventually returned to Richmond, Virginia, to rekindle a relationship with Sarah Royster, a childhood sweetheart.

The circumstances surrounding Poe's death remain shrouded in mystery. Found on the streets of Baltimore, Maryland, delirious and dressed in clothes that weren't his, Poe was taken to Washington College Hospital, where he died on October 7, 1849. It was reported that his last words were "Lord help my poor soul," but this cannot be proven as all records surrounding his death have been lost. Edgar Allan Poe's death has been attributed to various causes, including delirium tremens, heart disease, epilepsy, or meningeal inflammation. He was buried in a Baltimore cemetery, where a mysterious figure has toasted Poe on the anniversary of his birth since 1949 by leaving cognac and three roses at his headstone.

Recognized primarily as a literary critic during his lifetime, Poe's work became popular in Europe after his death owing mainly to the translations of his stories and poems by Charles Baudelaire. Sir Arthur Conan Doyle cited him as the creator of the mystery short story with his C. Auguste Dupin stories, saying, "Where was the detective story until Poe breathed the breath of life into it?" Poe's work also inspired later authors of science fiction and fantasy, including Jules Verne and H. G. Wells. Today he is recognized as a literary master who both created new genres and reinvigorated old ones with a unique combination of story and style.

About the Mystery Writers of America's Edgar Award

· · · · · ·

In 1945, when the Mystery Writers of America was just being formed, the founders of the organization decided to give an award for the best first American mystery novel, as well as awards for the best and worst mystery reviews of the year. Initially they were going to call it the Edmund Wilson Memorial Award (partly in revenge for Wilson's disdain for the genre), but calmer heads prevailed. Although it is unknown exactly who came up with the idea of naming the award for "the Father of the Detective Story," it was an immediate success, and the "Edgar" was created.

The first Edgar Award was bestowed in 1946 on Julian Fast for his debut novel, *Watchful at Night,* and in the more than fifty years since, the stylized ceramic bust of the great author has become one of the top prizes in the field of mystery fiction. The award categories, in addition to Best First Novel, have been expanded over time to include Best Novel, Best Short Story, Best Paperback Original, Best Young Adult Novel, Best Juvenile Novel, Best Fact Crime, Best Critical/Biographical, Best Play, Best Television Episode, and Best Motion Picture. The Edgar has been won by many noted authors in the field, including Stuart Kaminsky, Michael Connelly, T. Jefferson Parker, Jan Burke, Lisa Scottoline, Laura Lippman, Laurie R. King, Steve Hamilton, Peter Robinson, Edward D. Hoch, S. J. Rozan, Thomas H. Cook, Joseph Wambaugh, Jeffery Deaver, Rupert Holmes, Anne Perry, Patricia Cornwell, Ira Levin, Thomas Harris, Dick Francis, Ruth Rendell, Lawrence Block, Elmore Leonard, Ken Follett, Frederick Forsyth, Harlan Ellison, and many, many others.

About the Illustrator

......

Harry Clarke (1889–1931) was a renowned stained-glass artist of the early twentieth century, and several examples of his work still exist today, most notably at the Honan Chapel in Cork, Ireland. It was during his education at Dublin Art School that he developed an interest in book illustration. After winning the gold medal in the stained-glass category at the 1910 Board of Education National Competition, he traveled to London to find work as an illustrator.

His first commission—illustrating a trade and deluxe edition of *Fairy Tales by Hans Christian Andersen*—came from George Harrap in 1913. For the next six years, he worked at the same time on illustrating the Edgar Allan Poe collection *Tales of Mystery and Imagination*. Clarke used the techniques he learned from working in stained glass on his macabre illustrations of Poe's dark stories. The resulting work, Poe's dark vision brought to stunning life by Clarke's detailed imagery, created a sensation when the first edition was published in October 1919. Other books that Clarke illustrated include *The Years at the Spring, Fairy Tales by Charles Perrault,* Goethe's *Faust,* and *Selected Poems of Algernon Charles Swinburne*. He also created more than 130 stained-glass windows, one of which, "The Baptism of St. Patrick," was selected for exhibition at the Louvre in Paris.

Unfortunately, the unceasing, grueling pace of his work, perhaps along with the toxic chemicals used in the stained-glass process, cut his life short. In 1931, at the age of forty-one, Harry Clarke died in Switzerland while trying to recover from tuberculosis.

What Poe Hath Wrought

· · · · · ·

BY MICHAEL CONNELLY

Happy birthday, Edgar Allan Poe. Seems strange using that name and that word "happy" in the same sentence. A tragic and morose figure in his short life, Poe is celebrated today, two hundred years after his birth, as the mad genius who started it all rolling in the genre of mystery fiction. His influence in other genres and fields of entertainment—from poetry to music to film—is incalculable. To put it simply, Edgar Allan Poe's work has echoed loudly across two centuries and will undoubtedly echo for at least two more. He walked across a field of pristine grass, not a single blade broken. Today that path has been worn down to a deep trench that crosses the imagination of the whole world. If you look at best-seller lists, movie charts, and television ratings, they are simply dominated by the mystery genre and its many offshoots. The tendrils of imagination behind these contemporary works can be traced all the way back to Poe.

This collection is presented to you by the Mystery Writers of America. Since day one this organization has held Edgar Allan Poe as its symbol of excellence. The annual award bestowed by the

MWA on the authors of books, television shows, and films of merit is a bust of Edgar Allan Poe. It is a caricature, and what is most notable about it is that the figure's head is oversized to the point of being as wide as his shoulders. Having the honor of guest-editing this collection of stories and essays, I now realize why Edgar's head is so big.

I'm not going to get analytical about Poe's life or work here. I leave that to his disciples. Gathered here with his most notable works are the long and short thoughts of those who follow Poe—the writers who directly or not so directly have taken inspiration from him. These are Edgar winners, best-selling authors, and practitioners of the short story. From Stephen King, who writes so eloquently of his connection to Poe, to Sue Grafton, who lovingly, grudgingly, gives Poe his due, to the late Edward Hoch, who penned over nine hundred seventy-five short stories, these writers are the modern masters of the world Poe created. The idea here is simple. This is a birthday party. The twenty guests invited here by the Mystery Writers of America have come to honor Edgar Allan Poe on his two hundredth birthday. We celebrate his work, and we celebrate all that his work has wrought.

I wonder what Poe would think of this. My guess is that it would give him a big head.

MYSTERY WRITERS OF AMERICA PRESENTS

In the Shadow of the Master

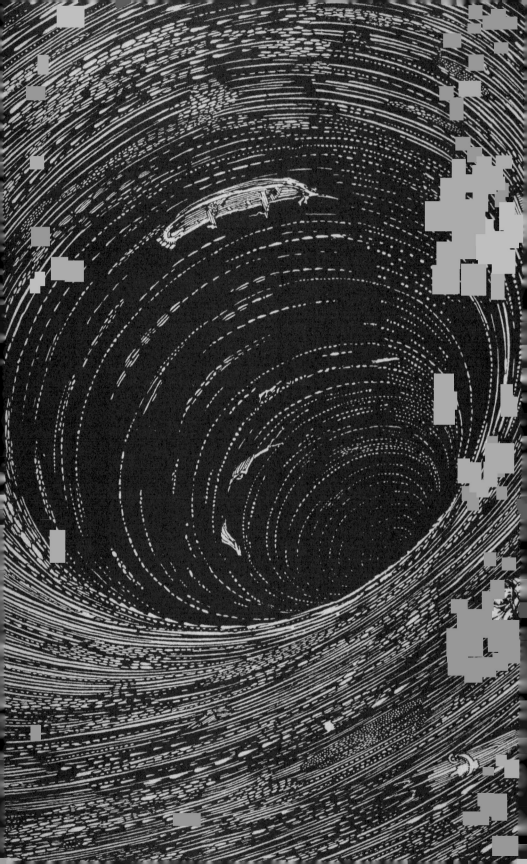

A Descent into the Maelström

> The ways of God in Nature, as in Providence, are not as our ways;
> nor are the models that we frame any way commensurate to the
> vastness, profundity, and unsearchableness of His works, *which
> have a depth in them greater than the well of Democritus.*

—JOSEPH GLANVILL

WE HAD NOW REACHED the summit of the loftiest crag.
For some minutes the old man seemed too much exhausted
to speak. "Not long ago," said he at length, "and I could
have guided you on this route as well as the youngest of
my sons; but, about three years past, there happened to me

an event such as never happened before to mortal man—or at least such as no man ever survived to tell of—and the six hours of deadly terror which I then endured have broken me up body and soul. You suppose me a *very* old man—but I am not. It took less than a single day to change these hairs from a jetty black to white, to weaken my limbs, and to unstring my nerves, so that I tremble at the least exertion, and am frightened at a shadow. Do you know I can scarcely look over this little cliff without getting giddy?"

The "little cliff," upon whose edge he had so carelessly thrown himself down to rest that the weightier portion of his body hung over it, while he was only kept from falling by the tenure of his elbow on its extreme and slippery edge—this "little cliff" arose, a sheer unobstructed precipice of black shining rock, some fifteen or sixteen hundred feet from the world of crags beneath us. Nothing would have tempted me to be within half a dozen yards of its brink. In truth so deeply was I excited by the perilous position of my companion, that I fell at full length upon the ground, clung to the shrubs around me, and dared not even glance upward at the sky—while I struggled in vain to divest myself of the idea that the very foundations of the mountain were in danger from the fury of the winds. It was long before I could reason myself into sufficient courage to sit up and look out into the distance.

"You must get over these fancies," said the guide, "for I have brought you here that you might have the best possible view of the scene of that event I mentioned—and to tell you the whole story with the spot just under your eye."

"We are now," he continued, in that particularizing manner which distinguished him—"we are now close upon the Norwegian coast—in the sixty-eighth degree of latitude—in the great province of Nordland—and in the dreary district of Lofoden. The mountain upon whose top we sit is Helseggen, the Cloudy. Now raise yourself up a little higher—hold on to the grass if you feel giddy—so—and look out, beyond the belt of vapor beneath us, into the sea."

I looked dizzily, and beheld a wide expanse of ocean, whose waters wore so inky a hue as to bring at once to my mind the Nubian geographer's account of the *Mare Tenebrarum.* A panorama more deplorably desolate no human imagination can conceive. To the right and left, as far as the eye could reach, there lay outstretched, like ramparts of the world, lines of horridly black and beetling cliff, whose character of gloom was but the more forcibly illustrated by the surf which reared high up against its white and ghastly crest, howling and shrieking for ever. Just opposite the promontory upon whose apex we were placed, and at a distance of some five or six miles out at sea, there was visible a small, bleak-looking island; or, more properly, its position was discernible through the wilderness of surge in which it was enveloped. About two miles nearer the land, arose another of smaller size, hideously craggy and barren, and encompassed at various intervals by a cluster of dark rocks.

The appearance of the ocean, in the space between the more distant island and the shore, had something very unusual about it. Although, at the time, so strong a gale was blowing landward that a brig in the remote offing lay to under a double-reefed trysail, and constantly plunged her whole hull out of sight, still there was here nothing like a regular swell, but only a short, quick, angry cross dashing of water in every direction—as well in the teeth of the wind as otherwise. Of foam there was little except in the immediate vicinity of the rocks.

"The island in the distance," resumed the old man, "is called by the Norwegians Vurrgh. The one midway is Moskoe. That a mile to the northward is Ambaaren. Yonder are Islesen, Hotholm, Keildhelm, Suarven, and Buckholm. Farther off—between Moskoe and Vurrgh—are Otterholm, Flimen, Sandflesen, and Stockholm. These are the true names of the places—but why it has been thought necessary to name them at all, is more than either you or I can understand. Do you hear any thing? Do you see any change in the water?"

We had now been about ten minutes upon the top of Helseggen, to which we had ascended from the interior of Lofoden, so that we had caught no glimpse of the sea until it had burst upon us from the summit. As the old man spoke, I became aware of a loud and gradually increasing sound, like the moaning of a vast herd of buffaloes upon an American prairie; and at the same moment I perceived that what seamen term the *chopping* character of the ocean beneath us, was rapidly changing into a current which set to the eastward. Even while I gazed, this current acquired a monstrous velocity. Each moment added to its speed—to its headlong impetuosity. In five minutes the whole sea, as far as Vurrgh, was lashed into ungovernable fury; but it was between Moskoe and the coast that the main uproar held its sway. Here the vast bed of the waters, seamed and scarred into a thousand conflicting channels, burst suddenly into phrensied convulsion—heaving, boiling, hissing—gyrating in gigantic and innumerable vortices, and all whirling and plunging on to the eastward with a rapidity which water never elsewhere assumes except in precipitous descents.

In a few minutes more, there came over the scene another radical alteration. The general surface grew somewhat more smooth, and the whirlpools, one by one, disappeared, while prodigious streaks of foam became apparent where none had been seen before. These streaks, at length, spreading out to a great distance, and entering into combination, took unto themselves the gyratory motion of the subsided vortices, and seemed to form the germ of another more vast. Suddenly—very suddenly—this assumed a distinct and definite existence, in a circle of more than a mile in diameter. The edge of the whirl was represented by a broad belt of gleaming spray; but no particle of this slipped into the mouth of the terrific funnel, whose interior, as far as the eye could fathom it, was a smooth, shining, and jet-black wall of water, inclined to the horizon at an angle of some forty-five degrees, speeding dizzily round and round with a swaying and sweltering motion, and sending forth to the winds an appalling voice, half shriek, half roar, such as not even the mighty cataract of Niagara ever lifts up in its agony to Heaven.

The mountain trembled to its very base, and the rock rocked. I threw myself upon my face, and clung to the scant herbage in an excess of nervous agitation.

"This," said I at length, to the old man — "this *can* be nothing else than the great whirlpool of the Maelström."

"So it is sometimes termed," said he. "We Norwegians call it the Moskoe-ström, from the island of Moskoe in the midway."

The ordinary account of this vortex had by no means prepared me for what I saw. That of Jonas Ramus, which is perhaps the most circumstantial of any, cannot impart the faintest conception either of the magnificence, or of the horror of the scene — or of the wild bewildering sense of *the novel* which confounds the beholder. I am not sure from what point of view the writer in question surveyed it, nor at what time; but it could neither have been from the summit of Helseggen, nor during a storm. There are some passages of his description, nevertheless, which may be quoted for their details, although their effect is exceedingly feeble in conveying an impression of the spectacle.

"Between Lofoden and Moskoe," he says, "the depth of the water is between thirty-six and forty fathoms; but on the other side, toward Ver (Vurrgh) this depth decreases so as not to afford a convenient passage for a vessel, without the risk of splitting on the rocks, which happens even in the calmest weather. When it is flood, the stream runs up the country between Lofoden and Moskoe with a boisterous rapidity; but the roar of its impetuous ebb to the sea is scarce equalled by the loudest and most dreadful cataracts; the noise being heard several leagues off, and the vortices or pits are of such an extent and depth, that if a ship comes within its attraction, it is inevitably absorbed and carried down to the bottom, and there beat to pieces against the rocks; and when the water relaxes, the fragments thereof are thrown up again. But these intervals of tranquility are only at the turn of the ebb and flood, and in calm weather, and last but a quarter of an hour, its violence gradually returning. When the stream is most boisterous, and its fury heightened by a storm, it is dangerous to come within a Norway mile of it. Boats, yachts, and ships have been carried away by not guarding against it before they were within its reach. It likewise happens frequently, that whales come too near the stream, and are overpowered by its violence; and then it is impossible to describe their howlings and bellowings in their fruitless struggles to disengage themselves. A bear once, attempting to swim from Lofoden to Moskoe, was caught by the stream and borne down, while he roared terribly, so as to be heard on shore. Large stocks of firs and pine trees, after being absorbed by the current, rise again broken and torn to such a degree as if bristles grew upon them. This plainly shows the bottom to consist of craggy rocks, among which they are whirled to and fro. This stream is regulated by the flux and reflux of the sea—it being constantly high and low water every six hours. In the year 1645, early in the morning of Sexagesima Sunday, it raged with such noise and impetuosity that the very stones of the houses on the coast fell to the ground."

In regard to the depth of the water, I could not see how this could have been ascertained at all in the immediate vicinity of the vortex. The "forty fathoms" must have reference only to portions of the channel close upon the shore either of Moskoe or Lofoden. The depth in the centre of the Moskoe-ström must be unmeasurably greater; and no better proof of this fact is necessary than can be obtained from even the sidelong glance into the abyss of the whirl which may be had from the highest crag of Helseggen. Looking down from this pinnacle upon the howling Phlegethon below, I could not help smiling at the simplicity with which the honest Jonas Ramus records, as a matter difficult of belief, the anecdotes of the whales and the bears, for it appeared to me, in fact, a self-evident thing, that the largest ship of the line in existence, coming within the influence of that deadly attraction, could resist it as little as a feather the hurricane, and must disappear bodily and at once.

The attempts to account for the phenomenon—some of which I remember, seemed to me sufficiently plausible in perusal—now wore a very different and unsatisfactory aspect. The idea generally received is that this, as well as three smaller vortices among the Ferroe islands, "have no other cause than the collision of waves rising and falling, at flux and reflux, against a ridge of rocks and shelves, which confines the water so that it precipitates itself like a cataract; and thus the higher the flood rises, the deeper must the fall be, and the natural result of all is a whirlpool or vortex, the prodigious suction of which is sufficiently known by lesser experiments."—These are the words of the Encyclopaedia Britannica. Kircher and others imagine that in the centre of the channel of the maelström is an abyss penetrating the globe, and issuing in some very remote part—the Gulf of Bothnia being somewhat decidedly named in one instance. This opinion, idle in itself, was the one to which, as I gazed, my imagination most readily assented; and, mentioning it to the guide, I was rather surprised to hear him say that, although it was the view almost universally entertained of the subject by the Norwegians, it nevertheless was not his own. As to the former notion he confessed his inability to comprehend it; and here I agreed with him—for, however conclusive on paper, it becomes altogether unintelligible, and even absurd, amid the thunder of the abyss.

"You have had a good look at the whirl now," said the old man, "and if you will creep round this crag, so as to get in its lee, and deaden the roar of the water, I will tell you a story that will convince you I ought to know something of the Moskoe-ström."

I placed myself as desired, and he proceeded.

"Myself and my two brothers once owned a schooner-rigged

smack of about seventy tons burthen, with which we were in the habit of fishing among the islands beyond Moskoe, nearly to Vurrgh. In all violent eddies at sea there is good fishing, at proper opportunities, if one has only the courage to attempt it; but among the whole of the Lofoden coastmen, we three were the only ones who made a regular business of going out to the islands, as I tell you. The usual grounds are a great way lower down to the southward. There fish can be got at all hours, without much risk, and therefore these places are preferred. The choice spots over here among the rocks, however, not only yield the finest variety, but in far greater abundance; so that we often got in a single day, what the more timid of the craft could not scrape together in a week. In fact, we made it a matter of desperate speculation—the risk of life standing instead of labor, and courage answering for capital.

"We kept the smack in a cove about five miles higher up the coast than this; and it was our practice, in fine weather, to take advantage of the fifteen minutes' slack to push across the main channel of the Moskoe-ström, far above the pool, and then drop down upon anchorage somewhere near Otterholm, or Sandflesen, where the eddies are not so violent as elsewhere. Here we used to remain until nearly time for slack-water again, when we weighed and made for home. We never set out upon this expedition without a steady side wind for going and coming—one that we felt sure would not fail us before our return—and we seldom made a miscalculation upon this point. Twice, during six years, we were forced to stay all night at anchor on account of a dead calm, which is a rare thing indeed just about here; and once we had to remain on the grounds nearly a week, starving to death, owing to a gale which blew up shortly after our arrival, and made the channel too boisterous to be thought of. Upon this occasion we should have been driven out to sea in spite of everything, (for the whirlpools threw us round and round so violently, that, at length, we fouled our anchor and dragged it) if it

had not been that we drifted into one of the innumerable cross cur-
rents—here to-day and gone to-morrow—which drove us under the
lee of Flimen, where, by good luck, we brought up.

"I could not tell you the twentieth part of the difficulties we
encountered 'on the grounds'—it is a bad spot to be in, even in
good weather—but we make shift always to run the gauntlet of the
Moskoe-ström itself without accident; although at times my heart
has been in my mouth when we happened to be a minute or so
behind or before the slack. The wind sometimes was not as strong
as we thought it at starting, and then we made rather less way than
we could wish, while the current rendered the smack unmanage-
able. My eldest brother had a son eighteen years old, and I had two
stout boys of my own. These would have been of great assistance at
such times, in using the sweeps, as well as afterward in fishing—but,
somehow, although we ran the risk ourselves, we had not the heart
to let the young ones get into the danger—for, after all is said and
done, it *was* a horrible danger, and that is the truth.

"It is now within a few days of three years since what I am going
to tell you occurred. It was on the tenth day of July, 18—, a day
which the people of this part of the world will never forget—for it
was one in which blew the most terrible hurricane that ever came
out of the heavens. And yet all the morning, and indeed until late in
the afternoon, there was a gentle and steady breeze from the southwest, while the sun shone brightly, so that the oldest seaman among
us could not have foreseen what was to follow.

"The three of us—my two brothers and myself—had crossed
over to the islands about two o'clock P.M., and soon nearly loaded the
smack with fine fish, which, we all remarked, were more plenty that
day than we had ever known them. It was just seven, *by my watch,*
when we weighed and started for home, so as to make the worst of
the Ström at slack water, which we knew would be at eight.

"We set out with a fresh wind on our starboard quarter, and

for some time spanked along at a great rate, never dreaming of danger, for indeed we saw not the slightest reason to apprehend it. All at once we were taken aback by a breeze from over Helseggen. This was most unusual—something that had never happened to us before—and I began to feel a little uneasy, without exactly knowing why. We put the boat on the wind, but could make no headway at all for the eddies, and I was upon the point of proposing to return to the anchorage, when, looking astern, we saw the whole horizon covered with a singular copper-colored cloud that rose with the most amazing velocity.

"In the meantime the breeze that had headed us off fell away, and we were dead becalmed, drifting about in every direction. This state of things, however, did not last long enough to give us time to think about it. In less than a minute the storm was upon us—in less than two the sky was entirely overcast—and what with this and the driving spray, it became suddenly so dark that we could not see each other in the smack.

"Such a hurricane as then blew it is folly to attempt describing. The oldest seaman in Norway never experienced any thing like it. We had let our sails go by the run before it cleverly took us; but, at the first puff, both our masts went by the board as if they had been sawed off—the mainmast taking with it my youngest brother, who had lashed himself to it for safety.

"Our boat was the lightest feather of a thing that ever sat upon water. It had a complete flush deck, with only a small hatch near the bow, and this hatch it had always been our custom to batten down when about to cross the Ström, by way of precaution against the chopping seas. But for this circumstance we should have foundered at once—for we lay entirely buried for some moments. How my elder brother escaped destruction I cannot say, for I never had an opportunity of ascertaining. For my part, as soon as I had let the foresail run, I threw myself flat on deck, with my feet against the narrow gunwale of the bow, and with my hands grasping a ring-bolt near the foot of the fore-mast. It was mere instinct that prompted me to do this — which was undoubtedly the very best thing I could have done — for I was too much flurried to think.

"For some moments we were completely deluged, as I say, and all this time I held my breath, and clung to the bolt. When I could stand it no longer I raised myself upon my knees, still keeping hold with my hands, and thus got my head clear. Presently our little boat gave herself a shake, just as a dog does in coming out of the water, and thus rid herself, in some measure, of the seas. I was now trying to get the better of the stupor that had come over me, and to collect my senses so as to see what was to be done, when I felt somebody grasp my arm. It was my elder brother, and my heart leaped for joy, for I had made sure that he was overboard — but the next moment all this joy was turned into horror — for he put his mouth close to my ear, and screamed out the word *'Moskoe-ström!'*

"No one ever will know what my feelings were at that moment. I shook from head to foot as if I had had the most violent fit of the ague. I knew what he meant by that one word well enough — I knew what he wished to make me understand. With the wind that now drove us on, we were bound for the whirl of the Ström, and nothing could save us!

"You perceive that in crossing the Ström *channel*, we always went a long way up above the whirl, even in the calmest weather, and then had to wait and watch carefully for the slack — but now we were driving right upon the pool itself, and in such a hurricane as this! 'To be sure,' I thought, 'we shall get there just about the slack — there is some little hope in that' — but in the next moment I cursed myself for being so great a fool as to dream of hope at all. I knew very well that we were doomed, had we been ten times a ninety-gun ship.

"By this time the first fury of the tempest had spent itself, or perhaps we did not feel it so much, as we scudded before it, but at all events the seas, which at first had been kept down by the wind, and lay flat and frothing, now got up into absolute mountains. A singular change, too, had come over the heavens. Around in every direction it was still as black as pitch, but nearly overhead there burst out, all at once, a circular rift of clear sky—as clear as I ever saw—and of a deep bright blue—and through it there blazed forth the full moon with a lustre that I never before knew her to wear. She lit up every thing about us with the greatest distinctness—but, oh God, what a scene it was to light up!

"I now made one or two attempts to speak to my brother—but in some manner which I could not understand, the din had so increased that I could not make him hear a single word, although I screamed at the top of my voice in his ear. Presently he shook his head, looking as pale as death, and held up one of his fingers, as if to say '*listen!*'

"At first I could not make out what he meant—but soon a hideous thought flashed upon me. I dragged my watch from its fob. It was not going. I glanced at its face by the moonlight and then burst into tears as I flung it far away into the ocean. *It had run down at seven o'clock! We were behind the time of the slack, and the whirl of the Ström was in full fury!*

"When a boat is well built, properly trimmed, and not deep laden, the waves in a strong gale, when she is going large, seem always to slip from beneath her—which appears very strange to a landsman—and this is what is called *riding*, in sea phrase.

"Well, so far we had ridden the swells very cleverly; but presently a gigantic sea happened to take us right under the counter, and bore us with it as it rose—up—up—as if into the sky. I would not have believed that any wave could rise so high. And then down we came with a sweep, a slide, and a plunge that made me feel sick and dizzy, as if I was falling from some lofty mountain-top in a dream. But while we were up I had thrown a quick glance around—and that one glance was all-sufficient. I saw our exact position in an instant. The Moskoe-ström whirlpool was about a quarter of a mile dead ahead—but no more like the every-day Moskoe-ström than the whirl, as you now see it, is like a mill-race. If I had not known where we were, and what we had to expect, I should not have recognized the place at all. As it was, I involuntarily closed my eyes in horror. The lids clenched themselves together as if in a spasm.

"It could not have been more than two minutes afterwards until we suddenly felt the waves subside, and were enveloped in foam. The boat made a sharp half turn to larboard, and then shot off in its new direction like a thunderbolt. At the same moment the roaring noise of the water was completely drowned in a kind of shrill shriek—such a sound as you might imagine given out by the waste-pipes of many thousand steam-vessels letting off their steam all together. We were now in the belt of surf that always surrounds the whirl; and I thought, of course, that another moment would plunge us into the abyss, down which we could only see indistinctly on account of the amazing velocity with which we were borne along. The boat did not seem to sink into the water at all, but to skim like an air-bubble upon the surface of the surge. Her starboard side was next the whirl, and on the larboard arose the world of ocean we had left. It stood like a huge writhing wall between us and the horizon.

"It may appear strange, but now, when we were in the very jaws of the gulf, I felt more composed than when we were only approaching it. Having made up my mind to hope no more, I got rid of a great deal of that terror which unmanned me at first. I suppose it was despair that strung my nerves.

"It may look like boasting—but what I tell you is truth—I began to reflect how magnificent a thing it was to die in such a manner, and how foolish it was in me to think of so paltry a consideration as my own individual life, in view of so wonderful a manifestation of God's power. I do believe that I blushed with shame when this idea crossed my mind. After a little while I became possessed with the keenest curiosity about the whirl itself. I positively felt a *wish* to explore its depths, even at the sacrifice I was going to make; and my principal grief was that I should never be able to tell my old companions on shore about the mysteries I should see. These, no doubt, were singular fancies to occupy a man's mind in such extremity—and I have often thought since, that the revolutions of the boat around the pool might have rendered me a little light-headed.

"There was another circumstance which tended to restore my self-possession; and this was the cessation of the wind, which could not reach us in our present situation—for, as you saw yourself, the belt of surf is considerably lower than the general bed of the ocean, and this latter now towered above us, a high, black, mountainous ridge. If you have never been at sea in a heavy gale, you can form no idea of the confusion of mind occasioned by the wind and spray together. They blind, deafen, and strangle you, and take away all power of action or reflection. But we were now, in a great measure, rid of these annoyances—just as death-condemned felons in prison are allowed petty indulgences, forbidden them while their doom is yet uncertain.

"How often we made the circuit of the belt it is impossible to say. We careered round and round for perhaps an hour, flying rather than floating, getting gradually more and more into the middle of the surge, and then nearer and nearer to its horrible inner edge. All this time I had never let go of the ring-bolt. My brother was at the stern, holding on to a small empty water-cask which had been securely lashed under the coop of the counter, and was the only thing on deck that had not been swept overboard when the gale first took us. As we approached the brink of the pit he let go his hold upon this, and made for the ring, from which, in the agony of his terror, he endeavored to force my hands, as it was not large enough to afford us both a secure grasp. I never felt deeper grief than when I saw him attempt this act—although I knew he was a madman when he did it—a raving maniac through sheer fright. I did not care, however, to contest the point with him. I knew it could make no difference whether either of us held on at all; so I let him have the bolt, and went astern to the cask.

"This there was no great difficulty in doing; for the smack flew round steadily enough, and upon an even keel—only swaying to and fro, with the immense sweeps and swelters of the whirl. Scarcely had I secured myself in my new position, when we gave a wild lurch to starboard, and rushed headlong into the abyss. I muttered a hurried prayer to God, and thought all was over.

"As I felt the sickening sweep of the descent, I had instinctively tightened my hold upon the barrel, and closed my eyes. For some seconds I dared not open them—while I expected instant destruction, and wondered that I was not already in my death-struggles with the water. But moment after moment elapsed. I still lived. The sense of falling had ceased; and the motion of the vessel seemed much as it had been before, while in the belt of foam, with the exception that she now lay more along. I took courage and looked once again upon the scene.

"Never shall I forget the sensations of awe, horror, and admiration with which I gazed about me. The boat appeared to be hanging, as if by magic, midway down, upon the interior surface of a funnel vast in circumference, prodigious in depth, and whose perfectly smooth sides might have been mistaken for ebony, but for the bewildering rapidity with which they spun around, and for the gleaming and ghastly radiance they shot forth, as the rays of the full moon, from that circular rift amid the clouds which I have already described, streamed in a flood of golden glory along the black walls, and far away down into the inmost recesses of the abyss.

"At first I was too much confused to observe anything accurately. The general burst of terrific grandeur was all that I beheld. When I recovered myself a little, however, my gaze fell instinctively downward. In this direction I was able to obtain an unobstructed view, from the manner in which the smack hung on the inclined surface of the pool. She was quite upon an even keel—that is to say, her deck lay in a plane parallel with that of the water—but this latter sloped at an angle of more than forty-five degrees, so that we seemed to be lying upon our beam-ends. I could not help observing, nevertheless, that I had scarcely more difficulty in maintaining my hold and footing in this situation, than if we had been upon a dead level; and this, I suppose, was owing to the speed at which we revolved.

"The rays of the moon seemed to search the very bottom of the profound gulf; but still I could make out nothing distinctly on account of a thick mist in which everything there was enveloped, and over which there hung a magnificent rainbow, like that narrow and tottering bridge which Mussulmen say is the only pathway between Time and Eternity. This mist, or spray, was no doubt occasioned by the clashing of the great walls of the funnel, as they all met together at the bottom—but the yell that went up to the Heavens from out of that mist, I dare not attempt to describe.

"Our first slide into the abyss itself, from the belt of foam above, had carried us a great distance down the slope; but our farther descent was by no means proportionate. Round and round we swept—not with any uniform movement—but in dizzying swings and jerks, that sent us sometimes only a few hundred yards—sometimes nearly the complete circuit of the whirl. Our progress downward, at each revolution, was slow, but very perceptible.

"Looking about me upon the wide waste of liquid ebony on which we were thus borne, I perceived that our boat was not the only object in the embrace of the whirl. Both above and below us were visible fragments of vessels, large masses of building-timber and trunks of trees, with many smaller articles, such as pieces of house furniture, broken boxes, barrels and staves. I have already described the unnatural curiosity which had taken the place of my original terrors. It appeared to grow upon me as I drew nearer and nearer to my dreadful doom. I now began to watch, with a strange interest, the numerous things that floated in our company. I *must* have been delirious, for I even sought *amusement* in speculating upon the relative velocities of their several descents toward the foam below. 'This fir tree,' I found myself at one time saying, 'will certainly be the next thing that takes the awful plunge and disappears,'—and then I was disappointed to find that the wreck of a Dutch merchant ship overtook it and went down before. At length, after making several guesses of this nature, and being deceived in all—this fact—the fact of my invariable miscalculation, set me upon a train of reflection that made my limbs again tremble, and my heart beat heavily once more.

"It was not a new terror that thus affected me, but the dawn of a more exciting *hope*. This hope arose partly from memory, and partly from present observation. I called to mind the great variety of buoyant matter that strewed the coast of Lofoden, having been absorbed and then thrown forth by the Moskoe-ström. By far the greater number of the articles were shattered in the most extraordinary way—so chafed and roughened as to have the appearance of being stuck full of splinters—but then I distinctly recollected that there were *some* of them which were not disfigured at all. Now I could not account for this difference except by supposing that the roughened fragments were the only ones which had been *completely absorbed*—that the others had entered the whirl at so late a period of the tide, or, from some reason, had descended so slowly after entering, that they did not reach the bottom before the turn of the flood came, or of the ebb, as the case might be. I conceived it possible, in either instance, that they might thus be whirled up again to the level of the ocean, without undergoing the fate of those which had been drawn in more early or absorbed more rapidly. I made, also, three important observations. The first was, that as a general rule, the larger the bodies were, the more rapid their descent—the second, that, between two masses of equal extent, the one spherical, and the other *of any other shape,* the superiority in speed of descent was with the sphere—the third, that, between two masses of equal size, the one cylindrical, and the other of any other shape, the cylinder was absorbed the more slowly. Since my escape, I have had several conversations on this subject with an old school-master of the district; and it was from him that I learned the use of the words 'cylinder' and 'sphere.' He explained to me—although I have forgotten the explanation—how what I observed was, in fact, the natural consequence of the forms of the floating fragments—and showed me how it happened that a cylinder, swimming in a vortex, offered more resistance to its suction, and was drawn in with greater difficulty than an equally bulky body, of any form whatever.

"There was one startling circumstance which went a great way in enforcing these observations, and rendering me anxious to turn them to account, and this was that, at every revolution, we passed something like a barrel, or else the yard or the mast of a vessel, while many of these things, which had been on our level when I first opened my eyes upon the wonders of the whirlpool, were now high up above us, and seemed to have moved but little from their original station.

"I no longer hesitated what to do. I resolved to lash myself securely to the water-cask upon which I now held, to cut it loose from the counter, and to throw myself with it into the water. I attracted my brother's attention by signs, pointed to the floating barrels that came near us, and did every thing in my power to make him understand what I was about to do. I thought at length that he comprehended my design—but, whether this was the case or not, he shook his head despairingly, and refused to move from his station by the ring-bolt. It was impossible to reach him; the emergency admitted of no delay; and so, with a bitter struggle, I resigned him to his fate, fastened myself to the cask by means of the lashings which secured it to the counter, and precipitated myself with it into the sea, without another moment's hesitation.

"The result was precisely what I had hoped it might be. As it is myself who now tell you this tale—as you see that I *did* escape—and as you are already in possession of the mode in which this escape was effected, and must therefore anticipate all that I have farther to say—I will bring my story quickly to conclusion. It might have been an hour, or thereabout, after my quitting the smack, when, having descended to a vast distance beneath me, it made three or four wild gyrations in rapid succession, and, bearing my loved brother with it, plunged headlong, at once and forever, into the chaos of foam below. The barrel to which I was attached sunk very little farther than half the distance between the bottom of the gulf and the spot at which I leaped overboard, before a great change took place in the character of the whirlpool. The slope of the sides of the vast funnel became momently less and less steep. The gyrations of the whirl grew, gradually, less and less violent. By degrees, the froth and the rainbow disappeared, and the bottom of the gulf seemed slowly to uprise. The sky was clear, the winds had gone down, and the full moon was setting radiantly in the west, when I found myself on the surface of the ocean, in full view of the shores of Lofoden, and above the spot where the pool of the Moskoe-ström *had been*. It was the hour of the slack—but the sea still heaved in mountainous waves from the effects of the hurricane. I was borne violently into the channel of the Ström, and in a few minutes, was hurried down the coast into the 'grounds' of the fishermen. A boat picked me up—exhausted from fatigue—and (now that the danger was removed) speechless from the memory of its horror. Those who drew me on board were my old mates and daily companions—but they knew me no more than they would have known a traveller from the spirit-land. My hair, which had been raven-black the day before, was as white as you see it now. They say, too, that the whole expression of my countenance had changed. I told them my story—they did not believe it. I now tell it to *you*—and I can scarcely expect you to put more faith in it than did the merry fishermen of Lofoden."

On Edgar Allan Poe

......

BY T. JEFFERSON PARKER

Picture my suburban living room in Orange County, California, 1966: an orange carpet, pale turquoise walls, white Naugahyde furniture, white acoustic ceiling, a rabbit-eared black-and-white TV, and a wall-to-wall bookshelf six feet high and stuffed with books.

The bookcase was filled mostly with nonfiction—history and politics and outdoors adventure and travel. But we had Robert Louis Stevenson, and we had Jack London, and we had Edgar Allan Poe.

"Mom, why do we have Poe?" I asked her as a sixth-grader.

"He understood the guilty conscience. Read 'The Tell-Tale Heart' and you'll see what I mean."

So one evening, a school night, after my homework was done and my half-hour on the TV was over, I turned on the reading lamp and settled into the white Naugahyde recliner and opened *Complete Stories of Edgar Allan Poe.*

I read "The Tell-Tale Heart" and saw that Mom was right. I suspected that Mr. Poe also understood some things about insanity and murder—how else could he write in the voice of a madman who remembers to use a tub to catch the blood and gore when he "cut[s] off the head and the arms and the legs" of the old man he has murdered and places the parts beneath the floorboards?

I was intrigued. I was exploring a foreign mind. I was transfixed.

The next night I read "The Black Cat." And the night after that "The Cask of Amontillado," where I was confronted with what I still think is the best opening line I've ever read:

> *The thousand injuries of Fortunato I had borne as I best could; but when he ventured upon insult, I vowed revenge.*

I read all of those stories over the next six months. Some I loved, and some unsettled me, and some went far over my young head.

But I took them all into my young heart. What they taught me was this: there is darkness in the hearts of men; there are consequences of that darkness; those consequences will crash down upon us here in this life. They taught me that words can be beautiful and mysterious and full of truth.

These are the things I learned from Poe as I sat in the white recliner in my Orange County living room as a twelve-year-old, and these are the things I write about today.

That volume sits beside me now. There are still small red dots beside the stories I read that first month: "Ligeia," "A Descent into the Maelström," "The Masque of the Red Death."

When I open it, I can see that room of forty years ago, and I can remember my rising sense of foreboding and excitement when I read the first line of "The Fall of the House of Usher."

I still read those stories. I still love them, and they still unsettle me, and some of them still go over my no-longer-young head.

T. Jefferson Parker was born in L.A. and grew up in Orange County, California. He has worked as a waiter, an animal hospital night watchman, and a newspaper reporter. His first novel, Laguna Heat, was published in 1985. Fourteen books later, he is ridiculously lucky to have received two Edgar Awards for Best Mystery. He is also the proud owner of a brick salvaged from Edgar Allan Poe's last New York apartment, which occupies a place of honor on the Parker family room hearth.

The Cask of Amontillado

THE THOUSAND INJURIES of Fortunato I had borne as I best could; but when he ventured upon insult, I vowed revenge. You, who so well know the nature of my soul, will not suppose, however, that I gave utterance to a threat. *At length* I would be avenged; this was a point definitively settled—but the very definitiveness with which it was resolved, precluded the idea of risk. I must not only punish, but punish with impunity. A wrong is unredressed when retribution overtakes its redresser. It is equally unredressed when the avenger fails to make himself felt as such to him who has done the wrong.

It must be understood, that neither by word nor deed had I given Fortunato cause to doubt my good-will. I continued, as was my wont, to smile in his face, and he did not perceive that my smile *now* was at the thought of his immolation.

He had a weak point—this Fortunato—although in other regards he was a man to be respected and even feared. He prided himself on his connoisseurship in wine. Few Italians have the true virtuoso spirit. For the most part their enthusiasm is adopted to suit the time and opportunity—to practise imposture upon the British and Austrian *millionaires*. In painting and gemmary Fortunato, like his countrymen, was a quack—but in the matter of old wines he was sincere. In this respect I did not differ from him materially: I was skilful in the Italian vintages myself, and bought largely whenever I could.

It was about dusk, one evening during the supreme madness of the carnival season, that I encountered my friend. He accosted me with excessive warmth, for he had been drinking much. The man wore motley. He had on a tight-fitting parti-striped dress, and his head was surmounted by the conical cap and bells. I was so pleased to see him, that I thought I should never have done wringing his hand.

I said to him: "My dear Fortunato, you are luckily met. How remarkably well you are looking to-day! But I have received a pipe of what passes for Amontillado, and I have my doubts."

"How?" said he. "Amontillado? A pipe? Impossible! And in the middle of the carnival!"

"I have my doubts," I replied; "and I was silly enough to pay the full Amontillado price without consulting you in the matter. You were not to be found, and I was fearful of losing a bargain."

"Amontillado!"

"I have my doubts."

"Amontillado!"

"And I must satisfy them."

"Amontillado!"

"As you are engaged, I am on my way to Luchesi. If any one has a critical turn, it is he. He will tell me—"

"Luchesi cannot tell Amontillado from Sherry."

"And yet some fools will have it that his taste is a match for your own."

"Come, let us go."

"Whither?"

"To your vaults."

"My friend, no; I will not impose upon your good nature. I perceive you have an engagement. Luchesi—"

"I have no engagement;—come."

"My friend, no. It is not the engagement, but the severe cold with which I perceive you are afflicted. The vaults are insufferably damp. They are encrusted with nitre."

"Let us go, nevertheless. The cold is merely nothing. Amontillado! You have been imposed upon. And as for Luchesi, he cannot distinguish Sherry from Amontillado."

Thus speaking, Fortunato possessed himself of my arm. Putting on a mask of black silk, and drawing a *roquelaire* closely about my person, I suffered him to hurry me to my palazzo.

There were no attendants at home; they had absconded to make merry in honor of the time. I had told them that I should not return until the morning, and had given them explicit orders not to stir from the house. These orders were sufficient, I well knew, to insure their immediate disappearance, one and all, as soon as my back was turned.

I took from their sconces two flambeaux, and giving one to Fortunato, bowed him through several suites of rooms to the archway that led into the vaults. I passed down a long and winding staircase, requesting him to be cautious as he followed. We came at length to the foot of the descent, and stood together on the damp ground of the catacombs of the Montresors.

The gait of my friend was unsteady, and the bells upon his cap jingled as he strode.

"The pipe?" said he.

"It is farther on," said I; "but observe the white web-work which gleams from these cavern walls."

He turned toward me, and looked into my eyes with two filmy orbs that distilled the rheum of intoxication.

"Nitre?" he asked, at length.

"Nitre," I replied. "How long have you had that cough?"

"Ugh! ugh! ugh! —ugh! ugh! ugh! —ugh! ugh! ugh! —ugh! ugh! ugh! —ugh! ugh! ugh!"

My poor friend found it impossible to reply for many minutes.

"It is nothing," he said, at last.

"Come," I said, with decision, "we will go back; your health is precious. You are rich, respected, admired, beloved; you are happy, as once I was. You are a man to be missed. For me it is no matter. We will go back; you will be ill, and I cannot be responsible. Besides, there is Luchesi—"

"Enough," he said; "the cough is a mere nothing; it will not kill me. I shall not die of a cough."

"True—true," I replied; "and, indeed, I had no intention of alarming you unnecessarily; but you should use all proper caution. A draught of this Medoc will defend us from the damps."

Here I knocked off the neck of a bottle which I drew from a long row of its fellows that lay upon the mould.

"Drink," I said, presenting him the wine.

He raised it to his lips with a leer. He paused and nodded to me familiarly, while his bells jingled.

"I drink," he said, "to the buried that repose around us."

"And I to your long life."

He again took my arm, and we proceeded.

"These vaults," he said, "are extensive."

"The Montresors," I replied, "were a great and numerous family."

"I forget your arms."

"A huge human foot d'or, in a field azure; the foot crushes a serpent rampant whose fangs are imbedded in the heel."

"And the motto?"

"Nemo me impune lacessit."

"Good!" he said.

The wine sparkled in his eyes and the bells jingled. My own fancy grew warm with the Medoc. We had passed through walls of piled bones, with casks and puncheons intermingling, into the inmost recesses of the catacombs. I paused again, and this time I made bold to seize Fortunato by an arm above the elbow.

"The nitre!" I said; "see, it increases. It hangs like moss upon the vaults. We are below the river's bed. The drops of moisture trickle among the bones. Come, we will go back ere it is too late. Your cough—"

"It is nothing," he said; "let us go on. But first, another draught of the Medoc."

I broke and reached him a flagon of De Grâve. He emptied it at a breath. His eyes flashed with a fierce light. He laughed and threw the bottle upwards with a gesticulation I did not understand.

I looked at him in surprise. He repeated the movement—a grotesque one.

"You do not comprehend?" he said.

"Not I," I replied.

"Then you are not of the brotherhood."

"How?"

"You are not of the masons."

"Yes, yes," I said, "yes, yes."

"You? Impossible! A mason?"

"A mason," I replied.

"A sign," he said.

"It is this," I answered, producing a trowel from beneath the folds of my *roquelaire*.

"You jest," he exclaimed, recoiling a few paces. "But let us proceed to the Amontillado."

"Be it so," I said, replacing the tool beneath the cloak, and again offering him my arm. He leaned upon it heavily. We continued our route in search of the Amontillado. We passed through a range of low arches, descended, passed on, and descending again, arrived at a deep crypt, in which the foulness of the air caused our flambeaux rather to glow than flame.

At the most remote end of the crypt there appeared another less spacious. Its walls had been lined with human remains, piled to the vault overhead, in the fashion of the great catacombs of Paris. Three sides of this interior crypt were still ornamented in this manner. From the fourth the bones had been thrown down, and lay promiscuously upon the earth, forming at one point a mound of some size. Within the wall thus exposed by the displacing of the bones, we perceived a still interior recess, in depth about four feet, in width three, in height six or seven. It seemed to have been constructed for no especial use within itself, but formed merely the interval between two of the colossal supports of the roof of the catacombs, and was backed by one of their circumscribing walls of solid granite.

It was in vain that Fortunato, uplifting his dull torch, endeavored to pry into the depths of the recess. Its termination the feeble light did not enable us to see.

"Proceed," I said; "herein is the Amontillado. As for Luchesi—"

"He is an ignoramus," interrupted my friend, as he stepped unsteadily forward, while I followed immediately at his heels. In an instant he had reached the extremity of the niche, and finding his progress arrested by the rock, stood stupidly bewildered. A moment more and I had fettered him to the granite. In its surface were two iron staples, distant from each other about two feet, horizontally.

From one of these depended a short chain, from the other a padlock. Throwing the links about his waist, it was but the work of a few seconds to secure it. He was too much astounded to resist. Withdrawing the key I stepped back from the recess.

"Pass your hand," I said, "over the wall; you cannot help feeling the nitre. Indeed it is *very* damp. Once more let me *implore* you to return. No? Then I must positively leave you. But I must first render you all the little attentions in my power."

"The Amontillado!" ejaculated my friend, not yet recovered from his astonishment.

"True," I replied; "the Amontillado."

As I said these words I busied myself among the pile of bones of which I have before spoken. Throwing them aside, I soon uncovered a quantity of building stone and mortar. With these materials and with the aid of my trowel, I began vigorously to wall up the entrance of the niche.

I had scarcely laid the first tier of my masonry when I discovered that the intoxication of Fortunato had in a great measure worn off. The earliest indication I had of this was a low moaning cry from the depth of the recess. It was *not* the cry of a drunken man. There was then a long and obstinate silence. I laid the second tier, and the third, and the fourth; and then I heard the furious vibrations of the chain. The noise lasted for several minutes, during which, that I might hearken to it with the more satisfaction, I ceased my labors and sat down upon the bones. When at last the clanking subsided, I resumed the trowel, and finished without interruption the fifth, the sixth, and the seventh tier. The wall was now nearly upon a level with my breast. I again paused, and holding the flambeaux over the mason-work, threw a few feeble rays upon the figure within.

A succession of loud and shrill screams, bursting suddenly from the throat of the chained form, seemed to thrust me violently back. For a brief moment I hesitated—I trembled. Unsheathing my rapier, I began to grope with it about the recess; but the thought of an instant reassured me. I placed my hand upon the solid fabric of the catacombs, and felt satisfied. I reapproached the wall. I replied to the yells of him who clamored. I re-echoed — I aided — I surpassed them in volume and in strength. I did this, and the clamorer grew still.

It was now midnight, and my task was drawing to a close. I had completed the eighth, the ninth, and the tenth tier. I had finished a portion of the last and the eleventh; there remained but a single stone to be fitted and plastered in. I struggled with its weight; I placed it partially in its destined position. But now there came from out the niche a low laugh that erected the hairs upon my head. It was succeeded by a sad voice, which I had difficulty in recognizing as that of the noble Fortunato. The voice said —

"Ha! ha! ha! — he! he! — a very good joke indeed — an excellent jest. We will have many a rich laugh about it at the palazzo — he! he! he! — over our wine — he! he! he!"

"The Amontillado!" I said.

"He! he! he! — he! he! he! — yes, the Amontillado. But is it not getting late? Will not they be awaiting us at the palazzo, the Lady Fortunato and the rest? Let us be gone."

"Yes," I said, "let us be gone."

"For the love of God, Montresor!"

"Yes," I said, "for the love of God!"

But to these words I hearkened in vain for a reply. I grew impatient. I called aloud:

"Fortunato!"

No answer. I called again:

"Fortunato!"

No answer still. I thrust a torch through the remaining aperture and let it fall within. There came forth in return only a jingling of the bells. My heart grew sick—on account of the dampness of the catacombs. I hastened to make an end of my labor. I forced the last stone into its position; I plastered it up. Against the new masonry I re-erected the old rampart of bones. For the half of a century no mortal has disturbed them. *In pace requiescat!*

Under the Covers with
Fortunato and Montresor

. . . . . .

BY JAN BURKE

Some years ago, I heard concern voiced over the fact that children seemed to adore a series of horror books written for that audience, and recently a parent told me she feared *Harry Potter* was "too intense" for her fifth-grader. I'm not a parent, so I would never attempt to judge what a child of today could cope with, but I do recall who scared the socks off me at the age of ten: Edgar Allan Poe.

Upon hearing how much I had enjoyed being terrified by "The Tell-Tale Heart," my father suggested I read "The Cask of Amontillado." It had been a while since he had read it, but as he said the name of the story, he gave a little shiver in reminiscence. Naturally, I hurried to search out a copy of the story. Like many young booklovers, I used to read with a flashlight under the bedcovers long after I was supposed to be asleep. For reasons you'll understand as you read "The Cask of Amontillado," those covers got tossed back when I read this one. For some weeks after I read it, I repaid my father the favor of his recommendation by refusing to sleep with the bedroom door closed.

Every time I've reread "The Cask of Amontillado" as an adult,

I've found it's still a tale guaranteed to incite claustrophobia. Now, though, I better appreciate how skillfully Poe told this tale. "The Cask of Amontillado" is a master's lesson in storytelling. Every element — the voice of the narrator, the setting, the interplay between characters, even the clothing of the victim — contributes to its mood, its tension, and its relentless drive to its conclusion.

Consider how we are lured into a journey with a killer, much as Fortunato is lured into doing the same. At first, we feel sympathetic to Montresor. Who among us has not known a Fortunato and wished him his comeuppance? A pompous connoisseur of fine wines, he easily represents the know-it-alls we've encountered in our own lives. Perhaps we've also known someone who has dealt us a "thousand injuries" or insults we've been forced to bear in smiling silence.

Soon we realize, though, that Montresor is a madman, not to be trusted. He's prone to exaggerating slights all out of proportion, and he's bent on revenge. We begin to fear for Fortunato, dressed as a fool and behaving like one. We descend with this pair from the street, where the carnival season is in full swing, down into the catacombs beneath the Montresor palazzo. Every step inexorably takes us away from the excesses and frivolity of the celebrations above — down into a dark and chill place, where even the bells on a fool's cap become fuelfor nightmares. We may have seen more graphically violent representations of the mind of a killer in fiction, but Montresor, capable of mocking both his victim's prayers and his screams, is as heartless as any.

With the power of a conjurer, Poe knew exactly how to summon our fears. Read "The Cask of Amontillado." Then feel free to sleep with the light on and the bedroom door open.

Jan Burke is the Edgar-winning author of twelve novels, including Bones, Flight, Bloodlines, *and* Kidnapped. *Her newest is a supernatural thriller,* The Messenger. *She is currently at work on the next Irene Kelly novel.*

The Curse of Amontillado

......

BY LAWRENCE BLOCK

I knew I wanted an Edgar Award back in 1961, when my good friend Don Westlake failed to win one.

He'd just published *The Mercenaries,* and it was nominated for an Edgar for Best First Mystery. Someone else took home the statuette (for what was in fact a first mystery by a veteran science-fiction writer, which made it eligible under the letter if not the spirit of the rule), and we all assured Don that it was honor enough to be nominated, and he pretended to believe us. We don't need to feel sorry for the man, though; he has a whole shelf full of those porcelain busts now, plus a sheaf of nominations. Anyway, this isn't about him.

It's about me.

I began publishing paperback original crime novels in 1961 and hardcovers a few years later. And while I can't say I was obsessed with the idea of winning an Edgar, I had my hopes. One book I published in the mid-1970s, under a pen name (Chip Harrison) that was also the name of the book's narrator, was dedicated "To Barbara Bonham, Newgate Callendar, John Dickson Carr, and the Edgar Awards Committee of the Mystery Writers of America."

Barbara Bonham was the chief fiction reviewer for *Publish-ers Weekly*. Newgate Callendar was the pen name that music critic Harold Schonberg used for his crime column in the *New York Times Book Review*. And John Dickson Carr, master of the locked room, reviewed mysteries for *Ellery Queen's Mystery Magazine*.

I was shameless, and to no avail. Well, not much avail anyway. The book got a mention in the Callendar column, where its dedication was quoted and its literary merits overlooked. Carr and Bonham paid no attention, and when Edgar time rolled around, Chip Harrison was left out in the cold.

But a year or so later one of my Matthew Scudder novels, *Time to Murder and Create*, picked up a nomination for Best Paperback Original. I went to the dinner somehow convinced I was going to win, and I didn't. Someone else did. I sat there stunned, barely able to assure people that it was honor enough merely to be nominated.

A couple of years later I was nominated again, this time for *Eight Million Ways to Die*, short-listed for Best Novel. "Honor enough to be nominated," I muttered and went home.

It took years for me to realize what was holding me back. It was, quite simply, a curse.

The curse of Amontillado.

I realized the precise dimensions of this curse only recently, when Charles Ardai was editing an early pseudonymous book of mine for his "Hard Case Crime" imprint. He pointed out that I'd referred to "The Cask of Amontillado" as having been written by Robert Louis Stevenson. Gently he asked if my attributing Poe's story to Stevenson was deliberate, indicating something subtle about the character who'd made the error.

The mistake, I replied, was not the character's but my own, and he should by all means correct it.

And not a moment too soon. Because it was clearly responsible for a long train of misfortunes.

This misattribution, I must confess, was not an isolated slip-of-the-keyboard confined to a single forgettable book. While that may have been the only time I publicly handed Poe's classic tale to Stevenson, I'd been confused about its authorship ever since I read the story. Which, if memory serves (and you can already tell what ill service it tends to provide), came about in the seventh grade, some fifty-seven years ago.

One of our textbooks in English class was a small blue volume of short stories, one of which was "The Cask of Amontillado," and one was something by Stevenson. (I seem to recall the title of the Stevenson story as "The Master of Ballantrae," but that's impossible, because that's the title of a novel. So I don't know what the Stevenson story may have been, and, God forgive me, I don't care either.)

I don't know what else I may have retained from the seventh grade, but one thing I held on to was that story, "The Cask of Amontillado."

"For the love of God, Montresor!"
"Yes," I said, "for the love of God!"

They don't write 'em like that anymore, and I knew that even then. But somehow I got it into my head that the author's initials were R.L.S., not E.A.P. Now and then it would come up in conversation, and someone would say I meant Poe, didn't I? And I'd say yes, of course, and stand corrected—but not for long, because my memory remained inexplicably loyal to Stevenson.

Well, really. Where did I get off looking to win an Edgar? If the

Red Sox could go that long without a World Series win just because their cheapjack owner let go of Babe Ruth, what did I expect?

And then, of course, everything changed.

Because I started keeping company with a young woman named Lynne Wood.

And why, you may ask, should that serve to lift the curse of Amontillado? Perhaps the answer will become clear when I tell you that the maiden name of Ms. Wood's mother, Emilie, was Poe.

She was not the first person I'd met with that surname. Back in the eighth grade, a mere year after I'd read about Montresor and the ill-named Fortunato, I had a classmate named William Poe. His family had just moved north from Alabama, and that made him an exotic creature indeed at PS 66 in Buffalo, New York. We teased him relentlessly about his accent—and I wouldn't be surprised if that helped reinforce the curse, now that I think about it. I don't know that anyone asked if he was related to *the* Poe, but he very likely would have answered that he was, because they all are. The Poes, that is.

Of course, none of them are direct descendants of Edgar Allan, because the poor fellow had no living issue. But he has plenty of collateral descendants, and one of them was named Emilie, and she had a daughter named Lynne.

Reader, I married her.

And within the year my short story "By the Dawn's Early Light" was nominated for an Edgar. Lynne and I attended what I'd come to term the Always-A-Bridesmaid Dinner, but this time I went home with a porcelain bust of my bride's great-great-great-etc.-uncle.

It has, I blush to admit, been joined by others in the years that followed. Coincidence?

I don't think so.

Lawrence Block once read "The Bells" at a New York Parks Department event at the Poe House in the Bronx and, flying in the face of popular demand, repeated the performance at a similar gala a year or two later. As editor of Akashic's forthcoming anthology Manhattan Noir II—The Classics, he made a point of including "The Raven," figuring you can't get a whole lot noirer than that. His sole other connection to Edgar Allan Poe is, as he makes evident in his essay in this volume, by marriage. But he does collect busts of the great author and has five of them arrayed on a shelf where he can see them even as he types these lines.

The Black Cat

FOR THE MOST WILD yet most homely narrative which I am about to pen, I neither expect nor solicit belief. Mad indeed would I be to expect it, in a case where my very senses reject their own evidence. Yet, mad am I not—and very surely do I not dream. But to-morrow I die, and to-day I would unburden my soul. My immediate purpose is to place before the world, plainly, succinctly, and without comment, a series of mere household events. In their consequences, these events have terrified—have tortured—have destroyed me. Yet I will not attempt to expound them. To me, they have presented little but horror—to many they will seem less terrible than *baroques*. Hereafter, perhaps, some intellect may be found which will reduce my phantasm to the commonplace—some intellect more calm, more logical, and far less excitable than my own, which will perceive, in the circumstances I detail with awe, nothing more than an ordinary succession of very natural causes and effects.

From my infancy I was noted for the docility and humanity of my disposition. My tenderness of heart was even so conspicuous as to make me the jest of my companions. I was especially fond of animals, and was indulged by my parents with a great variety of pets. With these I spent most of my time, and never was so happy as when feeding and caressing them. This peculiarity of character grew with my growth, and, in my manhood, I derived from it one of my principal sources of pleasure. To those who have cherished an affection for a faithful and sagacious dog, I need hardly be at the trouble of explaining the nature or the intensity of the gratification thus derivable. There is something in the unselfish and self-sacrificing love of a brute, which goes directly to the heart of him who has had frequent occasion to test the paltry friendship and gossamer fidelity of mere *Man*.

I married early, and was happy to find in my wife a disposition not uncongenial with my own. Observing my partiality for domestic pets, she lost no opportunity of procuring those of the most agreeable kind. We had birds, gold-fish, a fine dog, rabbits, a small monkey, and a *cat*.

This latter was a remarkably large and beautiful animal, entirely black, and sagacious to an astonishing degree. In speaking of his intelligence, my wife, who at heart was not a little tinctured with superstition, made frequent allusion to the ancient popular notion, which regarded all black cats as witches in disguise. Not that she was ever *serious* upon this point—and I mention the matter at all for no better reason than that it happens, just now, to be remembered.

Pluto—this was the cat's name—was my favorite pet and playmate. I alone fed him, and he attended me wherever I went about the house. It was even with difficulty that I could prevent him from following me through the streets.

Our friendship lasted, in this manner, for several years, during which my general temperament and character—through the instrumentality of the Fiend Intemperance—had (I blush to confess it) experienced a radical alteration for the worse. I grew, day by day, more moody, more irritable, more regardless of the feelings of others. I suffered myself to use intemperate language to my wife. At length, I even offered her personal violence. My pets, of course, were made to feel the change in my disposition. I not only neglected, but ill-used them. For Pluto, however, I still retained sufficient regard to restrain me from maltreating him, as I made no scruple of maltreating the rabbits, the monkey, or even the dog, when by accident, or through affection, they came in my way. But my disease grew upon me—for what disease is like Alcohol!—and at length even Pluto, who was now becoming old, and consequently somewhat peevish—even Pluto began to experience the effects of my ill temper.

One night, returning home, much intoxicated, from one of my haunts about town, I fancied that the cat avoided my presence. I seized him; when, in his fright at my violence, he inflicted a slight wound upon my hand with his teeth. The fury of a demon instantly possessed me. I knew myself no longer. My original soul seemed, at once, to take its flight from my body; and a more than fiendish malevolence, gin-nurtured, thrilled every fibre of my frame. I took from my waistcoat-pocket a penknife, opened it, grasped the poor beast by the throat, and deliberately cut one of its eyes from the socket! I blush, I burn, I shudder, while I pen the damnable atrocity. When reason returned with the morning—when I had slept off the fumes of the night's debauch—I experienced a sentiment half of horror, half of remorse, for the crime of which I had been guilty; but it was, at best, a feeble and equivocal feeling, and the soul remained untouched. I again plunged into excess, and soon drowned in wine all memory of the deed.

In the meantime the cat slowly recovered. The socket of the lost eye presented, it is true, a frightful appearance, but he no longer appeared to suffer any pain. He went about the house as usual, but, as might be expected, fled in extreme terror at my approach. I had so much of my old heart left, as to be at first grieved by this evident dislike on the part of a creature which had once so loved me. But this feeling soon gave place to irritation. And then came, as if to my final and irrevocable overthrow, the spirit of PERVERSENESS. Of this spirit philosophy takes no account. Yet I am not more sure that my soul lives, than I am that perverseness is one of the primitive impulses of the human heart—one of the indivisible primary faculties, or sentiments, which give direction to the character of Man. Who has not, a hundred times, found himself committing a vile or a stupid action, for no other reason than because he knows he should *not*? Have we not a perpetual inclination, in the teeth of our best judgment, to violate that which is *Law*, merely because we understand it to be such? This spirit of perverseness, I say, came to my final overthrow. It was this unfathomable longing of the soul *to vex itself*—to offer violence to its own nature—to do wrong for the wrong's sake only—that urged me to continue and finally to consummate the injury I had inflicted upon the unoffending brute. One morning, in cool blood, I slipped a noose about its neck and hung it to the limb of a tree;—hung it with the tears streaming from my eyes, and with the bitterest remorse at my heart;—hung it *because* I knew that it had loved me, and *because* I felt it had given me no reason of offence;—hung it *because* I knew that in so doing I was committing a sin—a deadly sin that would so jeopardize my immortal soul as to place it—if such a thing were possible—even beyond the reach of the infinite mercy of the Most Merciful and Most Terrible God.

On the night of the day on which this most cruel deed was done, I was aroused from sleep by the cry of fire. The curtains of my bed were in flames. The whole house was blazing. It was with great difficulty that my wife, a servant, and myself, made our escape from the conflagration. The destruction was complete. My entire worldly wealth was swallowed up, and I resigned myself thenceforward to despair.

I am above the weakness of seeking to establish a sequence of cause and effect, between the disaster and the atrocity. But I am detailing a chain of facts—and wish not to leave even a possible link imperfect. On the day succeeding the fire, I visited the ruins. The walls, with one exception, had fallen in. This exception was found in a compartment wall, not very thick, which stood about the middle of the house, and against which had rested the head of my bed. The plastering had here, in great measure, resisted the action of the fire—a fact which I attributed to its having been recently spread. About this wall a dense crowd were collected, and many persons seemed to be examining a particular portion of it with very minute and eager attention. The words "strange!" "singular!" and other similar expressions, excited my curiosity. I approached and saw, as if graven in bas relief upon the white surface, the figure of a gigantic *cat*. The impression was given with an accuracy truly marvellous. There was a rope about the animal's neck.

When I first beheld this apparition—for I could scarcely regard it as less—my wonder and my terror were extreme. But at length reflection came to my aid. The cat, I remembered, had been hung in a garden adjacent to the house. Upon the alarm of fire, this garden had been immediately filled by the crowd—by some one of whom the animal must have been cut from the tree and thrown, through an open window, into my chamber. This had probably been done with the view of arousing me from sleep. The falling of other walls had compressed the victim of my cruelty into the substance of the freshly-spread plaster; the lime of which, with the flames, and the *ammonia* from the carcass, had then accomplished the portraiture as I saw it.

Although I thus readily accounted to my reason, if not altogether to my conscience, for the startling fact just detailed, it did not the less fail to make a deep impression upon my fancy. For months I could not rid myself of the phantasm of the cat; and, during this period, there came back into my spirit a half-sentiment that seemed, but was not, remorse. I went so far as to regret the loss of the animal, and to look about me, among the vile haunts which I now habitually frequented, for another pet of the same species, and of somewhat similar appearance, with which to supply its place.

One night as I sat, half stupefied, in a den of more than infamy, my attention was suddenly drawn to some black object, reposing upon the head of one of the immense hogsheads of gin, or of rum, which constituted the chief furniture of the apartment. I had been looking steadily at the top of this hogshead for some minutes, and what now caused me surprise was the fact that I had not sooner perceived the object thereupon. I approached it, and touched it with my hand. It was a black cat—a very large one—fully as large as Pluto, and closely resembling him in every respect but one. Pluto had not a white hair upon any portion of his body; but this cat had a large, although indefinite splotch of white, covering nearly the whole region of the breast.

Upon my touching him, he immediately arose, purred loudly, rubbed against my hand, and appeared delighted with my notice. This, then, was the very creature of which I was in search. I at once offered to purchase it of the landlord; but this person made no claim to it—knew nothing of it—had never seen it before. I continued my caresses, and when I prepared to go home, the animal evinced a disposition to accompany me. I permitted it to do so; occasionally stooping and patting it as I proceeded. When it reached the house it domesticated itself at once, and became immediately a great favorite with my wife.

For my own part, I soon found a dislike to it arising within me. This was just the reverse of what I had anticipated; but—I know not how or why it was—its evident fondness for myself rather disgusted and annoyed me. By slow degrees these feelings of disgust and annoyance rose into the bitterness of hatred. I avoided the creature;

a certain sense of shame, and the remembrance of my former deed of cruelty, preventing me from physically abusing it. I did not, for some weeks, strike, or otherwise violently ill use it; but gradually— very gradually—I came to look upon it with unutterable loathing, and to flee silently from its odious presence, as from the breath of a pestilence.

What added, no doubt, to my hatred of the beast, was the discovery, on the morning after I brought it home, that, like Pluto, it also had been deprived of one of its eyes. This circumstance, however, only endeared it to my wife, who, as I have already said, possessed, in a high degree, that humanity of feeling which had once been my distinguishing trait, and the source of many of my simplest and purest pleasures.

With my aversion to this cat, however, its partiality for myself seemed to increase. It followed my footsteps with a pertinacity which it would be difficult to make the reader comprehend. Whenever I sat, it would crouch beneath my chair, or spring upon my knees, covering me with its loathsome caresses. If I arose to walk it would get between my feet and thus nearly throw me down, or, fastening its long and sharp claws in my dress, clamber, in this manner, to my breast. At such times, although I longed to destroy it with a blow, I was yet withheld from so doing, partly by a memory of my former crime, but chiefly—let me confess it at once—by absolute *dread* of the beast.

This dread was not exactly a dread of physical evil—and yet I should be at a loss how otherwise to define it. I am almost ashamed to own—yes, even in this felon's cell, I am almost ashamed to own— that the terror and horror with which the animal inspired me, had been heightened by one of the merest chimeras it would be possible to conceive. My wife had called my attention, more than once, to the character of the mark of white hair, of which I have spoken, and which constituted the sole visible difference between the strange beast and the one I had destroyed. The reader will remember that this mark, although large, had been originally very indefinite; but, by slow degrees—degrees nearly imperceptible, and which for a long time my reason struggled to reject as fanciful—it had, at length, assumed a rigorous distinctness of outline. It was now the representation of an object that I shudder to name—and for this, above all, I loathed, and dreaded, and would have rid myself of the monster *had I dared*—it was now, I say, the image of a hideous—of a ghastly thing—of the GALLOWS!—oh, mournful and terrible engine of Horror and of Crime—of Agony and of Death!

And now was I indeed wretched beyond the wretchedness of mere Humanity. And *a brute beast*—whose fellow I had contemptuously destroyed—*a brute beast* to work out for *me*—for me, a man fashioned in the image of the High God—so much of insufferable woe! Alas! neither by day nor by night knew I the blessing of rest any more! During the former the creature left me no moment alone, and in the latter I started hourly from dreams of unutterable fear to find the hot breath of *the thing* upon my face, and its vast weight—an incarnate nightmare that I had no power to shake off—incumbent eternally upon my *heart*!

Beneath the pressure of torments such as these the feeble remnant of the good within me succumbed. Evil thoughts became my sole intimates—the darkest and most evil of thoughts. The moodiness of my usual temper increased to hatred of all things and of all mankind; while from the sudden, frequent, and ungovernable outbursts of a fury to which I now blindly abandoned myself, my uncomplaining wife, alas, was the most usual and the most patient of sufferers.

One day she accompanied me, upon some household errand, into the cellar of the old building which our poverty compelled us to inhabit. The cat followed me down the steep stairs, and, nearly throwing me headlong, exasperated me to madness. Uplifting an

axe, and forgetting in my wrath the childish dread which had hitherto stayed my hand, I aimed a blow at the animal which, of course,
would have proved instantly fatal had it descended as I wished. But
this blow was arrested by the hand of my wife. Goaded by the interference into a rage more than demoniacal, I withdrew my arm from
her grasp and buried the axe in her brain. She fell dead upon the
spot without a groan.

This hideous murder accomplished, I set myself forthwith, and
with entire deliberation, to the task of concealing the body. I knew
that I could not remove it from the house, either by day or by night,
without the risk of being observed by the neighbors. Many projects
entered my mind. At one period I thought of cutting the corpse into
minute fragments, and destroying them by fire. At another, I resolved to dig a grave for it in the floor of the cellar. Again, I deliber-
ated about casting it in the well in the yard—about packing it in a
box, as if merchandise, with the usual arrangements, and so getting
a porter to take it from the house. Finally I hit upon what I considered a far better expedient than either of these. I determined to wall
it up in the cellar, as the monks of the middle ages are recorded to
have walled up their victims.

For a purpose such as this the cellar was well adapted. Its walls
were loosely constructed, and had lately been plastered throughout
with a rough plaster, which the dampness of the atmosphere had
prevented from hardening. Moreover, in one of the walls was a pro-
jection, caused by a false chimney, or fireplace, that had been filled
up, and made to resemble the rest of the cellar. I made no doubt that
I could readily displace the bricks at this point, insert the corpse,
and wall the whole up as before, so that no eye could detect any
thing suspicious.

And in this calculation I was not deceived. By means of a crowbar I easily dislodged the bricks, and, having carefully deposited
the body against the inner wall, I propped it in that position, while

with little trouble I relaid the whole structure as it originally stood. Having procured mortar, sand, and hair, with every possible precaution, I prepared a plaster which could not be distinguished from the old, and with this I very carefully went over the new brick-work. When I had finished, I felt satisfied that all was right. The wall did not present the slightest appearance of having been disturbed. The rubbish on the floor was picked up with the minutest care. I looked around triumphantly, and said to myself: "Here at least, then, my labor has not been in vain."

My next step was to look for the beast which had been the cause of so much wretchedness; for I had, at length, firmly resolved to put it to death. Had I been able to meet with it at the moment, there could have been no doubt of its fate; but it appeared that the crafty animal had been alarmed at the violence of my previous anger, and forbore to present itself in my present mood. It is impossible to describe or to imagine the deep, the blissful sense of relief which the absence of the detested creature occasioned in my bosom. It did not make its appearance during the night; and thus for one night, at least, since its introduction into the house, I soundly and tranquilly slept; aye, *slept* even with the burden of murder upon my soul.

The second and the third day passed, and still my tormentor came not. Once again I breathed as a freeman. The monster, in terror, had fled the premises for ever! I should behold it no more! My happiness was supreme! The guilt of my dark deed disturbed me but little. Some few inquiries had been made, but these had been readily answered. Even a search had been instituted—but of course nothing was to be discovered. I looked upon my future felicity as secured.

Upon the fourth day of the assassination, a party of the police came, very unexpectedly, into the house, and proceeded again to make rigorous investigation of the premises. Secure, however, in the inscrutability of my place of concealment, I felt no embarrassment whatever. The officers bade me accompany them in their search. They left no nook or corner unexplored. At length, for the third or fourth time, they descended into the cellar. I quivered not in a muscle. My heart beat calmly as that of one who slumbers in innocence. I walked the cellar from end to end. I folded my arms upon my bosom, and roamed easily to and fro. The police were thoroughly satisfied and prepared to depart. The glee at my heart was too strong to be restrained. I burned to say if but one word, by way of triumph, and to render doubly sure their assurance of my guiltlessness.

"Gentlemen," I said at last, as the party ascended the steps, "I delight to have allayed your suspicions. I wish you all health and a little more courtesy. By the bye, gentlemen, this—this is a very well-constructed house," (in the rabid desire to say something easily, I scarcely knew what I uttered at all),—"I may say an *excellently* well-constructed house. These walls—are you going, gentlemen?—these walls are solidly put together"; and here, through the mere phrenzy of bravado, I rapped heavily with a cane which I held in my hand, upon that very portion of the brickwork behind which stood the corpse of the wife of my bosom.

But may God shield and deliver me from the fangs of the Arch-Fiend! No sooner had the reverberation of my blows sunk into silence, than I was answered by a voice from within the tomb!—by a cry, at first muffled and broken, like the sobbing of a child, and then quickly swelling into one long, loud, and continuous scream, utterly anomalous and inhuman—a howl—a wailing shriek, half of horror and half of triumph, such as might have arisen only out of hell, conjointly from the throats of the damned in their agony and of the demons that exult in the damnation.

Of my own thoughts it is folly to speak. Swooning, I staggered to the opposite wall. For one instant the party upon the stairs remained motionless, through extremity of terror and of awe. In the next a dozen stout arms were toiling at the wall. It fell bodily. The corpse, already greatly decayed and clotted with gore, stood erect before the eyes of the spectators. Upon its head, with red extended mouth and solitary eye of fire, sat the hideous beast whose craft had seduced me into murder, and whose informing voice had consigned me to the hangman. I had walled the monster up within the tomb!

Pluto's Heritage

······

BY P. J. PARRISH

The homeless man cornered us outside the supermarket.

"I found this in the Dumpster," he said, pointing to his dirty plaid shirt.

Poking out of his pocket was a kitten's head.

"I got no place for it," he said. "Can you give it a home?"

The tiny beast was wet with blood. It was dying.

My husband took it and handed the man a twenty. It was late on a Saturday night, but we drove to the emergency vet. An hour and two hundred dollars later, the vet sent us on our way with the kitten. It was fine, he said, just starving and missing an eye.

Cleaned up, the kitten didn't look that bad. It quickly grew fat and found its rank among our eight other cats.

"What should we name it?" my husband asked.

"Pluto," I said.

Which is, of course, the name of the tortured feline in Edgar Allan Poe's "The Black Cat." Not that I was any expert on Poe then. Far from it. Like most people, my first guide to Poe was B-director Roger Corman (Ray Milland in *Premature Burial* drinking maggots from a wine goblet!). My next guide was Professor Schneider, whose Introduction to American Literature course had me shoehorning the Poe short stories in between Twain and Hawthorne.

I remember finding "The Black Cat" dense and difficult. I had to look up a lot of words. I couldn't figure out what was going on. And what was the deal with this guy gouging out his cat's eye and planting an ax in his wife's head after claiming he adored them both? Was he a liar, confused, drunk, or just plain nuts?

Like most critics of Poe's day—Yeats called him "vulgar"—I was underwhelmed.

I didn't cross paths with "The Black Cat" for decades, writing it—and its creator—off as archaic and lightweight. It was only after I started writing fiction that I gave Poe a second chance. Although I had published a handful of crime novels, I was struggling with my first short story. Pluto was sitting on my lap at the computer one day as I stared at the blank screen. He wasn't the one who Googled "The Black Cat," but damn, wouldn't that have made a great Poe twist?

I was floored by the story and went on to read others. Poe hadn't gotten better; I had just gotten older. The Saturday-matinee Poe who scared the Jujubes out of me as a kid scared me in a completely different way as an adult. Now I could understand the thin line between promise and disappointment. Now I could imagine the terror of a mind unbalanced by demons or drink. Now I could see the rich mix of emotions, the delicate dance between the romantic and the macabre, the real and the supernatural. And as a writer, now I could appreciate the complex construction of Poe's puzzles and his use of what he called "the vivid effect" to grab the reader's emotions. What modern storyteller worth her salt doesn't strive to do that?

All writers today—crime, horror, romance, yes, even literary— owe him a debt. My favorite author, Joyce Carol Oates, asks in the afterword of her short-story collection *Haunted:* "Who has not been influenced by Poe?" Oates herself wrote a Poe paean called "The

White Cat" in which a husband becomes murderously jealous of his wife's Persian cat.

Writers can learn much from him still.

As for readers, there is much to savor in this sly little tale.

First, it is a very modern detective story, but one in which you, the reader, must follow the bread-crumb trail of clues. Why did this man kill his wife? You have to peel back the psychological layers of the killer's behavior—shades of *Silence of the Lambs*!—to find meaning for a brutal murder when none seems to exist.

Second, it is a chilling study of domestic violence, perversity, and guilt. Compare it with its bookend story, "The Tell-Tale Heart," the other great example in this collection. Both narrators deny that they are insane—but are they?

Third, "The Black Cat" is one of the first stories to use "the unreliable narrator." (This is when bias, instability, limited knowledge, or deliberate deceit makes the storyteller suspect.) With one line— "I neither expect nor solicit belief"—Poe paved the way for Nick Carraway in Fitzgerald's *The Great Gatsby*, the governess in Henry James's *The Turn of the Screw*, Dr. Sheppard in Agatha Christie's *The Murder of Roger Ackroyd*, the cook in Dean Koontz's *Odd Thomas*, and Teddy Daniels in Dennis Lehane's *Shutter Island*.

Fourth, "The Black Cat" is an early example of genre-crossing. Poe is known for horror, but in this story he blurs the line between realism and the supernatural. The paranormal, reincarnation, horror, mystery—it's all there and more.

And last? Well, it *is* the first cat mystery.

Which brings us back to Pluto. Mine is still hale and hearty at fourteen. The fictional Pluto, of course, dies horribly. Which didn't really bother me—until I started writing fiction. See, there's an axiom among mystery writers: kill an animal and your readers will turn on you.

Poe adored cats in real life. His beloved tabby Catarina even inspired him to write a scientific essay, "Instinct vs. Reason—A Black Cat."

Still, when he put pen to paper, he wasn't afraid to kill the cat. You have to admire a writer who takes big risks.

P. J. Parrish, a.k.a. Kristy Montee, is the author (with her sister Kelly Nichols) of two series of crime novels featuring biracial private eye Louis Kincaid and female homicide detective Joe Frye. Their books are New York Times *best-sellers and have won awards from the Private Eye Writers of America and International Thriller Writers. Their short stories have appeared in* Ellery Queen's Mystery Magazine, *in Mystery Writers of America's anthologies, and in Akashic Books'* Detroit Noir. *Like Poe, Kris has a love of wine and cats, an appreciation of all that is grotesque and depressing, and a distrust of critics (even though she once earned a living as one). Unfortunately, that is the limit of her kinship to Poe—unless one counts the fact that her second book was nominated for an Edgar.*

William Wilson

"What say of it? what say of CONSCIENCE grim,
That spectre in my path?"

—CHAMBERLAIN'S *PHARRONIDA*

LET ME CALL MYSELF, for the present, William Wilson. The fair page now lying before me need not be sullied with my real appellation. This has been already too much an object for the scorn—for the horror—for the detestation of my race. To the uttermost regions of the globe have not the indignant winds bruited its unparalleled infamy? Oh, outcast of all outcasts most abandoned!—to the earth art thou not for ever dead? to its honors, to its flowers, to its golden aspirations?—and a cloud, dense, dismal, and limitless, does it not hang eternally between thy hopes and heaven?

I would not, if I could, here or to-day, embody a record

of my later years of unspeakable misery, and unpardonable crime. This epoch—these later years—took unto themselves a sudden elevation in turpitude, whose origin alone it is my present purpose to assign. Men usually grow base by degrees. From me, in an instant, all virtue dropped bodily as a mantle. From comparatively trivial wickedness I passed, with the stride of a giant, into more than the enormities of an Elah-Gabalus. What chance—what one event brought this evil thing to pass, bear with me while I relate. Death approaches; and the shadow which foreruns him has thrown a softening influence over my spirit. I long, in passing through the dim valley, for the sympathy—I had nearly said for the pity—of my fellow men. I would fain have them believe that I have been, in some measure, the slave of circumstances beyond human control. I would wish them to seek out for me, in the details I am about to give, some little oasis of *fatality* amid a wilderness of error. I would have them allow—what they cannot refrain from allowing—that, although temptation may have erewhile existed as great, man was never *thus*, at least, tempted before—certainly, never *thus* fell. And is it therefore that he has never thus suffered? Have I not indeed been living in a dream? And am I not now dying a victim to the horror and the mystery of the wildest of all sublunary visions?

I am the descendant of a race whose imaginative and easily excitable temperament has at all times rendered them remarkable; and, in my earliest infancy, I gave evidence of having fully inherited the family character. As I advanced in years it was more strongly developed; becoming, for many reasons, a cause of serious disquietude to my friends, and of positive injury to myself. I grew self-willed, addicted to the wildest caprices, and a prey to the most ungovernable passions. Weak-minded, and beset with constitutional infirmities akin to my own, my parents could do but little to check the evil propensities which distinguished me. Some feeble and ill-directed efforts resulted in complete failure on their part, and, of course, in total triumph on mine. Thenceforward my voice was a household law; and at an age when few children have abandoned their leading-strings, I was left to the guidance of my own will, and became, in all but name, the master of my own actions.

My earliest recollections of a school-life, are connected with a large, rambling, Elizabethan house, in a misty-looking village of England, where were a vast number of gigantic and gnarled trees, and where all the houses were excessively ancient. In truth, it was a dream-like and spirit-soothing place, that venerable old town. At this moment, in fancy, I feel the refreshing chilliness of its deeply-shadowed avenues, inhale the fragrance of its thousand shrubberies, and thrill anew with undefinable delight, at the deep hollow note of the church-bell, breaking, each hour, with sullen and sudden roar, upon the stillness of the dusky atmosphere in which the fretted Gothic steeple lay imbedded and asleep.

It gives me, perhaps, as much of pleasure as I can now in any manner experience, to dwell upon minute recollections of the school and its concerns. Steeped in misery as I am—misery, alas! only too real—I shall be pardoned for seeking relief, however slight and temporary, in the weakness of a few rambling details. These, moreover, utterly trivial, and even ridiculous in themselves, assume, to my fancy, adventitious importance, as connected with a period and a locality when and where I recognize the first ambiguous monitions of the destiny which afterward so fully overshadowed me. Let me then remember.

The house, I have said, was old and irregular. The grounds were extensive, and a high and solid brick wall, topped with a bed of mortar and broken glass, encompassed the whole. This prison-like rampart formed the limit of our domain; beyond it we saw but thrice a week—once every Saturday afternoon, when, attended by two ushers, we were permitted to take brief walks in a body through some of the neighbouring fields—and twice during Sunday, when we were paraded in the same formal manner to the morning and evening service in the one church of the village. Of this church the principal of our school was pastor. With how deep a spirit of wonder and perplexity was I wont to regard him from our remote pew in the gallery, as, with step solemn and slow, he ascended the pulpit! This reverend man, with countenance so demurely benign, with robes so glossy and so clerically flowing, with wig so minutely powdered, so rigid and so vast,—could this be he who, of late, with sour visage, and in snuffy habiliments, administered, ferule in hand, the Draconian Laws of the academy? Oh, gigantic paradox, too utterly monstrous for solution!

At an angle of the ponderous wall frowned a more ponderous gate. It was riveted and studded with iron bolts, and surmounted with jagged iron spikes. What impressions of deep awe did it inspire! It was never opened save for the three periodical egressions and ingressions already mentioned; then, in every creak of its mighty hinges, we found a plenitude of mystery—a world of matter for solemn remark, or for more solemn meditation.

The extensive enclosure was irregular in form, having many capacious recesses. Of these, three or four of the largest constituted the play-ground. It was level, and covered with fine hard gravel. I well remember it had no trees, nor benches, nor any thing similar within it. Of course it was in the rear of the house. In front lay a small parterre, planted with box and other shrubs, but through this sacred division we passed only upon rare occasions indeed—such as a first advent to school or final departure thence, or perhaps, when a parent or friend having called for us, we joyfully took our way home for the Christmas or Midsummer holidays.

But the house!—how quaint an old building was this!—to me how veritably a palace of enchantment! There was really no end to its windings—to its incomprehensible subdivisions. It was difficult, at any given time, to say with certainty upon which of its two stories one happened to be. From each room to every other there were sure to be found three or four steps either in ascent or descent. Then the lateral branches were innumerable—inconceivable—and so returning in upon themselves, that our most exact ideas in regard to the whole mansion were not very far different from those with which we pondered upon infinity. During the five years of my residence here, I was never able to ascertain with precision, in what remote locality lay the little sleeping apartment assigned to myself and some eighteen or twenty other scholars.

The school-room was the largest in the house—I could not help thinking, in the world. It was very long, narrow, and dismally low, with pointed Gothic windows and a ceiling of oak. In a remote and terror-inspiring angle was a square enclosure of eight or ten feet, comprising the *sanctum*, "during hours," of our principal, the Reverend Dr. Bransby. It was a solid structure, with massy door, sooner than open which in the absence of the "Dominie," we would all have willingly perished by the *peine forte et dure*. In other angles were two other similar boxes, far less reverenced, indeed, but still greatly matters of awe. One of these was the pulpit of the "classical" usher, one of the "English and mathematical." Interspersed about the room, crossing and recrossing in endless irregularity, were innumerable benches and desks, black, ancient, and time-worn, piled desperately with much bethumbed books, and so beseamed with initial letters, names at full length, grotesque figures, and other multiplied efforts of the knife, as to have entirely lost what little of original form might have been their portion in days long departed. A huge bucket with water stood at one extremity of the room, and a clock of stupendous dimensions at the other.

Encompassed by the massy walls of this venerable academy, I passed, yet not in tedium or disgust, the years of the third lustrum of my life. The teeming brain of childhood requires no external world of incident to occupy or amuse it; and the apparently dismal monotony of a school was replete with more intense excitement than my riper youth has derived from luxury, or my full manhood from crime. Yet I must believe that my first mental development had in it much of the uncommon—even much of the *outré*. Upon mankind at large the events of very early existence rarely leave in mature age any definite impression. All is gray shadow—a weak and irregular remembrance—an indistinct regathering of feeble pleasures and phantasmagoric pains. With me this is not so. In childhood I must have felt with the energy of a man what I now find stamped upon memory in lines as vivid, as deep, and as durable as the *exergues* of the Carthaginian medals.

Yet in fact—in the fact of the world's view—how little was there to remember! The morning's awakening, the nightly summons to bed; the connings, the recitations; the periodical half-holidays, and perambulations; the play-ground, with its broils, its pastimes, its intrigues;—these, by a mental sorcery long forgotten, were made to involve a wilderness of sensation, a world of rich incident, an universe of varied emotion, of excitement the most passionate and spirit-stirring. *"Oh, le bon temps, que ce siècle de fer!"*

In truth, the ardor, the enthusiasm, and the imperiousness of my disposition, soon rendered me a marked character among my schoolmates, and by slow, but natural gradations, gave me an ascendancy over all not greatly older than myself;—over all with a single exception. This exception was found in the person of a scholar, who, although no relation, bore the same Christian and surname as myself;—a circumstance, in fact, little remarkable; for, notwithstanding a noble descent, mine was one of those everyday appellations which seem, by prescriptive right, to have been, time out of mind, the common property of the mob. In this narrative I have therefore designated myself as William Wilson,—a fictitious title not very dissimilar to the real. My namesake alone, of those who in school phraseology constituted "our set," presumed to compete with me in the studies of the class—in the sports and broils of the playground—to refuse implicit belief in my assertions, and submission to my will—indeed, to interfere with my arbitrary dictation in any respect whatsoever. If there is on earth a supreme and unqualified despotism, it is the despotism of a mastermind in boyhood over the less energetic spirits of its companions.

Wilson's rebellion was to me a source of the greatest embarrassment; the more so as, in spite of the bravado with which in public I made a point of treating him and his pretensions, I secretly felt that I feared him, and could not help thinking the equality which he maintained so easily with myself, a proof of his true superiority; since not to be overcome, cost me a perpetual struggle. Yet this superiority—even this equality—was in truth acknowledged by no one but myself; our associates, by some unaccountable blindness, seemed not even to suspect it. Indeed, his competition, his resistance, and especially his impertinent and dogged interference with my purposes, were not more pointed than private. He appeared to be destitute alike of the ambition which urged, and of the passionate energy of mind which enabled me to excel. In his rivalry he might have been supposed actuated solely by a whimsical desire to thwart, astonish, or mortify myself; although there were times when I could not help observing, with a feeling made up of wonder, abasement, and pique, that he mingled with his injuries, his insults, or his contradictions, a certain most inappropriate, and assuredly most unwelcome *affectionateness* of manner. I could only conceive this singular behavior to arise from a consummate self-conceit assuming the vulgar airs of patronage and protection.

Perhaps it was this latter trait in Wilson's conduct, conjoined with our identity of name, and the mere accident of our having entered the school upon the same day, which set afloat the notion that we were brothers, among the senior classes in the academy. These do not usually inquire with much strictness into the affairs of their juniors. I have before said, or should have said, that Wilson was not, in a most remote degree, connected with my family. But assuredly if we *had* been brothers we must have been twins; for, after leaving Dr. Bransby's, I casually learned that my namesake was born on the nineteenth of January, 1813—and this is a somewhat remarkable coincidence; for the day is precisely that of my own nativity.

It may seem strange that in spite of the continual anxiety occasioned me by the rivalry of Wilson, and his intolerable spirit of contradiction, I could not bring myself to hate him altogether. We had, to be sure, nearly every day a quarrel in which, yielding me publicly the palm of victory, he, in some manner, contrived to make me feel that it was he who had deserved it; yet a sense of pride on my part, and a veritable dignity on his own, kept us always upon what are called "speaking terms," while there were many points of strong congeniality in our tempers, operating to awake me in a sentiment which our position alone, perhaps, prevented from ripening into friendship. It is difficult, indeed, to define, or even to describe, my real feelings towards him. They formed a motley and heterogeneous admixture;—some petulant animosity, which was not yet hatred, some esteem, more respect, much fear, with a world of uneasy curiosity. To the moralist it will be unnecessary to say, in addition, that Wilson and myself were the most inseparable of companions.

It was no doubt the anomalous state of affairs existing between us, which turned all my attacks upon him, (and there were many, either open or covert) into the channel of banter or practical joke (giving pain while assuming the aspect of mere fun) rather than into a more serious and determined hostility. But my endeavours on this head were by no means uniformly successful, even when my plans were the most wittily concocted; for my namesake had much about him, in character of that unassuming and quiet austerity which, while enjoying the poignancy of its own jokes, has no heel of Achilles in itself, and absolutely refuses to be laughed at.

I could find, indeed, but one vulnerable point, and that, lying in a personal peculiarity, arising, perhaps, from constitutional disease, would have been spared by any antagonist less at his wit's end than myself;—my rival had a weakness in the faucial or guttural organs, which precluded him from raising his voice at any time *above a very low whisper.* Of this defect I did not fail to take what poor advantage lay in my power.

Wilson's retaliations in kind were many; and there was one form of his practical wit that disturbed me beyond measure. How his sagacity first discovered at all that so petty a thing would vex me, is a question I never could solve; but having discovered, he habitually practised the annoyance. I had always felt aversion to my uncourtly patronymic, and its very common, if not plebeian praenomen. The words were venom in my ears; and when, upon the day of my arrival, a second William Wilson came also to the academy, I felt angry with him for bearing the name, and doubly disgusted with the name because a stranger bore it, who would be the cause of its twofold repetition, who would be constantly in my presence, and whose concerns, in the ordinary routine of the school business, must inevitably, on account of the detestable coincidence, be often confounded with my own.

The feeling of vexation thus engendered grew stronger with every circumstance tending to show resemblance, moral or physical, between my rival and myself. I had not then discovered the remarkable fact that we were of the same age; but I saw that we were of the same height, and I perceived that we were even singularly alike in general contour of person and outline of feature. I was galled, too, by the rumor touching a relationship, which had grown current in the upper forms. In a word, nothing could more seriously disturb me (although I scrupulously concealed such disturbance) than any allusion to a similarity of mind, person, or condition existing between us. But, in truth, I had no reason to believe that (with the exception of the matter of relationship, and in the case of Wilson himself) this similarity had ever been made a subject of comment, or even observed at all by our schoolfellows. That *he* observed it in all its bearings, and as fixedly as I, was apparent; but that he could discover in such circumstances so fruitful a field of annoyance, can only be attributed, as I said before, to his more than ordinary penetration.

His cue, which was to perfect an imitation of myself, lay both in words and in actions; and most admirably did he play his part. My dress it was an easy matter to copy; my gait and general manner were, without difficulty, appropriated; in spite of his constitutional defect, even my voice did not escape him. My louder tones were, of course, unattempted, but then the key, — it was identical; *and his singular whisper, it grew the very echo of my own.*

How greatly this most exquisite portraiture harassed me, (for it could not justly be termed a caricature), I will not now venture to describe. I had but one consolation — in the fact that the imitation, apparently, was noticed by myself alone, and that I had to endure only the knowing and strangely sarcastic smiles of my namesake himself. Satisfied with having produced in my bosom the intended effect, he seemed to chuckle in secret over the sting he had inflicted, and was characteristically disregardful of the public applause which the success of his witty endeavours might have so easily elicited. That the school, indeed, did not feel his design, perceive its accomplishment, and participate in his sneer, was, for many anxious months, a riddle I could not resolve. Perhaps the *gradation* of his copy rendered it not so readily perceptible; or, more possibly, I owed my security to the master air of the copyist, who, disdaining the letter (which in a painting is all the obtuse can see), gave but the full spirit of his original for my individual contemplation and chagrin.

I have already more than once spoken of the disgusting air of patronage which he assumed toward me, and of his frequent officious interference with my will. This interference often took the ungracious character of advice; advice not openly given, but hinted or insinuated. I received it with a repugnance which gained strength as I grew in years. Yet, at this distant day, let me do him the simple justice to acknowledge that I can recall no occasion when the suggestions of my rival were on the side of those errors or follies so usual to his immature age and seeming inexperience; that his moral sense, at least, if not his general talents and worldly wisdom, was far keener than my own; and that I might, to-day, have been a better and thus a happier man, had I less frequently rejected the counsels embodied in those meaning whispers which I then but too cordially hated and too bitterly despised.

As it was I at length grew restive in the extreme under his distasteful supervision, and daily resented more and more openly, what I considered his intolerable arrogance. I have said that, in the first years of our connection as schoolmates, my feelings in regard to him might have been easily ripened into friendship; but, in the latter months of my residence at the academy, although the intrusion of his ordinary manner had, beyond doubt, in some measure, abated, my sentiments, in nearly similar proportion, partook very much of positive hatred. Upon one occasion he saw this, I think, and afterwards avoided, or made a show of avoiding me.

It was about the same period, if I remember aright, that, in an altercation of violence with him, in which he was more than usually thrown off his guard, and spoke and acted with an openness of demeanor rather foreign to his nature, I discovered, or fancied I discovered, in his accent, in his air, and general appearance, a something which first startled, and then deeply interested me, by bringing to mind dim visions of my earliest infancy—wild, confused and thronging memories of a time when memory herself was yet unborn. I cannot better describe the sensation which oppressed me, than by saying that I could with difficulty shake off the belief of my having been acquainted with the being who stood before me, at some epoch very long ago—some point of the past even infinitely remote. The delusion, however, faded as rapidly as it came; and I mention it at all but to define the day of the last conversation I there held with my singular namesake.

The huge old house, with its countless subdivisions, had several large chambers communicating with each other, where slept the greater number of the students. There were, however (as must necessarily happen in a building so awkwardly planned), many little nooks or recesses, the odds and ends of the structure; and these the economic ingenuity of Dr. Bransby had also fitted up as dormitories; although, being the merest closets, they were capable of accommodating but a single individual. One of these small apartments was occupied by Wilson.

One night, about the close of my fifth year at the school, and immediately after the altercation just mentioned, finding every one wrapped in sleep, I arose from bed, and, lamp in hand, stole through a wilderness of narrow passages, from my own bedroom to that of my rival. I had long been plotting one of those ill-natured pieces of practical wit at his expense in which I had hitherto been so uniformly unsuccessful. It was my intention, now, to put my scheme in operation and I resolved to make him feel the whole extent of the malice with which I was imbued. Having reached his closet, I noiselessly entered, leaving the lamp, with a shade over it, on the outside. I advanced a step, and listened to the sound of his tranquil breathing. Assured of his being asleep, I returned, took the light, and with it again approached the bed. Close curtains were around it, which, in the prosecution of my plan, I slowly and quietly withdrew, when the bright rays fell vividly upon the sleeper, and my eyes at the same moment, upon his countenance. I looked;—and a numbness, an iciness of feeling instantly pervaded my frame. My breast heaved, my knees tottered, my whole spirit became possessed with an objectless yet intolerable horror. Gasping for breath, I lowered the lamp in still nearer proximity to the face. Were these—*these* the lineaments of William Wilson? I saw, indeed, that they were his, but I shook as if with a fit of the ague, in fancying they were not. What *was* there about them to confound me in this manner? I gazed;—while my brain reeled with a multitude of incoherent thoughts. Not thus he appeared—assuredly not *thus*—in the vivacity of his waking hours. The same name! the same contour of person! the same day of arrival at the academy! And then his dogged and meaningless imitation of my gait, my voice, my habits, and my manner! Was it, in truth, within the bounds of human possibility, that *what I now saw* was the result, merely, of the habitual practice of this sarcastic imitation? Awe-stricken, and with a creeping shudder, I extinguished the lamp, passed silently from the chamber, and left, at once, the halls of that old academy, never to enter them again.

After a lapse of some months, spent at home in mere idleness, I found myself a student at Eton. The brief interval had been sufficient to enfeeble my remembrance of the events at Dr. Bransby's, or at least to effect a material change in the nature of the feelings with which I remembered them. The truth—the tragedy—of the drama was no more. I could now find room to doubt the evidence of my senses; and seldom called up the subject at all but with wonder at the extent of human credulity, and a smile at the vivid force of the imagination which I hereditarily possessed. Neither was this species of skepticism likely to be diminished by the character of the life I led at Eton. The vortex of thoughtless folly into which I there so immediately and so recklessly plunged, washed away all but the froth of my past hours, ingulfed at once every solid or serious impression, and left to memory only the veriest levities of a former existence.

I do not wish, however, to trace the course of my miserable profligacy here—a profligacy which set at defiance the laws, while it eluded the vigilance of the institution. Three years of folly, passed without profit, had but given me rooted habits of vice, and added, in a somewhat unusual degree, to my bodily stature, when, after a week of soulless dissipation, I invited a small party of the most dissolute students to a secret carousal in my chambers. We met at a late hour of the night; for our debaucheries were to be faithfully protracted until morning. The wine flowed freely, and there were not wanting other and perhaps more dangerous seductions; so that the gray dawn had already faintly appeared in the east, while our delirious extravagance was at its height. Madly flushed with cards and intoxication, I was in the act of insisting upon a toast of more than wonted profanity, when my attention was suddenly diverted by the violent, although partial, unclosing of the door of the apartment, and by the eager voice of a servant from without. He said that some person, apparently in great haste, demanded to speak with me in the hall.

Wildly excited with wine, the unexpected interruption rather delighted than surprised me. I staggered forward at once, and a few steps brought me to the vestibule of the building. In this low and small room there hung no lamp; and now no light at all was admitted, save that of the exceedingly feeble dawn which made its way through the semi-circular window. As I put my foot over the threshold, I became aware of the figure of a youth about my own height, and habited in a white kerseymere morning frock, cut in the novel fashion of the one I myself wore at the moment. This the faint light enabled me to perceive; but the features of his face I could not distinguish. Upon my entering, he strode hurriedly up to me, and, seizing me by the arm with a gesture of petulant impatience, whispered the words "William Wilson!" in my ear.

I grew perfectly sober in an instant.

There was that in the manner of the stranger, and in the tremulous shake of his uplifted finger, as he held it between my eyes and the light, which filled me with unqualified amazement; but it was not this which had so violently moved me. It was the pregnancy of solemn admonition in the singular, low, hissing utterance; and, above all, it was the character, the tone, the *key*, of those few, simple, and familiar, yet *whispered* syllables, which came with a thousand thronging memories of by-gone days, and struck upon my soul with the shock of a galvanic battery. Ere I could recover the use of my senses he was gone.

Although this event failed not of a vivid effect upon my disordered imagination, yet was it evanescent as vivid. For some weeks, indeed, I busied myself in earnest inquiry, or was wrapped in a cloud of morbid speculation. I did not pretend to disguise from my perception the identity of the singular individual who thus perseveringly interfered with my affairs, and harassed me with his insinuated counsel. But who and what was this Wilson?—and whence came he?—and what were his purposes? Upon neither of these points could I be satisfied—merely ascertaining, in regard to him, that a sudden accident in his family had caused his removal from Dr. Bransby's academy on the afternoon of the day in which I myself had eloped. But in a brief period I ceased to think upon the subject, my attention being all absorbed in a contemplated departure for Oxford. Thither I soon went; the uncalculating vanity of my parents furnishing me with an outfit and annual establishment, which would enable me to indulge at will in the luxury already so dear to my heart,—to vie in profuseness of expenditure with the haughtiest heirs of the wealthiest earldoms in Great Britain.

Excited by such appliances to vice, my constitutional temperament broke forth with redoubled ardor, and I spurned even the common restraints of decency in the mad infatuation of my revels. But it were absurd to pause in the detail of my extravagance. Let it suffice, that among spendthrifts I out-Heroded Herod, and that, giving name to a multitude of novel follies, I added no brief appendix to the long catalogue of vices then usual in the most dissolute university of Europe.

It could hardly be credited, however, that I had, even here, so utterly fallen from the gentlemanly estate, as to seek acquaintance with the vilest arts of the gambler by profession, and, having become an adept in his despicable science, to practice it habitually as a means of increasing my already enormous income at the expense of the weakminded among my fellow-collegians. Such, nevertheless, was the fact. And the very enormity of this offence against all manly and honorable sentiment proved, beyond doubt, the main if not the sole reason of the impunity with which it was committed. Who, indeed, among my most abandoned associates, would not rather have disputed the clearest evidence of his senses, than have suspected of such courses, the gay, the frank, the generous William Wilson—the noblest and most commoner at Oxford—him whose follies (said his parasites) were but the follies of youth and unbridled fancy—whose errors but inimitable whim—whose darkest vice but a careless and dashing extravagance?

I had been now two years successfully busied in this way, when there came to the university a young *parvenu* nobleman, Glendinning—rich, said report, as Herodes Atticus—his riches, too, as easily acquired. I soon found him of weak intellect, and, of course, marked him as a fitting subject for my skill. I frequently engaged him in play, and contrived, with the gambler's usual art, to let him win considerable sums, the more effectually to entangle him in my snares. At length, my schemes being ripe, I met him (with the full intention that this meeting should be final and decisive) at the chambers of a fellow-commoner (Mr. Preston), equally intimate with both, but who, to do him Justice, entertained not even a remote suspicion of my design. To give to this a better coloring, I had contrived to have assembled a party of some eight or ten, and was solicitously careful that the introduction of cards should appear accidental, and originate in the proposal of my contemplated dupe himself. To be brief upon a vile topic, none of the low finesse was omitted, so customary upon similar occasions, that it is a just matter for wonder how any are still found so besotted as to fall its victim.

We had protracted our sitting far into the night, and I had at length effected the manoeuvre of getting Glendinning as my sole antagonist. The game, too, was my favorite *écarté*. The rest of the company, interested in the extent of our play, had abandoned their own cards, and were standing around us as spectators. The *parvenu*, who had been induced by my artifices in the early part of the evening, to drink deeply, now shuffled, dealt, or played, with a wild nervousness of manner for which his intoxication, I thought, might partially, but could not altogether account. In a very short period he had become my debtor to a large amount, when, having taken a long draught of port, he did precisely what I had been coolly anticipating—he proposed to double our already extravagant stakes. With a well-feigned show of reluctance, and not until after my repeated refusal had seduced him into some angry words which gave a color of *pique* to my compliance, did I finally comply. The result, of course, did but prove how entirely the prey was in my toils: in less than an hour he had quadrupled his debt. For some time his countenance had been losing the florid tinge lent it by the wine; but now, to my astonishment, I perceived that it had grown to a pallor truly fearful. I say, to my astonishment. Glendinning had been represented to my eager inquiries as immeasurably wealthy; and the sums which he had as yet lost, although in themselves vast, could not, I supposed, very seriously annoy, much less so violently affect him. That he was overcome by the wine just swallowed, was the idea which most readily presented itself; and, rather with a view to the preservation of my own character in the eyes of my associates, than from any less interested motive, I was about to insist, peremptorily, upon a discontinuance of the play, when some expressions at my elbow from among the company, and an ejaculation evincing utter despair on the part of Glendinning, gave me to understand that I had effected his total ruin under circumstances which, rendering him an object for the pity of all, should have protected him from the ill offices even of a fiend.

What now might have been my conduct it is difficult to say. The pitiable condition of my dupe had thrown an air of embarrassed gloom over all; and, for some moments, a profound silence was maintained, during which I could not help feeling my cheeks tingle with the many burning glances of scorn or reproach cast upon me by the less abandoned of the party. I will even own that an intolerable weight of anxiety was for a brief instant lifted from my bosom by the sudden and extraordinary interruption which ensued. The wide, heavy folding doors of the apartment were all at once thrown open, to their full extent, with a vigorous and rushing impetuosity that extinguished, as if by magic, every candle in the room. Their light, in dying, enabled us just to perceive that a stranger had entered, about my own height, and closely muffled in a cloak. The darkness, however, was now total; and we could only *feel* that he was standing in our midst. Before any one of us could recover from the extreme astonishment into which this rudeness had thrown all, we heard the voice of the intruder.

"Gentlemen," he said, in a low, distinct, and never-to-be-forgotten *whisper* which thrilled to the very marrow of my bones, "Gentlemen, I make an apology for this behavior, because in thus behaving, I am fulfilling a duty. You are, beyond doubt, uninformed of the true character of the person who has to-night won at *écarté* a large sum of money from Lord Glendinning. I will therefore put you upon an expeditious and decisive plan of obtaining this very necessary information. Please to examine, at your leisure, the inner linings of the cuff of his left sleeve, and the several little packages which may be found in the somewhat capacious pockets of his embroidered morning wrapper."

While he spoke, so profound was the stillness that one might have heard a pin drop upon the floor. In ceasing, he departed at once, and as abruptly as he had entered. Can I—shall I describe my sensations? Must I say that I felt all the horrors of the damned? Most assuredly I had little time given for reflection. Many hands roughly seized me upon the spot, and lights were immediately re-procured. A search ensued. In the lining of my sleeve were found all the court cards essential in *écarté*, and, in the pockets of my wrapper, a number of packs, facsimiles of those used at our sittings, with the single exception that mine were of the species called, technically, *arrondées;* the honors being slightly convex at the ends, the lower cards slightly convex at the sides. In this disposition, the dupe who cuts, as customary, at the length of the pack, will invariably find that he cuts his antagonist an honor; while the gambler, cutting at the breadth, will, as certainly, cut nothing for his victim which may count in the records of the game.

Any burst of indignation upon this discovery would have affected me less than the silent contempt, or the sarcastic composure, with which it was received.

"Mr. Wilson," said our host, stooping to remove from beneath his feet an exceedingly luxurious cloak of rare furs, "Mr. Wilson, this is your property." (The weather was cold; and, upon quitting my own room, I had thrown a cloak over my dressing wrapper, putting it off upon reaching the scene of play.) "I presume it is supererogatory to seek here (eyeing the folds of the garment with a bitter smile) for any farther evidence of your skill. Indeed, we have had enough. You will see the necessity, I hope, of quitting Oxford—at all events, of quitting instantly my chambers."

Abased, humbled to the dust as I then was, it is probable that I should have resented this galling language by immediate personal violence, had not my whole attention been at the moment arrested by a fact of the most startling character. The cloak which I had worn was of a rare description of fur; how rare, how extravagantly costly,

I shall not venture to say. Its fashion, too, was of my own fantastic invention; for I was fastidious to an absurd degree of coxcombry, in matters of this frivolous nature. When, therefore, Mr. Preston reached me that which he had picked up upon the floor, and near the folding doors of the apartment, it was with an astonishment nearly bordering upon terror, that I perceived my own already hanging on my arm (where I had no doubt unwittingly placed it), and that the one presented me was but its exact counterpart in every, in even the minutest possible particular. The singular being who had so disastrously exposed me had been muffled, I remembered, in a cloak; and none had been worn at all by any of the members of our party, with the exception of myself. Retaining some presence of mind, I took the one offered me by Preston; placed it, unnoticed, over my own; left the apartment with a resolute scowl of defiance; and, next morning ere dawn of day, commenced a hurried journey from Oxford to the continent, in a perfect agony of horror and of shame.

I fled in vain. My evil destiny pursued me as if in exultation, and proved, indeed, that the exercise of its mysterious dominion had as yet only begun. Scarcely had I set foot in Paris, ere I had fresh evidence of the detestable interest taken by this Wilson in my concerns. Years flew, while I experienced no relief. Villain!—at Rome, with how untimely, yet with how spectral an officiousness, stepped he in between me and my ambition! at Vienna, too—at Berlin—and at Moscow! Where, in truth, had I *not* bitter cause to curse him within my heart? From his inscrutable tyranny did I at length flee, panic-stricken, as from a pestilence; and to the very ends of the earth *I fled in vain.*

And again, and again, in secret communion with my own spirit, would I demand the questions "Who is he?—whence came he?—and what are his objects?" But no answer was there found. And now I scrutinized, with a minute scrutiny, the forms, and the methods, and the leading traits of his impertinent supervision. But even here there was very little upon which to base a conjecture. It was notice-able, indeed, that, in no one of the multiplied instances in which he had of late crossed my path, had he so crossed it except to frustrate those schemes, or to disturb those actions, which, if fully carried out, might have resulted in bitter mischief. Poor justification this, in truth, for an authority so imperiously assumed! Poor indemnity for natural rights of self-agency so pertinaciously, so insultingly denied!

I had also been forced to notice that my tormentor, for a very long period of time (while scrupulously and with miraculous dex-terity maintaining his whim of an identity of apparel with myself) had so contrived it, in the execution of his varied interference with my will, that I saw not, at any moment, the features of his face. Be Wilson what he might, *this*, at least, was but the veriest of affecta-tion, or of folly. Could he, for an instant, have supposed that, in my admonisher at Eton—in the destroyer of my honor at Oxford,—in him who thwarted my ambition at Rome, my revenge at Paris, my passionate love at Naples, or what he falsely termed my avarice in Egypt,—that in this, my arch-enemy and evil genius, I could fail to recognize the William Wilson of my school-boy days,—the name-sake, the companion, the rival,—the hated and dreaded rival at Dr. Bransby's? Impossible!—But let me hasten to the last eventful scene of the drama.

Thus far I had succumbed supinely to this imperious domination. The sentiment of deep awe with which I habitually regarded the el-evated character, the majestic wisdom, the apparent omnipresence and omnipotence of Wilson, added to a feeling of even terror, with which certain other traits in his nature and assumptions inspired me, had operated, hitherto, to impress me with an idea of my own utter weakness and helplessness, and to suggest an implicit, although bit-terly reluctant submission to his arbitrary will. But, of late days, I had given myself up entirely to wine; and its maddening influence upon my hereditary temper rendered me more and more impatient of control. I began to murmur,—to hesitate,—to resist. And was it only fancy which induced me to believe that, with the increase of my own firmness, that of my tormentor underwent a proportional diminution? Be this as it may, I now began to feel the inspiration of a burning hope, and at length nurtured in my secret thoughts a stern and desperate resolution that I would submit no longer to be enslaved.

It was at Rome, during the Carnival of 18—, that I attended a masquerade in the palazzo of the Neapolitan Duke Di Broglio. I had indulged more freely than usual in the excesses of the wine-table; and now the suffocating atmosphere of the crowded rooms irritated me beyond endurance. The difficulty, too, of forcing my way through the mazes of the company contributed not a little to the ruffling of my temper; for I was anxiously seeking (let me not say with what unworthy motive) the young, the gay, the beauti-ful wife of the aged and doting Di Broglio. With a too unscrupu-lous confidence she had previously communicated to me the secret of the costume in which she would be habited, and now, having caught a glimpse of her person, I was hurrying to make my way into her presence. At this moment I felt a light hand placed upon my shoulder, and that ever-remembered, low, damnable *whisper* within my ear.

In an absolute frenzy of wrath, I turned at once upon him who had thus interrupted me, and seized him violently by the collar. He was attired, as I had expected, in a costume altogether similar to my own; wearing a Spanish cloak of blue velvet, begirt about the waist with a crimson belt sustaining a rapier. A mask of black silk entirely covered his face.

"Scoundrel!" I said, in a voice husky with rage, while every syl-lable I uttered seemed as new fuel to my fury; "scoundrel! impostor!

accursed villain! you shall not—you *shall not* dog me unto death! Follow me, or I stab you where you stand!"—and I broke my way from the ball-room into a small antechamber adjoining—dragging him unresistingly with me as I went.

Upon entering, I thrust him furiously from me. He staggered against the wall, while I closed the door with an oath, and commanded him to draw. He hesitated but for an instant; then, with a slight sigh, drew in silence, and put himself upon his defence.

The contest was brief indeed. I was frantic with every species of wild excitement, and felt within my single arm the energy and power of a multitude. In a few seconds I forced him by sheer strength against the wainscotting, and thus, getting him at mercy, plunged my sword with brute ferocity, repeatedly through and through his bosom.

At that instant some person tried the latch of the door. I hastened to prevent an intrusion, and then immediately returned to my dying antagonist. But what human language can adequately portray *that* astonishment, *that* horror which possessed me at the spectacle then presented to view? The brief moment in which I averted my eyes had been sufficient to produce, apparently, a material change in the arrangements at the upper or farther end of the room. A large mirror,—so at first it seemed to me in my confusion—now stood where none had been perceptible before; and as I stepped up to it in extremity of terror, mine own image, but with features all pale and dabbled in blood, advanced to meet me with a feeble and tottering gait.

Thus it appeared, I say, but was not. It was my antagonist—it was Wilson, who then stood before me in the agonies of his dissolution. His mask and cloak lay, where he had thrown them, upon the floor. Not a thread in all his raiment—not a line in all the marked and singular lineaments of his face which was not, even in the most absolute identity, *mine own*!

It was Wilson; but he spoke no longer in a whisper, and I could have fancied that I myself was speaking while he said:

"You have conquered, and I yield. Yet, henceforward art thou also dead—dead to the World, to Heaven, and to Hope! In me didst thou exist—and, in my death, see by this image, which is thine own, how utterly thou hast murdered thyself."

Identity Crisis

· · · · · ·

BY LISA SCOTTOLINE

Edgar Allan Poe was presented to me in high school the way he was probably presented to you.

As broccoli.

You know what I mean. It's good for you, so you have to eat it. You're fifteen, craving French fries and cheeseburgers, but all they have in the English syllabus is broccoli. Then they make you read it and try to convince you that reading is fun(damental).

No wonder it doesn't work.

Unfortunately, high school broccoli is the way that lots of great writing gets introduced to us, and the sad thing is that there could be French fries in there somewhere, but we'd never know it. We don't always give it a chance. We won't even taste it unless there's a pop quiz.

Teenagers are the picky eaters of literature.

Add to that the rebelliousness of youth, especially of a girl like me. I didn't do drugs and I didn't drink. I had braces until senior year, was president of the Latin Club, and should have been Most

Likely to Achieve Sainthood. The only way I could rebel was to skip Poe.

So I did.

And I confess, here in this classy anthology, for an organization I love, among the writers I admire the most, that I didn't read Poe until I was an adult. Until I finally grew up and, after my divorce, had no one left to rebel against. And when I won an Edgar, I felt like an impostor for never having read him. I couldn't take the secret shame another minute, so I picked up a copy of his collected works and read a few of the stories. They were terrific, but the one that stayed with me was "William Wilson," and I'll tell you why.

It's the story of a schoolboy, and at the very outset, his identity is uncertain. In fact, Poe starts the story, "Let me call myself, for the present, William Wilson. The fair page lying before me need not be sullied with my real appellation."

Think "Call me Ishmael," but more intriguing. Poe reportedly had an obsession with the color white, but we won't go into the parallels between him and Melville here. Suffice it to say that what happens in "William Wilson" is as epic a battle as with any white whale, but in Poe's story, the nemesis may be the hero himself.

Let me explain.

In the story, William Wilson meets a classmate who looks exactly like him. The other boy has the same name and even the same birthday. (Actually, William specifies their shared birthday is "the nineteenth of January," which is Poe's own birthday.) He's the same height too. They even enter the school on the same day, "by mere accident." The only difference between them is that the other boy has some defect in his throat that prevents him from raising his voice "above a very low whisper." Bottom line, the other boy is the double, or twin, of William Wilson.

The boys start out as uneasy friends, then the double does everything to make himself more like William Wilson, except that he can't copy his voice completely. William says, "His cue, which was to perfect an imitation of myself, lay both in words and in actions; and most admirably did he play his part. My dress it was an easy matter to copy; my gait and general manner were, without difficulty, appropriated; in spite of his constitutional defect, even my voice did not escape him. My louder tones were, of course, unattempted, but then the key, — it was identical; *and his singular whisper, it grew the very echo of my own.*"

It's *Single White Female*, only with boys.

And, of course, a great twist. Instead of the main character being the good one and the double being the bad one, in "William Wilson" the narrator is the bad one and the double is the good one. It's so much more interesting, and bolder. Imagine Goofus and Gallant, with Goofus as the storyteller. Isn't he more fun to listen to than the goody-goody Gallant? (Patricia Highsmith, in the Ripley series, and Jeff Lindsay, in the Dexter series, would make the same wise choice. Though the first to do so may have been John Milton, whom you remember from your college broccoli. In *Paradise Lost*, wasn't Satan more interesting than you-know-who?)

But to stay on point, in "William Wilson" the title character is witty, naughty, and an effete bully. He drinks too much, he uses profanity, he cheats at cards. His double is nicer, kinder, and more considerate in every respect. In time, William Wilson comes to dislike, then hate his double. He leaves school to get away from him, then time passes and he goes to Eton, where one day he invites "a small party of the most dissolute students" to his room for "a secret carousal." Bam! In walks his double, to spoil the fun. William Wilson says, "I grew perfectly sober in an instant."

The double is the buzz kill of the century.

William flees to Oxford, his thoughts haunted by his doppelgänger. He says, "[A]gain, and again, in secret communion with my own spirit, would I demand the questions 'Who is he? — whence came he?—and what are his objects?' But no answer was there found." At war with itself, William's psyche begins to disintegrate. He lapses into chronic gambling, drinking, and further debauchery until we see him at another card game, with an aristocratic "dupe" whom William plies with liquor to cheat him more easily. Suddenly, the double reappears and blows William's cover, exposing his hidden cards when he says: "Please to examine, at your leisure, the inner linings of the cuff of his left sleeve, and the several little packages which may be found in the somewhat capacious pockets of his embroidered morning wrapper."

Busted.

William hurries to Paris, then to Rome, decompensating further, and during a ball at carnival his lecherous eye falls upon the beautiful wife of a duke. Out of the blue, the double appears, this time masked and caped, to thwart our hero's misdeed. The two fall into a sword fight, and—

Well, I can't give away the surprise ending.

You're probably thinking that you can predict the ending, but it's more ambiguous than it first appears. I think I have a good guess about what happens, but I won't ruin it for you, and sometimes I'm not sure my guess is right anyway. I checked online to read criticisms of the story's ending, but all I found was a Web site called wiki .answers.com, which devotes an entire page to the ending of "William Wilson" but asks only, "What Does the Tale William Wilson by Edgar Allan Poe Mean? Show Us Your Smarts! Help Us Answer This Question!"

I declined to show my smarts.

Elsewhere on the Web are comments from people confused by the story's ending, and my favorite is from mister_noel_y2k of Cardiff, Wales, who posted: "for anyone who has read this story, could they perhaps explain what this story was about because I wasn't sure whether or not the two william wilson's were the same person or not or whether it was a jekyll and hyde kind of story or whether or not the narrator was obsessed with william wilson" (http://www .online-literature.com/forums/showthread.php?t=12581).

So why do I think this story is so great, and how does it speak to why Poe himself was so great? I think it's in the pull of its terrific premise, the doubling between William Wilson and his look-alike. As our friend mister_noel_y2k says, while it's unclear whether William and his double are two halves of the same whole, or in fact two separate people, the effect is the same. His fragmented or broken identity terrifies us at a profound level, and when it's the protagonist who's having an identity crisis, we're placed squarely in his very shaky shoes. So it's impossible to read "William Wilson" and not identify with William, feeling his anguish and his evil, both at once.

And the threat is so much greater when it comes from within, as in this story of psychological horror, than from without, as in a conventional ghost story. Poe must have known that no monster is half as scary as the evil within us, and it's tempting to wonder if he "wrote what he knew," considering his own personal unhappiness and the fact that he assigned William Wilson his own birthday. Read that way, the story is poignant indeed.

Plus, Poe may not have invented the Evil Twin, but he certainly anticipated it, as well as the spookiness that comes from the fragmenting or doubling of the self, and the splintering of identity. Sigmund Freud would later explain the psychology at work here in his essay "The Uncanny," written in 1919, but there's no doubt that the concept gives "William Wilson" its dramatic impact. And the hold that doubling has on our collective psyche is underlined by more recent examples in popular culture, from benign sitcoms like *The Patty Duke Show* to the comic-book conflict of Spider Man and his evil flip side, Venom. Think, too, of *Invasion of the Body Snatchers,* where the man looks like your husband but he's not your husband. Or vice versa, in *The Stepford Wives*, when the terrified wife stumbles upon her own replica.

Robert Ludlum's Jason Bourne novels trade on the doubling concept when our hero flashes back on a self he doesn't know, remember, or even recognize. Bourne's confusion about his own identity, and about whether he is fundamentally good or evil, echoes "William Wilson." And there's even a hint of identity duality, or a split self, in Stephen King's classic, *The Shining*, in which a frustrated writer takes a job as a hotel caretaker, loses his mind, and tries to kill his family. Not only is the caretaker a double of a previous caretaker, who had followed the same deranged path, but we see how easily Good Dad crosses the median to become Evil Dad when a hotel and a blank page drive him crazy.

The blank page I know well.

In fact, I was thinking of "William Wilson" when I wrote my novels *Mistaken Identity* and *Dead Ringer*. The main character in those books, Bennie Rosato, is a strong, independent, and clever woman whose life gets turned upside down when she's summoned to prison to meet with a look-alike inmate—who claims to be her long-lost twin sister. I didn't get the idea from Poe, I got it from my own life, when I learned I had a half sister I didn't know about. That she looked uncannily like me, down to the blue eyes we both got from our father, at first unsettled me at the deepest level, and by the time we got to know each other, I knew I had to write about the experience. You can't have this job and ignore something like that or you forfeit your advance.

I reread "William Wilson" for the inspiration to turn my life into fiction, and though my half sister is a lovely person, I made her into an Evil Twin (with her permission). The psychological journey that Bennie Rosato takes in my novels was informed not only by my own confused feelings but by those of the entirely fictional William Wilson, and I like to think they gave those novels an emotional truth.

So I owe Edgar Allan Poe quite a lot.

Thank you, sir, and Happy Birthday.

And what is the lesson in all this?

Eat your vegetables.

Lisa Scottoline will admit that she got interested in Edgar Allan Poe only after he got interested in her, which is the story of her social life in general and perhaps why she is twice divorced. After she won an Edgar, she picked up Poe's stories and fell in love with "William Wilson," a great tale of dual identity. She has mined that theme for many of her fifteen best-selling novels, which is a nice way of saying that she steals from the best. She has served on the board of MWA and teaches Justice and Fiction at the University of Pennsylvania Law School, her alma mater. She also writes a weekly column for the Philadelphia Inquirer, *because nine hundred words comes a lot easier than ninety thousand. She still lives in her hometown, Philadelphia, the rightful home of Edgar Allan Poe, but let's not get into that.*

Manuscript Found in a Bottle

Qui n'a plus qu'un moment a vivre
N'a plus rien a dissimuler.

—QUINAULT —Atys.

OF MY COUNTRY AND OF MY FAMILY I have little to say. Ill usage and length of years have driven me from the one, and estranged me from the other. Hereditary wealth afforded me an education of no common order, and a contemplative turn of mind enabled me to methodize the stores which early study very diligently garnered up. Beyond all things, the works of the German moralists gave me great delight; not from any ill-advised admiration of their eloquent madness, but from the ease with which my habits of rigid thought enabled me to detect their falsities. I have often been reproached with the aridity of my genius; a deficiency of imagination has been imputed to me as a crime; and the Pyrrhonism of my opinions has at all times rendered me notorious. Indeed, a strong relish for physical philosophy has, I fear, tinctured my mind with a very common error of this age—I mean the habit of referring occurrences, even the least susceptible of such reference, to the principles of that science. Upon the whole, no person could be less liable than myself to be led away from the severe precincts of truth by the *ignes fatui* of superstition. I have thought proper to premise thus much, lest the incredible tale I have to tell should be considered rather the raving of a crude imagination, than the positive experience of a mind to which the reveries of fancy have been a dead letter and a nullity.

After many years spent in foreign travel, I sailed in the year 18—, from the port of Batavia, in the rich and populous island of Java, on a voyage to the Archipelago Islands. I went as passenger—having no other inducement than a kind of nervous restlessness which haunted me as a fiend.

Our vessel was a beautiful ship of about four hundred tons, copperfastened, and built at Bombay of Malabar teak. She was freighted with cotton-wool and oil, from the Lachadive Islands. We had also on board coir, jaggeree, ghee, cocoanuts, and a few cases of opium. The stowage was clumsily done, and the vessel consequently crank.

We got under way with a mere breath of wind, and for many days stood along the eastern coast of Java, without any other incident to beguile the monotony of our course than the occasional meeting with some of the small grabs of the Archipelago to which we were bound.

One evening, leaning over the taffrail, I observed a very singular, isolated cloud, to the N.W. It was remarkable, as well from its color, as from its being the first we had seen since our departure from Batavia. I watched it attentively until sunset, when it spread all at once to the eastward and westward, girting in the horizon with a narrow strip of vapor, and looking like a long line of low beach. My notice was soon afterwards attracted by the dusky-red appearance of the moon, and the peculiar character of the sea. The latter was undergoing a rapid change, and the water seemed more than usually transparent. Although I could distinctly see the bottom, yet, heaving the lead, I found the ship in fifteen fathoms. The air now became intolerably hot, and was loaded with spiral exhalations similar to those arising from heated iron. As night came on, every breath of wind died away, and a more entire calm it is impossible to conceive. The flame of a candle burned upon the poop without the least perceptible motion, and a long hair, held between the finger and thumb, hung without the possibility of detecting a vibration. However, as the captain said he could perceive no indication of danger, and as we were drifting in bodily to shore, he ordered the sails to be furled, and the anchor let go. No watch was set, and the crew, consisting principally of Malays, stretched themselves deliberately upon deck. I went below — not without a full presentiment of evil. Indeed, every appearance warranted me in apprehending a simoom. I told the captain my fears; but he paid no attention to what I said, and left me without deigning to give a reply. My uneasiness, however, prevented me from sleeping, and about midnight I went upon deck. As I placed my foot upon the upper step of the companion-ladder, I was startled by a loud, humming noise, like that occasioned by the rapid revolution of a mill-wheel, and before I could ascertain its meaning, I found the ship quivering to its centre. In the next instant a wilderness of foam hurled us upon our beam-ends, and, rushing over us fore and aft, swept the entire decks from stem to stern.

The extreme fury of the blast proved, in a great measure, the salvation of the ship. Although completely water-logged, yet, as her masts had gone by the board, she rose, after a minute, heavily from the sea, and, staggering awhile beneath the immense pressure of the tempest, finally righted.

By what miracle I escaped destruction, it is impossible to say. Stunned by the shock of the water, I found myself, upon recovery, jammed in between the stern-post and rudder. With great difficulty I gained my feet, and looking dizzily around, was, at first, struck with the idea of our being among breakers; so terrific, beyond the wildest imagination, was the whirlpool of mountainous and foaming ocean within which we were engulfed. After a while I heard the voice of an old Swede, who had shipped with us at the moment of our leaving port. I hallooed to him with all my strength, and presently he came reeling aft. We soon discovered that we were the sole survivors of the accident. All on deck, with the exception of ourselves, had been swept overboard; the captain and mates must have perished as they slept, for the cabins were deluged with water. Without assistance we could expect to do little for the security of the ship, and our exertions were at first paralyzed by the momentary expectation of going down. Our cable had, of course, parted like pack-thread, at the first breath of the hurricane, or we should have been instantaneously overwhelmed. We scudded with frightful velocity before the sea, and the water made clear breaches over us. The framework of our stern was shattered excessively, and, in almost every respect, we had received considerable injury; but to our extreme joy we found the pumps unchoked, and that we had made no great shifting of our ballast. The main fury of the blast had already blown over, and we apprehended little danger from the violence of the wind; but we looked forward to its total cessation with dismay; well believing, that in our shattered condition, we should inevitably perish in the tremendous swell which would ensue. But this very just apprehension seemed by no means likely to be soon verified. For five entire days and nights — during which our only subsistence was a small quantity of jaggeree, procured with great difficulty from the forecastle — the hulk flew at a rate defying computation, before rapidly succeeding flaws of wind, which, without equalling the first violence of the simoom, were still more terrific than any tempest I had before encountered. Our course for the first four days was, with trifling variations, S.E. and by S.; and we must have run down the coast of New Holland. In the fifth day the cold became extreme, although the wind had hauled round a point more to the northward. The sun arose with a sickly yellow lustre, and clambered a very few degrees above the horizon — emitting no decisive light. There were no clouds apparent, yet the wind was upon the increase, and blew with a fitful and un-steady fury. About noon, as nearly as we could guess, our attention was again arrested by the appearance of the sun. It gave out no light, properly so called, but a dull and sullen glow without reflection, as if all its rays were polarized. Just before sinking within the turgid sea, its central fires suddenly went out, as if hurriedly extinguished by some unaccountable power. It was a dim, silver-like rim, alone, as it rushed down the unfathomable ocean.

We waited in vain for the arrival of the sixth day — that day to me has not yet arrived — to the Swede, never did arrive. Thenceforward we were enshrouded in patchy darkness, so that we could not have seen an object at twenty paces from the ship. Eternal night contin-ued to envelop us, all unrelieved by the phosphoric sea-brilliancy to which we had been accustomed in the tropics. We observed, too, that, although the tempest continued to rage with unabated vio-lence, there was no longer to be discovered the usual appearance of surf, or foam, which had hitherto attended us. All around were horror, and thick gloom, and a black sweltering desert of ebony. Su-perstitious terror crept by degrees into the spirit of the old Swede, and my own soul was wrapped up in silent wonder. We neglected all care of the ship, as worse than useless, and securing ourselves as well as possible, to the stump of the mizzen-mast, looked out bitterly into the world of ocean. We had no means of calculating time, nor could we form any guess of our situation. We were, however, well aware of having made farther to the southward than any previous navigators, and felt great amazement at not meeting with the usual impediments of ice. In the meantime every moment threatened to be our last—every mountainous billow hurried to overwhelm us. The swell surpassed anything I had imagined possible, and that we were not instantly buried is a miracle. My companion spoke of the lightness of our cargo, and reminded me of the excellent qualities of our ship; but I could not help feeling the utter hopelessness of hope itself, and prepared myself gloomily for that death which I thought nothing could defer beyond an hour, as, with every knot of way the ship made, the swelling of the black stupendous seas became more dismally appalling. At times we gasped for breath at an elevation beyond the albatross—at times became dizzy with the velocity of our descent into some watery hell, where the air grew stagnant, and no sound disturbed the slumbers of the kraken.

We were at the bottom of one of these abysses, when a quick scream from my companion broke fearfully upon the night. "See! see!" cried he, shrieking in my ears, "Almighty God! see! see!" As he spoke, I became aware of a dull, sullen glare of red light which streamed down the sides of the vast chasm where we lay, and threw a fitful brilliancy upon our deck. Casting my eyes upwards, I beheld a spectacle which froze the current of my blood. At a terrific height directly above us, and upon the very verge of the precipitous descent, hovered a gigantic ship of, perhaps, four thousand tons. Although upreared upon the summit of a wave more than a hundred times her own altitude, her apparent size exceeded that of any ship of the line or East Indiaman in existence. Her huge hull was of a deep dingy black, unrelieved by any of the customary carvings of a ship. A single row of brass cannon protruded from her open ports, and dashed from their polished surfaces the fires of innumerable battle-lanterns which swung to and fro about her rigging. But what mainly inspired us with horror and astonishment, was that she bore up under a press of sail in the very teeth of that supernatural sea, and of that ungovernable hurricane. When we first discovered her, her bows were alone to be seen, as she rose slowly from the dim and horrible gulf beyond her. For a moment of intense terror she paused upon the giddy pinnacle as if in contemplation of her own sublimity, then trembled, and tottered, and—came down.

At this instant, I know not what sudden self-possession came over my spirit. Staggering as far aft as I could, I awaited fearlessly the ruin that was to overwhelm. Our own vessel was at length ceasing from her struggles, and sinking with her head to the sea. The shock of the descending mass struck her, consequently, in that portion of her frame which was already under water, and the inevitable result was to hurl me, with irresistible violence, upon the rigging of the stranger.

As I fell, the ship hove in stays, and went about; and to the confusion ensuing I attributed my escape from the notice of the crew. With little difficulty I made my way unperceived to the main hatchway, which was partially open, and soon found an opportunity of secreting myself in the hold. Why I did so I can hardly tell. An indefinite sense of awe, which at first sight of the navigators of the ship had taken hold of my mind, was perhaps the principle of my concealment. I was unwilling to trust myself with a race of people who had offered, to the cursory glance I had taken, so many points of vague novelty, doubt, and apprehension. I therefore thought proper to contrive a hiding-place in the hold. This I did by removing a small portion of the shifting-boards, in such a manner as to afford me a convenient retreat between the huge timbers of the ship.

I had scarcely completed my work, when a footstep in the hold forced me to make use of it. A man passed by my place of concealment with a feeble and unsteady gait. I could not see his face, but had an opportunity of observing his general appearance. There was about it an evidence of great age and infirmity. His knees tottered beneath a load of years, and his entire frame quivered under the burthen. He muttered to himself, in a low broken tone, some words of a language which I could not understand, and groped in a corner among a pile of singular-looking instruments, and decayed charts of navigation. His manner was a wild mixture of the peevishness of second childhood, and the solemn dignity of a God. He at length went on deck, and I saw him no more.

A feeling, for which I have no name, has taken possession of my soul—a sensation which will admit of no analysis, to which the lessons of bygone times are inadequate, and for which I fear futurity itself will offer me no key. To a mind constituted like my own, the latter consideration is an evil. I shall never—I know that I shall never—be satisfied with regard to the nature of my conceptions. Yet it is not wonderful that these conceptions are indefinite, since they have their origin in sources so utterly novel. A new sense—a new entity is added to my soul.

It is long since I first trod the deck of this terrible ship, and the rays of my destiny are, I think, gathering to a focus. Incomprehensible men! Wrapped up in meditations of a kind which I cannot divine, they pass me by unnoticed. Concealment is utter folly on my part, for the people *will not see*. It is but just now that I passed directly before the eyes of the mate; it was no long while ago that I ventured into the captain's own private cabin, and took thence the materials with which I write, and have written. I shall from time to time continue this journal. It is true that I may not find an opportunity of transmitting it to the world, but I will not fail to make the endeavor. At the last moment I will enclose the MS. in a bottle, and cast it within the sea.

An incident has occurred which has given me new room for meditation. Are such things the operation of ungoverned chance? I had ventured upon deck and thrown myself down, without attracting any notice, among a pile of ratlin-stuff and old sails, in the bottom of the yawl. While musing upon the singularity of my fate, I unwittingly daubed with a tar-brush the edges of a neatly-folded studding-sail which lay near me on a barrel. The studding-sail is now bent upon the ship, and the thoughtless touches of the brush are spread out into the word DISCOVERY.

I have made many observations lately upon the structure of the vessel. Although well armed, she is not, I think, a ship of war. Her rigging, build, and general equipment, all negative a supposition of this kind. What she *is not*, I can easily perceive; what she *is*, I fear it is impossible to say. I know not how it is, but in scrutinizing her strange model and singular cast of spars, her huge size and over-grown suits of canvas, her severely simple bow and antiquated stern, there will occasionally flash across my mind a sensation of familiar things, and there is always mixed up with such indistinct shadows of recollection, an unaccountable memory of old foreign chronicles and ages long ago.

I have been looking at the timbers of the ship. She is built of a material to which I am a stranger. There is a peculiar character about the wood which strikes me as rendering it unfit for the purpose to which it has been applied. I mean its extreme *porousness*, considered independently by the worm-eaten condition which is a consequence of navigation in these seas, and apart from the rottenness attendant upon age. It will appear perhaps an observation somewhat overcurious, but this would have every characteristic of Spanish oak, if Spanish oak were distended by any unnatural means.

In reading the above sentence, a curious apothegm of an old weather-beaten Dutch navigator comes full upon my recollection. "It is as sure," he was wont to say, when any doubt was entertained of his veracity, "as sure as there is a sea where the ship itself will grow in bulk like the living body of the seaman."

About an hour ago, I made bold to trust myself among a group of the crew. They paid me no manner of attention, and, although I stood in the very midst of them all, seemed utterly unconscious of my presence. Like the one I had at first seen in the hold, they all bore about them the marks of a hoary old age. Their knees trembled with infirmity; their shoulders were bent double with decrepitude; their shrivelled skins rattled in the wind; their voices were low, tremulous, and broken; their eyes glistened with the rheum of years; and their gray hairs streamed terribly in the tempest. Around them, on every part of the deck, lay scattered mathematical instruments of the most quaint and obsolete construction.

I mentioned, some time ago, the bending of a studding-sail. From that period, the ship, being thrown dead off the wind, has continued her terrific course due south, with every rag of canvas packed upon her, from her trucks to her lower studding-sail booms, and rolling every moment her top-gallant yard-arms into the most appalling hell of water which it can enter into the mind of man to imagine. I have just left the deck, where I find it impossible to maintain a footing, although the crew seem to experience little inconvenience. It appears to me a miracle of miracles that our enormous bulk is not swallowed up at once and forever. We are surely doomed to hover continually upon the brink of eternity, without taking a final plunge into the abyss. From billows a thousand times more stupendous than any I have ever seen, we glide away with the facility of the arrowy sea-gull; and the colossal waters rear their heads above us like demons of the deep, but like demons confined to simple threats, and forbidden to destroy. I am led to attribute these frequent escapes to the only natural cause which can account for such effect. I must suppose the ship to be within the influence of some strong current, or impetuous undertow.

I have seen the captain face to face, and in his own cabin—but, as I expected, he paid me no attention. Although in his appearance there is, to a casual observer, nothing which might bespeak him more or less than man, still, a feeling of irrepressible reverence and awe mingled with the sensation of wonder with which I regarded him. In stature, he is nearly my own height; that is, about five feet eight inches. He is of a well-knit and compact frame of body, neither robust nor remarkably otherwise. But it is the singularity of the expression which reigns upon the face — it is the intense, the wonderful, the thrilling evidence of old age so utter, so extreme, which excites within my spirit a sense — a sentiment ineffable. His forehead, although little wrinkled, seems to bear upon it the stamp of a myriad of years. His gray hairs are records of the past, and his grayer eyes are sybils of the future. The cabin floor was thickly strewn with strange, iron-clasped folios, and mouldering instruments of science, and obsolete long-forgotten charts. His head was bowed down upon his hands, and he pored, with a fiery, unquiet eye, over a paper which I took to be a commission, and which, at all events, bore the signature of a monarch. He muttered to himself — as did the first seaman whom I saw in the hold — some low peevish syllables of a foreign tongue; and although the speaker was close at my elbow, his voice seemed to reach my ears from the distance of a mile.

The ship and all in it are imbued with the spirit of Eld. The crew glide to and fro like the ghosts of buried centuries; their eyes have an eager and uneasy meaning; and when their fingers fall athwart my path in the wild glare of the battle-lanterns, I feel as I have never felt before, although I have been all my life a dealer in antiquities, and have imbibed the shadows of fallen columns at Balbec, and Tadmor, and Persepolis, until my very soul has become a ruin.

When I look around me, I feel ashamed of my former apprehensions. If I trembled at the blast which has hitherto attended us, shall I not stand aghast at a warring of wind and ocean, to convey any idea of which, the words tornado and simoom are trivial and ineffective? All in the immediate vicinity of the ship, is the blackness of eternal night, and a chaos of foamless water; but, about a league on either side of us, may be seen, indistinctly and at intervals, stupendous ramparts of ice, towering away into the desolate sky, and looking like the walls of the universe.

As I imagined, the ship proves to be in a current—if that appellation can properly be given to a tide, which, howling and shrieking by the white ice, thunders on to the southward with a velocity like the headlong dashing of a cataract.

To conceive the horror of my sensations is, I presume, utterly impossible; yet a curiosity to penetrate the mysteries of these awful regions, predominates even over my despair, and will reconcile me to the most hideous aspect of death. It is evident that we are hurrying onwards to some exciting knowledge—some never-to-be-imparted secret, whose attainment is destruction. Perhaps this current leads us to the southern pole itself. It must be confessed that a supposition apparently so wild has every probability in its favor.

The crew pace the deck with unquiet and tremulous step; but there is upon their countenances an expression more of the eagerness of hope than of the apathy of despair.

In the meantime the wind is still in our poop, and, as we carry a crowd of canvas, the ship is at times lifted bodily from out the sea! Oh, horror upon horror!—the ice opens suddenly to the right, and to the left, and we are whirling dizzily, in immense concentric circles, round and round the borders of a gigantic amphitheatre, the summit of whose walls is lost in the darkness and the distance. But little time will be left me to ponder upon my destiny! The circles rapidly grow small—we are plunging madly within the grasp of the whirlpool—and amid a roaring, and bellowing, and thundering of ocean and of tempest, the ship is quivering, oh God! and—going down!

In a Strange City: Baltimore and the Poe Toaster

. . . . . .

BY LAURA LIPPMAN

Lo, Death has reared itself a throne
In a strange city, lying alone.

—EDGAR ALLAN POE, "THE CITY BY THE SEA"

I admit, the name is regrettable: the Poe Toaster. Can anyone say it without first picturing that old screen saver, the one with winged toasters shuttling through the cosmos, only this time adorned with little mustaches and those famously melancholy eyes? But the first thing you need to know is that the Poe Toaster is not an appliance but a person, one charged with a sacred duty: the annual visit to Poe's grave in the Westminster Burying Ground.

Admittedly, many of Baltimore's tributes to Poe seem just a little . . . off. His original grave site was unmarked for years. Then we have the Ravens, the NFL team that my hometown stole from Cleveland. There is the long-shuttered Telltale Hearth, a decent pizza joint in its day, and Edgar's Club, a billiards joint on the Baltimore Skywalk, which is everything one might expect in a billiards joint on the Baltimore Skywalk. There is the omnipresent squad car parked outside the Poe House, in case a tourist loses his way. There are the Poe Homes, a housing project, where the tourists are on their own. There is the fact that we've torn down the hospital where Poe died, failing to salvage a single item. And then there is the memorial erected to Poe in 1875, almost thirty years after his death. On it, the date of Poe's birthday is wrong, off by a day.

The Poe Toaster does not come to this site. That's the second thing you need to know. The Poe Toaster visits the original grave, at the rear of the old cemetery in downtown Baltimore. He arrives between midnight and 6:00 A.M. on January 19—for the Poe Toaster is not confused about the date of Poe's birth—and leaves three red roses and a half bottle of cognac. Cognac—a toast, hence the Poe Toaster. Yet no one, except the Poe Toaster, knows why he does this, the precise significance of those items, or even how many people have assumed the mantle of Poe Toaster since the custom began in 1949, precisely one hundred years after Poe's mysterious death in Baltimore.

A man in a nursing home came forward in the summer of 2007, claiming that he started the whole thing, but his version of events was so full of holes and inconsistencies that it would have been more polite to ignore him entirely. (If only the local newspaper had shared that opinion.) This is what we know: The visits started in 1949. A note was left in 1999, suggesting the torch had been passed at least once, if not twice. In 2001 another note was left, but this one was silly, exhorting the New York Giants to a Super Bowl win over the Ravens. Hmmm. I have always found that one a little dubious.

But in 2000 I was there, and I can describe very precisely what happened. Only—I won't. Because that is part of the promise I made to Jeff Jerome, the Poe House curator, who granted me entry to the annual watch party, an invitation he controls because the church is now a concert hall owned by the University of Maryland. Oh, anyone can go to the corner of Fayette and Greene and wait, in what is usually a frigid night, for a glimpse of the visitor. Go ahead, hang out on a corner in Baltimore at 2:00 A.M. I dare you. If you do, you will find that the sight lines from the street are compromised, especially since the construction of a new building behind the grave-yard. You can see Poe's second grave easily enough from outside the gates, but not the original one.

In 2000 I was the one who saw the Poe Toaster first. That's the way I remember it, but I bet everyone who was there that night thinks they had the first glimpse. I was in the right location, though, a second-story window that afforded a wide-open view of the grave-yard. It was a dreamlike moment, watching him approach, for he really did seem to appear out of thin air. His clothing, his aspect, how he moved, the route by which he left—I could probably share those things without breaking my promise to Jerome. Again, I won't. They belong to me, and the others who were there.

I suppose there are people who think it would be great sport to unmask the Toaster. Just as there are probably people who think it would be fun to tell young children that there is no Santa Claus and, by the way, you're not going to grow up to be a fireman or a ballerina either. All I can say is that I've never known of a true Bal-timorean—outside of an elderly man in a nursing home—who wants to unmask the visitor. The mystery is what makes it special. Every January 20, I awake with a queasy sensation. Did he come? Is it over? So far, so good.

Baltimore has a strange relationship with Poe. The city gave him an important leg up when, in 1838, a panel of judges here granted the struggling young writer a prize for his story "Manuscript Found in a Bottle." But he didn't write any of his best-known works in the brief time he lived here on Amity Street. Instead, Baltimore's primary claim to Poe is that he died here, under mysterious circum-stances. The last time I checked, there were more than twenty competing theories about Poe's death. Some have been knocked down definitively (rabies). Others are more plausible but not provable (cooping—the idea that Poe was rewarded with drink for voting repeatedly in a Baltimore election, then beaten). Some are just preposterous. (Sexual impotence? Only if a man can literally die of embarrassment.)

Then there is the theory of all theories—that Poe's body isn't even in his grave, that it was carried off by corpse-needy medical students long before the memorial was built. This idea, too, has been largely discredited, but it comes back to life again and again, a monster that cannot be slain.

In 1999, on the sesquicentennial weekend of Poe's death, I traveled to a symposium in Richmond, a city that can—and does—make a good case for its ownership of Poe. "Everyone wants a piece of Poe," I scribbled in my reporter's notebook. The Poe scholars are a contentious lot, proudly so. They agree to disagree about virtually everything. Almost a decade later, much of what I learned that weekend has vanished from my poor, porous memory. The only impressions I retain are a lecture on the problem of translating "The Raven" into Italian (the literal translation of "nevermore" was aurally inelegant, requiring a substitute) and my utter confusion at the vocabulary of literary criticism, some of which sailed so far over my head that I sat through an entire lecture with only these notes to show for my attendance: "Something about the X-files." And: "Wittgenstein, what?"

But my ignorance does not void the fact that I, too, have my piece of Poe. A moonless night, the view of a graveyard through the window of an old church. A figure approaches. How do you imagine him? Young, old? Dressed in a cape, or clad so as to attract no attention on a modern city street? Tall, short? Thin, fat? Male, female? How does he move? Stealthily or with a grand swagger? Is he capable of a quickness that suggests a younger man, or does he move with the stiffness of age? Does he saunter out the front gates or make a more devious exit?

This much I will tell you—yes.

Laura Lippman is the New York Times *best-selling author of thirteen novels and a short-story collection. She has been nominated for the Edgar five times and won the award in 1998 for* Charm City *—a book in which one character fronts a band called Poe White Trash.*

The Fall of the House of Usher

Son coeur est un luth suspendu;
Sitôt qu'on le touché il résonne.

—DE BÉRANGER

DURING THE WHOLE of a dull, dark, and soundless day in the autumn of the year, when the clouds hung oppressively low in the heavens, I had been passing alone, on horseback, through a singularly dreary tract of country; and at length found myself, as the shades of the evening drew on, within view of the melancholy House of Usher. I know not how it was—but, with the first glimpse of the building, a sense of insufferable gloom pervaded my spirit. I say insufferable; for the feeling was unrelieved by any of that half-pleasurable, because poetic, sentiment, with which the mind usually receives even the sternest natural images of the desolate or terrible. I looked upon the scene before me—upon the mere house, and the simple landscape features of the domain—upon the bleak walls—upon the vacant eye-like windows—upon a few rank sedges—and upon a few white trunks of decayed trees—with an utter depression of soul which I can compare to no earthly sensation more properly than to the after-dream of the reveller upon opium—the bitter lapse into everyday life—the hideous dropping off of the veil. There was an iciness, a sinking, a sickening of the heart—an unredeemed dreariness of thought which no goading of the imagination could torture into aught of the sublime. What was it—I paused to think—what was it that so unnerved me in the contemplation of the House of Usher?

It was a mystery all insoluble; nor could I grapple with the shadowy fancies that crowded upon me as I pondered. I was forced to fall back upon the unsatisfactory conclusion, that while, beyond doubt, there are combinations of very simple natural objects which have the power of thus affecting us, still the analysis of this power lies among considerations beyond our depth. It was possible, I reflected, that a mere different arrangement of the particulars of the scene, of the details of the picture, would be sufficient to modify, or perhaps to annihilate its capacity for sorrowful impression; and, acting upon this idea, I reined my horse to the precipitous brink of a black and lurid tarn that lay in unruffled lustre by the dwelling, and gazed down—but with a shudder even more thrilling than before—upon the remodelled and inverted images of the gray sedge, and the ghastly tree-stems, and the vacant and eye-like windows.

Nevertheless, in this mansion of gloom I now proposed to myself a sojourn of some weeks. Its proprietor, Roderick Usher, had been one of my boon companions in boyhood; but many years had elapsed since our last meeting. A letter, however, had lately reached me in a distant part of the country—a letter from him—which, in its wildly importunate nature, had admitted of no other than a personal reply. The MS. gave evidence of nervous agitation. The writer spoke of acute bodily illness—of a mental disorder which oppressed him—and of an earnest desire to see me, as his best, and indeed his only personal friend, with a view of attempting, by the cheerfulness of my society, some alleviation of his malady. It was the manner in which all this, and much more, was said—it was the apparent *heart* that went with his request—which allowed me no room for hesitation; and I accordingly obeyed forthwith what I still considered a very singular summons.

Although, as boys, we had been even intimate associates, yet I really knew little of my friend. His reserve had been always excessive and habitual. I was aware, however, that his very ancient family had been noted, time out of mind, for a peculiar sensibility of temperament, displaying itself, through long ages, in many works of exalted art, and manifested, of late, in repeated deeds of munificent yet unobtrusive charity, as well as in a passionate devotion to the intricacies, perhaps even more than to the orthodox and easily recognizable beauties, of musical science. I had learned, too, the very remarkable fact, that the stem of the Usher race, all time-honored as it was, had put forth, at no period, any enduring branch; in other words, that the entire family lay in the direct line of descent, and had always, with very trifling and very temporary variation, so lain. It was this deficiency, I considered, while running over in thought the perfect keeping of the character of the premises with the accredited character of the people, and while speculating upon the possible influence which the one, in the long lapse of centuries, might have exercised upon the other—it was this deficiency, perhaps, of collateral issue, and the consequent undeviating transmission, from sire to son, of the patrimony with the name, which had, at length, so identified the two as to merge the original title of the estate in the quaint and equivocal appellation of the "House of Usher"—an appellation which seemed to include, in the minds of the peasantry who used it, both the family and the family mansion.

I have said that the sole effect of my somewhat childish experiment—that of looking down within the tarn—had been to deepen the first singular impression. There can be no doubt that the consciousness of the rapid increase of my superstition—for why should I not so term it?—served mainly to accelerate the increase itself. Such, I have long known, is the paradoxical law of all sentiments having terror as a basis. And it might have been for this reason only, that, when I again uplifted my eyes to the house itself, from its image in the pool, there grew in my mind a strange fancy—a fancy so ridiculous, indeed, that I but mention it to show the vivid force of the sensations which oppressed me. I had so worked upon my imagination as really to believe that about the whole mansion and domain there hung an atmosphere peculiar to themselves and their immediate vicinity—an atmosphere which had no affinity with the air of heaven, but which had reeked up from the decayed trees, and the gray wall, and the silent tarn—a pestilent and mystic vapor, dull, sluggish, faintly discernible, and leaden-hued.

Shaking off from my spirit what *must* have been a dream, I scanned more narrowly the real aspect of the building. Its principal feature seemed to be that of an excessive antiquity. The discoloration of ages had been great. Minute fungi overspread the whole exterior, hanging in a fine tangled web-work from the eaves. Yet all this was apart from any extraordinary dilapidation. No portion of the masonry had fallen; and there appeared to be a wild inconsistency between its still perfect adaptation of parts, and the crumbling condition of the individual stones. In this there was much that reminded me of the specious totality of old wood-work which has rotted for long years in some neglected vault, with no disturbance from the breath of the external air. Beyond this indication of extensive decay, however, the fabric gave little token of instability. Perhaps the eye

of a scrutinizing observer might have discovered a barely perceptible fissure, which, extending from the roof of the building in front,
made its way down the wall in a zigzag direction, until it became lost
in the sullen waters of the tarn.

Noticing these things, I rode over a short causeway to the house.
A servant in waiting took my horse, and I entered the Gothic archway of the hall. A valet, of stealthy step, thence conducted me, in
silence, through many dark and intricate passages in my progress
to the *studio* of his master. Much that I encountered on the way contributed, I know not how, to heighten the vague sentiments of which
I have already spoken. While the objects around me—while the
carvings of the ceilings, the sombre tapestries of the walls, the ebon
blackness of the floors, and the phantasmagoric armorial trophies
which rattled as I strode, were but matters to which, or to such as
which, I had been accustomed from my infancy—while I hesitated
not to acknowledge how familiar was all this—I still wondered to
find how unfamiliar were the fancies which ordinary images were
stirring up. On one of the staircases, I met the physician of the
family. His countenance, I thought, wore a mingled expression of
low cunning and perplexity. He accosted me with trepidation and
passed on. The valet now threw open a door and ushered me into
the presence of his master.

The room in which I found myself was very large and lofty. The
windows were long, narrow, and pointed, and at so vast a distance
from the black oaken floor as to be altogether inaccessible from
within. Feeble gleams of encrimsoned light made their way through
the trellissed panes, and served to render sufficiently distinct the
more prominent objects around; the eye, however, struggled in vain
to reach the remoter angles of the chamber, or the recesses of the
vaulted and fretted ceiling. Dark draperies hung upon the walls.
The general furniture was profuse, comfortless, antique, and tattered. Many books and musical instruments lay scattered about, but

failed to give any vitality to the scene. I felt that I breathed an atmosphere of sorrow. An air of stern, deep, and irredeemable gloom hung over and pervaded all.

Upon my entrance, Usher arose from a sofa on which he had been lying at full length, and greeted me with a vivacious warmth which had much in it, I at first thought, of an overdone cordiality—of the constrained effort of the *ennuyé* man of the world. A glance, however, at his countenance, convinced me of his perfect sincerity. We sat down; and for some moments, while he spoke not, I gazed upon him with a feeling half of pity, half of awe. Surely, man had never before so terribly altered, in so brief a period, as had Roderick Usher! It was with difficulty that I could bring myself to admit the identity of the wan being before me with the companion of my early boyhood. Yet the character of his face had been at all times remarkable. A cadaverousness of complexion; an eye large, liquid, and luminous beyond comparison; lips somewhat thin and very pallid, but of a surpassingly beautiful curve; a nose of a delicate Hebrew model, but with a breadth of nostril unusual in similar formations; a finely moulded chin, speaking, in its want of prominence, of a want of moral energy; hair of a more than web-like softness and tenuity;—these features, with an inordinate expansion above the regions of the temple, made up altogether a countenance not easily to be forgotten. And now in the mere exaggeration of the prevailing character of these features, and of the expression they were wont to convey, lay so much of change that I doubted to whom I spoke. The now ghastly pallor of the skin, and the now miraculous lustre of the eye, above all things startled and even awed me. The silken hair, too, had been suffered to grow all unheeded, and as, in its wild gossamer texture, it floated rather than fell about the face, I could not, even with effort, connect its Arabesque expression with any idea of simple humanity.

In the manner of my friend I was at once struck with an incoherence—an inconsistency; and I soon found this to arise from a series of feeble and futile struggles to overcome an habitual trepidancy— an excessive nervous agitation. For something of this nature I had indeed been prepared, no less by his letter, than by reminiscences of certain boyish traits, and by conclusions deduced from his peculiar physical conformation and temperament. His action was alternately vivacious and sullen. His voice varied rapidly from a tremulous in-decision (when the animal spirits seemed utterly in abeyance) to that species of energetic concision—that abrupt, weighty, unhur-ried, and hollow-sounding enunciation—that leaden, self-balanced and perfectly modulated guttural utterance, which may be observed in the lost drunkard, or the irreclaimable eater of opium, during the periods of his most intense excitement.

It was thus that he spoke of the object of my visit, of his earnest desire to see me, and of the solace he expected me to afford him. He entered, at some length, into what he conceived to be the nature of his malady. It was, he said, a constitutional and a family evil, and one for which he despaired to find a remedy—a mere nervous affection, he immediately added, which would undoubtedly soon pass off. It displayed itself in a host of unnatural sensations. Some of these, as he detailed them, interested and bewildered me; although, perhaps, the terms, and the general manner of the narration had their weight. He suffered much from a morbid acuteness of the senses; the most insipid food was alone endurable; he could wear only garments of certain texture; the odors of all flowers were oppressive; his eyes were tortured by even a faint light; and there were but peculiar sounds, and these from stringed instruments, which did not inspire him with horror.

To an anomalous species of terror I found him a bounden slave. "I shall perish," said he, "I *must* perish in this deplorable folly. Thus, thus, and not otherwise, shall I be lost. I dread the events of the future, not in themselves, but in their results. I shudder at the thought of any, even the most trivial, incident, which may operate upon this intolerable agitation of soul. I have, indeed, no abhorrence of danger, except in its absolute effect—in terror. In this unnerved—in this pitiable condition—I feel that the period will sooner or later arrive when I must abandon life and reason together, in some struggle with the grim phantasm, FEAR."

I learned, moreover, at intervals, and through broken and equivocal hints, another singular feature of his mental condition. He was enchained by certain superstitious impressions in regard to the dwelling which he tenanted, and whence, for many years, he had never ventured forth—in regard to an influence whose supposititious force was conveyed in terms too shadowy here to be re-stated—an influence which some peculiarities in the mere form and substance of his family mansion, had, by dint of long sufferance, he said, obtained over his spirit—an effect which the *physique* of the gray walls and turrets, and of the dim tarn into which they all looked down, had, at length, brought about upon the *morale* of his existence.

He admitted, however, although with hesitation, that much of the peculiar gloom which thus afflicted him could be traced to a more natural and far more palpable origin—to the severe and long-continued illness—indeed to the evidently approaching dissolution—of a tenderly beloved sister—his sole companion for long years—his last and only relative on earth. "Her decease," he said, with a bitterness which I can never forget, "would leave him (him the hopeless and the frail) the last of the ancient race of the Ushers." While he spoke, the lady Madeline (for so was she called) passed slowly through a remote portion of the apartment, and, without having noticed my presence, disappeared. I regarded her with an utter astonishment not unmingled with dread—and yet I found it impossible to account for such feelings. A sensation of stupor oppressed me, as my eyes followed her retreating steps. When a door, at length, closed upon her, my glance sought instinctively and eagerly the countenance of the brother—but he had buried his face in his hands, and I could only perceive that a far more than ordinary wanness had overspread the emaciated fingers through which trickled many passionate tears.

The disease of the lady Madeline had long baffled the skill of her physicians. A settled apathy, a gradual wasting away of the person, and frequent although transient affections of a partially cataleptical character, were the unusual diagnosis. Hitherto she had steadily borne up against the pressure of her malady, and had not betaken herself finally to bed; but, on the closing in of the evening of my arrival at the house, she succumbed (as her brother told me at night with inexpressible agitation) to the prostrating power of the destroyer; and I learned that the glimpse I had obtained of her person would thus probably be the last I should obtain—that the lady, at least while living, would be seen by me no more.

For several days ensuing, her name was unmentioned by either Usher or myself; and during this period I was busied in earnest endeavors to alleviate the melancholy of my friend. We painted and read together; or I listened, as if in a dream, to the wild improvisations of his speaking guitar. And thus, as a closer and still closer intimacy admitted me more unreservedly into the recesses of his spirit, the more bitterly did I perceive the futility of all attempt at cheering a mind from which darkness, as if an inherent positive quality, poured forth upon all objects of the moral and physical universe, in one unceasing radiation of gloom.

I shall ever bear about me a memory of the many solemn hours I thus spent alone with the master of the House of Usher. Yet I should fail in any attempt to convey an idea of the exact character of the studies, or of the occupations, in which he involved me, or led me the way. An excited and highly distempered ideality threw a sulphureous lustre over all. His long, improvised dirges will ring forever in my ears. Among other things, I hold painfully in mind a certain singular perversion and amplification of the wild air of the last waltz of Von Weber. From the paintings over which his elaborate fancy brooded, and which grew, touch by touch, into vaguenesses at which I shuddered the more thrillingly, because I shuddered knowing not why—from these paintings (vivid as their images now are before me) I would in vain endeavor to educe more than a small portion which should lie within the compass of merely written words. By the utter simplicity, by the nakedness of his designs, he arrested and overawed attention. If ever mortal painted an idea, that mortal was Roderick Usher. For me at least—in the circumstances then surrounding me—there arose out of the pure abstractions which the hypochondriac contrived to throw upon his canvas, an intensity of intolerable awe, no shadow of which felt I ever yet in the contemplation of the certainly glowing yet too concrete reveries of Fuseli.

One of the phantasmagoric conceptions of my friend, partaking not so rigidly of the spirit of abstraction, may be shadowed forth, although feebly, in words. A small picture presented the interior of an immensely long and rectangular vault or tunnel, with low walls, smooth, white, and without interruption or device. Certain accessory points of the design served well to convey the idea that this excavation lay at an exceeding depth below the surface of the earth. No outlet was observed in any portion of its vast extent, and no torch, or other artificial source of light was discernible; yet a flood of intense rays rolled throughout, and bathed the whole in a ghastly and inappropriate splendor.

I have just spoken of that morbid condition of the auditory nerve which rendered all music intolerable to the sufferer, with the exception of certain effects of stringed instruments. It was, perhaps, the narrow limits to which he thus confined himself upon the guitar, which gave birth, in great measure, to the fantastic character of his performances. But the fervid *facility* of his *impromptus* could not be so accounted for. They must have been, and were, in the notes, as well as in the words of his wild fantasias (for he not unfrequently accompanied himself with rhymed verbal improvisations), the result of that intense mental collectedness and concentration to which I have previously alluded as observable only in particular moments of the highest artificial excitement. The words of one of these rhapsodies I have easily remembered. I was, perhaps, the more forcibly impressed with it, as he gave it, because, in the under or mystic current of its meaning, I fancied that I perceived, and for the first time, a full consciousness on the part of Usher, of the tottering of his lofty reason upon her throne. The verses, which were entitled "The Haunted Palace," ran very nearly, if not accurately, thus:

I.

In the greenest of our valleys,
    By good angels tenanted,
Once a fair and stately palace —
    Radiant palace — reared its head.
In the monarch Thought's dominion —
    It stood there!
Never seraph spread a pinion
    Over fabric half so fair.

II.

Banners yellow, glorious, golden,
    On its roof did float and flow;
(This — all this — was in the olden
    Time long ago)
And every gentle air that dallied,
    In that sweet day,

Along the ramparts plumed and pallid,
    A winged odor went away.

III.

Wanderers in that happy valley
    Through two luminous windows saw
Spirits moving musically
    To a lute's well-tunéd law,
Round about a throne, where sitting
    (Porphyrogene!)
In state his glory well befitting,
    The ruler of the realm was seen.

IV.

And all with pearl and ruby glowing
    Was the fair palace door,
Through which came flowing, flowing, flowing,
    And sparkling evermore,
A troop of Echoes whose sweet duty
    Was but to sing,
In voices of surpassing beauty,
    The wit and wisdom of their king.

V.

But evil things, in robes of sorrow,
    Assailed the monarch's high estate;

(Ah, let us mourn, for never morrow
    Shall dawn upon him, desolate!)
And, round about his home, the glory
    That blushed and bloomed
Is but a dim-remembered story
    Of the old time entombed.

VI.

And travellers now within that valley,
    Through the red-litten windows see
Vast forms that move fantastically
    To a discordant melody;
While, like a rapid ghastly river,
    Through the pale door,
A hideous throng rush out forever,
    And laugh—but smile no more.

I well remember that suggestions arising from this ballad, led us into a train of thought wherein there became manifest an opinion of Usher's which I mention not so much on account of its novelty, (for other men[1] have thought thus,) as on account of the pertinacity with which he maintained it. This opinion, in its general form, was that of the sentience of all vegetable things. But, in his disordered fancy, the idea had assumed a more daring character, and trespassed, under certain conditions, upon the kingdom of inorganization. I lack words to

1. Watson, Dr. Percival, Spallanzini, and especially the Bishop of Landaff.—See "Chemical Essays," vol. V.

express the full extent, or the earnest *abandon* of his persuasion. The belief, however, was connected (as I have previously hinted) with the gray stones of the home of his forefathers. The conditions of the sentience had been here, he imagined, fulfilled in the method of collocation of these stones—in the order of their arrangement, as well as in that of the many *fungi* which overspread them, and of the decayed trees which stood around—above all, in the long undisturbed endurance of this arrangement, and in its reduplication in the still waters of the tarn. Its evidence—the evidence of the sentience—was to be seen, he said, (and I here started as he spoke,) in the gradual yet certain condensation of an atmosphere of their own about the waters and the walls. The result was discoverable, he added, in that silent, yet importunate and terrible influence which for centuries had moulded the destinies of his family, and which made *him* what I now saw him—what he was. Such opinions need no comment, and I will make none.

Our books—the books which, for years, had formed no small portion of the mental existence of the invalid—were, as might be supposed, in strict keeping with this character of phantasm. We pored together over such works as the "Ververt et Chartreuse" of Gresset; the "Belphegor" of Machiavelli; the "Heaven and Hell" of Swedenborg; the "Subterranean Voyage of Nicholas Klimm" by Holberg; the "Chiromancy" of Robert Flud, of Jean D'Indaginé, and of De la Chambre; the "Journey into the Blue Distance" of Tieck; and the "City of the Sun" of Campanella. One favorite volume was a small octavo edition of the "Directorium Inquisitorium," by the Dominican Eymeric de Gironne; and there were passages in Pomponius Mela, about the old African Satyrs and Oegipans, over which Usher would sit dreaming for hours. His chief delight, however, was found in the perusal of an exceedingly rare and curious book in quarto Gothic—the manual of a forgotten church—the *Vigiliae Mortuorum secundum Chorum Ecclesiae Maguntinae.*

I could not help thinking of the wild ritual of this work, and of its probable influence upon the hypochondriac, when, one evening, having informed me abruptly that the lady Madeline was no more, he stated his intention of preserving her corpse for a fortnight, (previously to its final interment,) in one of the numerous vaults within the main walls of the building. The worldly reason, however, assigned for this singular proceeding, was one which I did not feel at liberty to dispute. The brother had been led to his resolution (so he told me) by consideration of the unusual character of the malady of the deceased, of certain obtrusive and eager inquiries on the part of her medical men, and of the remote and exposed situation of the burial-ground of the family. I will not deny that when I called to mind the sinister countenance of the person whom I met upon the staircase, on the day of my arrival at the house, I had no desire to oppose what I regarded as at best but a harmless, and by no means an unnatural, precaution.

At the request of Usher, I personally aided him in the arrangements for the temporary entombment. The body having been encoffined, we two alone bore it to its rest. The vault in which we placed it (and which had been so long unopened that our torches, half smothered in its oppressive atmosphere, gave us little opportunity for investigation) was small, damp, and entirely without means of admission for light; lying, at great depth, immediately beneath that portion of the building in which was my own sleeping apartment. It had been used, apparently, in remote feudal times, for the worst purposes of a donjon-keep, and, in later days, as a place of deposit for powder, or some other highly combustible substance, as a portion of its floor, and the whole interior of a long archway through which we reached it, were carefully sheathed with copper. The door, of massive iron, had been, also, similarly protected. Its immense weight caused an unusually sharp grating sound, as it moved upon its hinges.

Having deposited our mournful burden upon tressels within this region of horror, we partially turned aside the yet unscrewed lid of the coffin, and looked upon the face of the tenant. A striking similitude between the brother and sister now first arrested my attention; and Usher, divining, perhaps, my thoughts, murmured out some few words from which I learned that the deceased and himself had been twins, and that sympathies of a scarcely intelligible nature had always existed between them. Our glances, however, rested not long upon the dead—for we could not regard her unawed. The disease which had thus entombed the lady in the maturity of youth, had left, as usual in all maladies of a strictly cataleptical character, the mockery of a faint blush upon the bosom and the face, and that suspiciously lingering smile upon the lip which is so terrible in death. We replaced and screwed down the lid, and, having secured the door of iron, made our way, with toil, into the scarcely less gloomy apartments of the upper portion of the house.

And now, some days of bitter grief having elapsed, an observable change came over the features of the mental disorder of my friend. His ordinary manner had vanished. His ordinary occupations were neglected or forgotten. He roamed from chamber to chamber with hurried, unequal, and objectless step. The pallor of his countenance had assumed, if possible, a more ghastly hue—but the luminousness of his eye had utterly gone out. The once occasional huskiness of his tone was heard no more; and a tremulous quaver, as if of extreme terror, habitually characterized his utterance. There were times, indeed, when I thought his unceasingly agitated mind was laboring with some oppressive secret, to divulge which he struggled for the necessary courage. At times, again, I was obliged to resolve all into the mere inexplicable vagaries of madness, for I beheld him gazing upon vacancy for long hours, in an attitude of the profoundest attention, as if listening to some imaginary sound. It was no wonder that his condition terrified—that it infected me. I felt creeping upon me, by slow yet certain degrees, the wild influences of his own fantastic yet impressive superstitions.

It was, especially, upon retiring to bed late in the night of the seventh or eighth day after the placing of the lady Madeline within the donjon, that I experienced the full power of such feelings. Sleep came not near my couch—while the hours waned and waned away. I struggled to reason off the nervousness which had dominion over me. I endeavored to believe that much, if not all of what I felt, was due to the bewildering influence of the gloomy furniture of the room—of the dark and tattered draperies, which, tortured into motion by the breath of a rising tempest, swayed fitfully to and fro upon the walls, and rustled uneasily about the decorations of the bed. But my efforts were fruitless. An irrepressible tremor gradually pervaded my frame; and, at length, there sat upon my very heart an incubus of utterly causeless alarm. Shaking this off with a gasp and a struggle, I uplifted myself upon the pillows, and, peering earnestly within the intense darkness of the chamber, harkened—I know not why, except that an instinctive spirit prompted me—to certain low and indefinite sounds which came, through the pauses of the storm, at long intervals, I knew not whence. Overpowered by an intense sentiment of horror, unaccountable yet unendurable, I threw on my clothes with haste (for I felt that I should sleep no more during the night), and endeavored to arouse myself from the pitiable condition into which I had fallen, by pacing rapidly to and fro through the apartment.

I had taken but few turns in this manner, when a light step on an adjoining staircase arrested my attention. I presently recognised it as that of Usher. In an instant afterward he rapped, with a gentle touch, at my door, and entered, bearing a lamp. His countenance was, as usual, cadaverously wan—but, moreover, there was a species of mad hilarity in his eyes—an evidently restrained *hysteria* in his whole demeanor. His air appalled me—but anything was preferable to the solitude which I had so long endured, and I even welcomed his presence as a relief.

"And you have not seen it?" he said abruptly, after having stared about him for some moments in silence—"you have not then seen it?—but, stay! you shall." Thus speaking, and having carefully shaded his lamp, he hurried to one of the casements, and threw it freely open to the storm.

The impetuous fury of the entering gust nearly lifted us from our feet. It was, indeed, a tempestuous yet sternly beautiful night, and one wildly singular in its terror and its beauty. A whirlwind had apparently collected its force in our vicinity; for there were frequent and violent alterations in the direction of the wind; and the exceeding density of the clouds (which hung so low as to press upon the turrets of the house) did not prevent our perceiving the life-like velocity with which they flew careering from all points against each other, without passing away into the distance. I say that even their exceeding density did not prevent our perceiving this—yet we had no glimpse of the moon or stars—nor was there any flashing forth of the lightning. But the under surfaces of the huge masses of agitated vapor, as well as all terrestrial objects immediately around us, were glowing in the unnatural light of a faintly luminous and distinctly visible gaseous exhalation which hung about and enshrouded the mansion.

"You must not—you shall not behold this!" said I, shudderingly, to Usher, as I led him, with a gentle violence, from the window to a seat. "These appearances, which bewilder you, are merely electrical phenomena not uncommon—or it may be that they have their ghastly origin in the rank miasma of the tarn. Let us close this casement;—the air is chilling and dangerous to your frame. Here is one of your favorite romances. I will read, and you shall listen;—and so we will pass away this terrible night together."

The antique volume which I had taken up was the "Mad Trist"

of Sir Launcelot Canning; but I had called it a favorite of Usher's more in sad jest than in earnest; for, in truth, there is little in its uncouth and unimaginative prolixity which could have had interest for the lofty and spiritual ideality of my friend. It was, however, the only book immediately at hand; and I indulged a vague hope that the excitement which now agitated the hypochondriac, might find relief (for the history of mental disorder is full of similar anomalies) even in the extremeness of the folly which I should read. Could I have judged, indeed, by the wild overstrained air of vivacity with which he harkened, or apparently harkened, to the words of the tale, I might well have congratulated myself upon the success of my design.

I had arrived at that well-known portion of the story where Ethelred, the hero of the Trist, having sought in vain for peaceable admission into the dwelling of the hermit, proceeds to make good an entrance by force. Here, it will be remembered, the words of the narrative run thus:

"And Ethelred, who was by nature of a doughty heart, and who was now mighty withal, on account of the powerfulness of the wine which he had drunken, waited no longer to hold parley with the hermit, who, in sooth, was of an obstinate and maliceful turn, but, feeling the rain upon his shoulders, and fearing the rising of the tempest, uplifted his mace outright, and, with blows, made quickly room in the plankings of the door for his gauntleted hand; and now pulling therewith sturdily, he so cracked, and ripped, and tore all asunder, that the noise of the dry and hollow-sounding wood alarummed and reverberated throughout the forest."

At the termination of this sentence I started, and for a moment, paused; for it appeared to me (although I at once concluded that my excited fancy had deceived me)—it appeared to me that, from some very remote portion of the mansion, there came, indistinctly, to my ears, what might have been, in its exact similarity of character, the echo (but a stifled and dull one certainly) of the very cracking and ripping sound which Sir Launcelot had so particularly described. It was, beyond doubt, the coincidence alone which had arrested my attention; for, amid the rattling of the sashes of the casements, and the ordinary commingled noises of the still increasing storm, the sound, in itself, had nothing, surely, which should have interested or disturbed me. I continued the story:

"But the good champion Ethelred, now entering within the door, was sore enraged and amazed to perceive no signal of the maliceful hermit; but, in the stead thereof, a dragon of a scaly and prodigious demeanor, and of a fiery tongue, which sate in guard before a palace of gold, with a floor of silver; and upon the wall there hung a shield of shining brass with this legend enwritten —

Who entereth herein, a conqueror hath bin;
Who slayeth the dragon, the shield he shall win;

"And Ethelred uplifted his mace, and struck upon the head of the dragon, which fell before him, and gave up his pesty breath, with a shriek so horrid and harsh, and withal so piercing, that Ethelred had fain to close his ears with his hands against the dreadful noise of it, the like whereof was never before heard."

Here again I paused abruptly, and now with a feeling of wild amazement—for there could be no doubt whatever that, in this instance, I did actually hear (although from what direction it proceeded I found it impossible to say) a low and apparently distant, but harsh, protracted, and most unusual screaming or grating sound — the exact counterpart of what my fancy had already conjured up for the dragon's unnatural shriek as described by the romancer.

Oppressed, as I certainly was, upon the occurrence of this second and most extraordinary coincidence, by a thousand conflicting sensations, in which wonder and extreme terror were predominant, I still retained sufficient presence of mind to avoid exciting, by any observation, the sensitive nervousness of my companion. I was by no means certain that he had noticed the sounds in question; although, assuredly, a strange alteration had, during the last few minutes, taken place in his demeanor. From a position fronting my own, he had gradually brought round his chair, so as to sit with his face to the door of the chamber; and thus I could but partially perceive his features, although I saw that his lips trembled as if he were murmuring inaudibly. His head had dropped upon his breast—yet I knew that he was not asleep, from the wide and rigid opening of the eye as I caught a glance of it in profile. The motion of his body, too, was at variance with this idea—for he rocked from side to side with a gentle yet constant and uniform sway. Having rapidly taken notice of all this, I resumed the narrative of Sir Launcelot, which thus proceeded:

"And now, the champion, having escaped from the terrible fury of the dragon, bethinking himself of the brazen shield, and of the breaking up of the enchantment which was upon it, removed the carcass from out of the way before him, and approached valorously over the silver pavement of the castle to where the shield was upon the wall; which in sooth tarried not for his full coming, but fell down at his feet upon the silver floor, with a mighty great and terrible ringing sound."

No sooner had these syllables passed my lips, than—as if a shield of brass had indeed, at the moment, fallen heavily upon a floor of silver—I became aware of a distinct, hollow, metallic, and clangorous, yet apparently muffled reverberation. Completely unnerved, I leaped to my feet; but the measured rocking movement of Usher was undisturbed. I rushed to the chair in which he sat. His eyes were bent fixedly before him, and throughout his whole countenance there reigned a stony rigidity. But, as I placed my hand upon his shoulder, there came a strong shudder over his whole person; a sickly smile quivered about his lips; and I saw that he spoke in a low, hurried, and gibbering murmur, as if unconscious of my presence. Bending closely over him, I at length drank in the hideous import of his words.

"Not hear it?—yes, I hear it, and have heard it. Long—long—long—many minutes, many hours, many days, have I heard it—yet I dared not—oh, pity me, miserable wretch that I am!—I dared not—I *dared* not speak! *We have put her living in the tomb!* Said I not that my senses were acute? I *now* tell you that I heard her first feeble movements in the hollow coffin. I heard them—many, many days ago—yet I dared not—*I dared not speak!* And now—to-night—Ethelred—ha! ha!—the breaking of the hermit's door, and the death-cry of the dragon, and the clangor of the shield!—say, rather, the rending of her coffin, and the grating of the iron hinges of her prison, and her struggles within the coppered archway of the vault! Oh whither shall I fly? Will she not be here anon? Is she not hurrying to upbraid me for my haste? Have I not heard her footstep on the stair? Do I not distinguish that heavy and horrible beating of her heart? Madman!"—here he sprang furiously to his feet, and shrieked out his syllables, as if in the effort he were giving up his soul—*"Madman! I tell you that she now stands without the door!"*

As if in the superhuman energy of his utterance there had been found the potency of a spell—the huge antique pannels to which the speaker pointed, threw slowly back, upon the instant, their ponderous and ebony jaws. It was the work of the rushing gust—but then without those doors there *did* stand the lofty and enshrouded figure of the lady Madeline of Usher. There was blood upon her white robes, and the evidence of some bitter struggle upon every portion of her emaciated frame. For a moment she remained trembling and reeling to and fro upon the threshold—then, with a low moaning cry, fell heavily inward upon the person of her brother, and in her violent and now final death-agonies, bore him to the floor a corpse, and a victim to the terrors he had anticipated.

From that chamber, and from that mansion, I fled aghast. The storm was still abroad in all its wrath as I found myself crossing the old causeway. Suddenly there shot along the path a wild light, and I turned to see whence a gleam so unusual could have issued; for the vast house and its shadows were alone behind me. The radiance was that of the full, setting, and blood-red moon, which now shone vividly through that once barely-discernible fissure, of which I have before spoken as extending from the roof of the building, in a zigzag direction, to the base. While I gazed, this fissure rapidly widened—there came a fierce breath of the whirlwind—the entire orb of the satellite burst at once upon my sight—my brain reeled as I saw the mighty walls rushing asunder—there was a long tumultuous shouting sound like the voice of a thousand waters—and the deep and dank tarn at my feet closed sullenly and silently over the fragments of the *"House of Usher."*

Once Upon a Midnight Dreary

· · · · · ·

BY MICHAEL CONNELLY

The plan was simple: I would write a book about a cross-country killer who leaves obscure phrases from the work of Edgar Allan Poe as his calling card. I would borrow some of the gloomy menace of the master and infect my own book with it. It would amount to a perfect crime. A clever literary theft disguised as homage. And I would get away with it.

I packed a suitcase for the road trip I would take to research the locations where the killer would strike and made sure to include a two-volume set of Poe's collected works as well. By day I picked killing scenes for my novel—Phoenix, Denver, Chicago, Sarasota, and Baltimore. By night I sat in hotel rooms and re-immersed myself in the collected works of Edgar Allan Poe. For the most part I had been a short-story man when it came to Poe. I knew the poetry was well regarded and substantial—what high school graduate was unfamiliar with "The Raven"—but I had never been much interested in rhyming. I liked the blood and guts thrills of the stories. But now, on the road, I was reading the poetry because the short, tightly drawn lines, steeped in metaphors for death and loneliness, were what I needed for my book. All these years later I remember one stanza by heart.

I dwelt alone in the land of moan
and my soul was a stagnant tide

Has there ever been a more beautiful and concise summation of an existence at the bottom of the dark abyss? Could there possibly be a better line to self-describe a killer who roams the country in 1997? I didn't think so. So I decided my killer would use the line.

My research travels took me to Washington, D.C., where I spent a day walking around government buildings and trying to talk my way into a tour of the FBI headquarters. (Access denied.) Late in the day I checked into the Hilton near Dupont Circle. I wanted to stay specifically in the Hilton because the place had its own creep factor—about fifteen years earlier President Ronald Reagan stepped out of a side entrance after giving a speech and was shot by a would-be assassin seeking notoriety to feed his fixation on a movie star. I planned to include a reference to this in my book.

I checked out the spot of the assassination attempt, took some notes, and then went up to my room to order dinner in and spend the rest of the evening reading Poe. After eating and calling home, I stretched out on the bed and cracked open the volume containing the poetry. The work was morose and haunting. Death lurks in almost every stanza that Poe wrote. To say I was spooking myself would be an understatement. I kept all the lights on in the room and double-locked the door.

As the night wore on I became aware of voices out in the hallway. Fellow travelers talking in a muffled cacophony as they headed to or from the elevator. I could hear their footsteps as they trod past my door. It was late and I was somewhere in that gray area between wakefulness and sleep. But I read on and soon came across the poem "The Haunted Palace." The poem rang eerily familiar to me, yet I knew I was not aware of any of Poe's poetry outside of "The Raven." I checked the notes section and learned it was a ballad that had originally been contained in one of Poe's signature short stories, "The Fall of the House of Usher."

"Usher" was a story I had read somewhere long before, as a school assignment or during a voluntary immersion in Poe's work. I now took up the first volume, which contained the short stories, and began to read it once again. The story quickly enveloped me in its claustrophobic dread. I think there is no story of Poe's, or perhaps from any other writer, that so forcefully and completely ensures the reader's descent into the unexpected. It is a story steeped in mystery and fear and the unexpected twist. It is a story that rolls inexorably deeper into darkness from the very first word.

Deeply submerged in the story of Roderick Usher and the haunting malady of his head and home, I lost track of where I was until a loud SHOT rang out in the hallway. I leaped up in my bed, book flying to the floor, and stifled a scream. I stood stock-still and waited, my ears waiting for any further report. I then heard a peal of female laughter, a murmur of conversation, and the polite chime of an arriving elevator. I sat back on the bed shaken but realizing I had heard no shot. I had heard the slamming of the door across the hall. I had simply fallen under the spell of Edgar Allan Poe. I'd let him take me to a world of dark imagination, where common things become uncommon, where the routine becomes the ghastly unexpected, where a slamming door becomes a shot in the night.

I called my book *The Poet,* the name bestowed on my killer by the media when they attribute the lines left behind at the crime scenes to him rather than their true author, Poe. I put the Hilton Hotel scene in the book. I re-created it in as much detail as I could, placing my fictitious alter ego in the bed where I had been. It's one of my favorite moments in one of my favorite books. I am glad to have made a record of it. But the truth is that it wasn't necessary. For me there will be no forgetting that midnight dreary when Edgar Allan Poe reached across nearly two centuries to seek justice for what I had thought would be a perfect literary crime.

Michael Connelly was born in Philadelphia and has lived in various cities in California and Florida. A reformed journalist, he is a past president of the Mystery Writers of America as well as a recipient of the Edgar Award for Best First Novel by an American Author, bestowed for his 1992 debut, The Black Echo. *Eighteen novels later, he has received no further Edgar Awards. With the completion of this collection, he announces his retirement from editing anthologies.*

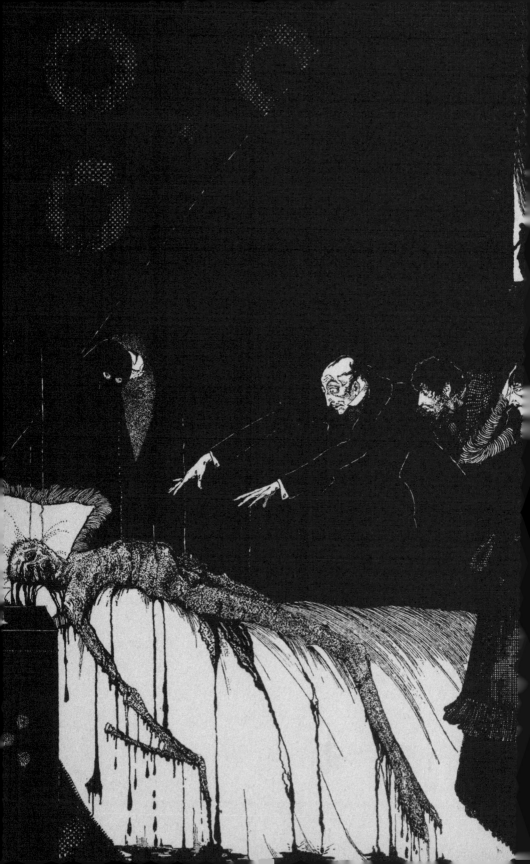

The Facts in the Case of M. Valdemar

OF COURSE I shall not pretend to consider it any matter for wonder, that the extraordinary case of M. Valdemar has excited discussion. It would have been a miracle had it not — especially under the circumstances. Through the desire of all parties concerned, to keep the affair from the public, at least for the present, or until we had further opportunities for investigation — through our endeavors to effect this — a garbled or exaggerated account made its way into society, and became the source of many unpleasant misrepresentations; and, very naturally, of a great deal of disbelief.

It is now rendered necessary that I give the *facts* — as far as I comprehend them myself. They are, succinctly, these:

My attention, for the last three years, had been repeatedly drawn to the subject of Mesmerism; and, about nine months ago, it occurred to me, quite suddenly, that in the series of experiments made hitherto, there had been a very remarkable and most unaccountable omission:—no person had as yet been mesmerized *in articulo mortis*. It remained to be seen, first, whether, in such condition, there existed in the patient any susceptibility to the magnetic influence; secondly, whether, if any existed, it was impaired or increased by the condition; thirdly, to what extent, or for how long a period, the encroachments of Death might be arrested by the process. There were other points to be ascertained, but these most excited my curiosity—the last in especial, from the immensely important character of its consequences.

In looking around me for some subject by whose means I might test these particulars, I was brought to think of my friend, M. Ernest Valdemar, the well-known compiler of the "Bibliotheca Forensica," and author (under the *nom de plume* of Issachar Marx) of the Polish versions of "Wallenstein" and "Gargantua." M. Valdemar, who has resided principally at Harlem, N.Y., since the year 1839, is (or was) particularly noticeable for the extreme spareness of his person—his lower limbs much resembling those of John Randolph; and, also, for the whiteness of his whiskers, in violent contrast to the blackness of his hair—the latter, in consequence, being very generally mistaken for a wig. His temperament was markedly nervous, and rendered him a good subject for mesmeric experiment. On two or three occasions I had put him to sleep with little difficulty, but was disappointed in other results which his peculiar constitution had naturally led me to anticipate. His will was at no period positively, or thoroughly, under my control, and in regard to *clairvoyance*, I could accomplish with him nothing to be relied upon. I always attributed my failure at these points to the disordered state of his health. For some months previous to my becoming acquainted with him, his physicians had declared him in a confirmed phthisis. It was his custom, indeed, to speak calmly of his approaching dissolution, as of a matter neither to be avoided nor regretted.

When the ideas to which I have alluded first occurred to me, it was of course very natural that I should think of M. Valdemar. I knew the steady philosophy of the man too well to apprehend any scruples from *him;* and he had no relatives in America who would be likely to interfere. I spoke to him frankly upon the subject; and, to my surprise, his interest seemed vividly excited. I say to my surprise; for, although he had always yielded his person freely to my experiments, he had never before given me any tokens of sympathy with what I did. His disease was of that character which would admit of exact calculation in respect to the epoch of its termination in death; and it was finally arranged between us that he would send for me about twenty-four hours before the period announced by his physicians as that of his decease.

It is now rather more than seven months since I received, from M. Valdemar himself, the subjoined note:

My DEAR P——

You may as well come now. D—— and F—— are agreed that I cannot hold out beyond to-morrow midnight; and I think they have hit the time very nearly.

VALDEMAR

I received this note within half an hour after it was written, and in fifteen minutes more I was in the dying man's chamber. I had not seen him for ten days, and was appalled by the fearful alteration which the brief interval had wrought in him. His face wore a leaden hue; the eyes were utterly lustreless; and the emaciation was so extreme, that the skin had been broken through by the cheek-bones. His expectoration was excessive. The pulse was barely perceptible.

He retained, nevertheless, in a very remarkable manner, both his mental power and a certain degree of physical strength. He spoke with distinctness — took some palliative medicines without aid — and, when I entered the room, was occupied in penciling memoranda in a pocket-book. He was propped up in the bed by pillows. Doctors D—— and F—— were in attendance.

After pressing Valdemar's hand, I took these gentlemen aside, and obtained from them a minute account of the patient's condition. The left lung had been for eighteen months in a semi-osseous or cartilaginous state, and was, of course, entirely useless for all purposes of vitality. The right, in its upper portion, was also partially, if not thoroughly, ossified, while the lower region was merely a mass of purulent tubercles, running one into another. Several extensive perforations existed; and, at one point, permanent adhesion to the ribs had taken place. These appearances in the right lobe were of comparatively recent date. The ossification had proceeded with very unusual rapidity; no sign of it had been discovered a month before, and the adhesion had only been observed during the three previous days. Independently of the phthisis, the patient was suspected of aneurism of the aorta; but on this point the osseous symptoms rendered an exact diagnosis impossible. It was the opinion of both physicians that M. Valdemar would die about midnight on the morrow (Sunday). It was then seven o'clock on Saturday evening.

On quitting the invalid's bedside to hold conversation with myself, Doctors D—— and F—— had bidden him a final farewell. It had not been their intention to return; but, at my request, they agreed to look in upon the patient about ten the next night.

When they had gone, I spoke freely with M. Valdemar on the subject of his approaching dissolution, as well as, more particularly, of the experiment proposed. He still professed himself quite willing and even anxious to have it made, and urged me to commence it at once.

A male and a female nurse were in attendance; but I did not feel myself altogether at liberty to engage in a task of this character with no more reliable witnesses than these people, in case of sudden accident, might prove. I therefore postponed operations until about eight the next night, when the arrival of a medical student, with whom I had some acquaintance (Mr. Theodore L——l,) relieved me from further embarrassment. It had been my design, originally, to wait for the physicians; but I was induced to proceed, first by the urgent entreaties of M. Valdemar, and secondly, by my conviction that I had not a moment to lose, as he was evidently sinking fast.

Mr. L——l was so kind as to accede to my desire that he would take notes of all that occurred; and it is from his memoranda that what I now have to relate is, for the most part, either condensed or copied *verbatim*.

It wanted about five minutes of eight when, taking the patient's hand, I begged him to state, as distinctly as he could, to Mr. L——l, whether he (M. Valdemar) was entirely willing that I should make the experiment of mesmerizing him in his then condition.

He replied feebly, yet quite audibly: "Yes, I wish to be mesmerized"—adding immediately afterward: "I fear you have deferred it too long."

While he spoke thus, I commenced the passes which I had already found most effectual in subduing him. He was evidently influenced with the first lateral stroke of my hand across his forehead; but, although I exerted all my powers, no further perceptible effect was induced until some minutes after ten o'clock, when Doctors D—— and F—— called, according to appointment. I explained to them, in a few words, what I designed, and as they opposed no objection, saying that the patient was already in the death agony, I proceeded without hesitation—exchanging, however, the lateral passes for downward ones, and directing my gaze entirely into the right eye of the sufferer. By this time his pulse was imperceptible and his breathing was stertorous, and at intervals of half a minute.

This condition was nearly unaltered for a quarter of an hour. At the expiration of this period, however, a natural although a very deep sigh escaped from the bosom of the dying man, and the stertorous breathing ceased—that is to say, its stertorousness was no longer apparent; the intervals were undiminished. The patient's extremities were of an icy coldness.

At five minutes before eleven, I perceived unequivocal signs of the mesmeric influence. The glassy roll of the eye was changed for that expression of uneasy *inward* examination which is never seen except in cases of sleep-waking, and which it is quite impossible to mistake. With a few rapid lateral passes I made the lids quiver, as in incipient sleep, and with a few more I closed them altogether. I was not satisfied, however, with this, but continued the manipulations vigorously, and with the fullest exertion of the will, until I had completely stiffened the limbs of the slumberer, after placing them in a seemingly easy position. The legs were at full length; the arms were nearly so, and reposed on the bed at a moderate distance from the loins. The head was very slightly elevated.

When I had accomplished this, it was fully midnight, and I requested the gentlemen present to examine M. Valdemar's condition. After a few experiments, they admitted him to be in an unusually perfect state of mesmeric trance. The curiosity of both the physicians was greatly excited. Dr. D—— resolved at once to remain with the patient all night, while Dr. F—— took leave with a promise to return at daybreak. Mr. L——l and the nurses remained.

We left M. Valdemar entirely undisturbed until about three o'clock in the morning, when I approached him and found him in precisely the same condition as when Dr. F—— went away—that is to say, he lay in the same position; the pulse was imperceptible; the breathing was gentle (scarcely noticeable, unless through the application of a mirror to the lips); the eyes were closed naturally;

and the limbs were as rigid and as cold as marble. Still, the general appearance was certainly not that of death.

As I approached M. Valdemar I made a kind of half effort to influence his right arm into pursuit of my own, as I passed the latter gently to and fro above his person. In such experiments with this patient, I had never perfectly succeeded before, and assuredly I had little thought of succeeding now; but to my astonishment, his arm very readily, although feebly, followed every direction I assigned it with mine. I determined to hazard a few words of conversation.

"M. Valdemar," I said, "are you asleep?" He made no answer, but I perceived a tremor about the lips, and was thus induced to repeat the question, again and again. At its third repetition, his whole frame was agitated by a very slight shivering; the eyelids unclosed themselves so far as to display a white line of the ball; the lips moved sluggishly, and from between them, in a barely audible whisper, issued the words:

"Yes;—asleep now. Do not wake me!—let me die so!"

I here felt the limbs, and found them as rigid as ever. The right arm, as before, obeyed the direction of my hand. I questioned the sleep-waker again:

"Do you still feel pain in the breast, M. Valdemar?"

The answer now was immediate, but even less audible than before:

"No pain—I am dying!"

I did not think it advisable to disturb him further just then, and nothing more was said or done until the arrival of Dr. F——, who came a little before sunrise, and expressed unbounded astonishment at finding the patient still alive. After feeling the pulse and applying a mirror to the lips, he requested me to speak to the sleep-waker again. I did so, saying:

"M. Valdemar, do you still sleep?"

As before, some minutes elapsed ere a reply was made; and during the interval the dying man seemed to be collecting his energies to speak. At my fourth repetition of the question, he said very faintly, almost inaudibly:

"Yes; still asleep—dying."

It was now the opinion, or rather the wish, of the physicians, that M. Valdemar should be suffered to remain undisturbed in his present apparently tranquil condition, until death should supervene—and this, it was generally agreed, must now take place within a few minutes. I concluded, however, to speak to him once more, and merely repeated my previous question.

While I spoke, there came a marked change over the countenance of the sleep-waker. The eyes rolled themselves slowly open, the pupils disappearing upwardly; the skin generally assumed a cadaverous hue, resembling not so much parchment as white paper; and the circular hectic spots which, hitherto, had been strongly defined in the centre of each cheek, *went out* at once. I use this expression, because the suddenness of their departure put me in mind of nothing so much as the extinguishment of a candle by a puff of the breath. The upper lip, at the same time, writhed itself away from the teeth, which it had previously covered completely; while the lower jaw fell with an audible jerk, leaving the mouth widely extended, and disclosing in full view the swollen and blackened tongue. I presume that no member of the party then present had been unaccustomed to death-bed horrors; but so hideous beyond conception was the appearance of M. Valdemar at this moment, that there was a general shrinking back from the region of the bed. I now feel that I have reached a point of this narrative at which every reader will be startled into positive disbelief. It is my business, however, simply to proceed.

There was no longer the faintest sign of vitality in M. Valdemar; and concluding him to be dead, we were consigning him to the charge of the nurses, when a strong vibratory motion was observable in the tongue. This continued for perhaps a minute. At the expiration of this period, there issued from the distended and motionless jaws a voice—such as it would be madness in me to attempt describing. There are, indeed, two or three epithets which might be considered as applicable to it in part; I might say, for example, that the sound was harsh, and broken and hollow; but the hideous whole is indescribable, for the simple reason that no similar sounds have ever jarred upon the ear of humanity. There were two particulars, nevertheless, which I thought then, and still think, might fairly be stated as characteristic of the intonation—as well adapted to convey some idea of its unearthly peculiarity. In the first place, the voice seemed to reach our ears—at least mine—from a vast distance, or from some deep cavern within the earth. In the second place, it impressed me (I fear, indeed, that it will be impossible to make myself comprehended) as gelatinous or glutinous matters impress the sense of touch.

I have spoken both of "sound" and of "voice." I mean to say that the sound was one of distinct—of even wonderfully, thrillingly distinct—syllabification. M. Valdemar *spoke*—obviously in reply to the question I had propounded to him a few minutes before. I had asked him, it will be remembered, if he still slept.

He now said:

"Yes;—no;—I *have been* sleeping—and now—now—*I am dead.*"

No person present even affected to deny, or attempted to repress, the unutterable, shuddering horror which these few words, thus uttered, were so well calculated to convey. Mr. L——l (the student) swooned. The nurses immediately left the chamber, and could not be induced to return. My own impressions I would not pretend to render intelligible to the reader. For nearly an hour, we busied ourselves, silently—without utterance of a word—in endeavors to revive Mr. L——l. When he came to himself, we addressed ourselves again to an investigation of M. Valdemar's condition.

It remained in all respects as I have last described it, with the exception that the mirror no longer afforded evidence of respiration. An attempt to draw blood from the arm failed. I should mention, too, that this limb was no further subject to my will. I endeavored in vain to make it follow the direction of my hand. The only real indication, indeed, of the mesmeric influence, was now found in the vibratory movement of the tongue, whenever I addressed M. Valdemar a question. He seemed to be making an effort to reply, but had no longer sufficient volition. To queries put to him by any other person than myself he seemed utterly insensible—although I endeavored to place each member of the company in mesmeric *rapport* with him. I believe that I have now related all that is necessary to an understanding of the sleep-waker's state at this epoch. Other nurses were procured; and at ten o'clock I left the house in company with the two physicians and Mr. L——l.

In the afternoon we all called again to see the patient. His condition remained precisely the same. We had now some discussion as to the propriety and feasibility of awakening him; but we had little difficulty in agreeing that no good purpose would be served by so doing. It was evident that, so far, death (or what is usually termed death) had been arrested by the mesmeric process. It seemed clear to us all that to awaken M. Valdemar would be merely to insure his instant, or at least his speedy, dissolution.

From this period until the close of last week—*an interval of nearly seven months*—we continued to make daily calls at M. Valdemar's house, accompanied, now and then, by medical and other friends. All this time the sleeper-waker remained *exactly* as I have last described him. The nurses' attentions were continual.

It was on Friday last that we finally resolved to make the experi-

ment of awakening, or attempting to awaken him; and it is the (perhaps) unfortunate result of this latter experiment which has given
rise to so much discussion in private circles—to so much of what I
cannot help thinking unwarranted popular feeling.

For the purpose of relieving M. Valdemar from the mesmeric
trance, I made use of the customary passes. These for a time were
unsuccessful. The first indication of revival was afforded by a partial
descent of the iris. It was observed, as especially remarkable, that
this lowering of the pupil was accompanied by the profuse outflow-
ing of a yellowish ichor (from beneath the lids) of a pungent and
highly offensive odor.

It was now suggested that I should attempt to influence the patient's arm as heretofore. I made the attempt and failed. Dr. F—— then
intimated a desire to have me put a question. I did so, as follows:

"M. Valdemar, can you explain to us what are your feelings or
wishes now?"

There was an instant return of the hectic circles on the cheeks:
the tongue quivered, or rather rolled violently in the mouth (although the jaws and lips remained rigid as before), and at length the
same hideous voice which I have already described, broke forth:

"For God's sake!—quick!—quick!—put me to sleep—or, quick!
—waken me!—quick!—*I say to you that I am dead!*"

I was thoroughly unnerved, and for an instant remained unde-
cided what to do. At first I made an endeavor to recompose the patient; but, failing in this through total abeyance of the will, I retraced
my steps and as earnestly struggled to awaken him. In this attempt I
soon saw that I should be successful—or at least I soon fancied that
my success would be complete—and I am sure that all in the room
were prepared to see the patient awaken.

For what really occurred, however, it is quite impossible that any
human being could have been prepared.

As I rapidly made the mesmeric passes, amid ejaculations of

"dead! dead!" absolutely *bursting* from the tongue and not from the lips of the sufferer, his whole frame at once—within the space of a single minute, or less, shrunk—crumbled—absolutely *rotted* away beneath my hands. Upon the bed, before that whole company, there lay a nearly liquid mass of loathsome—of detestable putrescence.

The Thief

· · · · · ·

BY LAURIE R. KING

It is a well-known criticism of William Shakespeare that, despite being universally celebrated for his fresh originality, the man's work is basically one cliché after another. Marching through his plays and poems, one finds the most timeworn of expressions: *All the world's a stage. To be or not to be. What's in a name?* A person really has to wonder why the Bard of Avon couldn't scrape together a more creative turn of phrase than Shylock's *bated breath*, the *elbow room* of King John's soul, Trinculo's lament that misery brings *strange bedfellows*—from *foul play* to *mind's eye*, *sorry sight* to *tower of strength*, the truth of the matter is, William Shakespeare was simply grinding out the same trite clichés that we lesser mortals still wrestle with. He was just very lucky to be the first to get them into print, that's all.

The same critique, I fear, must be leveled at our own Edgar Allan Poe. The man is credited with being the inventor of crime fiction, but when you look more closely, you find that Poe is just reworking the same old tired ideas the rest of us depend on.

An example? Okay: Some years ago, I'm writing a story about a young woman who is—I freely admit this—a female version of

Sherlock Holmes. Now, Holmes, you may know, is an extraordinarily clever analytical mind who solves peculiar crimes and discusses them with a partner who isn't quite so bright. What does it matter that Edgar Allan Poe also wrote (in "The Murders in the Rue Morgue") about an extraordinarily clever analytical mind who solves peculiar crimes and discusses them with a partner who isn't quite so bright? I mean, how else could you tell this kind of story, really? It doesn't mean Arthur Conan Doyle was a plagiarist, any more than I am.

So I tell myself this and keep writing my story, and I come up with a solution to one aspect of the crime that revolves around an enigmatic cipher. Which is fine—even Dorothy Sayers has a cipher in one of her stories—except that when I later sit down to read "The Gold-Bug" I see that it, too, contains an enigmatic cipher. Hmm.

Then, a few years later, I'm working on another novel, where the characters use hypnotism to solve a case, and when I finish it, I'm pleased with how clever those characters—and of course, their author—are. Until I find that Poe has used mesmerism as well, in "The Facts in the Case of M. Valdemar."

By now, I'm starting to get a little sensitive about old E.A.P. I wonder if there's some kind of weird linkup between his brain and my laptop, a century and a half apart. It sure would explain a lot. But no, I'm just being paranoid, it's coincidence.

So I sit down to write a book about a noble family and their idiosyncratic manor house, only to discover that, sure enough, Poe has the same kind of setup in "The Fall of the House of Usher." But so what, so *damned* what? The man's a thief, there's nothing I can do about it.

However, I decide that, no matter how he's doing it, I can get around him by writing a book with an absolutely unique central character, a person no one but Laurie King would ever think of. And to make matters really secure, I'll write it with a pen, not on the laptop. Not that I think there's anything paranormal going on here, don't be ridiculous. But just in case. . . . So out trots Brother Erasmus, a holy fool in a modern city, who is surely one of the most quirky, unlikely, singular characters in fiction. Nobody will ever duplicate him.

And then I turn the pages of "The Cask of Amontillado" and find—oh, bugger! The sneaky bastard's done it again: *the man wore motley.*

I tell you, Edgar Allan Poe is a blatant and unscrupulous thief of all the best ideas. If he wasn't dead, we mystery writers would have to band together and start legal proceedings.

I have to say, it gets a person down when everything one writes is tainted with a whiff of the derivative. I'm thinking about moving out of crime fiction for a while since, with Poe in the field, it's feeling a little crowded. Maybe I'll write poetry for a change. I've even started playing with some nice ideas about this gloomy bird and a lost lover. . . .

Laurie R. King regretfully admits that she won, and kept, the award named after Edgar Allan Poe, for her first novel in 1993. Since then, she has written eighteen novels and a number of short stories, absolutely none of which were influenced in the least by the work of any other writer. (And for anyone keeping score, the L.R.K. titles referred to above are: The Beekeeper's Apprentice, A Letter of Mary, Justice Hall, *and* To Play the Fool.*)*

Ligeia

And the will therein lieth, which dieth not. Who knoweth the
mysteries of the will, with its vigor? For God is but a great will
pervading all things by nature of its intentness. Man doth not
yield himself to the angels, nor unto death utterly, save
only through the weakness of his feeble will.

—JOSEPH GLANVILL

I CANNOT, FOR MY SOUL, remember how, when, or
even precisely where, I first became acquainted with the lady
Ligeia. Long years have since elapsed, and my memory is
feeble through much suffering. Or, perhaps, I cannot *now*
bring these points to mind, because, in truth, the character of
my beloved, her rare learning, her singular yet placid cast of
beauty, and the thrilling and enthralling eloquence of her low
musical language, made their way into my heart by paces so
steadily and stealthily progressive, that they have been unnoticed and unknown. Yet I believe that I met her first and

most frequently in some large, old, decaying city near the Rhine. Of her family—I have surely heard her speak. That it is of a remotely ancient date cannot be doubted. Ligeia! Ligeia! Buried in studies of a nature more than all else adapted to deaden impressions of the outward world, it is by that sweet word alone—by Ligeia—that I bring before mine eyes in fancy the image of her who is no more.

And now, while I write, a recollection flashes upon me that I have *never known* the paternal name of her who was my friend and my betrothed, and who became the partner of my studies, and finally the wife of my bosom. Was it a playful charge on the part of my Ligeia? or was it a test of my strength of affection, that I should institute no inquiries upon this point? or was it rather a caprice of my own—a wildly romantic offering on the shrine of the most passionate devotion? I but indistinctly recall the fact itself—what wonder that I have utterly forgotten the circumstances which originated or attended it? And, indeed, if ever that spirit which is entitled *Romance*—if ever she, the wan and the misty-winged *Ashtophet* of idolatrous Egypt, presided, as they tell, over marriages ill-omened, then most surely she presided over mine.

There is one dear topic, however, on which my memory fails me not. It is the *person* of Ligeia. In stature she was tall, somewhat slender, and, in her latter days, even emaciated. I would in vain attempt to portray the majesty, the quiet ease of her demeanor, or the incomprehensible lightness and elasticity of her footfall. She came and departed as a shadow. I was never made aware of her entrance into my closed study, save by the dear music of her low sweet voice, as she placed her marble hand upon my shoulder. In beauty of face no maiden ever equalled her. It was the radiance of an opium-dream—an airy and spirit-lifting vision more wildly divine than the phantasies which hovered vision about the slumbering souls of the daughters of Delos. Yet her features were not of that regular mould which we have been falsely taught to worship in the classical labors of the heathen. "There is no exquisite beauty," says Bacon, Lord Verulam, speaking truly of all the forms and *genera* of beauty, "without some *strangeness* in the proportion." Yet, although I saw that the features of Ligeia were not of a classic regularity—although I perceived that her loveliness was indeed "exquisite," and felt that there was much of "strangeness" pervading it, yet I have tried in vain to detect the irregularity and to trace home my own perception of "the strange." I examined the contour of the lofty and pale forehead—it was faultless—how cold indeed that word when applied to a majesty so divine!—the skin rivalling the purest ivory, the commanding extent and repose, the gentle prominence of the regions above the temples; and then the raven-black, the glossy, the luxuriant and naturally-curling tresses, setting forth the full force of the Homeric epithet, "hyacinthine!" I looked at the delicate out-lines of the nose—and nowhere but in the graceful medallions of the Hebrews had I beheld a similar perfection. There were the same luxurious smoothness of surface, the same scarcely perceptible ten-dency to the aquiline, the same harmoniously curved nostrils speak-ing the free spirit. I regarded the sweet mouth. Here was indeed the triumph of all things heavenly—the magnificent turn of the short upper lip—the soft, voluptuous slumber of the under—the dimples which sported, and the color which spoke—the teeth glancing back, with a brilliancy almost startling, every ray of the holy light which fell upon them in her serene and placid yet most exultingly radi-ant of all smiles. I scrutinized the formation of the chin—and here, too, I found the gentleness of breadth, the softness and the majesty, the fulness and the spirituality, of the Greek—the contour which the god Apollo revealed but in a dream, to Cleomenes, the son of the Athenian. And then I peered into the large eyes of Ligeia.

For eyes we have no models in the remotely antique. It might have been, too, that in these eyes of my beloved lay the secret to which Lord Verulam alludes. They were, I must believe, far larger than the ordinary eyes of our own race. They were even fuller than the fullest of the gazelle eyes of the tribe of the valley of Nourjahad. Yet it was only at intervals—in moments of intense excitement—that this peculiarity became more than slightly noticeable in Ligeia. And at such moments was her beauty—in my heated fancy thus it appeared perhaps—the beauty of beings either above or apart from the earth—the beauty of the fabulous Houri of the Turk. The hue of the orbs was the most brilliant of black, and, far over them, hung jetty lashes of great length. The brows, slightly irregular in outline, had the same tint. The "strangeness," however, which I found in the eyes was of a nature distinct from the formation, or the color, or the brilliancy of the features, and must, after all, be referred to the *expression*. Ah, word of no meaning! behind whose vast latitude of mere sound we intrench our ignorance of so much of the spiritual. The expression of the eyes of Ligeia! How for long hours have I pondered upon it! How have I, through the whole of a midsummer night, struggled to fathom it! What was it—that something more profound than the well of Democritus—which lay far within the pupils of my beloved? What *was* it? I was possessed with a passion to discover. Those eyes! those large, those shining, those divine orbs! they became to me twin stars of Leda, and I to them devoutest of astrologers.

There is no point, among the many incomprehensible anomalies of the science of mind, more thrillingly exciting than the fact—never, I believe, noticed in the schools—that, in our endeavors to recall to memory something long forgotten, we often find ourselves *upon the very verge* of remembrance, without being able, in the end, to remember. And thus how frequently, in my intense scrutiny of Ligeia's eyes, have I felt approaching the full knowledge of their expression—felt it approaching—yet not quite be mine—and so at length entirely depart! And (strange, oh, strangest mystery of all!) I found, in the commonest objects of the universe, a circle of analogies to that expression. I mean to say that, subsequently to the period when Ligeia's beauty passed into my spirit, there dwelling as in a shrine, I derived, from many existences in the material world, a sentiment such as I felt always around, within me, by her large and luminous orbs. Yet not the more could I define that sentiment, or analyze, or even steadily view it. I recognized it, let me repeat, sometimes in the survey of a rapidly growing vine—in the contemplation of a moth, a butterfly, a chrysalis, a stream of running water. I have felt it in the ocean—in the falling of a meteor. I have felt it in the glances of unusually aged people. And there are one or two stars in heaven (one especially, a star of the sixth magnitude, double and changeable, to be found near the large star in Lyra) in a telescopic scrutiny of which I have been made aware of the feeling. I have been filled with it by certain sounds from stringed instruments, and not unfrequently by passages from books. Among innumerable other instances, I well remember something in a volume of Joseph Glanvill, which (perhaps merely from its quaintness—who shall say?) never failed to inspire me with the sentiment: "And the will therein lieth, which dieth not. Who knoweth the mysteries of the will, with its vigor? For God is but a great will pervading all things by nature of its intentness. Man doth not yield him to the angels, nor unto death utterly, save only through the weakness of his feeble will."

Length of years and subsequent reflection have enabled me to trace, indeed, some remote connection between this passage in the English moralist and a portion of the character of Ligeia. An *intensity* in thought, action, or speech was possibly, in her, a result, or at least an index, of that gigantic volition which, during our long intercourse, failed to give other and more immediate evidence of its existence. Of all the women whom I have ever known, she, the outwardly calm, the ever-placid Ligeia, was the most violently a prey to the tumultuous vultures of stern passion. And of such passion I could form no estimate save by the miraculous expansion of those eyes which at once so delighted and appalled me,—by the almost magical melody, modulation, distinctness, and placidity of her very low voice,—and by the fierce energy (rendered doubly effective by contrast with her manner of utterance) of the wild words which she habitually uttered.

I have spoken of the learning of Ligeia: it was immense — such as I have never known in woman. In the classical tongues was she deeply proficient, and as far as my own acquaintance extended in regard to the modern dialects of Europe, I have never known her at fault. Indeed upon any theme of the most admired because simply the most abstruse of the boasted erudition of the Academy, have I *ever* found Ligeia at fault? How singularly — how thrillingly, this one point in the nature of my wife has forced itself, at this late period only, upon my attention! I said her knowledge was such as I have never known in woman — but where breathes the man who has traversed, and successfully, *all* the wide areas of moral, physical, and mathematical science? I saw not then what I now clearly perceive, that the acquisitions of Ligeia were gigantic, were astounding; yet I was sufficiently aware of her infinite supremacy to resign myself, with a child-like confidence, to her guidance through the chaotic world of metaphysical investigation at which I was most busily occupied during the earlier years of our marriage. With how vast a triumph — with how vivid a delight — with how much of all that is ethereal in hope did I *feel,* as she bent over me in studies but little sought — but less known, — that delicious vista by slow degrees expanding before me, down whose long, gorgeous, and all untrodden path, I might at length pass onward to the goal of a wisdom too divinely precious not to be forbidden!

How poignant, then, must have been the grief with which, after some years, I beheld my well-grounded expectations take wings to themselves and fly away! Without Ligeia I was but as a child groping benighted. Her presence, her readings alone, rendered vividly luminous the many mysteries of the transcendentalism in which we were immersed. Wanting the radiant lustre of her eyes, letters, lambent and golden, grew duller than Saturnian lead. And now those eyes shone less and less frequently upon the pages over which I pored. Ligeia grew ill. The wild eyes blazed with a too—too glorious effulgence; the pale fingers became of the transparent waxen hue of the grave; and the blue veins upon the lofty forehead swelled and sank impetuously with the tides of the gentle emotion. I saw that she must die—and I struggled desperately in spirit with the grim Azrael. And the struggles of the passionate wife were, to my astonishment, even more energetic than my own. There had been much in her stern nature to impress me with the belief that, to her, death would have come without its terrors; but not so. Words are impotent to convey any just idea of the fierceness of resistance with which she wrestled with the Shadow. I groaned in anguish at the pitiable spectacle. I would have soothed—I would have reasoned; but in the intensity of her wild desire for life—for life—*but* for life—solace and reason were alike the uttermost of folly. Yet not until the last instance, amid the most convulsive writhings of her fierce spirit, was shaken the external placidity of her demeanor. Her voice grew more gentle—grew more low—yet I would not wish to dwell upon the wild meaning of the quietly uttered words. My brain reeled as I hearkened, entranced to a melody more than mortal—to assumptions and aspirations which mortality had never before known.

That she loved me I should not have doubted; and I might have been easily aware that, in a bosom such as hers, love would have reigned no ordinary passion. But in death only was I fully impressed with the strength of her affection. For long hours, detaining my hand, would she pour out before me the overflowing of a heart whose more than passionate devotion amounted to idolatry. How had I deserved to be so blessed by such confessions?—how had I deserved to be so cursed with the removal of my beloved in the hour of her making them? But upon this subject I cannot bear to dilate. Let me say only, that in Ligeia's more than womanly abandonment to a love, alas! all unmerited, all unworthily bestowed, I at length recognized the

principle of her longing, with so wildly earnest a desire, for the life
which was now fleeing so rapidly away. It is this wild longing—it is
this eager vehemence of desire for life—*but* for life—that I have no
power to portray—no utterance capable of expressing.

At high noon of the night in which she departed, beckoning me,
peremptorily, to her side, she bade me repeat certain verses composed
by herself not many days before. I obeyed her. They were these:—

Lo! 'tis a gala night
    Within the lonesome latter years!
An angel throng, bewinged, bedight
    In veils, and drowned in tears,
Sit in a theatre, to see
    A play of hopes and fears,
While the orchestra breathes fitfully
    The music of the spheres.

Mimes, in the form of God on high,
    Mutter and mumble low,
And hither and thither fly;
    Mere puppets they, who come and go
At bidding of vast formless things
    That shift the scenery to and fro,
Flapping from out their condor wings
    Invisible Woe!

That motley drama!—oh, be sure
    It shall not be forgot!
With its Phantom chased for evermore,
    By a crowd that seize it not,
Through a circle that ever returneth in
    To the self-same spot,

And much of Madness, and more of Sin
    And Horror, the soul of the plot!

But see, amid the mimic rout
    A crawling shape intrude!
A blood-red thing that writhes from out
    The scenic solitude!
It writhes! — it writhes! — with mortal pangs
    The mimes become its food,
And the seraphs sob at vermin fangs
    In human gore imbued.

Out — out are the lights — out all!
    And over each quivering form,
The curtain, a funeral pall,
    Comes down with the rush of a storm —
And the angels, all pallid and wan,
    Uprising, unveiling, affirm
That the play is the tragedy, "Man,"
    And its hero, the Conqueror Worm.

"O God!" half shrieked Ligeia, leaping to her feet and extending her arms aloft with a spasmodic movement, as I made an end of these lines — "O God! O Divine Father! — shall these things be undeviatingly so? — shall this conqueror be not once conquered? Are we not part and parcel in Thee? Who — who knoweth the mysteries of the will with its vigor? Man doth not yield him to the angels, *nor unto death utterly,* save only through the weakness of his feeble will."

And now, as if exhausted with emotion, she suffered her white arms to fall, and returned solemnly to her bed of death. And as she breathed her last sighs, there came mingled with them a low murmur from her lips. I bent to them my ear, and distinguished, again, the concluding words of the passage in Glanvill: *"Man doth not yield him to the angels, nor unto death utterly, save only through the weakness of his feeble will."*

She died; and I, crushed into the very dust with sorrow, could no longer endure the lonely desolation of my dwelling in the dim and decaying city by the Rhine. I had no lack of what the world calls wealth. Ligeia had brought me far more, very far more, than ordinarily falls to the lot of mortals. After a few months, therefore, of weary and aimless wandering, I purchased and put in some repair, an abbey, which I shall not name, in one of the wildest and least frequented portions of fair England. The gloomy and dreary grandeur of the building, the almost savage aspect of the domain, the many melancholy and time-honored memories connected with both, had much in unison with the feelings of utter abandonment which had driven me into that remote and unsocial region of the country. Yet although the external abbey, with its verdant decay hanging about it, suffered but little alteration, I gave way, with a child-like perversity, and perchance with a faint hope of alleviating my sorrows, to a display of more than regal magnificence within. For such follies, even in childhood, I had imbibed a taste, and now they came back to me as if in the dotage of grief. Alas, I feel how much even of incipient madness might have been discovered in the gorgeous and fantastic draperies, in the solemn carvings of Egypt, in the wild cornices and furniture, in the Bedlam patterns of the carpets of tufted gold! I had become a bounden slave in the trammels of opium, and my labors and my orders had taken a coloring from my dreams. But these absurdities must not pause to detail. Let me speak only of that one chamber, ever accursed, whither, in a moment of mental alienation, I led from the altar as my bride—as the successor of the unforgotten Ligeia—the fair-haired and blue-eyed Lady Rowena Trevanion, of Tremaine.

There is no individual portion of the architecture and decoration of that bridal chamber which is not now visibly before me. Where were the souls of the haughty family of the bride, when, through

thirst of gold, they permitted to pass the threshold of an apartment
so bedecked, a maiden and a daughter so beloved? I have said, that
I minutely remember the details of the chamber—yet I am sadly
forgetful on topics of deep moment; and here there was no system,
no keeping, in the fantastic display, to take hold upon the memory.
The room lay in a high turret of the castellated abbey, was pentago-
nal in shape, and of capacious size. Occupying the whole southern
face of the pentagon was the sole window—an immense sheet of
unbroken glass from Venice—a single pane, and tinted of a leaden
hue, so that the rays of either the sun or moon passing through it,
fell with a ghastly lustre on the objects within. Over the upper portion of this huge window, extended the trellis-work of an aged vine,
which clambered up the massy walls of the turret. The ceiling, of
gloomy-looking oak, was excessively lofty, vaulted, and elaborately
fretted with the wildest and most grotesque specimens of a semi-
Gothic, semi-Druidical device. From out the most central recess of
this melancholy vaulting, depended, by a single chain of gold with
long links, a huge censer of the same metal, Saracenic in pattern,
and with many perforations so contrived that there writhed in and
out of them, as if endued with a serpent vitality, a continual succession of parti-colored fires.

Some few ottomans and golden candelabra, of Eastern figure,
were in various stations about; and there was the couch, too—the
bridal couch—of an Indian model, and low, and sculptured of solid
ebony, with a pall-like canopy above. In each of the angles of the
chamber stood on end a gigantic sarcophagus of black granite, from
the tombs of the kings over against Luxor, with their aged lids full of
immemorial sculpture. But in the draping of the apartment lay, alas!
the chief phantasy of all. The lofty walls, gigantic in height—even
unproportionably so—were hung from summit to foot, in vast folds,
with a heavy and massive-looking tapestry—tapestry of a material
which was found alike as a carpet on the floor, as a covering for the

ottomans and the ebony bed, as a canopy for the bed and as the gorgeous volutes of the curtains which partially shaded the window. The material was the richest cloth of gold. It was spotted all over, at irregular intervals, with arabesque figures, about a foot in diameter, and wrought upon the cloth in patterns of the most jetty black. But these figures partook of the true character of the arabesque only when regarded from a single point of view. By a contrivance now common, and indeed traceable to a very remote period of antiquity, they were made changeable in aspect. To one entering the room, they bore the appearance of simple monstrosities; but upon a farther advance, this appearance gradually departed; and step by step, as the visitor moved his station in the chamber, he saw himself surrounded by an endless succession of the ghastly forms which belong to the superstition of the Norman, or arise in the guilty slumbers of the monk. The phantasmagoric effect was vastly heightened by the artificial introduction of a strong continual current of wind behind the draperies—giving a hideous and uneasy animation to the whole.

In halls such as these—in a bridal chamber such as this—I passed, with the Lady of Tremaine, the unhallowed hours of the first month of our marriage—passed them with but little disquietude. That my wife dreaded the fierce moodiness of my temper—that she shunned me, and loved me but little—I could not help perceiving; but it gave me rather pleasure than otherwise. I loathed her with a hatred belonging more to demon than to man. My memory flew back, (oh, with what intensity of regret!) to Ligeia, the beloved, the august, the beautiful, the entombed. I revelled in recollections of her purity, of her wisdom, of her lofty—her ethereal nature, of her passionate, her idolatrous love. Now, then, did my spirit fully and freely burn with more than all the fires of her own. In the excitement of my opium dreams (for I was habitually fettered in the shackles of the drug) I would call aloud upon her name, during the silence of the night, or among the sheltered recesses of the glens by day, as if, through the wild eagerness, the solemn passion, the consuming ardor of my longing for the departed, I could restore her to the pathway she had abandoned—ah, *could* it be for ever?—upon the earth.

About the commencement of the second month of the marriage, the Lady Rowena was attacked with sudden illness, from which her recovery was slow. The fever which consumed her rendered her nights uneasy; and in her perturbed state of half-slumber, she spoke of sounds, and of motions, in and about the chamber of the turret, which I concluded had no origin save in the distemper of her fancy, or perhaps in the phantasmagoric influences of the chamber itself. She became at length convalescent—finally, well. Yet but a brief period elapsed, ere a second more violent disorder again threw her upon a bed of suffering; and from this attack her frame, at all times feeble, never altogether recovered. Her illnesses were, after this epoch, of alarming character, and of more alarming recurrence, defying alike the knowledge and the great exertions of her physicians. With the increase of the chronic disease, which had thus, apparently, taken too sure hold upon her constitution to be eradicated by human means, I could not fail to observe a similar increase in the nervous irritation of her temperament, and in her excitability by trivial causes of fear. She spoke again, and now more frequently and pertinaciously, of the sounds—of the slight sounds—and of the unusual motions among the tapestries, to which she had formerly alluded.

One night, near the closing in of September, she pressed this distressing subject with more than usual emphasis upon my attention. She had just awakened from an unquiet slumber, and I had been watching, with feelings half of anxiety, half of vague terror, the workings of her emaciated countenance. I sat by the side of her ebony bed, upon one of the ottomans of India. She partly arose, and spoke, in an earnest low whisper, of sounds which she *then* heard, but which I could not hear—of motions which she *then* saw, but which I could not perceive. The wind was rushing hurriedly behind the tapestries, and I wished to show her (what, let me confess it, I could not *all* believe) that those almost inarticulate breathings, and those very gentle variations of the figures upon the wall, were but the natural effects of that customary rushing of the wind. But a deadly pallor, overspreading her face, had proved to me that my exertions to reassure her would be fruitless. She appeared to be fainting, and no attendants were within call. I remembered where was deposited a decanter of light wine which had been ordered by her physicians, and hastened across the chamber to procure it. But, as I stepped beneath the light of the censer, two circumstances of a startling nature attracted my attention. I had felt that some palpable although invisible object had passed lightly by my person; and I saw that there lay upon the golden carpet, in the very middle of the rich lustre thrown from the censer, a shadow—a faint, indefinite shadow of angelic aspect—such as might be fancied for the shadow of a shade. But I was wild with the excitement of an immoderate dose of opium, and heeded these things but little, nor spoke of them to Rowena. Having found the wine, I recrossed the chamber, and poured out a gobletful, which I held to the lips of the fainting lady. She had now partially recovered, however, and took the vessel herself, while I sank upon an ottoman near me, with my eyes fastened upon her person. It was then that I became distinctly aware of a gentle footfall upon the carpet, and near the couch; and in a second thereafter, as Rowena was in the act of raising the wine to her lips, I saw, or may have dreamed that I saw, fall within the goblet, as if from some invisible spring in the atmosphere of the room, three or four large drops of a brilliant and ruby colored fluid. If this I saw—not so Rowena. She swallowed the wine unhesitatingly, and I forbore to speak to her of a circumstance which must, after all, I considered, have been but the suggestion of a vivid imagination, rendered morbidly active by the terror of the lady, by the opium, and by the hour.

Yet I cannot conceal it from my own perception that, immediately subsequent to the fall of the ruby-drops, a rapid change for the worse took place in the disorder of my wife; so that, on the third subsequent night, the hands of her menials prepared her for the tomb, and on the fourth, I sat alone, with her shrouded body, in that fantastic chamber which had received her as my bride. Wild visions, opium-engendered, flitted, shadow-like, before me. I gazed with un-quiet eye upon the sarcophagi in the angles of the room, upon the varying figures of the drapery, and upon the writhing of the parti-colored fires in the censer overhead. My eyes then fell, as I called to mind the circumstances of a former night, to the spot beneath the glare of the censer where I had seen the faint traces of the shadow. It was there, however, no longer; and breathing with greater free-dom, I turned my glances to the pallid and rigid figure upon the bed. Then rushed upon me a thousand memories of Ligeia—and then came back upon my heart, with the turbulent violence of a flood, the whole of that unutterable woe with which I had regarded *her* thus enshrouded. The night waned; and still, with a bosom full of bitter thoughts of the one only and supremely beloved, I remained gazing upon the body of Rowena.

It might have been midnight, or perhaps earlier, or later, for I had taken no note of time, when a sob, low, gentle, but very dis-tinct, startled me from my revery. I *felt* that it came from the bed of ebony—the bed of death. I listened in an agony of supersti-tious terror—but there was no repetition of the sound. I strained my vision to detect any motion in the corpse—but there was not the slightest perceptible. Yet I could not have been deceived. I *had* heard the noise, however faint, and my soul was awakened within me. I resolutely and perseveringly kept my attention riveted upon the body. Many minutes elapsed before any circumstance occurred tending to throw light upon the mystery. At length it became evident that a slight, a very feeble, and barely noticeable tinge of color had flushed up within the cheeks, and along the sunken small veins of the eyelids. Through a species of unutterable horror and awe, for which the language of mortality has no sufficiently energetic expression, I felt my heart cease to beat, my limbs grow rigid where I sat. Yet a sense of duty finally operated to restore my self-possession. I could no longer doubt that we had been precipitate in our preparations—that Rowena still lived. It was necessary that some immediate exertion be made; yet the turret was altogether apart from the portion of the abbey tenanted by the servants—there were none within call—I had no means of summoning them to my aid without leaving the room for many minutes—and this I could not venture to do. I therefore struggled alone in my endeavors to call back the spirit still hovering. In a short period it was certain, however, that a relapse had taken place; the color disappeared from both eyelid and cheek, leaving a wanness even more than that of marble; the lips became doubly shrivelled and pinched up in the ghastly expression of death; a repulsive clamminess and coldness overspread rapidly the surface of the body; and all the usual rigorous stiffness immediately supervened. I fell back with a shudder upon the couch from which I had been so startlingly aroused, and again gave myself up to passionate waking visions of Ligeia. An hour thus elapsed when (could it be possible?) I was a second time aware of some vague sound issuing from the region of the bed.

I listened—in extremity of horror. The sound came again—it was a sigh. Rushing to the corpse, I saw—distinctly saw—a tremor upon the lips. In a minute afterward they relaxed, disclosing a bright line of the pearly teeth. Amazement now struggled in my bosom with the profound awe which had hitherto reigned there alone. I felt that my vision grew dim, that my reason wandered; and it was only by a violent effort that I at length succeeded in nerving myself to the task which duty thus once more had pointed out. There was now a partial glow upon the forehead and upon the cheek and throat; a perceptible warmth pervaded the whole frame; there was even a slight pulsation at the heart. The lady *lived;* and with redoubled ardor I betook myself to the task of restoration. I chafed and bathed the temples and the hands, and used every exertion which experience, and no little medical reading, could suggest. But in vain. Suddenly, the color fled, the pulsation ceased, the lips resumed the expression of the dead, and, in an instant afterward, the whole body took upon itself the icy chilliness, the livid hue, the intense rigidity, the sunken outline, and all the loathsome peculiarities of that which has been, for many days, a tenant of the tomb.

And again I sunk into visions of Ligeia—and again, (what marvel that I shudder while I write?) *again* there reached my ears a low sob from the region of the ebony bed. But why shall I minutely detail the unspeakable horrors of that night? Why shall I pause to relate how, time after time, until near the period of the gray dawn, this hideous drama of revivification was repeated; how each terrific relapse was only into a sterner and apparently more irredeemable death; how each agony wore the aspect of a struggle with some invisible foe; and how each struggle was succeeded by I know not what of wild change in the personal appearance of the corpse? Let me hurry to a conclusion.

The greater part of the fearful night had worn away, and she who had been dead, once again stirred—and now more vigorously than hitherto, although arousing from a dissolution more appalling in its utter hopelessness than any. I had long ceased to struggle or to move, and remained sitting rigidly upon the ottoman, a helpless prey to a whirl of violent emotions, of which extreme awe was perhaps the least terrible, the least consuming. The corpse, I repeat, stirred, and now more vigorously than before. The hues of life flushed up with unwonted energy into the countenance—the limbs relaxed— and, save that the eyelids were yet pressed heavily together, and that the bandages and draperies of the grave still imparted their char- nel character to the figure, I might have dreamed that Rowena had indeed shaken off, utterly, the fetters of Death. But if this idea was not, even then, altogether adopted, I could at least doubt no longer, when, arising from the bed, tottering, with feeble steps, with closed eyes, and with the manner of one bewildered in a dream, the thing that was enshrouded advanced boldly and palpably into the middle of the apartment.

I trembled not—I stirred not—for a crowd of unutterable fancies connected with the air, the stature, the demeanor, of the figure, rushing hurriedly through my brain, had paralyzed—had chilled me into stone. I stirred not—but gazed upon the apparition. There was a mad disorder in my thoughts—a tumult unappeasable. Could it, indeed, be the *living* Rowena who confronted me? Could it, indeed, be Rowena *at all*—the fair-haired, the blue-eyed Lady Rowena Trevanion of Tremaine? Why, *why* should I doubt it? The bandage lay heavily about the mouth—but then might it not be the mouth of the breathing Lady of Tremaine? And the cheeks—there were the roses as in her noon of life—yes, these might indeed be the fair cheeks of the living Lady of Tremaine. And the chin, with its dimples, as in health, might it not be hers?—but *had she then grown taller since her malady?* What inexpressible madness seized me with that thought? One bound, and I had reached her feet! Shrinking from my touch, she let fall from her head, unloosened, the ghastly cerements which had confined it, and there streamed forth, into the rushing atmosphere of the chamber huge masses of long and dishevelled hair; *it was blacker than the raven wings of the midnight!* And now slowly opened *the eyes* of the figure which stood before me. "Here then, at least," I shrieked aloud, "can I never—can I never be mistaken—these are the full, and the black, and the wild eyes—of my lost love—of the Lady—of the LADY LIGEIA."

Poe and Me at the Movies

......

BY TESS GERRITSEN

My introduction to Edgar Allan Poe wasn't on the page, but in a darkened movie theater, my fingers clenched in fear around my mother's hand. I wish I could say I was already an avid fan of Poe's written work, but I had a good excuse for not reading him. I was only seven years old at the time, too young to appreciate his dense prose and his convoluted themes. But I was certainly old enough to be thrilled by the movies that were loosely based on his stories. There were seven Poe films made by legendary director Roger Corman, and I saw every single one of them, usually the very week they arrived in the theaters.

I had no choice but to go; my mother made me.

My mother is a Chinese immigrant who arrived in the United States in her early twenties, speaking almost no English. Even to this day her grasp of the English language is shaky at best. Back then, in 1960, it was truly a struggle for her to read an English-language book or newspaper. What she did grasp, however, were American horror films. How much English do you need to know, after all, to feel the terror of a good old-fashioned movie monster?

And so she dragged me and my younger brother to the theater. At the time there were no MPAA ratings to guide parents, no ominous PG-13 labels to deter her. She took us to them all. I spent my childhood cowering in dark theaters, tormented by nightmares of killer ants and pod people.

I also learned to love Poe—at least, the B-movie versions of Poe. Starting with *House of Usher* (1960), all the way to *The Tomb of Ligeia* (1963), I was captivated by those cheap sets and the hammy acting and happy to be caught up in the pure pleasure of being utterly, even sickeningly, terrified. I was no judge of what constituted a great film; my favorite was *Premature Burial,* which is generally considered by critics to be the worst of the lot. But to this day one shocking scene from that film (at least, I think it was from *Premature Burial*) still haunts me: a thirsty Ray Milland lifting a wine goblet to his lips, only to recoil in horror when he finds it brimming with maggots.

That's the kind of image that tends to stick with a nine-year-old.

Everything I know about thriller writing, I learned by watching those B-movie versions of Edgar Allan Poe. I know they were hardly faithful translations. I have since read the tales bearing the same titles, and I can scarcely recognize most of them. As an adult, I can appreciate Poe's groundbreaking literary work. But as a kid, I certainly would not have. I'm sure I would have thought him inaccessible and wordy and—if I had known the word at the time—pretentious.

It took a Roger Corman to translate Poe's work into a form that even a seven-year-old kid could understand. He distilled it down to campy horror. Some would contend that by doing so he undermined the dignity of the literary works. I think not. I think Corman gave a whole generation of kids our very first look at Poe's genius—and what an enticing peek it was.

Tess Gerritsen's father was a restaurant chef, and her immigrant mother is the granddaughter of a prominent Chinese poet, so she grew up enjoying great food, great books . . . and scary B movies. She's convinced that a childhood spent watching films based on Edgar Allan Poe stories helped turn her into the thriller writer she is today, with fifteen million copies of her books sold in thirty-two countries. She lives in Maine.

The Tell-Tale Heart

TRUE! —nervous—very, very dreadfully nervous I had been and am; but why *will* you say that I am mad? The disease had sharpened my senses—not destroyed—not dulled them. Above all was the sense of hearing acute. I heard all things in the heaven and in the earth. I heard many things in hell. How, then, am I mad? Hearken! and observe how healthily—how calmly I can tell you the whole story.

It is impossible to say how first the idea entered my brain; but once conceived, it haunted me day and night. Object there was none. Passion there was none. I loved the old man. He had never wronged me. He had never given me insult. For his gold I had no desire. I think it was his eye! yes, it was this! One of his eyes resembled that of a vulture—a pale blue eye, with a film over it. Whenever it fell upon me, my blood ran cold; and so by degrees—very gradually—I made up my mind to take the life of the old man, and thus rid myself of the eye for ever.

Now this is the point. You fancy me mad. Madmen know nothing. But you should have seen *me*. You should have seen how wisely I proceeded—with what caution—with what foresight—with what dissimulation I went to work! I was never kinder to the old man than during the whole week before I killed him. And every night, about midnight, I turned the latch of his door and opened it—oh, so gently! And then, when I had made an opening sufficient for my head, I put in a dark lantern, all closed, closed, so that no light shone out, and then I thrust in my head. Oh, you would have laughed to see how cunningly I thrust it in! I moved it slowly—very, very slowly, so that I might not disturb the old man's sleep. It took me an hour to place my whole head within the opening so far that I could see him as he lay upon his bed. Ha!—would a madman have been so wise as this? And then, when my head was well in the room, I undid the lantern cautiously—oh, so cautiously—cautiously (for the hinges creaked)—I undid it just so much that a single thin ray fell upon the vulture eye. And this I did for seven long nights—every night just at midnight—but I found the eye always closed; and so it was impossible to do the work; for it was not the old man who vexed me, but his Evil Eye. And every morning, when the day broke, I went boldly into the chamber, and spoke courageously to him, calling him by name in a hearty tone, and inquiring how he had passed the night. So you see he would have been a very profound old man, indeed, to suspect that every night, just at twelve, I looked in upon him while he slept.

Upon the eighth night I was more than usually cautious in opening the door. A watch's minute hand moves more quickly than did mine. Never before that night had I *felt* the extent of my own powers — of my sagacity. I could scarcely contain my feelings of triumph. To think that there I was, opening the door, little by little, and he not even to dream of my secret deeds or thoughts. I fairly chuckled at the idea; and perhaps he heard me; for he moved on the bed suddenly, as if startled. Now you may think that I drew back — but no. His room was as black as pitch with the thick darkness (for the shutters were close fastened, through fear of robbers), and so I knew that he could not see the opening of the door, and I kept pushing it on steadily, steadily.

I had my head in, and was about to open the lantern, when my thumb slipped upon the tin fastening, and the old man sprang up in the bed, crying out — "Who's there?"

I kept quite still and said nothing. For a whole hour I did not move a muscle, and in the meantime I did not hear him lie down. He was still sitting up in the bed listening; — just as I have done, night after night, hearkening to the death watches in the wall.

Presently I heard a slight groan, and I knew it was the groan of mortal terror. It was not a groan of pain or of grief — oh, no! — it was the low stifled sound that arises from the bottom of the soul when overcharged with awe. I knew the sound well. Many a night, just at midnight, when all the world slept, it has welled up from my own bosom, deepening, with its dreadful echo, the terrors that distracted me. I say I knew it well. I knew what the old man felt, and pitied him, although I chuckled at heart. I knew that he had been lying awake ever since the first slight noise, when he had turned in the bed. His fears had been ever since growing upon him. He had been trying to fancy them causeless, but could not. He had been saying to himself — "It is nothing but the wind in the chimney — it is only a mouse crossing the floor," or "It is merely a cricket which has made a single chirp." Yes, he had been trying to comfort himself with these suppositions; but he had found all in vain. *All in vain;* because Death, in approaching him, had stalked with his black shadow before him, and enveloped the victim. And it was the mournful influence of the unperceived shadow that caused him to feel—although he neither saw nor heard—to *feel* the presence of my head within the room.

When I had waited a long time, very patiently, without hearing him lie down, I resolved to open a little—a very, very little crevice in the lantern. So I opened it—you cannot imagine how stealthily, stealthily—until, at length, a simple dim ray, like the thread of the spider, shot from out the crevice and fell upon the vulture eye.

It was open—wide, wide open—and I grew furious as I gazed upon it. I saw it with perfect distinctness—all a dull blue, with a hideous veil over it that chilled the very marrow in my bones; but I could see nothing else of the old man's face or person: for I had directed the ray as if by instinct, precisely upon the damned spot.

And now have I not told you that what you mistake for madness is but over-acuteness of the sense?—now, I say, there came to my ears a low, dull, quick sound, such as a watch makes when enveloped in cotton. I knew *that* sound well too. It was the beating of the old man's heart. It increased my fury, as the beating of a drum stimulates the soldier into courage.

But even yet I refrained and kept still. I scarcely breathed. I held the lantern motionless. I tried how steadily I could maintain the ray upon the eye. Meantime the hellish tattoo of the heart increased. It grew quicker and quicker, and louder and louder every instant. The old man's terror *must* have been extreme! It grew louder, I say, louder every moment!—do you mark me well? I have told you that I am nervous: so I am. And now at the dead hour of the night, amid the dreadful silence of that old house, so strange a noise as this excited me to uncontrollable terror. Yet, for some minutes longer I refrained and stood still. But the beating grew louder, louder! I thought the heart must burst. And now a new anxiety seized me—the sound would be heard by a neighbor! The old man's hour had come! With a loud yell, I threw open the lantern and leaped into the room. He shrieked once—once only. In an instant I dragged him to the floor, and pulled the heavy bed over him. I then smiled gaily, to find the deed so far done. But, for many minutes, the heart beat on with a muffled sound. This, however, did not vex me; it would not be heard through the wall. At length it ceased. The old man was dead. I removed the bed and examined the corpse. Yes, he was stone, stone dead. I placed my hand upon the heart and held it there many minutes. There was no pulsation. He was stone dead. His eye would trouble me no more.

If still you think me mad, you will think so no longer when I describe the wise precautions I took for the concealment of the body. The night waned, and I worked hastily, but in silence. First of all I dismembered the corpse. I cut off the head and the arms and the legs.

I then took up three planks from the flooring of the chamber, and deposited all between the scantlings. I then replaced the boards so cleverly, so cunningly, that no human eye—not even *his*—could have detected any thing wrong. There was nothing to wash out—no stain of any kind—no blood-spot whatever. I had been too wary for that. A tub had caught all—ha! ha!

When I had made an end of these labors, it was four o'clock— still dark as midnight. As the bell sounded the hour, there came a knocking at the street door. I went down to open it with a light heart,—for what had I *now* to fear? There entered three men, who introduced themselves, with perfect suavity, as officers of the police. A shriek had been heard by a neighbor during the night; suspicion of foul play had been aroused; information had been lodged at the police office, and they (the officers) had been deputed to search the premises.

I smiled,—for *what* had I to fear? I bade the gentlemen welcome. The shriek, I said, was my own in a dream. The old man, I mentioned, was absent in the country. I took my visitors all over the house. I bade them search—search *well*. I led them, at length, to *his* chamber. I showed them his treasures, secure, undisturbed. In the enthusiasm of my confidence, I brought chairs into the room, and desired them *here* to rest from their fatigues, while I myself, in the wild audacity of my perfect triumph, placed my own seat upon the very spot beneath which reposed the corpse of the victim.

The officers were satisfied. My *manner* had convinced them. I was singularly at ease. They sat, and while I answered cheerily, they chatted of familiar things. But, ere long, I felt myself getting pale and wished them gone. My head ached, and I fancied a ringing in my ears: but still they sat and still chatted. The ringing became more distinct:—it continued and became more distinct: I talked more freely to get rid of the feeling: but it continued and gained definiteness—until, at length, I found that the noise was *not* within my ears.

No doubt I now grew *very* pale;—but I talked more fluently, and with a heightened voice. Yet the sound increased—and what could I do? It was *a low dull, quick sound—much such a sound as a watch makes when enveloped in cotton.* I gasped for breath—and yet the officers heard it not. I talked more quickly—more vehemently; but the noise steadily increased. I arose and argued about trifles, in a high key and with violent gesticulations, but the noise steadily increased. Why *would* they not be gone? I paced the floor to and fro with heavy strides, as if excited to fury by the observations of the men—but the noise steadily increased. Oh God! what *could* I do? I foamed—I raved—I swore! I swung the chair upon which I had been sitting, and grated it upon the boards, but the noise arose over all and continually increased. It grew louder—louder—*louder*! And still the men chatted pleasantly, and smiled. Was it possible they heard not? Almighty God!—no, no! They heard!—they suspected!—they *knew*!—they were making a mockery of my horror!—this I thought, and this I think. But any thing was better than this agony! Any thing was more tolerable than this derision! I could bear those hypocritical smiles no longer! I felt that I must scream or die!—and now—again!—hark! louder! louder! louder! *louder!*

"Villains!" I shrieked, "dissemble no more! I admit the deed!—tear up the planks! here, here!—it is the beating of his hideous heart!"

The Genius of
"The Tell-Tale Heart"

· · · · · ·

BY STEPHEN KING

When I do public appearances, I'm often—no, *always*—asked what scares me. The answer is almost everything, from express elevators in very tall buildings to the idea of a zealot loose with a suitcase nuke in one of the great cities of the world. But if the question is refined to "What works of fiction have scared you?" two always leap immediately to mind: *Lord of the Flies* by William Golding and "The Tell-Tale Heart" by Edgar Allan Poe.

Most people know that Poe invented the modern detective story (Conan Doyle's Sherlock Holmes is in many ways the same detective as Poe's C. Auguste Dupin), but few are aware that he also created the first work of criminal sociopathy in "The Tell-Tale Heart," a story originally published in 1843. Many great crime writers of the twentieth century, from Jim Thompson and John D. MacDonald to Thomas Harris (who in Hannibal Lecter may have created the greatest sociopath of them all), are the children of Poe.

The details of the story are still gruesome enough to produce nightmares (the cutting up of the victim's body, for instance, or the old man's one dying shriek), but the terror that lingers—and the story's genius—lies in the superficially reasonable voice of the narrator. He is never named, and that is fitting, because we have no idea how he picked his victim, or what drove him to the crime. Oh, we know what he *says:* it was the old man's gruesomely veiled eye. But of course, Jeffrey Dahmer said he wanted to create zombies, and the Son of Sam at one point claimed his dog told him to do it. We understand, I think, that psychopaths offer such wacky motivations because they are as helpless as the rest of us to explain their terrible acts.

This is, above all, a persuasive story of lunacy, and Poe never offers any real explanations. Nor has to. The narrator's cheerful laughter ("A tub had caught . . . all [the blood]—ha! ha!") tells us all we need to know. Here is a creature who looks like a man but who really belongs to another species. That's scary. What elevates this story beyond merely scary and into the realm of genius, though, is that Poe foresaw the darkness of generations far beyond his own.

Ours, for instance.

Stephen King was born in Portland, Maine, in 1947, the second son of Donald and Nellie Ruth Pillsbury King. He made his first professional short-story sale in 1967 to Startling Mystery Stories. In the fall of 1973, he began teaching high school English classes at Hampden Academy, the public high school in Hampden, Maine. Writing in the evenings and on the weekends, he continued to produce short stories and work on novels. In the spring of 1973, Doubleday & Company accepted the novel Carrie *for publication, and the book's success provided him with the means to leave teaching and write full-time. He has since published more than forty books and become one of the world's most successful writers. Stephen lives in Maine and Florida with his wife, novelist Tabitha King. They are regular contributors to a number of charities, including many libraries, and have been honored locally for their philanthropic activities.*

The First Time

· · · · · ·

BY STEVE HAMILTON

I read my first Poe story, "The Murders in the Rue Morgue," in 1974. I was thirteen years old. I read that story, then another, working my way through an old hardback anthology while sitting on a hard plastic chair in the most miserable place in the world.

That place was Highland Junior High School, in Highland, Michigan. Nobody is supposed to like junior high school, I know, but seriously, HJH was a two-year prison sentence. The worst part was wintertime, when the sun didn't even start coming up until the end of first period. As a bonus, sometimes a few of the worst kids would escape outside, push open the windows, and then pelt everyone with ice balls. If you weren't quick enough, you were a goner.

That first class of the day, the world outside still pitch-black, was seventh-grade English. The teacher was a man named Vincent Lucius. I still remember him because at the time I thought he was probably insane. First of all, he was always in an unnaturally cheerful mood, even on Monday mornings in January. And even worse, he actually seemed to enjoy his job. He loved teaching. He loved being around seventh-graders, if you can even imagine that. More than anything, he loved good writing.

The first time he made us all write something, I came up with some strange story about me and my best friend catching a burglar. Mr. Lucius stood up in front of the class and read it out loud. Having a teacher single you out in seventh grade was a seriously uncool thing in 1974, and I don't imagine that's changed much since. But he made me keep writing. I ended up giving him more crime stories, always me and my friend catching grown-up bad guys. I was reading a lot of Hardy Boys then, along with Encyclopedia Brown and the Three Investigators. That's what I thought a mystery should be. A little bit of danger to keep things interesting, but everything turning out right in the end. One day Mr. Lucius gave me the collected stories of Edgar Allan Poe and told me to give it a try. "I think you're ready for something a little 'darker,'" he said to me. "Just leave this on my desk at the end of class. You can read some more tomorrow."

He must have known what those stories would do to me. The nineteenth-century language was a little tough to get through at first, but once I got the hang of it . . . damn. This was a little darker, all right. This was the real thing. This was what it looked like when things *didn't* turn out right in the end. And Poe wasn't just standing on the outside of it, looking in. He *lived* there.

"The Pit and the Pendulum." "The Tell-Tale Heart." Every time I go back to these stories, I'm right back there in junior high school again, dodging ice balls. I'm back to that one hour when I could lose myself in this other world, as dark and mysterious as anything I'd ever imagined, created whole by a man who died 112 years before I was born. Back to that feeling I had when I first started reading the real thing. And wondering if there was any way I'd ever be able to write that way myself. It was in that seventh-grade class, in 1974, when I decided exactly what I wanted to be when I grew up.

So thanks, Mr. Vincent Lucius, wherever you are. And thanks to you, Mr. Edgar Allan Poe.

Born and raised in Detroit, Steve Hamilton graduated from the University of Michigan, where he won the prestigious Hopwood Award for Fiction. In 2006 he won the Michigan Author Award for his outstanding body of work. His novels have won numerous awards and media acclaim, beginning with the very first in the Alex McKnight series, A Cold Day in Paradise, *which won the Private Eye Writers of America/St. Martin's Press Award for Best First Mystery by an Unpublished Writer. Once published, it went on to win the MWA Edgar and the PWA Shamus Awards for Best First Novel, and it was short-listed for the Anthony and Barry awards. The awards didn't stop there, but he's too modest to crow about them. Hamilton currently works for IBM in upstate New York, where he lives with his wife, Julia, and their two children.*

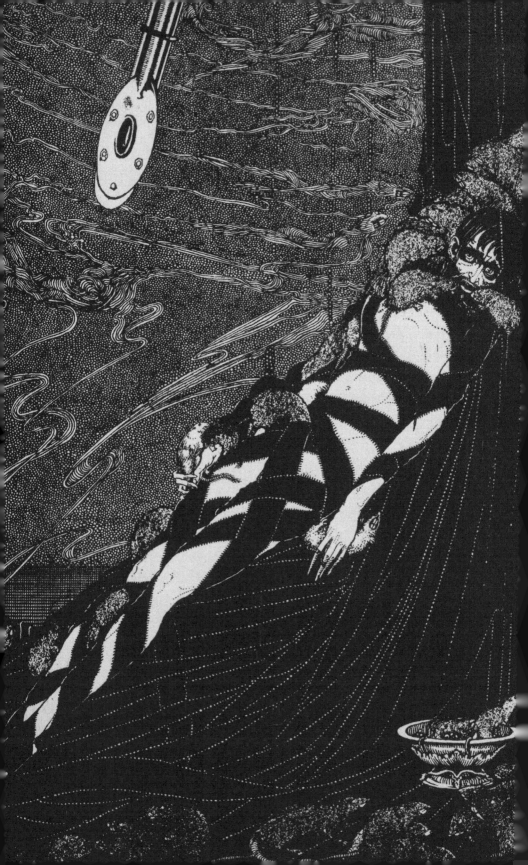

The Pit and the Pendulum

I WAS SICK — sick unto death with that long agony; and when they at length unbound me, and I was permitted to sit, I felt that my senses were leaving me. The sentence — the dread sentence of death — was the last of distinct accentuation which reached my ears. After that, the sound of the inquisitorial voices seemed merged in one dreamy indeterminate hum. It conveyed to my soul the idea of *revolution* — perhaps from its association in fancy with the burr of a mill-wheel. This only for a brief period, for presently I heard no more. Yet, for a while, I saw — but with how terrible an exaggeration! I saw the lips of the black-robed judges. They appeared to me white — whiter than the sheet upon which I trace these words — and thin even to grotesqueness; thin with the intensity of their expression of firmness — of immoveable resolution — of stern contempt of human torture. I saw that the decrees of what to me was Fate were still issuing from those lips. I saw them writhe with a deadly locution. I saw them fashion the syllables of my name; and I shuddered because no sound succeeded. I saw, too, for a few moments of delirious horror, the soft and nearly imperceptible waving of the sable draperies which enwrapped the walls of the apartment. And then my vision fell upon the seven tall candles upon the table. At first they wore the aspect of charity, and seemed white slender angels who would save me; but then, all at once, there came a most deadly nausea over my spirit, and I felt every fibre in my frame thrill as if I had touched the wire of a galvanic battery, while the angel forms became meaningless spectres, with heads of flame, and I saw that from them there would be no help.

And then there stole into my fancy, like a rich musical note, the thought of what sweet rest there must be in the grave. The thought came gently and stealthily, and it seemed long before it attained full appreciation; but just as my spirit came at length properly to feel and entertain it, the figures of the judges vanished, as if magically, from before me; the tall candles sank into nothingness; their flames went out utterly; the blackness of darkness supervened; all sensations appeared swallowed up in a mad rushing descent as of the soul into Hades. Then silence, and stillness, and night were the universe.

I had swooned; but still will not say that all of consciousness was lost. What of it there remained, I will not attempt to define, or even to describe; yet all was not lost. In the deepest slumber—no! In delirium—no! In a swoon—no! In death—no! even in the grave all *is not* lost. Else there is no immortality for man. Arousing from the most profound of slumbers, we break the gossamer web of *some* dream. Yet in a second afterward (so frail may that web have been) we remember not that we have dreamed. In the return to life from the swoon there are two stages: first, that of the sense of mental or spiritual; secondly, that of the sense of physical, existence. It seems probable that if, upon reaching the second stage, we could recall the impressions of the first, we should find these impressions eloquent in memories of the gulf beyond. And that gulf is—what? How at least shall we distinguish its shadows from those of the tomb? But if the impressions of what I have termed the first stage are not, at will, recalled, yet, after long interval, do they not come unbidden, while we marvel whence they come? He who has never swooned, is not he who finds strange palaces and wildly familiar faces in coals that glow; is not he who beholds floating in mid-air the sad visions that the many may not view; is not he who ponders over the perfume of some novel flower; is not he whose brain grows bewildered with the meaning of some musical cadence which has never before arrested his attention.

Amid frequent and thoughtful endeavors to remember, amid earnest struggles to regather some token of the state of seeming nothingness into which my soul had lapsed, there have been moments when I have dreamed of success; there have been brief, very brief periods when I have conjured up remembrances which the lucid reason of a later epoch assures me could have had reference only to that condition of seeming unconsciousness. These shadows of memory tell, indistinctly, of tall figures that lifted and bore me in silence down—down—still down—till a hideous dizziness oppressed me at the mere idea of the interminableness of the descent. They tell also of a vague horror at my heart, on account of that heart's unnatural stillness. Then comes a sense of sudden motionlessness throughout all things; as if those who bore me (a ghastly train!) had outrun, in their descent, the limits of the limitless, and paused from the wearisomeness of their toil. After this I call to mind flatness and dampness; and then all is *madness*—the madness of a memory which busies itself among forbidden things. Very suddenly there came back to my soul motion and sound—the tumultuous motion of the heart, and, in my ears, the sound of its beating. Then a pause in which all is blank. Then again sound, and motion, and touch—a tingling sensation pervading my frame. Then the mere consciousness of existence, without thought—a condition which lasted long. Then, very suddenly, *thought*, and shuddering terror, and earnest endeavor to comprehend my true state. Then a strong desire to lapse into insensibility. Then a rushing revival of soul and a successful effort to move. And now a full memory of the trial, of the judges, of the sable draperies, of the sentence, of the sickness, of the swoon. Then entire forgetfulness of all that followed; of all that a later day and much earnestness of endeavor have enabled me vaguely to recall.

So far, I had not opened my eyes. I felt that I lay upon my back, unbound. I reached out my hand, and it fell heavily upon something damp and hard. There I suffered it to remain for many minutes, while I strove to imagine where and *what* I could be. I longed, yet dared not, to employ my vision. I dreaded the first glance at objects around me. It was not that I feared to look upon things horrible, but that I grew aghast lest there should be *nothing* to see. At length, with a wild desperation at heart, I quickly unclosed my eyes. My worst thoughts, then, were confirmed. The blackness of eternal night encompassed me. I struggled for breath. The intensity of the darkness seemed to oppress and stifle me. The atmosphere was intolerably close. I still lay quietly, and made effort to exercise my reason. I brought to mind the inquisitorial proceedings, and attempted from that point to deduce my real condition. The sentence had passed; and it appeared to me that a very long interval of time had since elapsed. Yet not for a moment did I suppose myself actually dead. Such a supposition, notwithstanding what we read in fiction, is altogether inconsistent with real existence;—but where and in what state was I? The condemned to death, I knew, perished usually at the *auto-da-fés*, and one of these had been held on the very night of the day of my trial. Had I been remanded to my dungeon, to await the next sacrifice, which would not take place for many months?

This I at once saw could not be. Victims had been in immediate demand. Moreover, my dungeon, as well as all the condemned cells at Toledo, had stone floors, and light was not altogether excluded.

A fearful idea now suddenly drove the blood in torrents upon my heart, and for a brief period I once more relapsed into insensibility. Upon recovering, I at once started to my feet, trembling convulsively in every fibre. I thrust my arms wildly above and around me in all directions. I felt nothing; yet dreaded to move a step, lest I should be impeded by the walls of a *tomb*. Perspiration burst from every pore, and stood in cold big beads upon my forehead. The agony of suspense grew at length intolerable, and I cautiously moved forward, with my arms extended, and my eyes straining from their sockets in the hope of catching some faint ray of light. I proceeded for many paces; but still all was blackness and vacancy. I breathed more freely. It seemed evident that mine was not, at least, the most hideous of fates. And now, as I still continued to step cautiously onward, there came thronging upon my recollection a thousand vague rumors of the horrors of Toledo. Of the dungeons there had been strange things narrated—fables I had always deemed them,—but yet strange, and too ghastly to repeat, save in a whisper. Was I left to perish of starvation in this subterranean world of darkness; or what fate, perhaps even more fearful, awaited me? That the result would be death, and a death of more than customary bitterness, I knew too well the character of my judges to doubt. The mode and the hour were all that occupied or distracted me.

My outstretched hands at length encountered some solid obstruction. It was a wall, seemingly of stone masonry—very smooth, slimy, and cold. I followed it up; stepping with all the careful distrust with which certain antique narratives had inspired me. This process, however, afforded me no means of ascertaining the dimensions of my dungeon, as I might make its circuit and return to the point whence I set out without being aware of the fact; so perfectly uniform seemed the wall. I therefore sought the knife which had been in my pocket when led into the inquisitorial chamber; but it was gone; my clothes had been exchanged for a wrapper of coarse serge. I had thought of forcing the blade in some minute crevice of the masonry, so as to identify my point of departure. The difficulty, nevertheless, was but trivial; although, in the disorder of my fancy, it seemed at first insuperable. I tore a part of the hem from the robe and placed the fragment at full length, and at right angles to the wall. In groping my way around the prison, I could not fail to encounter this rag upon completing the circuit. So, at least, I thought; but I had not counted upon the extent of the dungeon, or upon my own weakness. The ground was moist and slippery. I staggered onward for some time, when I stumbled and fell. My excessive fatigue induced me to remain prostrate; and sleep soon overtook me as I lay.

Upon awaking, and stretching forth an arm, I found beside me a loaf and a pitcher with water. I was too much exhausted to reflect upon this circumstance, but ate and drank with avidity. Shortly afterward, I resumed my tour around the prison, and with much toil, came at last upon the fragment of the serge. Up to the period when I fell, I had counted fifty-two paces, and, upon resuming my walk, I had counted forty-eight more—when I arrived at the rag. There were in all, then, a hundred paces; and, admitting two paces to the yard, I presumed the dungeon to be fifty yards in circuit. I had met, however, with many angles in the wall, and thus I could form no guess at the shape of the vault; for vault I could not help supposing it to be.

I had little object—certainly no hope—in these researches; but a vague curiosity prompted me to continue them. Quitting the wall, I resolved to cross the area of the enclosure. At first, I proceeded with extreme caution, for the floor, although seemingly of solid material, was treacherous with slime. At length, however, I took courage, and did not hesitate to step firmly—endeavoring to cross in as direct a line as possible. I had advanced some ten or twelve paces in this manner, when the remnant of the torn hem of my robe became entangled between my legs. I stepped on it, and fell violently on my face.

In the confusion attending my fall, I did not immediately apprehend a somewhat startling circumstance, which yet, in a few seconds afterward, and while I still lay prostrate, arrested my attention. It was this: my chin rested upon the floor of the prison, but my lips, and the upper portion of my head, although seemingly at a less elevation than the chin, touched nothing. At the same time, my forehead seemed bathed in a clammy vapor, and the peculiar smell of decayed fungus arose to my nostrils. I put forward my arm, and shuddered to find that I had fallen at the very brink of a circular pit, whose extent, of course, I had no means of ascertaining at the moment. Groping about the masonry just below the margin, I succeeded in dislodging a small fragment, and let it fall into the abyss. For many seconds I hearkened to its reverberations as it dashed against the sides of the chasm in its descent; at length, there was a sullen plunge into water, succeeded by loud echoes. At the same moment, there came a sound resembling the quick opening and as rapid closing of a door overhead, while a faint gleam of light flashed suddenly through the gloom, and as suddenly faded away.

I saw clearly the doom which had been prepared for me, and congratulated myself upon the timely accident by which I had escaped. Another step before my fall, and the world had seen me no more. And the death just avoided was of that very character which I had regarded as fabulous and frivolous in the tales respecting the Inquisition. To the victims of its tyranny, there was the choice of death with its direst physical agonies, or death with its most hideous moral horrors. I had been reserved for the latter. By long suffering my nerves had been unstrung, until I trembled at the sound of my own voice, and had become in every respect a fitting subject for the species of torture which awaited me.

Shaking in every limb, I groped my way back to the wall—resolving there to perish rather than risk the terrors of the wells, of which my imagination now pictured many in various positions about the dungeon. In other conditions of mind, I might have had courage to end my misery at once, by a plunge into one of these abysses; but now I was the veriest of cowards. Neither could I forget what I had read of these pits—that the *sudden* extinction of life formed no part of their most horrible plan.

Agitation of spirit kept me awake for many long hours, but at length I again slumbered. Upon arousing, I found by my side, as before, a loaf and a pitcher of water. A burning thirst consumed me, and I emptied the vessel at a draught. It must have been drugged—for scarcely had I drunk, before I became irresistibly drowsy. A deep sleep fell upon me—a sleep like that of death. How long it lasted, of course I know not; but when, once again, I unclosed my eyes, the objects around me were visible. By a wild, sulphurous lustre, the origin of which I could not at first determine, I was enabled to see the extent and aspect of the prison.

In its size I had been greatly mistaken. The whole circuit of its walls did not exceed twenty-five yards. For some minutes this fact occasioned me a world of vain trouble; vain indeed—for what could be of less importance, under the terrible circumstances which environed me, than the mere dimensions of my dungeon? But my soul took a wild interest in trifles, and I busied myself in endeavors to account for the error I had committed in my measurement. The truth at length flashed upon me. In my first attempt at exploration I had counted fifty-two paces, up to the period when I fell: I must then have been within a pace or two of the fragment of serge; in fact, I had nearly performed the circuit of the vault. I then slept—and,

upon awaking, I must have returned upon my steps—thus supposing the circuit nearly double what it actually was. My confusion of
mind prevented me from observing that I began my tour with the
wall to the left, and ended it with the wall to the right.

I had been deceived, too, in respect to the shape of the enclosure.
In feeling my way I had found many angles, and thus deduced an
idea of great irregularity; so potent is the effect of total darkness
upon one arousing from lethargy or sleep! The angles were simply
those of a few slight depressions, or niches, at odd intervals. The
general shape of the prison was square. What I had taken for masonry seemed now to be iron, or some other metal in huge plates,
whose sutures or joints occasioned the depression. The entire surface of this metallic enclosure was rudely daubed in all the hideous
and repulsive devices to which the charnel superstition of the monks
has given rise. The figures of fiends in aspects of menace, with skeleton forms, and other more really fearful images, overspread and
disfigured the walls. I observed that the outlines of these monstrosities were sufficiently distinct, but that the colors seemed faded and
blurred, as if from the effects of a damp atmosphere. I now noticed
the floor, too, which was of stone. In the centre yawned the circular
pit from whose jaws I had escaped; but it was the only one in the
dungeon.

All this I saw indistinctly and by much effort—for my personal
condition had been greatly changed during slumber. I now lay upon
my back, and at full length, on a species of low framework of wood.
To this I was securely bound by a long strap resembling a surcingle.
It passed in many convolutions about my limbs and body, leaving at
liberty only my head, and my left arm to such extent, that I could,
by dint of much exertion, supply myself with food from an earthen
dish which lay by my side on the floor. I saw, to my horror, that the
pitcher had been removed. I say to my horror—for I was consumed
with intolerable thirst. This thirst it appeared to be the design of my

persecutors to stimulate—for the food in the dish was meat pungently seasoned.

Looking upward, I surveyed the ceiling of my prison. It was some thirty or forty feet overhead, and constructed much as the side walls. In one of its panels a very singular figure riveted my whole attention. It was the painted figure of Time as he is commonly represented, save that, in lieu of a scythe, he held what, at a casual glance, I supposed to be the pictured image of a huge pendulum, such as we see on antique clocks. There was something, however, in the appearance of this machine which caused me to regard it more attentively. While I gazed directly upward at it (for its position was immediately over my own) I fancied that I saw it in motion. In an instant afterward the fancy was confirmed. Its sweep was brief, and of course slow. I watched it for some minutes somewhat in fear, but more in wonder. Wearied at length with observing its dull movement, I turned my eyes upon the other objects in the cell.

A slight noise attracted my notice, and, looking to the floor, I saw several enormous rats traversing it. They had issued from the well which lay just within view to my right. Even then, while I gazed, they came up in troops, hurriedly, with ravenous eyes, allured by the scent of the meat. From this it required much effort and attention to scare them away.

It might have been half an hour, perhaps even an hour, (for I could take but imperfect note of time), before I again cast my eyes upward. What I then saw confounded and amazed me. The sweep of the pendulum had increased in extent by nearly a yard. As a natural consequence its velocity was also much greater. But what mainly disturbed me was the idea that it had perceptibly *descended*. I now observed—with what horror it is needless to say—that its nether extremity was formed of a crescent of glittering steel, about a foot in length from horn to horn; the horns upward, and the under edge evidently as keen as that of a razor. Like a razor also, it seemed massy

and heavy, tapering from the edge into a solid and broad structure
above. It was appended to a weighty rod of brass, and the whole
hissed as it swung through the air.

I could no longer doubt the doom prepared for me by monkish
ingenuity in torture. My cognizance of the pit had become known
to the inquisitorial agents — *the pit*, whose horrors had been destined
for so bold a recusant as myself — *the pit*, typical of hell and regarded
by rumor as the Ultima Thule of all their punishments. The plunge
into this pit I had avoided by the merest of accidents, and I knew
that surprise, or entrapment into torment, formed an important portion of all the grotesquerie of these dungeon deaths. Having failed to
fall, it was no part of the demon plan to hurl me into the abyss, and
thus (there being no alternative) a different and a milder destruction
awaited me. Milder! I half smiled in my agony as I thought of such
application of such a term.

What boots it to tell of the long, long hours of horror more than
mortal, during which I counted the rushing oscillations of the steel!
Inch by inch — line by line — with a descent only appreciable at intervals that seemed ages — down and still down it came! Days passed —
it might have been that many days passed — ere it swept so closely
over me as to fan me with its acrid breath. The odor of the sharp
steel forced itself into my nostrils. I prayed — I wearied heaven with
my prayer for its more speedy descent. I grew frantically mad, and
struggled to force myself upward against the sweep of the fearful
scimitar. And then I fell suddenly calm, and lay smiling at the glittering death, as a child at some rare bauble.

There was another interval of utter insensibility; it was brief; for,
upon again lapsing into life, there had been no perceptible descent in
the pendulum. But it might have been long — for I knew there were
demons who took note of my swoon, and who could have arrested
the vibration at pleasure. Upon my recovery, too, I felt very — oh!
inexpressibly — sick and weak, as if through long inanition. Even

amid the agonies of that period, the human nature craved food. With painful effort I outstretched my left arm as far as my bonds permitted, and took possession of the small remnant which had been spared me by the rats. As I put a portion of it within my lips, there rushed to my mind a half-formed thought of joy—of hope. Yet what business had *I* with hope? It was, as I say, a half-formed thought—man has many such, which are never completed. I felt that it was of joy—of hope; but I felt also that it had perished in its formation. In vain I struggled to perfect—to regain it. Long suffering had nearly annihilated all my ordinary powers of mind. I was an imbecile—an idiot.

The vibration of the pendulum was at right angles to my length. I saw that the crescent was designed to cross the region of the heart. It would fray the serge of my robe—it would return and repeat its operations—again—and again. Notwithstanding its terrifically wide sweep (some thirty feet or more), and the hissing vigor of its descent, sufficient to sunder these very walls of iron, still the fraying of my robe would be all that, for several minutes, it would accomplish. And at this thought I paused. I dared not go further than this reflection. I dwelt upon it with a pertinacity of attention—as if, in so dwelling, I could arrest *here* the descent of the steel. I forced myself to ponder upon the sound of the crescent as it should pass across the garment—upon the peculiar thrilling sensation which the friction of cloth produces on the nerves. I pondered upon all this frivolity until my teeth were on edge.

Down—steadily down it crept. I took a frenzied pleasure in contrasting its downward with its lateral velocity. To the right—to the left—far and wide—with the shriek of a damned spirit! to my heart, with the stealthy pace of the tiger! I alternately laughed and howled, as the one or the other idea grew predominant.

Down—certainly, relentlessly down! It vibrated within three inches of my bosom! I struggled violently—furiously—to free my left arm. This was free only from the elbow to the hand. I could reach the latter, from the platter beside me, to my mouth, with great effort, but no farther. Could I have broken the fastenings above the elbow, I would have seized and attempted to arrest the pendulum. I might as well have attempted to arrest an avalanche!

Down—still unceasingly—still inevitably down! I gasped and struggled at each vibration. I shrunk convulsively at its every sweep. My eyes followed its outward or upward whirls with the eagerness of the most unmeaning despair; they closed themselves spasmodically at the descent, although death would have been a relief, oh, how unspeakable! Still I quivered in every nerve to think how slight a sinking of the machinery would precipitate that keen, glistening axe upon my bosom. It was *hope* that prompted the nerve to quiver—the frame to shrink. It was *hope*—the hope that triumphs on the rack—that whispers to the death-condemned even in the dungeons of the Inquisition.

I saw that some ten or twelve vibrations would bring the steel in actual contact with my robe—and with this observation there suddenly came over my spirit all the keen, collected calmness of despair. For the first time during many hours—or perhaps days—I *thought*. It now occurred to me, that the bandage, or surcingle, which enveloped me, was *unique*. I was tied by no separate cord. The first stroke of the razor-like crescent athwart any portion of the band would so detach it that it might be unwound from my person by means of my left hand. But how fearful, in that case, the proximity of the steel! The result of the slightest struggle, how deadly! Was it likely, moreover, that the minions of the torturer had not foreseen and provided for this possibility? Was it probable that the bandage crossed my bosom in the track of the pendulum? Dreading to find my faint and, as it seemed, my last hope frustrated, I so far elevated my head as to obtain a distinct view of my breast. The surcingle enveloped my limbs and body close in all directions—*save in the path of the destroying crescent.*

Scarcely had I dropped my head back into its original position, when there flashed upon my mind what I cannot better describe than as the unformed half of that idea of deliverance to which I have previously alluded, and of which a moiety only floated indeterminately through my brain when I raised food to my burning lips. The whole thought was now present—feeble, scarcely sane, scarcely definite—but still entire. I proceeded at once, with the nervous energy of despair, to attempt its execution.

For many hours the immediate vicinity of the low framework upon which I lay had been literally swarming with rats. They were wild, bold, ravenous—their red eyes glaring upon me as if they waited but for motionlessness on my part to make me their prey. "To what food," I thought, "have they been accustomed in the well?"

They had devoured, in spite of all my efforts to prevent them, all but a small remnant of the contents of the dish. I had fallen into an habitual see-saw or wave of the hand about the platter; and, at length, the unconscious uniformity of the movement deprived it of effect. In their voracity, the vermin frequently fastened their sharp fangs in my fingers. With the particles of the oily and spicy viand which now remained, I thoroughly rubbed the bandage wherever I could reach it; then, raising my hand from the floor, I lay breathlessly still.

At first, the ravenous animals were startled and terrified at the change—at the cessation of movement. They shrank alarmedly back; many sought the well. But this was only for a moment. I had not counted in vain upon their voracity. Observing that I remained without motion, one or two of the boldest leaped upon the framework, and smelt at the surcingle. This seemed the signal for a general rush. Forth from the well they hurried in fresh troops. They clung to the wood—they overran it, and leaped in hundreds upon my person. The measured movement of the pendulum disturbed them not at all. Avoiding its strokes, they busied themselves with the anointed bandage. They pressed—they swarmed upon me in ever accumulating heaps. They writhed upon my throat; their cold lips sought my own; I was half stifled by their thronging pressure; disgust, for which the world has no name, swelled my bosom, and chilled, with a heavy clamminess, my heart. Yet one minute, and I felt that the struggle would be over. Plainly I perceived the loosening of the bandage. I knew that in more than one place it must be already severed. With a more than human resolution I lay *still*.

Nor had I erred in my calculations—nor had I endured in vain. I at length felt that I was *free*. The surcingle hung in ribands from my body. But the stroke of the pendulum already pressed upon my bosom. It had divided the serge of the robe. It had cut through the linen beneath. Twice again it swung, and a sharp sense of pain shot through every nerve. But the moment of escape had arrived. At a wave of my hand my deliverers hurried tumultuously away. With a steady movement—cautious, side-long, shrinking and slow—I slid from the embrace of the bandage and beyond the reach of the scimitar. For the moment, at least, *I was free*.

Free!—and in the grasp of the Inquisition! I had scarcely stepped from my wooden bed of horror upon the stone floor of the prison, when the motion of the hellish machine ceased, and I beheld it drawn up, by some invisible force, through the ceiling. This was a lesson which I took desperately to heart. My every motion was undoubtedly watched. Free!—I had but escaped death in one form of agony, to be delivered unto worse than death in some other. With that thought I rolled my eyes nervously around on the barriers of iron that hemmed me in. Something unusual—some change which, at first, I could not appreciate distinctly—it was obvious, had taken place in the apartment. For many minutes of a dreamy and trembling abstraction, I busied myself in vain, unconnected conjecture. During this period, I became aware, for the first time, of the origin of the sulphurous light which illumined the cell. It proceeded from a fissure, about half an inch in width, extending entirely around the prison at the base of the walls, which thus appeared, and were completely separated from the floor. I endeavored, but of course in vain, to look through the aperture.

As I arose from the attempt, the mystery of the alteration in the chamber broke at once upon my understanding. I have observed that, although the outlines of the figures upon the walls were sufficiently distinct, yet the colors seemed blurred and indefinite. These colors had now assumed, and were momentarily assuming, a startling and most intense brilliancy, that gave to the spectral and fiendish portraitures an aspect that might have thrilled even firmer nerves than my own. Demon eyes, of a wild and ghastly vivacity, glared upon me in a thousand directions, where none had been visible before, and gleamed with the lurid lustre of a fire that I could not force my imagination to regard as unreal.

Unreal!—Even while I breathed there came to my nostrils the breath of the vapor of heated iron! A suffocating odor pervaded the prison! A deeper glow settled each moment in the eyes that glared at my agonies! A richer tint of crimson diffused itself over the pictured horrors of blood. I panted! I gasped for breath! There could be no doubt of the design of my tormentors—oh! most unrelenting! oh! most demoniac of men! I shrank from the glowing metal to the centre of the cell. Amid the thought of the fiery destruction that impended, the idea of the coolness of the well came over my soul like balm. I rushed to its deadly brink. I threw my straining vision below. The glare from the enkindled roof illumined its inmost recesses. Yet, for a wild moment, did my spirit refuse to comprehend the meaning of what I saw. At length it forced—it wrestled its way into my soul—it burned itself in upon my shuddering reason. Oh! for a voice to speak!—oh! horror!—oh! any horror but this! With a shriek, I rushed from the margin, and buried my face in my hands—weeping bitterly.

The heat rapidly increased, and once again I looked up, shuddering as with a fit of the ague. There had been a second change in the cell—and now the change was obviously in the *form*. As before, it was in vain that I at first endeavored to appreciate or understand what was taking place. But not long was I left in doubt. The Inquisitorial vengeance had been hurried by my two-fold escape, and there was to be no more dallying with the King of Terrors. The room had been square. I saw that two of its iron angles were now acute—two, consequently, obtuse. The fearful difference quickly increased with a low rumbling or moaning sound. In an instant the apartment had shifted its form into that of a lozenge. But the alteration stopped not here—I neither hoped nor desired it to stop. I could have clasped the red walls to my bosom as a garment of eternal peace. "Death," I said, "any death but that of the pit!" Fool! might I not have known that *into the pit* it was the object of the burning iron to urge me? Could I resist its glow? or if even that, could I withstand its pressure? And now, flatter and flatter grew the lozenge, with a rapidity that left me no time for contemplation. Its centre, and of course its greatest width, came just over the yawning gulf. I shrank back—but the closing walls pressed me resistlessly onward. At length for my seared and writhing body there was no longer an inch of foothold on the firm floor of the prison. I struggled no more, but the agony of my soul found vent in one loud, long, and final scream of despair. I felt that I tottered upon the brink—I averted my eyes—

There was a discordant hum of human voices! There was a loud blast as of many trumpets! There was a harsh grating as of a thousand thunders! The fiery walls rushed back! An outstretched arm caught my own as I fell, fainting, into the abyss. It was that of General Lasalle. The French army had entered Toledo. The Inquisition was in the hands of its enemies.

The Pit, the Pendulum, and Perfection

. . . . . .

BY EDWARD D. HOCH

I have written elsewhere that my lifetime commitment to mystery fiction can be traced to an early exposure to the novels of Ellery Queen. But my love for the short story dates from my first reading of Edgar Allan Poe. It was in my school textbook that I discovered "The Pit and the Pendulum," a near-perfect example of the horror and suspense that marked so much of Poe's work.

From the very beginning with its description of the Inquisition chamber, the reader is caught up in the narrator's terrible plight. We are to be his companion in the tortures that follow, and it seems that death will be his only release. He drifts between a conscious and dreamlike state, facing first the fate of execution by a swinging, razor-sharp pendulum, a method Poe had no doubt seen described in a contemporary history of the Inquisition. As his narrator describes the slow descent of the pendulum and the scurrying of rats about his chamber, there seems to be no chance of survival.

When he miraculously escapes death by the pendulum, he is immediately faced with an even graver danger. The red-hot walls of his cell begin to close in upon him, forcing him ever closer to the gaping abyss at the center of the room. The suspense builds to a terrifying pitch that holds the reader until the story's final paragraph. Poe's ending may be a bit far-fetched, but it has a historical basis. To the reader it is supremely satisfying, the perfect ending to a half hour of nail-biting suspense.

For anyone who wishes to write short stories, there is no better teacher than Edgar Allan Poe. And there is no better example of suspenseful perfection in a short story than "The Pit and the Pendulum."

Edward D. Hoch (1930–2008) was a past president of Mystery Writers of America and winner of its Edgar Award for Best Short Story. In 2001 he received MWA's Grand Master Award. He was a guest of honor at Bouchercon, two-time winner of its Anthony Award, and recipient of its Lifetime Achievement Award. The Private Eye Writers of America honored him with its Life Achievement Award as well. Author of some 975 published stories, he appeared in every issue of Ellery Queen's Mystery Magazine *in the past thirty-five years.*

The Pit and the Pendulum at the Palace

. . . . . .

BY PETER ROBINSON

If I hadn't become a crime writer, I think it most likely I would have written horror or science fiction. I certainly did when I was a teenager; then, after many years of poetry, I turned to crime. While Poe's stories of "ratiocination" featuring Auguste Dupin never really thrilled me (even back then I just couldn't believe in that Ourang-Outang!), his tales of mystery and imagination enthralled me from the start. And I came to them first through the films of Roger Corman, many of them scripted by the excellent Richard Matheson.

In England in the early 1960s there were three ratings for films: U, A, and X. The first was general admission, for an A film you had to be accompanied by an adult, and you had to be over sixteen to see an X film. X ratings weren't reserved for films about sex and violence but were applied to just about every exciting horror and science fiction film that came out in that golden age—from *The Blob* to *Psycho*. For a twelve-year-old fan, the pickings were pretty slim. You might get something decent with an A rating, which meant that you had to hang around outside the cinema and ask some adult stranger to take you in—something I'm sure would be inconceivable in this day and age. But we did it and survived.

Luckily, though, there was one local fleapit, incredibly named the Palace, where the old woman in the ticket booth didn't really care how old you were. At twelve or thirteen, I was tall enough that I could pass for sixteen there, or so I thought. At any rate, she took my money and let me in without a second glance. I can still recall the sense of excitement and anticipation I felt before the lush red velvet curtains parted. I was doing something I shouldn't be doing, seeing something forbidden—at least to kids my age—and I had no idea what wonders to expect. My previous horror and science fiction experiences had included *A for Andromeda* and *Quatermass and the Pit* on television, and the latter had scared the living daylights out of me. Now here I was, alone in a dark cinema, waiting for the ultimate experience in terror—in living color on a large screen—*The Pit and the Pendulum*. No wonder my stomach clenched as I lit a Woodbine and slunk down in my seat.

When the curtains opened, the swirl of colors was much like that of light shows I was to see later in the decade, but at the time, combined with a quirky, contemporary score, it was just enough to set the juices flowing. This was going to be weird. Then came the impossible castle on its hill, surrounded by a ring of mist, and the coach driver who would only take his passenger so far. (Quickly developing a taste for these horror films, I also devoured everything Hammer produced around the same time and got used to seeing such openings over and over again!) But it wasn't so much the castle and the cobwebs and the dungeon and the strange colors and the distortion used in flashbacks and dream sequences that made me squirm in my seat. Poe, I discovered through Corman, was a master of morbid psychology, master of the language of grief and loss and how they could lead a man (usually Vincent Price) to madness beyond the grave.

Of course, in retrospect, it's hard to say how much I understood at the time. Probably the whole element of adultery that underpins the tale was lost on me, though the hints of illicit sex and debauchery certainly weren't—heaving cleavage was as much a feature of the Corman films as it was with Hammer—and the way Elizabeth expresses her fascination with the torture chamber, rushing around feverishly, touching the implements with a kind of sexual longing, was both disturbing and exciting. I knew about the Spanish Inquisition (though this was several years before it was immortalized by Monty Python) and its tortures—the Iron Maiden, the rack, and the rest—but perhaps the adult relationships were somewhat lost on me.

Certainly there are moments of pure shock—the opening of the stone tomb to reveal the skeleton of a woman who had obviously died trying to claw her way out, the reappearance of Elizabeth in the flesh, the revelation of the "ultimate torture device" itself, and the heavy swishing sound it made as it got faster and faster. (Apparently, Corman cut every other frame to get this effect.) But mostly it was atmosphere, the unspoken, the hint of terrible mysteries beyond the grave, a world where people are condemned to relive terrible acts or suffer the ancient curses of their ancestors, and the realm of the opium dream/nightmare that Corman fashioned from Poe's story. And of course, you couldn't go home after seeing any of these films without being absolutely terrified of being buried alive.

No doubt I slept uneasily that night, but the next day I went out and bought *Tales of Mystery and Imagination*. In no time I was immersed in "The Tell-Tale Heart," "Berenice" (the teeth, my God, the teeth!), and "The Cask of Amontillado" and probably produced my own pale imitations in the notebooks I filled with drivel in those days. It also didn't take me long to discover that Corman's movie had little to do with the actual plot of Poe's story, though he excelled in re-creating the atmosphere of Poe's work. In later life I studied

Poe along with Melville when I was doing my Ph.D. in English literature, and his work has since given me hours of pleasure (and many sleepless nights).

And I went back to the Palace. I went to see *The House of Usher, The Masque of the Red Death, The Tomb of Ligeia, Tales of Terror,* and *The Premature Burial.* I enjoyed them all, though I don't think any had quite the same impact as the first one I saw — *The Pit and the Pendulum.*

Peter Robinson was born in England and now splits his time between Toronto and Richmond, North Yorkshire. He is the author of the Inspector Banks series of novels, the latest of which is Friend of the Devil, *and many short stories, one of which, "Missing in Action," won the MWA Edgar Award in 2000. In his spare time, he enjoys mesmerism, building model torture chambers, and extracting teeth from dead bodies.*

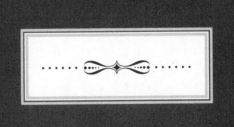

The Masque
of the
Red Death

THE "RED DEATH" had long devastated the country.
No pestilence had ever been so fatal, or so hideous. Blood
was its Avatar and its seal—the redness and the horror of
blood. There were sharp pains, and sudden dizziness, and
then profuse bleeding at the pores, with dissolution. The
scarlet stains upon the body and especially upon the face
of the victim, were the pest ban which shut him out from
the aid and from the sympathy of his fellow-men. And the
whole seizure, progress, and termination of the disease,
were the incidents of half an hour.

But the Prince Prospero was happy and dauntless and
sagacious. When his dominions were half depopulated, he

summoned to his presence a thousand hale and light-hearted friends from among the knights and dames of his court, and with these retired to the deep seclusion of one of his castellated abbeys. This was an extensive and magnificent structure, the creation of the prince's own eccentric yet august taste. A strong and lofty wall girdled it in. This wall had gates of iron. The courtiers, having entered, brought furnaces and massy hammers and welded the bolts. They resolved to leave means neither of ingress nor egress to the sudden impulses of despair or of frenzy from within. The abbey was amply provisioned. With such precautions the courtiers might bid defiance to contagion. The external world could take care of itself. In the meantime it was folly to grieve, or to think. The prince had provided all the appliances of pleasure. There were buffoons, there were improvisatori, there were ballet-dancers, there were musicians, there was Beauty, there was wine. All these and security were within. Without was the "Red Death."

It was toward the close of the fifth or sixth month of his seclusion, and while the pestilence raged most furiously abroad, that the Prince Prospero entertained his thousand friends at a masked ball of the most unusual magnificence.

It was a voluptuous scene, that masquerade. But first let me tell of the rooms in which it was held. There were seven—an imperial suite. In many palaces, however, such suites form a long and straight vista, while the folding doors slide back nearly to the walls on either hand, so that the view of the whole extent is scarcely impeded. Here the case was very different; as might have been expected from the duke's love of the *bizarre*. The apartments were so irregularly disposed that the vision embraced but little more than one at a time. There was a sharp turn at every twenty or thirty yards, and at each turn a novel effect. To the right and left, in the middle of each wall, a tall and narrow Gothic window looked out upon a closed corridor which pursued the windings of the suite. These windows were of

stained glass whose color varied in accordance with the prevailing
hue of the decorations of the chamber into which it opened. That at
the eastern extremity was hung, for example, in blue—and vividly
blue were its windows. The second chamber was purple in its ornaments and tapestries, and here the panes were purple. The third
was green throughout, and so were the casements. The fourth was
furnished and lighted with orange—the fifth with white—the sixth
with violet. The seventh apartment was closely shrouded in black
velvet tapestries that hung all over the ceiling and down the walls,
falling in heavy folds upon a carpet of the same material and hue.
But in this chamber only, the color of the windows failed to cor-
respond with the decorations. The panes here were scarlet—a deep
blood color. Now in no one of the seven apartments was there any
lamp or candelabrum, amid the profusion of golden ornaments that
lay scattered to and fro or depended from the roof. There was no
light of any kind emanating from lamp or candle within the suite of
chambers. But in the corridors that followed the suite, there stood,
opposite to each window, a heavy tripod, bearing a brazier of fire,
that protected its rays through the tinted glass and so glaringly illumined the room. And thus were produced a multitude of gaudy
and fantastic appearances. But in the western or black chamber the
effect of the fire-light that streamed upon the dark hangings through
the blood-tinted panes was ghastly in the extreme, and produced so
wild a look upon the countenances of those who entered, that there
were few of the company bold enough to set foot within its precincts
at all.

It was in this apartment, also, that there stood against the western
wall, a gigantic clock of ebony. Its pendulum swung to and fro with a
dull, heavy, monotonous clang; and when the minute-hand made the
circuit of the face, and the hour was to be stricken, there came from
the brazen lungs of the clock a sound which was clear and loud and
deep and exceedingly musical, but of so peculiar a note and empha-

sis that, at each lapse of an hour, the musicians of the orchestra were constrained to pause, momentarily, in their performance, to hearken to the sound; and thus the waltzers perforce ceased their evolutions; and there was a brief disconcert of the whole gay company; and, while the chimes of the clock yet rang, it was observed that the giddiest grew pale, and the more aged and sedate passed their hands over their brows as if in confused revery or meditation. But when the echoes had fully ceased, a light laughter at once pervaded the assembly; the musicians looked at each other and smiled as if at their own nervousness and folly, and made whispering vows, each to the other, that the next chiming of the clock should produce in them no similar emotion; and then, after the lapse of sixty minutes (which embrace three thousand and six hundred seconds of the Time that flies), there came yet another chiming of the clock, and then were the same disconcert and tremulousness and meditation as before.

But, in spite of these things, it was a gay and magnificent revel. The tastes of the duke were peculiar. He had a fine eye for colors and effects. He disregarded the *decora* of mere fashion. His plans were bold and fiery, and his conceptions glowed with barbaric lustre. There are some who would have thought him mad. His followers felt that he was not. It was necessary to hear and see and touch him to be *sure* that he was not.

He had directed, in great part, the moveable embellishments of the seven chambers, upon occasion of this great *fête;* and it was his own guiding taste which had given character to the masqueraders. Be sure they were grotesque. There were much glare and glitter and piquancy and phantasm—much of what has been since seen in "Hernani." There were arabesque figures with unsuited limbs and appointments. There were delirious fancies such as the madman fashions. There were much of the beautiful, much of the wanton, much of the *bizarre,* something of the terrible, and not a little of that which might have excited disgust. To and fro in the seven chambers there stalked, in fact, a multitude of dreams. And these—the dreams—writhed in and about, taking hue from the rooms, and causing the wild music of the orchestra to seem as the echo of their steps. And, anon, there strikes the ebony clock which stands in the hall of the velvet. And then, for a moment, all is still, and all is silent save the voice of the clock. The dreams are stiff-frozen as they stand. But the echoes of the chime die away—they have endured but an instant—and a light, half-subdued laughter floats after them as they depart. And now again the music swells, and the dreams live, and writhe to and fro more merrily than ever, taking hue from the many-tinted windows through which stream the rays from the tripods. But to the chamber which lies most westwardly of the seven there are now none of the maskers who venture; for the night is waning away; and there flows a ruddier light through the blood-colored panes; and the blackness of the sable drapery appals; and to him whose foot falls upon the sable carpet, there comes from the near clock of ebony a muffled peal more solemnly emphatic than any which reaches *their* ears who indulge in the more remote gaieties of the other apartments.

But these other apartments were densely crowded, and in them beat feverishly the heart of life. And the revel went whirlingly on, until at length there commenced the sounding of midnight upon the clock. And then the music ceased, as I have told; and the evolutions of the waltzers were quieted; and there was an uneasy cessation of all things as before. But now there were twelve strokes to be sounded by the bell of the clock; and thus it happened, perhaps, that more of thought crept, with more of time, into the meditations of the thoughtful among those who revelled. And thus, too, it happened, perhaps, that before the last echoes of the last chime had utterly sunk into silence, there were many individuals in the crowd who had found leisure to become aware of the presence of a masked figure which had arrested the attention of no single individual before. And the rumor of this new presence having spread itself whisperingly around, there arose at length from the whole company a buzz, or murmur, expressive of disapprobation and surprise—then, finally, of terror, of horror, and of disgust.

In an assembly of phantasms such as I have painted, it may well be supposed that no ordinary appearance could have excited such sensation. In truth the masquerade license of the night was nearly unlimited; but the figure in question had out-Heroded Herod, and gone beyond the bounds of even the prince's indefinite decorum. There are chords in the hearts of the most reckless which cannot be touched without emotion. Even with the utterly lost, to whom life and death are equally jests, there are matters of which no jest can be made. The whole company, indeed, seemed now deeply to feel that in the costume and bearing of the stranger neither wit nor propriety existed. The figure was tall and gaunt, and shrouded from head to foot in the habiliments of the grave. The mask which concealed the visage was made so nearly to resemble the countenance of a stiffened corpse that the closest scrutiny must have had difficulty in detecting the cheat. And yet all this might have been endured, if not approved, by the mad revellers around. But the mummer had gone so far as to assume the type of the Red Death. His vesture was dabbled in *blood*—and his broad brow, with all the features of the face, was besprinkled with the scarlet horror.

When the eyes of Prince Prospero fell upon this spectral image (which, with a slow and solemn movement, as if more fully to sustain its *rôle*, stalked to and fro among the waltzers) he was seen to be convulsed, in the first moment with a strong shudder either of terror or distaste; but, in the next, his brow reddened with rage.

"Who dares"—he demanded hoarsely of the courtiers who stood near him—"who dares insult us with this blasphemous mockery? Seize him and unmask him—that we may know whom we have to hang, at sunrise, from the battlements!"

It was in the eastern or blue chamber in which stood the Prince Prospero as he uttered these words. They rang throughout the seven rooms loudly and clearly—for the prince was a bold and robust man, and the music had become hushed at the waving of his hand.

It was in the blue room where stood the prince, with a group of pale courtiers by his side. At first, as he spoke, there was a slight rushing movement of this group in the direction of the intruder, who, at the moment was also near at hand, and now, with deliberate and stately step, made closer approach to the speaker. But from a certain nameless awe with which the mad assumptions of the murmur had inspired the whole party, there were found none who put forth hand to seize him; so that, unimpeded, he passed within a yard of the prince's person; and, while the vast assembly, as if with one impulse, shrank from the centres of the rooms to the walls, he made his way uninterruptedly, but with the same solemn and measured step which had distinguished him from the first, through the blue chamber to the purple—through the purple to the green—through the green to the orange—through this again to the white—and even thence to the violet, ere a decided movement had been made to arrest him. It was then, however, that the Prince Prospero, maddening with rage and the shame of his own momentary cowardice, rushed hurriedly through the six chambers, while none followed him on account of a deadly terror that had seized upon all.

He bore aloft a drawn dagger, and had approached, in rapid impetuosity, to within three or four feet of the retreating figure, when the latter, having attained the extremity of the velvet apartment, turned suddenly and confronted his pursuer. There was a sharp cry—and the dagger dropped gleaming upon the sable carpet, upon which, instantly afterward, fell prostrate in death the Prince Prospero. Then, summoning the wild courage of despair, a throng of the revellers at once threw themselves into the black apartment, and, seizing the mummer, whose tall figure stood erect and motionless within the shadow of the ebony clock, gasped in unutterable horror at finding the grave cerements and corpse-like mask, which they handled with so violent a rudeness, untenanted by any tangible form.

And now was acknowledged the presence of the Red Death. He had come like a thief in the night. And one by one dropped the revellers in the blood-bedewed halls of their revel, and died each in the despairing posture of his fall. And the life of the ebony clock went out with that of the last of the gay. And the flames of the tripods expired. And Darkness and Decay and the Red Death held illimitable dominion over all.

Edgar Allan Poe, Mark Twain, and Me

. . . . . .

BY S. J. ROZAN

When I was twelve, I had pneumonia, complicated by a bad case of strep. I wasn't hospitalized, but I was confined to my room to keep me from causing havoc among my sibs. My mother heroically ferried chicken soup and ice cream from downstairs. Other than that, I was pretty much on my own—for two weeks. Luckily, we had a complete set of Mark Twain, and a complete set of Edgar Allan Poe. My mom deposited them in my room in a couple of tall piles, and they made me what I am today.

From Twain I learned about character and narrative structure. And humor. Poe didn't have a lot of that. But from Poe I learned about language. The beauty of Poe's language still shines—I defy anyone to find a story more perfect in rhythm, cadence, and sound, sentence by sentence, than "The Tell-Tale Heart." (Twain's language, of course, is also gorgeous, but more subtle. I was twelve. I didn't want subtle. I wanted my socks knocked off.) And I also found in Poe something less tangible, but which resonated with me and still does: inevitability, and the laughable nature of human intention.

This thread runs all through Poe's work—for example, in poems like "Conqueror Worm"—including the above-mentioned "Tell-Tale

Heart." It's not the still-beating heart of the dead man that gives the killer away, after all; it's his own fearful, guilty heart that does. But the example I remember most vividly is "The Masque of the Red Death." In the middle of a plague, an array of wealthy citizens lock themselves away and throw a party, a big masked ball. The danger outside doesn't matter; they congratulate one another on how cleverly they've isolated themselves from it. Except, of course, they haven't. They've made it worse. One of the "guests," dressed as the Red Death (everyone laughs and applauds, he's so-o-o-o amusing), really *is* the Red Death. And far from being locked away from him, they're locked in with him. He dances with them all, and they all die.

This is "the best laid plans / gang aft agley," this is "man proposes, God disposes." It ain't news. But it was to me, at twelve. Or, no, it wasn't. It was better than that. It was the first time someone had said, out loud as it were, something I'd suspected but, as a member of a rational, hardworking, optimistic family and society, not been allowed to think. It's what much, much later, in a review of the movie *Chinatown*, I saw referred to as "the disastrous consequences of good intentions." Was I a bleak twelve-year-old? Sure I was. But I had always been like that. What reading Poe for two solid weeks gave me was the relief of knowing I wasn't alone. I don't think I've ever felt closer to a writer than I did to Poe those two weeks.

But I was luckier than Poe. I had Mark Twain, right beside us, showing at least one of us how to laugh despite, or at, it all.

Bless both their beating hearts.

S. J. Rozan grew up in the Bronx and as a child visited the Poe Cottage many times, where she looked for but never found the Tell-Tale Heart. The author of ten novels and dozens of short stories, she's won most of crime writing's major awards, including two Edgars that make the cat-sitter so nervous he puts hats over their faces whenever S.J.'s out of town.

The Murders in the Rue Morgue

What song the Syrens sang, or what name Achilles assumed
when he hid himself among women, although puzzling
questions, are not beyond all conjecture.

—SIR THOMAS BROWNE

THE MENTAL FEATURES discoursed of as the analytical, are, in themselves, but little susceptible of analysis. We appreciate them only in their effects. We know of them, among other things, that they are always to their possessor, when inordinately possessed, a source of the liveliest enjoyment. As the strong man exults in his physical ability, delighting in such exercises as call his muscles into action, so glories the analyst in that moral activity which *disentangles*. He derives pleasure from even the most trivial occupations bringing his talent into play. He is fond of enigmas, of conundrums, of hieroglyphics; exhibiting in his solutions of each a degree of *acumen* which appears to the ordinary apprehension praeternatural. His results, brought about by the very soul and essence of method, have, in truth, the whole air of intuition.

The faculty of re-solution is possibly much invigorated by mathematical study, and especially by that highest branch of it which, unjustly, and merely on account of its retrograde operations, has been called, as if *par excellence,* analysis. Yet to calculate is not in itself to analyse. A chess-player, for example, does the one, without effort at the other. It follows that the game of chess, in its effects upon mental character, is greatly misunderstood. I am not now writing a treatise, but simply prefacing a somewhat peculiar narrative by observations very much at random; I will, therefore, take occasion to assert that the higher powers of the reflective intellect are more decidedly and more usefully tasked by the unostentatious game of draughts than by all the elaborate frivolity of chess. In this latter, where the pieces have different and *bizarre* motions, with various and variable values, what is only complex, is mistaken (a not unusual error) for what is profound. The *attention* is here called powerfully into play. If it flag for an instant, an oversight is committed, resulting in injury or defeat. The possible moves being not only manifold, but involute, the chances of such oversights are multiplied; and in nine cases out of ten, it is the more concentrative rather than the more acute player who conquers. In draughts, on the contrary, where the moves are *unique* and have but little variation, the probabilities of inadvertence are diminished, and the mere attention being left comparatively unemployed, what advantages are obtained by either party are obtained by superior *acumen*. To be less abstract, let us suppose a game of draughts where the pieces are reduced to four kings, and where, of course, no over-sight is to be expected. It is obvious that here the victory can be decided (the players being at all equal) only by some *recherché* move-ment, the result of some strong exertion of the intellect.

Deprived of ordinary resources, the analyst throws himself into the spirit of his opponent, identifies himself therewith, and not un-frequently sees thus, at a glance, the sole methods (sometimes indeed absurdly simple ones) by which he may seduce into error or hurry into miscalculation.

Whist has long been noted for its influence upon what is termed the calculating power; and men of the highest order of intellect have been known to take an apparently unaccountable delight in it, while eschewing chess as frivolous. Beyond doubt there is nothing of a similar nature so greatly tasking the faculty of analysis. The best chess-player in Christendom *may* be little more than the best player of chess; but proficiency in whist implies capacity for success in all these more important undertakings where mind struggles with mind. When I say proficiency, I mean that perfection in the game which includes a comprehension of *all* the sources whence legitimate ad-vantage may be derived. These are not only manifold but multiform, and lie frequently among recesses of thought altogether inaccessible to the ordinary understanding. To observe attentively is to remem-ber distinctly; and, so far, the concentrative chess-player will do very well at whist; while the rules of Hoyle (themselves based upon the mere mechanism of the game) are sufficiently and generally com-prehensible. Thus to have a retentive memory, and proceed by "the book," are points commonly regarded as the sum total of good play-ing. But it is in matters beyond the limits of mere rule that the skill of the analyst is evinced. He makes, in silence, a host of observations and inferences. So, perhaps, do his companions; and the difference in the extent of the information obtained, lies not so much in the validity of the inference as in the quality of the observation. The necessary knowledge is that of *what* to observe. Our player confines himself not at all; nor, because the game is the object, does he reject deductions from things external to the game. He examines the countenance of his partner, comparing it carefully with that of each of his opponents. He considers the mode of assorting the cards in each hand; often counting trump by trump, and honor by honor, through the glances bestowed by their holders upon each. He notes every variation of face as the play progresses, gathering a fund of thought from the differences in the expression of certainty, of surprise, of triumph, or chagrin. From the manner of gathering up a trick he judges whether the person taking it, can make another in the suit. He recognizes what is played through feint, by the manner with which it is thrown upon the table. A casual or inadvertent word; the accidental dropping or turning of a card, with the accompanying anxiety or carelessness in regard to its concealment; the counting of the tricks, with the order of their arrangement; embarrassment, hesitation, eagerness, or trepidation—all afford, to his apparently intuitive perception, indications of the true state of affairs. The first two or three rounds having been played, he is in full possession of the contents of each hand, and thenceforward puts down his cards with as absolute a precision of purpose as if the rest of the party had turned outward the faces of their own.

The analytical power should not be confounded with simple ingenuity; for while the analyst is necessarily ingenious, the ingenious man is often remarkably incapable of analysis. The constructive or combining power, by which ingenuity is usually manifested, and to which the phrenologists (I believe erroneously) have assigned a separate organ, supposing it a primitive faculty, has been so frequently seen in those whose intellect bordered otherwise upon idiocy, as to have attracted general observation among writers on morals. Between ingenuity and the analytic ability there exists a difference far greater, indeed, than that between the fancy and the imagination, but of a character very strictly analogous. It will be found, in fact, that the ingenious are always fanciful, and the *truly* imaginative never otherwise than analytic.

The narrative which follows will appear to the reader somewhat in the light of a commentary upon the propositions just advanced.

Residing in Paris during the spring and part of the summer of 18—, I there became acquainted with a Monsieur C. Auguste Dupin. This young gentleman was of an excellent, indeed of an illustrious family, but, by a variety of untoward events, had been reduced to such poverty that the energy of his character succumbed beneath it, and he ceased to bestir himself in the world, or to care for the retrieval of his fortunes. By courtesy of his creditors, there still remained in his possession a small remnant of his patrimony; and, upon the income arising from this, he managed, by means of a rigorous economy, to procure the necessaries of life, without troubling himself about its superfluities. Books, indeed, were his sole luxuries, and in Paris these are easily obtained.

Our first meeting was at an obscure library in the Rue Montmartre, where the accident of our both being in search of the same very rare and very remarkable volume, brought us into closer communion. We saw each other again and again. I was deeply interested in the little family history which he detailed to me with all that candor which a Frenchman indulges whenever mere self is his theme. I was astonished, too, at the vast extent of his reading; and, above all, I felt my soul enkindled within me by the wild fervor, and the vivid freshness of his imagination. Seeking in Paris the objects I then sought, I felt that the society of such a man would be to me a treasure beyond price; and this feeling I frankly confided to him. It was at length arranged that we should live together during my stay in the city; and as my worldly circumstances were somewhat less embarrassed than his own, I was permitted to be at the expense of renting, and furnishing in a style which suited the rather fantastic gloom of our common temper, a time-eaten and grotesque mansion, long deserted through superstitions into which we did not inquire, and tottering to its fall in a retired and desolate portion of the Faubourg St. Germain.

Had the routine of our life at this place been known to the world, we should have been regarded as madmen—although, perhaps, as madmen of a harmless nature. Our seclusion was perfect. We admitted no visitors. Indeed the locality of our retirement had been carefully kept a secret from my own former associates; and it had been many years since Dupin had ceased to know or be known in Paris. We existed within ourselves alone.

It was a freak of fancy in my friend (for what else shall I call it?) to be enamored of the night for her own sake; and into this *bizarrerie*, as into all his others, I quietly fell; giving myself up to his wild whims with a perfect *abandon*. The sable divinity would not herself dwell with us always; but we could counterfeit her presence. At the first dawn of the morning we closed all the massy shutters of our old building; lighting a couple of tapers which, strongly perfumed, threw out only the ghastliest and feeblest of rays. By the aid of these we then busied our souls in dreams—reading, writing, or conversing, until warned by the clock of the advent of the true Darkness. Then we sallied forth into the streets, arm in arm, continuing the topics of the day, or roaming far and wide until a late hour, seeking, amid the wild lights and shadows of the populous city, that infinity of mental excitement which quiet observation can afford.

At such times I could not help remarking and admiring (although from his rich ideality I had been prepared to expect it) a peculiar analytic ability in Dupin. He seemed, too, to take an eager delight in its exercise—if not exactly in its display—and did not hesitate to confess the pleasure thus derived. He boasted to me, with a low chuckling laugh, that most men, in respect to himself, wore windows in their bosoms, and was wont to follow up such assertions by direct and very startling proofs of his intimate knowledge of my own. His manner at these moments was frigid and abstract; his eyes were vacant in expression; while his voice, usually a rich tenor, rose into a treble which would have sounded petulant but for the deliberateness and entire distinctness of the enunciation. Observing him in these moods, I often dwelt meditatively upon the old philosophy of the Bi-Part Soul, and amused myself with the fancy of a double Dupin—the creative and the resolvent.

Let it not be supposed, from what I have just said, that I am detailing any mystery, or penning any romance. What I have described in the Frenchman was merely the result of an excited, or perhaps of a diseased, intelligence. But of the character of his remarks at the periods in question an example will best convey the idea.

We were strolling one night down a long dirty street, in the vicinity of the Palais Royal. Being both, apparently, occupied with thought, neither of us had spoken a syllable for fifteen minutes at least. All at once Dupin broke forth with these words:

"He is a very little fellow, that's true, and would do better for the *Théâtre des Variétés*."

"There can be no doubt of that," I replied, unwittingly, and not at first observing (so much had I been absorbed in reflection) the extraordinary manner in which the speaker had chimed in with my meditations. In an instant afterward I recollected myself, and my astonishment was profound.

"Dupin," said I, gravely, "this is beyond my comprehension. I do not hesitate to say that I am amazed, and can scarcely credit my senses. How was it possible you should know I was thinking of—?" Here I paused, to ascertain beyond a doubt whether he really knew of whom I thought.

"—of Chantilly," said he, "why do you pause? You were remarking to yourself that his diminutive figure unfitted him for tragedy."

This was precisely what had formed the subject of my reflections. Chantilly was a *quondam* cobbler of the Rue St. Denis, who, becoming stage-mad, had attempted the *rôle* of Xerxes, in Crébillon's tragedy so called, and been notoriously Pasquinaded for his pains.

"Tell me, for Heaven's sake," I exclaimed, "the method—if method there is—by which you have been enabled to fathom my soul in this matter." In fact, I was even more startled than I would have been willing to express.

"It was the fruiterer," replied my friend, "who brought you to the conclusion that the mender of soles was not of sufficient height for Xerxes *et id genus omne.*"

"The fruiterer!—you astonish me—I know no fruiterer whomsoever."

"The man who ran up against you as we entered the street—it may have been fifteen minutes ago."

I now remembered that, in fact, a fruiterer, carrying upon his head a large basket of apples, had nearly thrown me down, by accident, as we passed from the Rue C—— into the thoroughfare where we stood; but what this had to do with Chantilly I could not possibly understand.

There was not a particle of *charlatânerie* about Dupin. "I will explain," he said, "and that you may comprehend all clearly, we will first retrace the course of your meditations, from the moment in which I spoke to you until that of the *rencontre* with the fruiterer in question. The larger links of the chain run thus—Chantilly, Orion, Dr. Nichols, Epicurus, Stereotomy, the street stones, the fruiterer."

There are few persons who have not, at some period of their lives, amused themselves in retracing the steps by which particular conclusions of their own minds have been attained. The occupation is often full of interest; and he who attempts it for the first time is astonished by the apparently illimitable distance and incoherence between the starting-point and the goal. What, then, must have been my amazement, when I heard the Frenchman speak what he had just spoken, and when I could not help acknowledging that he had spoken the truth. He continued:

"We had been talking of horses, if I remember aright, just before leaving the Rue C——. This was the last subject we discussed. As we crossed into this street, a fruiterer, with a large basket upon his head, brushing quickly past us, thrust you upon a pile of paving-stones collected at a spot where the causeway is undergoing repair. You stepped upon one of the loose fragments, slipped, slightly strained your ankle, appeared vexed or sulky, muttered a few words, turned to look at the pile, and then proceeded in silence. I was not particularly attentive to what you did; but observation has become with me, of late, a species of necessity.

"You kept your eyes upon the ground—glancing, with a petulant expression, at the holes and ruts in the pavement, (so that I saw you were still thinking of the stones), until we reached the little alley called Lamartine, which has been paved, by way of experiment, with the overlapping and riveted blocks. Here your countenance brightened up, and, perceiving your lips move, I could not doubt that you murmured the word 'stereotomy,' a term very affectedly applied to this species of pavement. I knew that you could not say to yourself 'stereotomy' without being brought to think of atomies, and thus of the theories of Epicurus; and since, when we discussed this subject not very long ago, I mentioned to you how singularly, yet with how little notice, the vague guesses of that noble Greek had met with confirmation in the late nebular cosmogony, I felt that you could not avoid casting your eyes upward to the great *nebula* in Orion, and I certainly expected that you would do so. You did look up; and I was now assured that I had correctly followed your steps. But in that bitter *tirade* upon Chantilly, which appeared in yesterday's '*Musée*,' the satirist, making some disgraceful allusions to the cobbler's change of name upon assuming the buskin, quoted a Latin line about which we have often conversed. I mean the line

Perdidit antiquum litera prima sonum.

I had told you that this was in reference to Orion, formerly written Urion; and, from certain pungencies connected with this explanation, I was aware that you could not have forgotten it. It was clear, therefore, that you would not fail to combine the two ideas of Orion and Chantilly. That you did combine them I saw by the character of the smile which passed over your lips. You thought of the poor cobbler's immolation. So far, you had been stooping in your gait; but now I saw you draw yourself up to your full height. I was then sure that you reflected upon the diminutive figure of Chantilly. At this point I interrupted your meditations to remark that as, in fact, he *was* a very little fellow—that Chantilly—he would do better at the *Théâtre des Variétés*."

Not long after this, we were looking over an evening edition of the *Gazette des Tribunaux*, when the following paragraphs arrested our attention.

EXTRAORDINARY MURDERS. —This morning, about three o'clock, the inhabitants of the Quartier St. Roch were roused from sleep by a succession of terrific shrieks, issuing, apparently, from the fourth story of a house in the Rue Morgue, known to be in the sole occupancy of one Madame L'Espanaye, and her daughter, Mademoiselle Camille L'Espanaye. After some delay, occasioned by a fruitless attempt to procure admission in the usual manner, the gateway was broken in with a crowbar, and eight or ten of the neighbors entered, accompanied by two gendarmes. By this time the cries had ceased; but, as the party rushed up the first flight of stairs, two or more rough voices, in angry contention, were distinguished, and seemed to proceed from the upper part of the house. As the second landing was reached, these sounds, also, had ceased, and every thing remained perfectly quiet. The party spread themselves, and hurried from room to room. Upon arriving at a large back chamber in the fourth story (the door of which, being found locked, with the key inside, was forced open), a spectacle presented itself which struck every one present not less with horror than with astonishment.

The apartment was in the wildest disorder—the furniture broken and thrown about in all directions. There was only one bedstead; and from this the bed had been removed, and thrown into the middle of the floor. On a chair lay a razor, besmeared with blood. On the hearth were two or three long and thick tresses of gray human hair, also dabbled with blood, and seeming to have been pulled out by the roots. Upon the floor were found four Napoleons, an ear-ring of topaz, three large silver spoons, three smaller of métal d'Alger, and two bags, containing nearly four thousand francs in gold. The drawers of a bureau, which stood in one corner were open, and had been, apparently, rifled, although many articles still remained in them. A small iron safe was discovered under the bed (not under the bedstead). It was open, with the key still in the door. It had no contents beyond a few old letters, and other papers of little consequence.

Of Madame L'Espanaye no traces were here seen; but an unusual quantity of soot being observed in the fire-place, a search was made in the chimney, and (horrible to relate!) the corpse of the daughter, head downward, was dragged therefrom; it having been thus forced up the narrow aperture for a considerable distance. The body was quite warm. Upon examining it, many excoriations were perceived, no doubt occasioned by the violence with which it had been thrust up and disengaged. Upon the face were many severe scratches, and, upon the throat, dark bruises, and deep indentations of finger nails, as if the deceased had been throttled to death.

After a thorough investigation of every portion of the house without farther discovery, the party made its way into a small paved yard in the rear of the building, where lay the corpse of the old lady, with her *throat so entirely cut that, upon an attempt to raise her, the head fell off. The body, as well as the head, was fearfully mutilated — the former so much so as scarcely to retain any semblance of humanity.*

To this horrible mystery there is not as yet, we believe, the slightest clue.

The next day's paper had these additional particulars:

THE TRAGEDY IN THE RUE MORGUE. — Many individuals have been examined in relation to this most extraordinary and frightful affair, [The word 'affaire' has not yet, in France, that levity of import which it conveys with us] but nothing whatever has transpired to throw light upon it. We give below all the material testimony elicited.

Pauline Dubourg, laundress, deposes that she has known both the deceased for three years, having washed for them during that period. The old lady and her daughter seemed on good terms — very affectionate towards each other. They were excellent pay. Could not speak in regard to their mode or means of living. Believed that Madame L. told fortunes for a living. Was reputed to have money put by. Never met any persons in the house when she called for the clothes or took them home. Was sure that they had no servant in employ. There appeared to be no furniture in any part of the building except in the fourth story.

Pierre Moreau, tobacconist, deposes that he has been in the habit of selling small quantities of tobacco and snuff to Madame L'Espanaye for nearly four years. Was born in the neighborhood, and has always resided there. The deceased and her daughter had occupied the house in which the corpses were found, for more than six years. It was formerly occupied by a jeweller, who under-let the upper rooms to various persons. The house was the property of Madame L., who became dissatisfied with the abuse of the premises by her tenant, and moved into them herself, refusing to let any portion. The old lady was childish. Witness had seen the daughter some five or six times during the six years. The two lived an exceedingly retired life—were reputed to have money. Had heard it said among the neighbors that Madame L. told fortunes—did not believe it. Had never seen any person enter the door except the old lady and her daughter, a porter once or twice, and a physician some eight or ten times.

Many other persons, neighbors, gave evidence to the same effect. No one was spoken of as frequenting the house. It was not known whether there were any living connections of Madame L. and her daughter. The shutters of the front windows were seldom opened. Those in the rear were always closed, with the exception of the large back room, fourth story. The house was a good house—not very old.

Isidore Musèt, gendarme, deposes that he was called to the house about three o'clock in the morning, and found some twenty or thirty persons at the gateway, endeavoring to gain admittance. Forced it open, at length, with a bayonet—not with a crowbar. Had but little difficulty in getting it open, on account of its being a double or folding gate, and bolted neither at bottom nor top. The shrieks were continued until the gate was forced—and then suddenly ceased. They seemed to be screams of some person (or persons) in great agony—were loud and drawn out, not short and quick. Witness led the way up stairs. Upon reaching the first landing, heard two voices in loud and angry contention—the one a gruff voice, the other much shriller—a very strange voice. Could distinguish some words of the former, which was that of a Frenchman. Was positive that it was not a woman's voice. Could distinguish the words "sacré" and "diable." The shrill voice was that of a foreigner. Could not be sure whether it was the voice of a man or of a woman. Could not make out what was said, but believed the language to be Spanish. The state of the room and of the bodies was described by this witness as we described them yesterday.

Henri Duval, a neighbor, and by trade a silver-smith, deposes that he was one of the party who first entered the house. Corroborates the testimony of Musèt in general. As soon as they forced an entrance, they re-closed the door, to keep out the crowd, which collected very fast, notwithstanding the lateness of the hour. The shrill voice, this witness thinks, was that of an Italian. Was certain it was not French. Could not be sure that it was a man's voice. It might have been a woman's. Was not acquainted with the Italian language. Could not distinguish the words, but was convinced by the intonation that the speaker was an Italian. Knew Madame L. and her daughter. Had conversed with both frequently. Was sure that the shrill voice was not that of either of the deceased.

—Odenheimer, restaurateur.—This witness volunteered his testimony. Not speaking French, was examined through an interpreter. Is a native of Amsterdam. Was passing the house at the time of the shrieks. They lasted for several minutes—probably ten. They were long and loud—very awful and distressing. Was one of those who entered the building. Corroborated the previous evidence in every respect but one. Was sure that the shrill voice was that of a man—of a Frenchman. Could not distinguish the words uttered. They were loud and quick—unequal—spoken apparently in fear as well as in anger. The voice was harsh—not so much shrill as harsh. Could not call it a shrill voice. The gruff voice said repeatedly "sacré," "diable," and once "mon Dieu."

Jules Mignaud, banker, of the firm of Mignaud et Fils, Rue Deloraine. Is the elder Mignaud. Madame L'Espanaye had some property. Had opened an account with his banking house in the spring of the year—(eight years previously). Made frequent deposits in small sums. Had checked for nothing until the third day before her death, when she took out in person the sum of 4000 francs. This sum was paid in gold, and a clerk sent home with the money.

Adolphe Le Bon, clerk to Mignaud et Fils, deposes that on the day in question, about noon, he accompanied Madame L'Espanaye to her residence with the 4000 francs, put up in two bags. Upon the door being opened, Mademoiselle L. appeared and took from his hands one of the bags, while the old lady relieved him of the other. He then bowed and departed. Did not see any person in the street at the time. It is a bye-street—very lonely.

William Bird, tailor, deposes that he was one of the party who entered the house. Is an Englishman. Has lived in Paris two years. Was one of the first to ascend the stairs. Heard the voices in contention. The gruff voice was that of a Frenchman. Could make out several words, but cannot now remember all. Heard distinctly "sacré" and "mon Dieu." There was a sound at the moment as if of several persons struggling—a scraping and scuffling sound. The shrill voice was very loud—louder than the gruff one. Is sure that it was not the voice of an Englishman. Appeared to be that of a German. Might have been a woman's voice. Does not understand German.

Four of the above-named witnesses, being recalled, deposed that the door of the chamber in which was found the body of Mademoiselle L. was locked on the inside when the party reached it. Every thing was perfectly silent—no groans or noises of any kind. Upon forcing the door no person was seen. The windows, both of the back and front room, were down and firmly fastened from within. A door between the two rooms was closed but not locked. The door leading from the front room into the passage was locked, with the key on the inside. A small room in the front of the house, on the fourth story, at the head of the passage, was open, the door being ajar. This room was crowded with old beds, boxes, and so forth. These were carefully removed and searched. There was not an inch of any portion of the house which was not carefully searched. Sweeps were sent up and down the chimneys.

The house was a four-story one, with garrets (mansardes). A trap-door on the roof was nailed down very securely—did not appear to have been opened for years. The time elapsing between the hearing of the voices in contention and the breaking open of the room door was variously stated by the witnesses. Some made it as short as three minutes—some as long as five. The door was opened with difficulty.

Alfonzo Garcio, undertaker, deposes that he resides in the Rue Morgue. Is a native of Spain. Was one of the party who entered the house. Did not proceed upstairs. Is nervous, and was apprehensive of the consequences of agitation. Heard the voices in contention. The gruff voice was that of a Frenchman. Could not distinguish what was said. The shrill voice was that of an Englishman—is sure of this. Does not understand the English language, but judges by the intonation.

Alberto Montani, confectioner, deposes that he was among the first to ascend the stairs. Heard the voices in question. The gruff voice was that of a Frenchman. Distinguished several words. The speaker appeared to be expostulating. Could not make out the words of the shrill voice. Spoke quick and unevenly. Thinks it the voice of a Russian. Corroborates the general testimony. Is an Italian. Never conversed with a native of Russia.

Several witnesses, recalled, here testified that the chimneys of all the rooms on the fourth story were too narrow to admit the passage of a human being. By "sweeps" were meant cylindrical sweeping-brushes, such as are employed by those who clean chimneys. These brushes were passed up and down every flue in the house. There is no back passage by which any one could have descended while the party proceeded upstairs. The body of Mademoiselle L'Espanaye was so firmly wedged in the chimney that it could not be got down until four or five of the party united their strength.

Paul Dumas, physician, deposes that he was called to view the bodies about daybreak. They were both then lying on the sacking of the bedstead in the chamber where Mademoiselle L. was found. The corpse of the young lady was much bruised and excoriated. The fact that it had been thrust up the chimney would sufficiently account for these appearances. The throat was greatly chafed. There were several deep scratches just below the chin, together with a series of livid spots which were evidently the impression of fingers. The face was fearfully discolored, and the eyeballs protruded. The tongue had been partially bitten through.

A large bruise was discovered upon the pit of the stomach, produced, apparently, by the pressure of a knee. In the opinion of M. Dumas, Mademoiselle L'Espanaye had been throttled to death by some person or persons unknown. The corpse of the mother was horribly mutilated. All the bones of the right leg and arm were more or less shattered. The left tibia much splintered, as well as all the ribs of the left side.

Whole body dreadfully bruised and discolored. It was not possible to say how the injuries had been inflicted. A heavy club of wood, or a broad bar of iron—a chair—any large, heavy, and obtuse weapon would have produced such results, if wielded by the hands of a very powerful man. No woman could have inflicted the blows with any weapon. The head of the deceased, when seen by witness, was entirely separated from the body, and was also greatly shattered. The throat had evidently been cut with some very sharp instrument—probably with a razor.

Alexandre Etienne, surgeon, was called with M. Dumas to view the bodies. Corroborated the testimony, and the opinions of M. Dumas. Nothing farther of importance was elicited, although several other persons were examined. A murder so mysterious, and so perplexing in all its particulars, was never before committed in Paris—if indeed a murder has been committed at all. The police are entirely at fault— an unusual occurrence in affairs of this nature. There is not, however, the shadow of a clue apparent.

The evening edition of the paper stated that the greatest excitement still continued in the Quartier St. Roch—that the premises in question had been carefully re-searched, and fresh examinations of witnesses instituted, but all to no purpose. A post-script, however, mentioned that Adolphe Le Bon had been arrested and imprisoned—although nothing appeared to criminate him beyond the facts already detailed. Dupin seemed singularly interested in the progress of this affair—at least so I judged from his manner, for he made no comments. It was only after the announcement that Le Bon had been imprisoned, that he asked me my opinion respecting the murders.

I could merely agree with all Paris in considering them an insoluble mystery. I saw no means by which it would be possible to trace the murderer.

"We must not judge of the means," said Dupin, "by this shell of an examination. The Parisian police, so much extolled for *acumen*, are cunning, but no more. There is no method in their proceedings, beyond the method of the moment. They make a vast parade of measures; but, not unfrequently, these are so ill-adapted to the objects proposed, as to put us in mind of Monsieur Jourdain's calling for his *robe-de-chambre—pour mieux entendre la musique*. The results attained by them are not unfrequently surprising, but, for the most part, are brought about by simple diligence and activity. When these qualities are unavailing, their schemes fail. Vidocq, for example, was a good guesser and a persevering man. But, without educated thought, he erred continually by the very intensity of his investigations. He impaired his vision by holding the object too close. He might see, perhaps, one or two points with unusual clearness, but in so doing he, necessarily, lost sight of the matter as a whole. Thus there is such a thing as being too profound. Truth is not always in a well. In fact, as regards the more important knowledge, I do believe that she is invariably superficial. The depth lies in the valleys where we seek her, and not upon the mountain-tops where she is found. The modes and sources of this kind of error are well typified in the contemplation of the heavenly bodies. To look at a star by glances—to view it in a side-long way, by turning toward it the exterior portions of the *retina* (more susceptible of feeble impressions of light than the interior), is to behold the star distinctly—is to have the best appreciation of its lustre—a lustre which grows dim just in proportion as we turn our vision *fully* upon it. A greater number of rays actually fall upon the eye in the latter case, but in the former, there is the more refined capacity for comprehension. By undue profundity we perplex and enfeeble thought; and it is possible to make even Venus herself vanish from the firmament by a scrutiny too sustained, too concentrated, or too direct.

"As for these murders, let us enter into some examinations for ourselves, before we make up an opinion respecting them. An inquiry will afford us amusement," [I thought this an odd term, so applied, but said nothing] "and besides, Le Bon once rendered me a service for which I am not ungrateful. We will go and see the premises with our own eyes. I know G——, the Prefect of Police, and shall have no difficulty in obtaining the necessary permission."

The permission was obtained, and we proceeded at once to the Rue Morgue. This is one of those miserable thoroughfares which intervene between the Rue Richelieu and the Rue St. Roch. It was late in the afternoon when we reached it; as this quarter is at a great distance from that in which we resided. The house was readily found; for there were still many persons gazing up at the closed shutters, with an objectless curiosity, from the opposite side of the way. It was an ordinary Parisian house, with a gateway, on one side of which was a glazed watch-box, with a sliding panel in the window, indicating a *loge de concierge*. Before going in we walked up the street, turned down an alley, and then, again turning, passed in the rear of the building—Dupin, meanwhile, examining the whole neighborhood, as well as the house, with a minuteness of attention for which I could see no possible object.

Retracing our steps, we came again to the front of the dwelling, rang, and, having shown our credentials, were admitted by the agents in charge. We went upstairs—into the chamber where the body of Mademoiselle L'Espanaye had been found, and where both the deceased still lay. The disorders of the room had, as usual, been suffered to exist. I saw nothing beyond what had been stated in the *Gazette des Tribunaux*. Dupin scrutinized every thing—not excepting the bodies of the victims. We then went into the other rooms, and into the yard; a *gendarme* accompanying us throughout. The examination occupied us until dark, when we took our departure. On our way home my companion stepped in for a moment at the office of one of the daily papers.

I have said that the whims of my friend were manifold, and that *Je les ménageais:*—for this phrase there is no English equivalent. It was his humor, now, to decline all conversation on the subject of the murder, until about noon the next day. He then asked me, suddenly, if I had observed any thing *peculiar* at the scene of the atrocity.

There was something in his manner of emphasizing the word *"peculiar,"* which caused me to shudder, without knowing why.

"No, nothing *peculiar,*" I said; "nothing more, at least, than we both saw stated in the paper."

"The *Gazette,*" he replied, "has not entered, I fear, into the unusual horror of the thing. But dismiss the idle opinions of this print. It appears to me that this mystery is considered insoluble, for the very reason which should cause it to be regarded as easy of solution—I mean for the *outré* character of its features. The police are confounded by the seeming absence of motive—not for the murder itself—but for the atrocity of the murder. They are puzzled, too, by the seeming impossibility of reconciling the voices heard in contention, with the facts that no one was discovered upstairs but the assassinated Mademoiselle L'Espanaye, and that there were no means of egress without the notice of the party ascending. The wild disorder of the room; the corpse thrust, with the head downward, up the chimney; the frightful mutilation of the body of the old lady; these considerations, with those just mentioned, and others which I need not mention, have sufficed to paralyze the powers, by putting completely at fault the boasted *acumen,* of the government agents. They have fallen into the gross but common error of confounding the unusual with the abstruse. But it is by these deviations from the plane of the ordinary, that reason feels its way, if at all, in its search for the true. In investigations such as we are now pursuing, it should not be so much asked 'what has occurred,' as 'what has occurred that has never occurred before.' In fact, the facility with which I shall arrive, or have arrived, at the solution of this mystery, is in the direct ratio of its apparent insolubility in the eyes of the police."

I stared at the speaker in mute astonishment.

"I am now awaiting," continued he, looking toward the door of our apartment—"I am now awaiting a person who, although perhaps not the perpetrator of these butcheries, must have been in some measure implicated in their perpetration. Of the worst portion of the crimes committed, it is probable that he is innocent. I hope that I am right in this supposition; for upon it I build my expectation of reading the entire riddle. I look for the man here—in this room—every moment. It is true that he may not arrive; but the probability is that he will. Should he come, it will be necessary to detain him. Here are pistols; and we both know how to use them when occasion demands their use."

I took the pistols, scarcely knowing what I did, or believing what I heard, while Dupin went on, very much as if in a soliloquy. I have already spoken of his abstract manner at such times. His discourse was addressed to myself; but his voice, although by no means loud, had that intonation which is commonly employed in speaking to some one at a great distance. His eyes, vacant in expression, regarded only the wall.

"That the voices heard in contention," he said, "by the party upon the stairs, were not the voices of the women themselves, was fully proved by the evidence. This relieves us of all doubt upon the question whether the old lady could have first destroyed the daughter, and afterward have committed suicide. I speak of this point chiefly for the sake of method; for the strength of Madame L'Espanaye would have been utterly unequal to the task of thrusting her daughter's corpse up the chimney as it was found; and the nature of the wounds upon her own person entirely preclude the idea of self-destruction. Murder, then, has been committed by some third party; and the voices of this third party were those heard in contention. Let me now advert—not to the whole testimony respecting these voices—but to what was *peculiar* in that testimony. Did you observe any thing peculiar about it?"

I remarked that, while all the witnesses agreed in supposing the gruff voice to be that of a Frenchman, there was much disagreement in regard to the shrill, or, as one individual termed it, the harsh voice.

"That was the evidence itself," said Dupin, "but it was not the peculiarity of the evidence. You have observed nothing distinctive. Yet there *was* something to be observed. The witnesses, as you remark, agreed about the gruff voice; they were here unanimous. But in regard to the shrill voice, the peculiarity is—not that they disagreed—but that, while an Italian, an Englishman, a Spaniard, a Hollander, and a Frenchman attempted to describe it, each one spoke of it as that *of a foreigner.* Each is sure that it was not the voice of one of his own countrymen. Each likens it—not to the voice of an individual of any nation with whose language he is conversant—but the converse. The Frenchman supposes it the voice of a Spaniard, and 'might have distinguished some words *had he been acquainted with the Spanish.*' The Dutchman maintains it to have been that of a Frenchman; but we find it stated that '*not understanding French this witness was examined through an interpreter.*' The Englishman thinks it the voice of a German, and '*does not understand German.*' The Spaniard 'is sure' that it was that of an Englishman, but 'judges by the intonation' altogether, '*as he has no knowledge of the English.*' The Italian believes it the voice of a Russian, but '*has never conversed with a native of Russia.*' A second Frenchman differs, moreover, with the first, and is positive that the voice was that of an Italian; but, *not being cognizant of that tongue,* is, like the Spaniard, 'convinced by the intonation.' Now, how strangely unusual must that voice have really been, about which such testimony as this *could* have been elicited!—in whose *tones,* even, denizens of the five great divisions of Europe could recognize nothing familiar! You will say that it might have been the voice of an Asiatic—of an African. Neither Asiatics nor Africans abound in Paris; but, without denying the inference, I will now merely call your attention to three points. The voice is termed by one witness 'harsh rather than shrill.' It is represented by two others to have been 'quick and *unequal.*' No words—no sounds resembling words—were by any witness mentioned as distinguishable.

"I know not," continued Dupin, "what impression I may have made, so far, upon your own understanding; but I do not hesitate to say that legitimate deductions even from this portion of the testimony—the portion respecting the gruff and shrill voices—are in themselves sufficient to engender a suspicion which should give direction to all farther progress in the investigation of the mystery. I said 'legitimate deductions'; but my meaning is not thus fully expressed. I designed to imply that the deductions are the *sole* proper ones, and that the suspicion arises *inevitably* from them as the single result. What the suspicion is, however, I will not say just yet. I merely wish you to bear in mind that, with myself, it was sufficiently forcible to give a definite form—a certain tendency—to my inquiries in the chamber.

"Let us now transport ourselves, in fancy, to this chamber. What shall we first seek here? The means of egress employed by the murderers. It is not too much to say that neither of us believe in praeternatural events. Madame and Mademoiselle L'Espanaye were not destroyed by spirits. The doers of the deed were material and escaped materially. Then how? Fortunately there is but one mode of reasoning upon the point, and that mode *must* lead us to a definite decision. Let us examine, each by each, the possible means of egress.

It is clear that the assassins were in the room where Mademoiselle L'Espanaye was found, or at least in the room adjoining, when the party ascended the stairs. It is, then, only from these two apartments that we have to seek issues. The police have laid bare the floors, the ceilings, and the masonry of the walls, in every direction. No *secret* issues could have escaped their vigilance. But, not trusting to *their* eyes, I examined with my own. There were, then, *no* secret issues. Both doors leading from the rooms into the passage were securely locked, with the keys inside. Let us turn to the chimneys. These, although of ordinary width for some eight or ten feet above the hearths, will not admit, throughout their extent, the body of a large cat. The impossibility of egress, by means already stated, being thus absolute, we are reduced to the windows. Through those of the front room no one could have escaped without notice from the crowd in the street. The murderers *must* have passed, then, through those of the back room. Now, brought to this conclusion in so unequivocal a manner as we are, it is not our part, as reasoners, to reject it on account of apparent impossibilities. It is only left for us to prove that these apparent 'impossibilities' are, in reality, not such.

"There are two windows in the chamber. One of them is unobstructed by furniture, and is wholly visible. The lower portion of the other is hidden from view by the head of the unwieldy bedstead which is thrust close up against it. The former was found securely fastened from within. It resisted the utmost force of those who endeavored to raise it. A large gimlet-hole had been pierced in its frame to the left, and a very stout nail was found fitted therein, nearly to the head. Upon examining the other window, a similar nail was seen similarly fitted in it; and a vigorous attempt to raise this sash failed also. The police were now entirely satisfied that egress had not been in these directions. And, *therefore*, it was thought a matter of supererogation to withdraw the nails and open the windows.

"My own examination was somewhat more particular, and was

so for the reason I have just given—because here it was, I knew, that all apparent impossibilities *must* be proved to be not such in reality.

"I proceeded to think thus—*a posteriori*. The murderers *did* escape from one of these windows. This being so, they could not have re-fastened the sashes from the inside, as they were found fastened;—the consideration which put a stop, through its obviousness, to the scrutiny of the police in this quarter. Yet the sashes *were* fastened. They *must*, then, have the power of fastening themselves. There was no escape from this conclusion. I stepped to the unobstructed case-ment, withdrew the nail with some difficulty, and attempted to raise the sash. It resisted all my efforts, as I had anticipated. A concealed spring must, I now know, exist; and this corroboration of my idea convinced me that my premises, at least, were correct, however mysterious still appeared the circumstances attending the nails. A careful search soon brought to light the hidden spring. I pressed it, and, satisfied with the discovery, forbore to upraise the sash.

"I now replaced the nail and regarded it attentively. A person passing out through this window might have reclosed it, and the spring would have caught—but the nail could not have been re-placed. The conclusion was plain, and again narrowed in the field of my investigations. The assassins *must* have escaped through the other window. Supposing, then, the springs upon each sash to be the same, as was probable, there *must* be found a difference between the nails, or at least between the modes of their fixture. Getting upon the sacking of the bedstead, I looked over the head-board minutely at the second casement. Passing my hand down behind the board, I readily discovered and pressed the spring, which was, as I had sup-posed, identical in character with its neighbor. I now looked at the nail. It was as stout as the other, and apparently fitted in the same manner—driven in nearly up to the head.

"You will say that I was puzzled; but, if you think so, you must have misunderstood the nature of the inductions. To use a sporting phrase, I had not been once 'at fault.' The scent had never for an instant been lost. There was no flaw in any link of the chain. I had traced the secret to its ultimate result, —and that result was *the nail*. It had, I say, in every respect, the appearance of its fellow in the other window; but this fact was an absolute nullity (conclusive as it might seem to be) when compared with the consideration that here, at this point, terminated the clue. 'There *must* be something wrong,' I said, 'about the nail.' I touched it; and the head, with about a quarter of an inch of the shank, came off in my fingers. The rest of the shank was in the gimlet-hole where it had been broken off. The fracture was an old one (for its edges were incrusted with rust), and had apparently been accomplished by the blow of a hammer, which had partially imbedded, in the top of the bottom sash, the head portion of the nail. I now carefully replaced this head portion in the indentation whence I had taken it, and the resemblance to a perfect nail was complete—the fissure was invisible. Pressing the spring, I gently raised the sash for a few inches; the head went up with it, remaining firm in its bed. I closed the window, and the semblance of the whole nail was again perfect.

"The riddle, so far, was now unriddled. The assassin had escaped through the window which looked upon the bed. Dropping of its own accord upon his exit (or perhaps purposely closed), it had become fastened by the spring; and it was the retention of this spring which had been mistaken by the police for that of the nail, —farther inquiry being thus considered unnecessary.

"The next question is that of the mode of descent. Upon this point I had been satisfied in my walk with you around the building. About five feet and a half from the casement in question there runs a lightning-rod. From this rod it would have been impossible for any one to reach the window itself, to say nothing of entering it. I observed, however, that the shutters of the fourth story were of the peculiar kind called by Parisian carpenters *ferrades*—a kind rarely employed at the present day, but frequently seen upon very old mansions at Lyons and Bordeaux. They are in the form of an ordinary door, (a single, not a folding door), except that the lower half is latticed or worked in open trellis—thus affording an excellent hold for the hands. In the present instance these shutters are fully three feet and a half broad. When we saw them from the rear of the house, they were both about half open—that is to say, they stood off at right angles from the wall. It is probable that the police, as well as myself, examined the back of the tenement; but, if so, in looking at these *ferrades* in the line of their breadth (as they must have done), they did not perceive this great breadth itself, or, at all events, failed to take it into due consideration. In fact, having once satisfied themselves that no egress could have been made in this quarter, they would naturally bestow here a very cursory examination. It was clear to me, however, that the shutter belonging to the window at the head of the bed, would, if swung fully back to the wall, reach to within two feet of the lightning-rod. It was also evident that, by exertion of a very unusual degree of activity and courage, an entrance into the window, from the rod, might have been thus effected. By reaching to the distance of two feet and a half (we now suppose the shutter open to its whole extent) a robber might have taken a firm grasp upon the trellis-work. Letting go, then, his hold upon the rod, placing his feet securely against the wall, and springing boldly from it, he might have swung the shutter so as to close it, and, if we imagine the window open at the time, might even have swung himself into the room.

"I wish you to bear especially in mind that I have spoken of a *very* unusual degree of activity as requisite to success in so hazardous and so difficult a feat. It is my design to show you first, that the thing might possibly have been accomplished:—but, secondly and *chiefly,*

I wish to impress upon your understanding the *very extraordinary* — the almost praeternatural character of that agility which could have accomplished it.

"You will say, no doubt, using the language of the law, that to make out my case, I should rather undervalue, than insist upon a full estimation of the activity required in this matter. This may be the practice in law, but it is not the usage of reason. My ultimate object is only the truth. My immediate purpose is to lead you to place in juxtaposition, that *very unusual* activity of which I have just spoken with that *very peculiar* shrill (or harsh) and *unequal* voice, about whose nationality no two persons could be found to agree, and in whose utterance no syllabification could be detected."

At these words a vague and half-formed conception of the meaning of Dupin flitted over my mind. I seemed to be upon the verge of comprehension without power to comprehend — as men, at times, find themselves upon the brink of remembrance, without being able, in the end, to remember. My friend went on with his discourse.

"You will see," he said, "that I have shifted the question from the mode of egress to that of ingress. It was my design to convey the idea that both were effected in the same manner, at the same point. Let us now revert to the interior of the room. Let us survey the appearances here. The drawers of the bureau, it is said, had been rifled, although many articles of apparel still remained within them. The conclusion here is absurd. It is a mere guess — a very silly one — and no more. How are we to know that the articles found in the drawers were not all these drawers had originally contained? Madame L'Espanaye and her daughter lived an exceedingly retired life — saw no company — seldom went out — had little use for numerous changes of habiliment. Those found were at least of as good quality as any likely to be possessed by these ladies. If a thief had taken any, why did he not take the best — why did he not take all? In a word, why did he abandon four thousand francs in gold to encumber himself with a bundle of linen? The gold *was* abandoned. Nearly the whole sum mentioned by Monsieur Mignaud, the banker, was discovered, in bags, upon the floor. I wish you therefore, to discard from your thoughts the blundering idea of *motive*, engendered in the brains of the police by that portion of the evidence which speaks of money delivered at the door of the house. Coincidences ten times as remarkable as this (the delivery of the money, and murder committed within three days upon the party receiving it), happen to all of us every hour of our lives, without attracting even momentary notice. Coincidences, in general, are great stumbling-blocks in the way of that class of thinkers who have been educated to know nothing of the theory of probabilities — that theory to which the most glorious objects of human research are indebted for the most glorious of illustration. In the present instance, had the gold been gone, the fact of its delivery three days before would have formed something more than a coincidence. It would have been corroborative of this idea of motive. But, under the real circumstances of the case, if we are to suppose gold the motive of this outrage, we must also imagine the perpetrator so vacillating an idiot as to have abandoned his gold and his motive together.

"Keeping now steadily in mind the points to which I have drawn your attention — that peculiar voice, that unusual agility, and that startling absence of motive in a murder so singularly atrocious as this — let us glance at the butchery itself. Here is a woman strangled to death by manual strength, and thrust up a chimney, head downward. Ordinary assassins employ no such modes of murder as this. Least of all, do they thus dispose of the murdered. In the manner of thrusting the corpse up the chimney, you will admit that there was something *excessively outré* — something altogether irreconcilable with our common notions of human action, even when we suppose the actors the most depraved of men. Think, too, how great must have been that strength which could have thrust the body *up* such an aperture so forcibly that the united vigor of several persons was found barely sufficient to drag it *down*!

"Turn, now, to other indications of the employment of a vigor most marvellous. On the hearth were thick tresses—very thick tresses—of grey human hair. These had been torn out by the roots. You are aware of the great force necessary in tearing thus from the head even twenty or thirty hairs together. You saw the locks in question as well as myself. Their roots (a hideous sight!) were clotted with fragments of the flesh of the scalp—sure token of the prodigious power which had been exerted in uprooting perhaps half a million of hairs at a time. The throat of the old lady was not merely cut, but the head absolutely severed from the body: the instrument was a mere razor. I wish you also to look at the *brutal* ferocity of these deeds. Of the bruises upon the body of Madame L'Espanaye I do not speak. Monsieur Dumas, and his worthy coadjutor Monsieur Etienne, have pronounced that they were inflicted by some obtuse instrument; and so far these gentlemen are very correct. The obtuse instrument was clearly the stone pavement in the yard, upon which the victim had fallen from the window which looked in upon the bed. This idea, however simple it may now seem, escaped the police for the same reason that the breadth of the shutters escaped them—because, by the affair of the nails, their perceptions had been hermetically sealed against the possibility of the windows having ever been opened at all.

"If now, in addition to all these things, you have properly reflected upon the odd disorder of the chamber, we have gone so far as to combine the ideas of an agility astounding, a strength superhuman, a ferocity brutal, a butchery without motive, a *grotesquerie* in horror absolutely alien from humanity, and a voice foreign in tone to the ears of men of many nations, and devoid of all distinct or intelligible syllabification. What result, then, has ensued? What impression have I made upon your fancy?"

I felt a creeping of the flesh as Dupin asked me the question. "A madman," I said, "has done this deed — some raving maniac, escaped from a neighboring *Maison de Santé*."

"In some respects," he replied, "your idea is not irrelevant. But the voices of madmen, even in their wildest paroxysms, are never found to tally with that peculiar voice heard upon the stairs. Madmen are of some nation, and their language, however incoherent in its words, has always the coherence of syllabification. Besides, the hair of a madman is not such as I now hold in my hand. I disentangled this little tuft from the rigidly clutched fingers of Madame L'Espanaye. Tell me what you can make of it."

"Dupin!" I said, completely unnerved; "this hair is most unusual — this is no *human* hair."

"I have not asserted that it is," said he; "but before we decide this point, I wish you to glance at the little sketch I have here traced upon this paper. It is a *facsimile* drawing of what has been described in one portion of the testimony as 'dark bruises and deep indentations of finger nails,' upon the throat of Mademoiselle L'Espanaye, and in another, (by Messrs. Dumas and Etienne) as a 'series of livid spots, evidently the impression of fingers.' You will perceive," continued my friend, spreading out the paper upon the table before us, "that this drawing gives the idea of a firm and fixed hold. There is no *slipping* apparent. Each finger has retained — possibly until the death of the victim — the fearful grasp by which it originally imbedded itself. Attempt, now, to place all your fingers, at the same time, in the respective impressions as you see them."

I made the attempt in vain.

"We are possibly not giving this matter a fair trial," he said. "The paper is spread out upon a plane surface; but the human throat is cylindrical. Here is a billet of wood, the circumference of which is about that of the throat. Wrap the drawing around it, and try the experiment again."

I did so; but the difficulty was even more obvious than before. "This," I said, "is the mark of no human hand."

"Read now," replied Dupin, "this passage from Cuvier."

It was a minute anatomical and generally descriptive account of the large fulvous Ourang-Outang of the East Indian Islands. The gigantic stature, the prodigious strength and activity, the wild ferocity, and the imitative propensities of these mammalia are sufficiently well known to all. I understood the full horrors of the murder at once.

"The description of the digits," said I, as I made an end of reading, "is in exact accordance with this drawing. I see that no animal but an Ourang-Outang, of the species here mentioned, could have impressed the indentations as you have traced them. This tuft of tawny hair, too, is identical in character with that of the beast of Cuvier. But I cannot possibly comprehend the particulars of this frightful mystery. Besides, there were *two* voices heard in contention, and one of them was unquestionably the voice of a Frenchman."

"True; and you will remember an expression attributed almost unanimously, by the evidence, to this voice,—the expression, '*mon Dieu!*' This, under the circumstances, has been justly characterized by one of the witnesses (Montani, the confectioner) as an expression of remonstrance or expostulation. Upon these two words, therefore, I have mainly built my hopes of a full solution of the riddle. A Frenchman was cognizant of the murder. It is possible—indeed it is far more than probable—that he was innocent of all participation in the bloody transactions which took place. The Ourang-Outang may have escaped from him. He may have traced it to the chamber; but, under the agitating circumstances which ensued, he could never have re-captured it. It is still at large. I will not pursue these guesses—for I have no right to call them more—since the shades of reflection upon which they are based are scarcely of sufficient depth to be appreciable by my own intellect, and since I could not pretend to make them intelligible to the understanding of another. We will call them guesses, then, and speak of them as such. If the Frenchman in question is indeed, as I suppose, innocent of this atrocity, this advertisement, which I left last night, upon our return home, at the office of *Le Monde*, (a paper devoted to the shipping interest, and much sought by sailors), will bring him to our residence."

He handed me a paper, and I read thus:

Caught—In the Bois de Boulogne, early in the morning of the — inst.
(the morning of the murder), a very large, tawny Ourang-Outang
of the Bornese species. The owner (who is ascertained to be a sailor,
belonging to a Maltese vessel) may have the animal again, upon
identifying it satisfactorily, and paying a few charges arising from
its capture and keeping. Call at No. ——, Rue ——, Faubourg St.
Germain—au troisième.

"How was it possible," I asked, "that you should know the man to be a sailor, and belonging to a Maltese vessel?"

"I do *not* know it," said Dupin. "I am not *sure* of it. Here, however, is a small piece of ribbon, which from its form, and from its greasy appearance, has evidently been used in tying the hair in one of those long *queues* of which sailors are so fond. Moreover, this knot is one which few besides sailors can tie, and is peculiar to the Maltese. I picked the ribbon up at the foot of the lightning-rod. It could not have belonged to either of the deceased. Now if, after all, I am wrong in my induction from this ribbon, that the Frenchman was a sailor belonging to a Maltese vessel, still I can have done no harm in saying what I did in the advertisement. If I am in error, he will merely suppose that I have been misled by some circumstance into which he will not take the trouble to inquire. But if I am right, a great point is gained. Cognizant although innocent of the murder, the Frenchman will naturally hesitate about replying to the advertisement—about demanding the Ourang-Outang. He will reason thus:—'I am innocent; I am poor; my Ourang-Outang is of great value—to one in my circumstances a fortune of itself—why should I lose it through idle apprehensions of danger? Here it is, within my grasp. It was found in the Bois de Boulogne—at a vast distance from the scene of that butchery. How can it ever be suspected that a brute beast should have done the deed? The police are at fault—they have failed to procure the slightest clue. Should they even trace the animal, it would be impossible to prove me cognizant of the murder, or to implicate me in guilt on account of that cognizance. Above all, *I am known*. The advertiser designates me as the possessor of the beast. I am not sure to what limit his knowledge may extend. Should I avoid claiming a property of so great value, which it is known that I possess, I will render the animal at least, liable to suspicion. It is not my policy to attract attention either to myself or to the beast. I will answer the advertisement, get the Ourang-Outang, and keep it close until this matter has blown over.'"

At this moment we heard a step upon the stairs.

"Be ready," said Dupin, "with your pistols, but neither use them nor show them until at a signal from myself."

The front door of the house had been left open, and the visitor had entered, without ringing, and advanced several steps upon the staircase. Now, however, he seemed to hesitate. Presently we heard him descending. Dupin was moving quickly to the door, when we again heard him coming up. He did not turn back a second time, but stepped up with decision, and rapped at the door of our chamber.

"Come in," said Dupin, in a cheerful and hearty tone.

A man entered. He was a sailor, evidently,—a tall, stout, and muscular-looking person, with a certain dare-devil expression of countenance, not altogether unprepossessing. His face, greatly sunburnt, was more than half hidden by whisker and *mustachio*. He had with him a huge oaken cudgel, but appeared to be otherwise unarmed. He bowed awkwardly, and bade us "good evening," in French accents, which, although somewhat Neufchatelish, were still sufficiently indicative of a Parisian origin.

"Sit down, my friend," said Dupin. "I suppose you have called about the Ourang-Outang. Upon my word, I almost envy you the possession of him; a remarkably fine, and no doubt a very valuable animal. How old do you suppose him to be?"

The sailor drew a long breath, with the air of a man relieved of some intolerable burden, and then replied, in an assured tone:

"I have no way of telling—but he can't be more than four or five years old. Have you got him here?"

"Oh no; we had no conveniences for keeping him here. He is at a livery stable in the Rue Dubourg, just by. You can get him in the morning. Of course you are prepared to identify the property?"

"To be sure I am, sir."

"I shall be sorry to part with him," said Dupin.

"I don't mean that you should be at all this trouble for nothing, sir," said the man. "Couldn't expect it. Am very willing to pay a reward for the finding of the animal—that is to say, any thing in reason."

"Well," replied my friend, "that is all very fair, to be sure. Let me think!—what should I have? Oh! I will tell you. My reward shall be this. You shall give me all the information in your power about these murders in the Rue Morgue."

Dupin said the last words in a very low tone, and very quietly. Just as quietly, too, he walked toward the door, locked it, and put the key in his pocket. He then drew a pistol from his bosom and placed it, without the least flurry, upon the table.

The sailor's face flushed up as if he were struggling with suffocation. He started to his feet and grasped his cudgel; but the next moment he fell back into his seat, trembling violently, and with the countenance of death itself. He spoke not a word. I pitied him from the bottom of my heart.

"My friend," said Dupin, in a kind tone, "you are alarming your-self unnecessarily—you are indeed. We mean you no harm what-ever. I pledge you the honor of a gentleman, and of a Frenchman, that we intend you no injury. I perfectly well know that you are innocent of the atrocities in the Rue Morgue. It will not do, how-ever, to deny that you are in some measure implicated in them. From what I have already said, you must know that I have had means of information about this matter—means of which you could never have dreamed. Now the thing stands thus. You have done nothing which you could have avoided—nothing, certainly, which renders you culpable. You were not even guilty of robbery, when you might have robbed with impunity. You have nothing to conceal. You have no reason for concealment. On the other hand, you are bound by every principle of honor to confess all you know. An innocent man is now imprisoned, charged with that crime of which you can point out the perpetrator."

The sailor had recovered his presence of mind, in a great mea-sure, while Dupin uttered these words; but his original boldness of bearing was all gone.

"So help me God!" said he, after a brief pause, "I *will* tell you all I know about this affair;—but I do not expect you to believe one half I say—I would be a fool indeed if I did. Still, I *am* innocent, and I will make a clean breast if I die for it."

What he stated was, in substance, this. He had lately made a voyage to the Indian Archipelago. A party, of which he formed one, landed at Borneo, and passed into the interior on an excursion of pleasure. Himself and a companion had captured the Ourang-Outang. This companion dying, the animal fell into his own exclu-sive possession. After great trouble, occasioned by the intractable

ferocity of his captive during the home voyage, he at length succeeded in lodging it safely at his own residence in Paris, where, not
to attract toward himself the unpleasant curiosity of his neighbors,
he kept it carefully secluded, until such time as it should recover
from a wound in the foot, received from a splinter on board ship.
His ultimate design was to sell it.

Returning home from some sailors' frolic on the night, or rather
in the morning, of the murder, he found the beast occupying his own
bed-room, into which it had broken from a closet adjoining, where
it had been, as was thought, securely confined. Razor in hand, and
fully lathered, it was sitting before a looking-glass, attempting the
operation of shaving, in which it had no doubt previously watched
its master through the key-hole of the closet. Terrified at the sight
of so dangerous a weapon in the possession of an animal so fero-
cious, and so well able to use it, the man, for some moments, was at
a loss what to do. He had been accustomed, however, to quiet the
creature, even in its fiercest moods, by the use of a whip, and to this
he now resorted. Upon sight of it, the Ourang-Outang sprang at
once through the door of the chamber, down the stairs, and thence,
through a window, unfortunately open, into the street.

The Frenchman followed in despair; the ape, razor still in hand,
occasionally stopping to look back and gesticulate at its pursuer,
until the latter had nearly come up with it. It then again made off.
In this manner the chase continued for a long time. The streets were
profoundly quiet, as it was nearly three o'clock in the morning. In
passing down an alley in the rear of the Rue Morgue, the fugitive's
attention was arrested by a light gleaming from the open window
of Madame L'Espanaye's chamber, in the fourth story of her house.
Rushing to the building, it perceived the lightning rod, clambered
up with inconceivable agility, grasped the shutter, which was thrown
fully back against the wall, and, by its means, swung itself directly
upon the headboard of the bed. The whole feat did not occupy a

minute. The shutter was kicked open again by the Ourang-Outang as it entered the room.

The sailor, in the meantime, was both rejoiced and perplexed. He had strong hopes of now recapturing the brute, as it could scarcely escape from the trap into which it had ventured, except by the rod, where it might be intercepted as it came down. On the other hand, there was much cause for anxiety as to what it might do in the house. This latter reflection urged the man still to follow the fugitive. A lightning-rod is ascended without difficulty, especially by a sailor; but, when he had arrived as high as the window, which lay far to his left, his career was stopped; the most that he could accomplish was to reach over so as to obtain a glimpse of the interior of the room. At this glimpse he nearly fell from his hold through excess of horror. Now it was that those hideous shrieks arose upon the night, which had startled from slumber the inmates of the Rue Morgue. Madame L'Espanaye and her daughter, habited in their night clothes, had apparently been occupied in arranging some papers in the iron chest already mentioned, which had been wheeled into the middle of the room. It was open, and its contents lay beside it on the floor. The victims must have been sitting with their backs toward the window; and, from the time elapsing between the ingress of the beast and the screams, it seems probable that it was not immediately perceived. The flapping-to of the shutter would naturally have been attributed to the wind.

As the sailor looked in, the gigantic animal had seized Madame L'Espanaye by the hair, (which was loose, as she had been combing it), and was flourishing the razor about her face, in imitation of the motions of a barber. The daughter lay prostrate and motionless; she had swooned. The screams and struggles of the old lady (during which the hair was torn from her head) had the effect of changing the probably pacific purposes of the Ourang-Outang into those of wrath. With one determined sweep of its muscular arm it nearly severed her head from her body. The sight of blood inflamed its anger into phrenzy. Gnashing its teeth, and flashing fire from its eyes, it flew upon the body of the girl, and imbedded its fearful talons in her throat, retaining its grasp until she expired. Its wandering and wild glances fell at this moment upon the head of the bed, over which the face of its master, rigid with horror, was just discernible. The fury of the beast, who no doubt bore still in mind the dreaded whip, was instantly converted into fear. Conscious of having deserved punishment, it seemed desirous of concealing its bloody deeds, and skipped about the chamber in an agony of nervous agitation; throwing down and breaking the furniture as it moved, and dragging the bed from the bedstead. In conclusion, it seized first the corpse of the daughter, and thrust it up the chimney, as it was found; then that of the old lady, which it immediately hurled through the window headlong.

As the ape approached the casement with its mutilated burden, the sailor shrank aghast to the rod, and, rather gliding than clambering down it, hurried at once home — dreading the consequences of the butchery, and gladly abandoning, in his terror, all solicitude about the fate of the Ourang-Outang. The words heard by the party upon the staircase were the Frenchman's exclamations of horror and affright, commingled with the fiendish jabberings of the brute.

I have scarcely anything to add. The Ourang-Outang must have escaped from the chamber, by the rod, just before the break of the door. It must have closed the window as it passed through it. It was subsequently caught by the owner himself, who obtained for it a very large sum at the *Jardin des Plantes*. Le Bon was instantly released, upon our narration of the circumstances (with some comments from Dupin) at the *bureau* of the Prefect of Police. This functionary, however well disposed to my friend, could not altogether conceal his chagrin at the turn which affairs had taken, and was fain to indulge in a sarcasm or two, about the propriety of every person minding his own business.

"Let him talk," said Dupin, who had not thought it necessary to reply. "Let him discourse; it will ease his conscience. I am satisfied with having defeated him in his own castle. Nevertheless, that he failed in the solution of this mystery, is by no means that matter for wonder which he supposes it; for, in truth, our friend the Prefect is somewhat too cunning to be profound. In his wisdom is no *stamen*. It is all head and no body, like the pictures of the Goddess Laverna—or, at best, all head and shoulders, like a codfish. But he is a good creature after all. I like him especially for one master stroke of cant, by which he has attained his reputation for ingenuity. I mean the way he has '*de nier ce qui est, et d'expliquer ce qui n'est pas.*'"

The Quick and the Undead

. . . . . .

BY NELSON DEMILLE

So much commentary has been written about Edgar Allan Poe over the last century and a half that it seems unnecessary to add more. Unless, of course, one has something new to say, which is unlikely, though that's never stopped academic writers.

This is my way of saying that I'm not going to try to outshine the Poe scholars who delve deep into the mind and writings of Edgar Allan Poe and who allude to Jung, Freud, and the collective un-consciousness. Not to mention mythopoeic inevitability. Instead, I'm going to fall back on the safety of a personal narrative, which recounts my introduction to Edgar Allan Poe.

This story begins in 1954 when I was eleven years old, so if the details seem fuzzy, you'll understand.

Three-D movies were big in the mid-1950s, and I made it a point not to miss any of them, no matter how badly they'd been reviewed by my peers who'd scraped up the twenty-five cents before I did. In 1954 the hot 3-D movie that everyone was raving about was *Phantom of the Rue Morgue*. I didn't know what a rue morgue was, but I did know that *The Phantom* was a good comic strip. I'd also never heard of Edgar Allan Poe, and I didn't know that Poe's short story, upon which the movie was loosely based, had been titled "The Murders in the Rue Morgue." That was irrelevant to me, and apparently, also to Hollywood. In any case, my classmates who'd seen the movie set me straight on the meaning of the title (a rue is like a street) and gave the movie a solid rating of "piss your pants."

I grew up in Elmont, a small community on Long Island, New York, which consisted mostly of postwar housing tracts. Within this community was a new movie theater within walking distance of my house, which in those days meant two miles. Lying between the theater and my house was—spooky music, please—a cemetery. But this was not the kind of horror-flick churchyard cemetery that I associated with ghosts, ghouls, zombies, werewolves, vampires, or any other species of the living dead; this was a nice Jewish cemetery, and who ever heard of a Jewish vampire? The cemetery, Beth David by name, actually bordered the backyard of my house, and lying as it did in the center of the town, it was a good shortcut to and from a lot of places, including the movie theater.

I had lived peacefully with this cemetery since we'd moved into the house, about six or seven years before, and from my second-floor bedroom window I could see the neat green acres of Beth David and rows and rows of polished granite tombstones. During the day the cemetery was filled with funeral processions, workers, and visitors, and my only fear in crossing this burial ground was the possibility of getting chased by the cemetery guards who patrolled in marked cars. I never got caught, and years later I became the star sprinter (one-hundred-yard dash in ten flat) of the Elmont Memorial High School track team.

My only experience with the cemetery at night was to stare at it now and then from my bedroom window. In five or six years of look- ing, I never once saw anything come out of a grave, or move that shouldn't move; the trees moved in the wind, the headlights of patrol cars moved on the roads. That was about it. So my proximity to, and trespassing in, the cemetery in my backyard made it a familiar place that held no terrors for me and caused no childhood mental trauma that needed to be addressed, then or now.

Except for that one time when I took the shortcut through the cemetery following a late-Saturday-afternoon showing of *Phantom of the Rue Morgue* in 3-D color.

The movie, by today's standards, would barely raise a hair on the back of anyone's neck. But in 1954, when you're eleven, weird makeup, creepy music, and blood-splatter patterns can easily send you sprinting up the aisle to the popcorn stand.

A quick Internet search of Edgar Allan Poe filmography informs me that Karl Malden, before he learned how to act, played the part of the Rue Morgue mad scientist, Dr. Marais. Logging in a better performance was a trained gorilla, whose name is lost to cinema history, and also Merv Griffin, of all people, who played a French medical student. I remember the mad scientist and the gorilla, but not Merv. The plot, such as it is, is simple: Dr. Marais uses the gorilla to exact revenge on various beautiful women who have spurned him. Each of these ladies has been given a jingling bracelet that attracts the killer gorilla. I know you want more of this plot, but I don't want to spoil your next Netflix selection. Suffice it to say, whenever these young ladies walk along a street, alone, at night, the tinkling bracelet is heard by the sharp-eared, preprogrammed gorilla. Why no one notices this gorilla is not something to be examined too closely; I never gave it much thought myself, and neither did the adults who made the movie. We're talking here of a *major* suspension of disbelief, and kids are good at that. Kids are also good at Pavlovian response and getting themselves scared out of their susceptible little minds, so when those pretty ladies jangled their bracelets, the movie theater let out a collective gasp and a few involuntary squeals. The future do-gooders among the mostly preadolescent crowd yelled out warnings to the strutting tarts.

The *really* scary parts of the movie, however, were the 3-D shock effects. You just never knew when something was going to hurtle at you from the screen, and if you can remember this, you'll verify that literally the entire audience in a 3-D shocker screamed and ducked. I mean, popcorn flying, Cokes splashing, and 3-D glasses being ripped from faces by the G-forces created by rapidly moving heads, arms, and bodies.

Bottom line on *Phantom of the Rue Morgue* is, it sucked. But it *was* scary.

It was fall or maybe winter, and by the time I and a few friends left the theater about 5:00 P.M., it was getting dark. The rule was, "Get home as soon as the streetlights come on." They'd come on, and I was late. My cell phone hadn't been invented yet, and the pay phone on the corner cost a nickel, or maybe a dime, and no one wanted to splurge on that just to say we were alive and running late. We mostly walked or biked wherever we went, and the concept of a parent coming to pick us up was not part of the zeitgeist of that simpler, safer, and unpampered age. Our parents had taught us well: however you got there, get back the same way.

Well, I'd walked to the movie theater, and now I had to walk home.

From the corner of Elmont Road and Hempstead Turnpike, where the theater was, it was about two miles, if I took the circuitous street route. However, if I took the direct route through the cemetery . . .

Two of the three guys I was with lived in the opposite direction, so the cemetery was not part of their plan. But the third guy—who I'll call Jack so as not to embarrass him a half century later or call into question the size of his developing cojones—lived down the block from me, so quite naturally I thought I'd have company on my quick trip through the land of the living dead. Jack, however, had other ideas and informed me that he'd rather be late for dinner than *be* dinner for a werewolf.

I should have followed his line of reasoning, but I was in the early stages of mastering the art of the bad decision—really nothing more than macho recklessness—that would later reach its crowning stupidity when I quit college, joined the Army, and volunteered for Vietnam.

At this point in my life, however, I really wanted company on my road toward discovering the limits of my courage and idiocy, so I said to Jack, "You're a chicken!"

"Am not!"

"Chicken, chicken!" And I imitated a chicken.

Today, Jack would tell me to go f**k myself, but I think he replied, "Ah, you're nuts!" and ran off toward the safety of home along lighted streets, slowing only long enough to turn and deliver a Parthian shot. "You're gonna diiiie!"

Of course, I should have reconsidered my route home and sprinted after him, and when I caught up with him, I could have pushed him on his face, then challenged him to a race home. But the idea I held on to was to cut about half a mile or more off my route and beat him home, stopping only long enough to ring his bell and tell his parents that Jack had stopped at the candy store to gorge on Snickers before dinner.

My other motivation for the cemetery route was less spiteful; I needed to get home as soon after the streetlight curfew as possible. I wasn't sure what would happen if I didn't, and I didn't want to find out.

I crossed Elmont Road and ran along the sidewalk that bordered the cemetery, which was enclosed by a wrought-iron fence about eight feet high, posted at intervals with signs that said KEEP OUT.

The streetlights always came on before it was really dark, so there was some light left in the sky, but it was fading fast. A half mile up ahead were the main gates and the guard booth of the cemetery, and I needed to scale the fence well before I reached the gates in order to benefit from the most direct route, which I'd used many times in the daylight. So, without giving it much thought, I scrambled up the wrought-iron fence and dropped into Beth David Cemetery.

I knelt, motionless, listening for any sign that I'd been seen or heard. I gave it ten seconds, then I was up and running.

It was fun at first. I stuck to the rows between the gravestones, avoiding the roads, which were patrolled by guard vehicles. I needed to cover about a mile and a half, and at the speed I was moving, I could do that in less than fifteen minutes. One time I did it in under twelve minutes. In the daylight.

The obvious problem was the sinking sun, and I found it was becoming more difficult to see. I spotted a few freshly dug open graves, covered only by green tarps, awaiting occupants, and I didn't want to fall into one of those six-foot holes. So I slowed up, cursed Jack, and within a few minutes realized I was disoriented. In fact, I was f**king lost.

It was almost pitch-dark now, and I couldn't recognize any landmarks. It was also cold, and I wished I'd taken my mother's advice about wearing a hat.

To cut to the chase, I was becoming frightened. I mean, *really, really* scared. Everybody in that place, except for me and a few guards, was dead. Or undead.

Because it was such an open space, there was a wind that I hadn't noticed back on the road, and the wind was making things move—tree limbs, dead leaves, litter, and the white shrouds that cover Jewish tombstones until the day of unveiling. And along with these movements came sounds and shadows that startled me every few seconds.

To make matters worse, if that were possible, I now heard something I'd never heard before in the cemetery—dogs.

The guards had one or two dogs, but these dogs that I heard were not those well-trained guard animals; these were wild dogs, and a lot of them, baying and barking into the black night. Or were they werewolves?

I mean, if you still believe in Santa Claus at age eleven, and you believe in good fairies, then it stands to reason that you will also believe in ghosts, witches, warlocks, werewolves, vampires, zombies, and flesh-eating ghouls, and if you're particularly gullible, killer mummies.

I could stretch things here and say I had visions of the killer gorilla and the creepy Dr. Marais, but I really didn't; those guys were wimps compared to the undead. I was, however, pre-spooked by the 3-D shock effects, and my spine had tingled about ten times already in the movie theater. So whatever it is in our psyches that causes us to become frightened by a horror flick, this feeling stays with us for a while, and when we go to bed, we pull the sheets over our heads and listen for vampires trying to get in the window or zombies banging on the door.

This, in retrospect, may have been why my imagination was running wild in the cemetery and why I froze with fear as I crouched in the dark, listening to the wind blowing between the tombstones and the dogs, or werewolves, barking in the distance.

So, quick segue to Edgar Allan Poe, master of the macabre, manipulator of our minds, and a very elegant writer. Long before the study of the mind became a quasi-scientific discipline, Poe was able to grasp what frightened us, and he transformed that understanding into spooky and entertaining tales that were far ahead of their time and which have endured through the nineteenth and twentieth centuries and into the twenty-first—which is more than I can say about that 3-D schlocker shocker I saw fifty years ago.

You could analyze this guy to death, and people have—and maybe Poe had that coming—but in the final non-analysis, just read this extraordinary writer, enjoy his prose with a glass of sherry, and read aloud the poetry—especially "The Raven"—to some kid in a dimly lit room. Don't forget the sound effects.

Cut to Beth David Cemetery, 1954, exterior, evening.

A calm, fatalistic sensation passed over me. I knew I was going to die, and I'd accepted that. I just wasn't sure if I was going to get eaten by dogs or werewolves. I wasn't thinking much about the killer gorilla, though somewhere in the back of my mind I could still see him jumping at me out of the movie screen.

I stood and began walking toward my Fate, wondering what I had missed for dinner.

Eventually, I came across a familiar road, and I allowed myself a small glimmer of hope. I pointed myself in the right direction and ran like hell. I could see house lights now, and I knew I was less than a minute from the chain-link fence that separated the living from the dead.

I honestly don't even remember climbing the fence; I think I ran up it. Then I remember being in someone's backyard and dashing down their driveway, then running on the sidewalk, then home.

My mother said, "Jack's mother called and said you were cutting through the cemetery. We were worried."

I replied, "It's a *shortcut,* Mom."

My father said, "Don't cut through the cemetery again." He explained, "The ghosts come out at night."

Thanks, Pop. I'll remember that.

Nelson DeMille was born in New York City but grew up next door to a cemetery on Long Island. He spent four undistinguished years at Hofstra University, where he was introduced to the works of Edgar Allan Poe (Cliff Notes) and was inspired by Poe to excessive drinking and growing a weird beard and mustache. DeMille is the author of fourteen best-selling novels, a member of the Authors Guild, and maybe a member of PEN and Poets & Writers, though he's not sure. He was president of the Mystery Writers of America in 2007 and served without mishap.

The Gold-Bug

What ho! what ho! this fellow is dancing mad!
He hath been bitten by the Tarantula.

—ALL IN THE WRONG

MANY YEARS AGO, I contracted an intimacy with a Mr. William Legrand. He was of an ancient Huguenot family, and had once been wealthy; but a series of misfortunes had reduced him to want. To avoid the mortification consequent upon his disasters, he left New Orleans, the city of his forefathers, and took up his residence at Sullivan's Island, near Charleston, South Carolina.

This island is a very singular one. It consists of little else than the sea sand, and is about three miles long. Its breadth at no point exceeds a quarter of a mile. It is separated from the mainland by a scarcely perceptible creek, oozing its way through a wilderness of reeds and slime, a favorite resort of the marsh-hen. The vegetation, as might be supposed, is scant, or at least dwarfish. No trees of any magnitude are to be seen. Near the western extremity, where Fort Moultrie stands, and where are some miserable frame buildings, tenanted, during summer, by the fugitives from Charleston dust and fever, may be found, indeed, the bristly palmetto; but the whole island, with the exception of this western point, and a line of hard, white beach on the sea-coast, is covered with a dense undergrowth of the sweet myrtle so much prized by the horticulturists of England. The shrub here often attains the height of fifteen or twenty feet, and forms an almost impenetrable coppice, burthening the air with its fragrance.

In the inmost recesses of this coppice, not far from the eastern or more remote end of the island, Legrand had built himself a small hut, which he occupied when I first, by mere accident, made his acquaintance. This soon ripened into friendship—for there was much in the recluse to excite interest and esteem. I found him well educated, with unusual powers of mind, but infected with misanthropy, and subject to perverse moods of alternate enthusiasm and melancholy. He had with him many books, but rarely employed them. His chief amusements were gunning and fishing, or sauntering along the beach and through the myrtles, in quest of shells or entomological specimens—his collection of the latter might have been envied by a Swammerdamm. In these excursions he was usually accompanied by an old negro, called Jupiter, who had been manumitted before the reverses of the family, but who could be induced, neither by threats nor by promises, to abandon what he considered his right of attendance upon the footsteps of his young "Massa Will." It is not improbable that the relatives of Legrand, conceiving him to be somewhat unsettled in intellect, had contrived to instill this obstinacy into Jupiter, with a view to the supervision and guardianship of the wanderer.

The winters in the latitude of Sullivan's Island are seldom very severe, and in the fall of the year it is a rare event indeed when a fire is considered necessary. About the middle of October, 18—, there occurred, however, a day of remarkable chilliness. Just before sunset I scrambled my way through the evergreens to the hut of my friend, whom I had not visited for several weeks—my residence being, at that time, in Charleston, a distance of nine miles from the island, while the facilities of passage and re-passage were very far behind those of the present day. Upon reaching the hut I rapped, as was my custom, and getting no reply, sought for the key where I knew it was secreted, unlocked the door, and went in. A fine fire was blazing upon the hearth. It was a novelty, and by no means an ungrateful one. I threw off an overcoat, took an arm-chair by the crackling logs, and awaited patiently the arrival of my hosts.

Soon after dark they arrived, and gave me a most cordial welcome. Jupiter, grinning from ear to ear, bustled about to prepare some marsh-hens for supper. Legrand was in one of his fits—how else shall I term them?—of enthusiasm. He had found an unknown bivalve, forming a new genus, and, more than this, he had hunted down and secured with Jupiter's assistance, a *scarabaeus* which he believed to be totally new, but in respect to which he wished to have my opinion on the morrow.

"And why not to-night?" I asked, rubbing my hands over the blaze, and wishing the whole tribe of *scarabaei* at the devil.

"Ah, if I had only known you were here!" said Legrand, "but it's so long since I saw you; and how could I foresee that you would pay me a visit this very night of all others? As I was coming home I met Lieutenant G——, from the fort, and, very foolishly, I lent him the bug; so it will be impossible for you to see it until the morning. Stay here to-night, and I will send Jup down for it at sunrise. It is the loveliest thing in creation!"

"What?—sunrise?"

"Nonsense! no!—the bug. It is of a brilliant gold color—about the size of a large hickory-nut—with two jet black spots near one extremity of the back, and another, somewhat longer, at the other. The *antennae* are—"

"Dey ain't *no* tin in him, Massa Will, I keep a tellin' on you," here interrupted Jupiter; "de bug is a goole-bug, solid, ebery bit of him, inside and all, sep him wing—neber feel half so hebby a bug in my life."

"Well, suppose it is, Jup," replied Legrand, somewhat more earnestly, it seemed to me, than the case demanded; "is that any reason for your letting the birds burn? The color"—here he turned to me—"is really almost enough to warrant Jupiter's idea. You never saw a more brilliant metallic luster than the scales emit—but of this you cannot judge till to-morrow. In the meantime I can give you some idea of the shape." Saying this, he seated himself at a small table, on which were a pen and ink, but no paper. He looked for some in a drawer, but found none.

"Never mind," he said at length, "this will answer"; and he drew from his waistcoat pocket a scrap of what I took to be very dirty foolscap, and made upon it a rough drawing with the pen. While he did this, I retained my seat by the fire, for I was still chilly. When the design was complete, he handed it to me without rising. As I received it, a loud growl was heard, succeeded by a scratching at the door. Jupiter opened it, and a large Newfoundland, belonging to Legrand, rushed in, leaped upon my shoulders, and loaded me with caresses; for I had shown him much attention during previous visits. When his gambols were over, I looked at the paper, and, to speak the truth, found myself not a little puzzled at what my friend had depicted.

"Well!" I said, after contemplating it for some minutes, "this *is* a strange *scarabaeus*, I must confess; new to me; never saw any thing like it before—unless it was a skull, or a death's-head, which it more

nearly resembles than any thing else that has come under *my* observation."

"A death's-head!" echoed Legrand. "Oh—yes—well, it has something of that appearance upon paper, no doubt. The two upper black
spots look like eyes, eh? and the longer one at the bottom like a
mouth—and then the shape of the whole is oval."

"Perhaps so," said I; "but, Legrand, I fear you are no artist. I
must wait until I see the beetle itself, if I am to form any idea of its
personal appearance."

"Well, I don't know," said he, a little nettled, "I draw tolerably—
should do it at least—have had good masters, and flatter myself that
I am not quite a blockhead."

"But, my dear fellow, you are joking then," said I, "this is a very
passable *skull*—indeed, I may say that it is a very *excellent* skull, according to the vulgar notions about such specimens of physiology—
and your *scarabaeus* must be the queerest *scarabaeus* in the world if it
resembles it. Why, we may get up a very thrilling bit of superstition
upon this hint. I presume you will call the bug *scarabaeus caput homi-
nis*, or something of that kind—there are many similar titles in the
Natural Histories. But where are the *antennae* you spoke of?"

"The *antennae*!" said Legrand, who seemed to be getting unaccountably warm upon the subject; "I am sure you must see the *antennae*. I made them as distinct as they are in the original insect, and I
presume that is sufficient."

"Well, well," I said, "perhaps you have—still I don't see them";
and I handed him the paper without additional remark, not wishing to ruffle his temper; but I was much surprised at the turn affairs had taken; his ill humor puzzled me—and, as for the drawing
of the beetle, there were positively *no antennae* visible, and the
whole *did* bear a very close resemblance to the ordinary cuts of a
death's-head.

He received the paper very peevishly, and was about to crumple it, apparently to throw it in the fire, when a casual glance at the design seemed suddenly to rivet his attention. In an instant his face grew violently red—in another as excessively pale. For some minutes he continued to scrutinize the drawing minutely where he sat. At length he arose, took a candle from the table, and proceeded to seat himself upon a sea-chest in the farthest corner of the room. Here again he made an anxious examination of the paper; turning it in all directions. He said nothing, however, and his conduct greatly astonished me; yet I thought it prudent not to exacerbate the growing moodiness of his temper by any comment. Presently he took from his coat-pocket a wallet, placed the paper carefully in it, and deposited both in a writing-desk, which he locked. He now grew more composed in his demeanor; but his original air of enthusiasm had quite disappeared. Yet he seemed not so much sulky as abstracted. As the evening wore away he became more and more absorbed in revery, from which no sallies of mine could arouse him. It had been my intention to pass the night at the hut, as I had frequently done before, but, seeing my host in this mood, I deemed it proper to take leave. He did not press me to remain, but, as I departed, he shook my hand with even more than his usual cordiality.

It was about a month after this (and during the interval I had seen nothing of Legrand) when I received a visit, at Charleston, from his man, Jupiter. I had never seen the good old negro look so dispirited, and I feared that some serious disaster had befallen my friend.

"Well, Jup," said I, "what is the matter now?—how is your master?"

"Why, to speak de troof, massa, him not so berry well as mought be."

"Not well! I am truly sorry to hear it. What does he complain of?"

"Dar! dat's it!—him neber 'plain of notin'—but him berry sick for all dat."

"*Very* sick, Jupiter!—why didn't you say so at once? Is he confined to bed?"

"No, dat he aint!—he aint 'fin'd nowhar—dat's just whar de shoe pinch—my mind is got to be berry hebby 'bout poor Massa Will."

"Jupiter, I should like to understand what it is you are talking about. You say your master is sick. Hasn't he told you what ails him?"

"Why, massa, 'taint worf while for to git mad about de matter—Massa Will say noffin at all aint de matter wid him—but den what make him go about looking dis here way, wid he head down and he soldiers up, and as white as a goose? And den he keep a syphon all de time—"

"Keeps a what, Jupiter?"

"Keeps a syphon wid de figgurs on de slate—de queerest figgurs I ebber did see. Ise gittin' to be skeered, I tell you. Hab for to keep mighty tight eye 'pon him 'noovers. Todder day he gib me slip 'fore de sun up and was gone de whole ob de blessed day. I had a big stick ready cut for to gib him deuced good beating when he did come—but Ise sich a fool dat I hadn't de heart arter all—he looked so berry poorly."

"Eh?—what?—ah yes!—upon the whole I think you had better not be too severe with the poor fellow—don't flog him, Jupiter—he can't very well stand it—but can you form no idea of what has occasioned this illness, or rather this change of conduct? Has any thing unpleasant happened since I saw you?"

"No, massa, dey aint bin noffin onpleasant *since* den—'twas '*fore* den I'm feared—'twas de berry day you was dare."

"How? what do you mean."

"Why, massa, I mean de bug—dare now."

"The what?"

"De bug—I'm berry sartain dat Massa Will bin bit somewhere 'bout de head by dat goole-bug."

"And what cause have you, Jupiter, for such a supposition?"

"Claws enuff, massa, and mouff too. I nebber did see sich a deuced bug—he kick and he bite ebery ting what cum near him. Massa Will cotch him fuss, but had for to let him go 'gin mighty quick, I tell you—den was de time he must ha' got de bite. I didn't like de look ob de bug mouff, myself, nohow, so I wouldn't take hold ob him wid my finger, but I cotch him wid a piece ob paper dat I found. I rap him up in de paper and stuff a piece of it in he mouff—dat was de way."

"And you think, then, that your master was really bitten by the beetle, and that the bite made him sick?"

"I don't think noffin' about it—I nose it. What make him dream 'bout de goole so much, if 'taint cause he bit by the goole-bug? Ise heerd 'bout dem goole-bugs 'fore dis."

"But how do you know he dreams about gold?"

"How I know? why, 'cause he talk about it in he sleep—dat's how I nose."

"Well, Jup, perhaps you are right; but to what fortunate circumstance am I to attribute the honor of a visit from you to-day?"

"What de matter, massa?"

"Did you bring any message from Mr. Legrand?"

"No, massa, I bring dis here pissel"; and here Jupiter handed me a note which ran thus:

MY DEAR ——

Why have I not seen you for so long a time? I hope you have not been so foolish as to take offense at any little brusquerie *of mine; but no, that is improbable.*

Since I saw you I have had great cause for anxiety. I have something to tell you, yet scarcely know how to tell it, or whether I should tell it at all.

I have not been quite well for some days past, and poor old Jup annoys me, almost beyond endurance, by his well-meant attentions. Would you believe it?—he had prepared a huge stick, the other day, with which to chastise me for giving him the slip, and spending the day, solus, among the hills on the main-land. I verily believe that my ill looks alone saved me a flogging.

I have made no addition to my cabinet since we met.

If you can, in any way, make it convenient, come over with Jupiter. Do come. I wish to see you to-night, upon business of importance. I assure you that it is of the highest importance.

Ever yours,
WILLIAM LEGRAND

There was something in the tone of this note which gave me great uneasiness. Its whole style differed materially from that of Legrand. What could he be dreaming of? What new crotchet possessed his excitable brain? What "business of the highest importance" could *he* possibly have to transact? Jupiter's account of him boded no good. I dreaded lest the continued pressure of misfortune had, at length, fairly unsettled the reason of my friend. Without a moment's hesitation, therefore, I prepared to accompany the negro.

Upon reaching the wharf, I noticed a scythe and three spades, all apparently new, lying in the bottom of the boat in which we were to embark.

"What is the meaning of all this, Jup?" I inquired.

"Him syfe, massa, and spade."

"Very true; but what are they doing here?"

"Him de syfe and de spade what Massa Will sis 'pon my buying for him in de town, and de debbil's own lot of money I had to gib for 'em."

"But what, in the name of all that is mysterious, is your 'Massa Will' going to do with scythes and spades?"

"Dat's more dan *I* know, and debbil take me if I don't b'lieve 'tis more dan he know too. But it's all cum ob de bug."

Finding that no satisfaction was to be obtained of Jupiter, whose whole intellect seemed to be absorbed by "de bug," I now stepped into the boat, and made sail. With a fair and strong breeze we soon ran into the little cove to the northward of Fort Moultrie, and a walk of some two miles brought us to the hut. It was about three in the afternoon when we arrived. Legrand had been waiting us in eager expectation. He grasped my hand with a nervous *empressement* which alarmed me and strengthened the suspicions already entertained. His countenance was pale even to ghastliness, and his deep-set eyes glared with unnatural luster. After some inquiries respecting his health, I asked him, not knowing what better to say, if he had yet obtained the *scarabaeus* from Lieutenant G——.

"Oh, yes," he replied, coloring violently, "I got it from him the next morning. Nothing should tempt me to part with that *scarabaeus*. Do you know that Jupiter is quite right about it?"

"In what way?" I asked, with a sad foreboding at heart.

"In supposing it to be a bug of *real gold*." He said this with an air of profound seriousness, and I felt inexpressibly shocked.

"This bug is to make my fortune," he continued, with a triumphant smile; "to reinstate me in my family possessions. Is it any wonder, then, that I prize it? Since Fortune has thought fit to bestow it upon me, I have only to use it properly, and I shall arrive at the gold of which it is the index. Jupiter, bring me that *scarabaeus*!"

"What! de bug, massa? I'd rudder not go fer trubble dat bug; you mus' git him for your own self." Hereupon Legrand arose, with a grave and stately air, and brought me the beetle from a glass case in which it was enclosed. It was a beautiful *scarabaeus*, and, at that time, unknown to naturalists—of course a great prize in a scientific point of view. There were two round black spots near one extremity of the back, and a long one near the other. The scales were exceedingly hard and glossy, with all the appearance of burnished gold. The weight of the insect was very remarkable, and, taking all things into consideration, I could hardly blame Jupiter for his opinion respecting it; but what to make of Legrand's concordance with that opinion, I could not, for the life of me, tell.

"I sent for you," said he, in a grandiloquent tone, when I had completed my examination of the beetle, "I sent for you that I might have your counsel and assistance in furthering the views of Fate and of the bug—"

"My dear Legrand," I cried, interrupting him, "you are certainly unwell, and had better use some little precautions. You shall go to bed, and I will remain with you a few days, until you get over this. You are feverish and—"

"Feel my pulse," said he.

I felt it, and, to say the truth, found not the slightest indication of fever.

"But you may be ill and yet have no fever. Allow me this once to prescribe for you. In the first place go to bed. In the next—"

"You are mistaken," he interposed, "I am as well as I can expect to be under the excitement which I suffer. If you really wish me well, you will relieve this excitement."

"And how is this to be done?"

"Very easily. Jupiter and myself are going upon an expedition into the hills, upon the main-land, and, in this expedition, we shall need the aid of some person in whom we can confide. You are the only one we can trust. Whether we succeed or fail, the excitement which you now perceive in me will be equally allayed."

"I am anxious to oblige you in any way," I replied; "but do you mean to say that this infernal beetle has any connection with your expedition into the hills?"

"It has."

"Then, Legrand, I can become a party to no such absurd proceeding."

"I am sorry—very sorry—for we shall have to try it by ourselves."

"Try it by yourselves! The man is surely mad!—but stay!—how long do you propose to be absent?"

"Probably all night. We shall start immediately, and be back, at all events, by sunrise."

"And will you promise me, upon your honor, that when this freak of yours is over, and the bug business (good God!) settled to your satisfaction, you will then return home and follow my advice implicitly, as that of your physician?"

"Yes; I promise; and now let us be off, for we have no time to lose."

With a heavy heart I accompanied my friend. We started about four o'clock—Legrand, Jupiter, the dog, and myself. Jupiter had with him the scythe and spades—the whole of which he insisted upon carrying—more through fear, it seemed to me, of trusting either of the implements within reach of his master, than from any excess of industry or complaisance. His demeanor was dogged in the extreme, and "dat deuced bug" were the sole words which escaped his lips during the journey. For my own part, I had charge of a couple of dark lanterns, while Legrand contented himself with the *scarabaeus*, which he carried attached to the end of a bit of whipcord; twirling it to and fro, with the air of a conjurer, as he went. When I observed this last, plain evidence of my friend's aberration of mind, I could scarcely refrain from tears. I thought it best, however, to humor his fancy, at least for the present, or until I could adopt some more energetic measures with a chance of success. In the meantime I endeavored, but all in vain, to sound him in regard to the object of the expedition. Having succeeded in inducing me to accompany him, he seemed unwilling to hold conversation upon any topic of minor importance, and to all my questions vouchsafed no other reply than "we shall see!"

We crossed the creek at the head of the island by means of a skiff, and, ascending the high grounds on the shore of the mainland, proceeded in a northwesterly direction, through a tract of country excessively wild and desolate, where no trace of a human footstep was to be seen. Legrand led the way with decision; pausing only for an instant, here and there, to consult what appeared to be certain landmarks of his own contrivance upon a former occasion.

In this manner we journeyed for about two hours, and the sun was just setting when we entered a region infinitely more dreary than any yet seen. It was a species of table-land, near the summit of an almost inaccessible hill, densely wooded from base to pinnacle, and interspersed with huge crags that appeared to lie loosely upon the soil, and in many cases were prevented from precipitating themselves into the valleys below, merely by the support of the trees against which they reclined. Deep ravines, in various directions, gave an air of still sterner solemnity to the scene.

The natural platform to which we had clambered was thickly overgrown with brambles, through which we soon discovered that it would have been impossible to force our way but for the scythe; and Jupiter, by direction of his master, proceeded to clear for us a path to the foot of an enormously tall tulip-tree, which stood, with some eight or ten oaks, upon the level, and far surpassed them all, and all other trees which I had then ever seen, in the beauty of its foliage and form, in the wide spread of its branches, and in the general majesty of its appearance. When we reached this tree, Legrand turned to Jupiter, and asked him if he thought he could climb it. The old man seemed a little staggered by the question, and for some moments made no reply. At length he approached the huge trunk, walked slowly around it, and examined it with minute attention. When he had completed his scrutiny, he merely said:

"Yes, massa, Jup climb any tree he ebber see in he life."

"Then up with you as soon as possible, for it will soon be too dark to see what we are about."

"How far mus' go up, massa?" inquired Jupiter.

"Get up the main trunk first, and then I will tell you which way to go—and here—stop! take this beetle with you."

"De bug, Massa Will!—de goole-bug!" cried the negro, drawing back in dismay—"what for mus' tote de bug way up de tree?—d——n if I do!"

"If you are afraid, Jup, a great big negro like you, to take hold of a harmless little dead beetle, why you can carry it up by this string— but, if you do not take it up with you in some way, I shall be under the necessity of breaking your head with this shovel."

"What de matter now, massa?" said Jup, evidently shamed into compliance; "always want for to raise fuss wid old nigger. Was only funnin anyhow. *Me* feered de bug! what I keer for de bug?" Here he took cautiously hold of the extreme end of the string, and, maintaining the insect as far from his person as circumstances would permit, prepared to ascend the tree.

In youth, the tulip-tree, or *Liriodendron tulipiferum,* the most magnificent of American foresters, has a trunk peculiarly smooth, and often rises to a great height without lateral branches; but, in its riper age, the bark becomes gnarled and uneven, while many short limbs make their appearance on the stem. Thus the difficulty of ascension, in the present case, lay more in semblance than in reality. Embracing the huge cylinder, as closely as possible with his arms and knees, seizing with his hands some projections, and resting his naked toes upon others, Jupiter, after one or two narrow escapes from falling, at length wriggled himself into the first great fork, and seemed to consider the whole business as virtually accomplished. The *risk* of the achievement was, in fact, now over, although the climber was some sixty or seventy feet from the ground.

"Which way mus' go now, Massa Will?" he asked.

"Keep up the largest branch—the one on this side," said Legrand. The negro obeyed him promptly, and apparently with but little trouble; ascending higher and higher, until no glimpse of his squat figure could be obtained through the dense foliage which enveloped it. Presently his voice was heard in a sort of halloo.

"How much fudder is got to go?"

"How high up are you?" asked Legrand.

"Ebber so fur," replied the negro; "can see de sky fru de top ob de tree."

"Never mind the sky, but attend to what I say. Look down the trunk and count the limbs below you on this side. How many limbs have you passed?"

"One, two, tree, four, fibe—I done pass fibe big limb, massa, 'pon dis side."

"Then go one limb higher."

In a few minutes the voice was heard again, announcing that the seventh limb was attained.

"Now, Jup," cried Legrand, evidently much excited, "I want you to work your way out upon that limb as far as you can. If you see anything strange let me know."

By this time what little doubt I might have entertained of my poor friend's insanity was put finally at rest. I had no alternative but to conclude him stricken with lunacy, and I became seriously anxious about getting him home. While I was pondering upon what was best to be done, Jupiter's voice was again heard.

"Mos' feered for to venture 'pon dis limb berry far—'tis dead limb putty much all de way."

"Did you say it was a *dead* limb, Jupiter?" cried Legrand in a quavering voice.

"Yes, massa, him dead as de door-nail—done up for sartain— done departed dis here life."

"What in the name of heaven shall I do?" asked Legrand, seemingly in the greatest distress.

"Do!" said I, glad of an opportunity to interpose a word, "why come home and go to bed. Come now!—that's a fine fellow. It's getting late, and, besides, you remember your promise."

"Jupiter," cried he, without heeding me in the least, "do you hear me?"

"Yes, Massa Will, hear you ebber so plain."

"Try the wood well, then, with your knife, and see if you think it *very* rotten."

"Him rotten, massa, sure nuff," replied the negro in a few moments, "but not so berry rotten as mought be. Mought venture out leetle way 'pon de limb by myself, dat's true."

"By yourself!—what do you mean?"

"Why, I mean de bug. 'Tis *berry* hebby bug. Spose I drop him down fuss, an den de limb won't break wid just de weight of one nigger."

"You infernal scoundrel!" cried Legrand, apparently much relieved, "what do you mean by telling me such nonsense as that? As sure as you drop that beetle I'll break your neck. Look here, Jupiter, do you hear me?"

"Yes, massa, needn't hollo at poor nigger dat style."

"Well! now listen!—if you will venture out on the limb as far as you think safe, and not let go the beetle, I'll make you a present of a silver dollar as soon as you get down."

"I'm gwine, Massa Will—deed I is," replied the negro very promptly—"mos' out to de eend now."

"*Out to the End!*" here fairly screamed Legrand; "do you say you are out to the end of that limb?"

"Soon be to de eend, massa—o-o-o-o-oh! Lor-gol-a-marcy! what *is* dis here pon de tree?"

"Well!" cried Legrand, highly delighted, "what is it?"

"Why taint noffin but a skull—somebody bin left him head up de tree, and de crows done gobble ebery bit ob de meat off."

"A skull, you say!—very well,—how is it fastened to the limb?—what holds it on?"

"Sure nuff, massa; mus' look. Why dis berry curous sarcumstance, 'pon my word—dare's a great big nail in de skull, what fastens ob it on to de tree."

"Well now, Jupiter, do exactly as I tell you—do you hear?"

"Yes, massa."

"Pay attention, then—find the left eye of the skull."

"Hum! hoo! dat's good! why dey ain't no eye lef' at all."

"Curse your stupidity! do you know your right hand from your left?"

"Yes, I knows dat—knows all about dat—'tis my lef' hand what I chops de wood wid."

"To be sure! you are left-handed; and your left eye is on the same side as your left hand. Now, I suppose, you can find the left eye of the skull, or the place where the left eye has been. Have you found it?"

Here was a long pause. At length the negro asked:

"Is de lef' eye of de skull 'pon de same side as de lef' hand ob de skull too?—cause de skull aint got not a bit ob a hand at all—nebber mind! I got de lef' eye now—here de lef' eye! what mus' do wid it?"

"Let the beetle drop through it, as far as the string will reach—but be careful and not let go your hold of the string."

"All dat done, Massa Will; mighty easy ting for to put de bug fru de hole—look out for him dare below!"

During this colloquy no portion of Jupiter's person could be seen; but the beetle, which he had suffered to descend, was now visible at the end of the string, and glistened, like a globe of burnished gold, in the last rays of the setting sun, some of which still faintly illumined the eminence upon which we stood. The *scarabaeus* hung quite clear of any branches, and, if allowed to fall, would have fallen at our feet. Legrand immediately took the scythe, and cleared with it a circular space, three or four yards in diameter, just beneath the insect, and, having accomplished this, ordered Jupiter to let go the string and come down from the tree.

Driving a peg, with great nicety, into the ground, at the precise spot where the beetle fell, my friend now produced from his pocket a tape-measure. Fastening one end of this at that point of the trunk of the tree which was nearest the peg, he unrolled it till it reached the peg and thence further unrolled it, in the direction already established by the two points of the tree and the peg, for the distance of fifty feet — Jupiter clearing away the brambles with the scythe. At the spot thus attained a second peg was driven, and about this, as a center, a rude circle, about four feet in diameter, described. Taking now a spade himself, and giving one to Jupiter and one to me, Legrand begged us to set about digging as quickly as possible.

To speak the truth, I had no especial relish for such amusement at any time, and, at that particular moment, would most willingly have declined it; for the night was coming on, and I felt much fatigued with the exercise already taken; but I saw no mode of escape, and was fearful of disturbing my poor friend's equanimity by a refusal. Could I have depended, indeed, upon Jupiter's aid, I would have had no hesitation in attempting to get the lunatic home by force; but I was too well assured of the old negro's disposition, to hope that he would assist me, under any circumstances, in a personal contest with his master.

I made no doubt that the latter had been infected with some of the innumerable Southern superstitions about money buried, and that his phantasy had received confirmation by the finding of the *scarabaeus*, or, perhaps, by Jupiter's obstinacy in maintaining it to be "a bug of real gold." A mind disposed to lunacy would readily be led away by such suggestions — especially if chiming in with favorite preconceived ideas — and then I called to mind the poor fellow's speech about the beetle's being "the index of his fortune." Upon the whole, I was sadly vexed and puzzled, but, at length, I concluded to make a virtue of necessity—to dig with a good will, and thus the sooner to convince the visionary, by ocular demonstration, of the fallacy of the opinion he entertained.

The lanterns having been lit, we all fell to work with a zeal worthy of a more rational cause; and, as the glare fell upon our persons and implements, I could not help thinking how picturesque a group we composed, and how strange and suspicious our labors must have appeared to any interloper who, by chance, might have stumbled upon our whereabouts.

We dug very steadily for two hours. Little was said; and our chief embarrassment lay in the yelpings of the dog, who took exceeding interest in our proceedings. He, at length, became so obstreperous that we grew fearful of his giving the alarm to some stragglers in the vicinity,—or, rather, this was the apprehension of Legrand;—for myself, I should have rejoiced at any interruption which might have enabled me to get the wanderer home. The noise was, at length, very effectually silenced by Jupiter, who, getting out of the hole with a dogged air of deliberation, tied the brute's mouth up with one of his suspenders, and then returned, with a grave chuckle, to his task.

When the time mentioned had expired, we had reached a depth of five feet, and yet no signs of any treasure became manifest. A general pause ensued, and I began to hope that the farce was at an end. Legrand, however, although evidently much disconcerted, wiped his brow thoughtfully and recommenced. We had excavated the entire circle of four feet diameter, and now we slightly enlarged the limit, and went to the farther depth of two feet. Still nothing appeared. The gold-seeker, whom I sincerely pitied, at length clambered from the pit, with the bitterest disappointment imprinted upon every feature, and proceeded, slowly and reluctantly, to put on his coat, which he had thrown off at the beginning of his labor. In the meantime I made no remark. Jupiter, at a signal from his master, began to gather up his tools. This done, and the dog having been unmuzzled, we turned in profound silence toward home.

We had taken, perhaps, a dozen steps in this direction, when, with a loud oath, Legrand strode up to Jupiter, and seized him by the collar. The astonished negro opened his eyes and mouth to the fullest extent, let fall the spades, and fell upon his knees.

"You scoundrel!" said Legrand, hissing out the syllables from between his clenched teeth — "you infernal black villain! — speak, I tell you! — answer me this instant, without prevarication! — which — which is your left eye?"

"Oh, my golly, Massa Will! aint dis here my lef' eye for sartain?" roared the terrified Jupiter, placing his hand upon his *right* organ of vision, and holding it there with a desperate pertinacity, as if in immediate dread of his master's attempt at a gouge.

"I thought so! — I knew it! hurrah!" vociferated Legrand, letting the negro go and executing a series of curvets and caracols, much to the astonishment of his valet, who, arising from his knees, looked, mutely, from his master to myself, and then from myself to his master.

"Come! we must go back," said the latter, "the game's not up yet"; and he again led the way to the tulip-tree.

"Jupiter," said he, when we reached its foot, "come here! Was the skull nailed to the limb with the face outward, or with the face to the limb?"

"De face was out, massa, so dat de crows could get at de eyes good, widout any trouble."

"Well, then, was it this eye or that through which you dropped the beetle?" here Legrand touched each of Jupiter's eyes.

" 'Twas dis eye, massa — de lef' eye — jis as you tell me," and here it was his right eye that the negro indicated.

"That will do — we must try it again."

Here my friend, about whose madness I now saw, or fancied that I saw, certain indications of method, removed the peg which marked the spot where the beetle fell, to a spot about three inches to the westward of its former position. Taking, now, the tape-measure from the nearest point of the trunk to the peg, as before, and continuing the extension in a straight line to the distance of fifty feet, a spot was indicated, removed, by several yards, from the point at which we had been digging.

Around the new position a circle, somewhat larger than in the former instance, was now described, and we again set to work with the spade. I was dreadfully weary, but, scarcely understanding what had occasioned the change in my thoughts, I felt no longer any great aversion from the labor imposed. I had become most unaccountably interested—nay, even excited. Perhaps there was something, amid all the extravagant demeanor of Legrand—some air of forethought, or of deliberation, which impressed me. I dug eagerly, and now and then caught myself actually looking, with something that very much resembled expectation, for the fancied treasure, the vision of which had demented my unfortunate companion. At a period when such vagaries of thought most fully possessed me, and when we had been at work perhaps an hour and a half, we were again interrupted by the violent howlings of the dog. His uneasiness, in the first instance, had been, evidently, but the result of playfulness or caprice, but he now assumed a bitter and serious tone. Upon Jupiter's again attempting to muzzle him, he made furious resistance, and, leaping into the hole, tore up the mould frantically with his claws. In a few seconds he had uncovered a mass of human bones, forming two complete skeletons, intermingled with several buttons of metal, and what appeared to be the dust of decayed woolen. One or two strokes of a spade up-turned the blade of a large Spanish knife, and, as we dug farther, three or four loose pieces of gold and silver coin came to light.

At sight of these the joy of Jupiter could scarcely be restrained, but the countenance of his master wore an air of extreme disappointment. He urged us, however, to continue our exertions, and the words were hardly uttered when I stumbled and fell forward, having caught the toe of my boot in a large ring of iron that lay half buried in the loose earth.

We now worked in earnest, and never did I pass ten minutes of more intense excitement. During this interval we had fairly unearthed an oblong chest of wood, which, from its perfect preservation and wonderful hardness, had plainly been subjected to some mineralizing process—perhaps that of the bi-chloride of mercury. This box was three feet and a half long, three feet broad, and two and a half feet deep. It was firmly secured by bands of wrought iron, riveted, and forming a kind of open trelliswork over the whole. On each side of the chest, near the top, were three rings of iron—six in all—by means of which a firm hold could be obtained by six persons. Our utmost united endeavors served only to disturb the coffer very slightly in its bed. We at once saw the impossibility of removing so great a weight. Luckily, the sole fastenings of the lid consisted of two sliding bolts. These we drew back—trembling and panting with anxiety. In an instant, a treasure of incalculable value lay gleaming before us. As the rays of the lanterns fell within the pit, there flashed upward a glow and a glare, from a confused heap of gold and of jewels, that absolutely dazzled our eyes.

I shall not pretend to describe the feelings with which I gazed. Amazement was, of course, predominant. Legrand appeared exhausted with excitement, and spoke very few words. Jupiter's countenance wore, for some minutes, as deadly a pallor as it is possible, in the nature of things, for any negro's visage to assume. He seemed stupefied—thunderstricken. Presently he fell upon his knees in the pit, and burying his naked arms up to the elbows in gold, let them there remain, as if enjoying the luxury of a bath. At length, with a deep sigh, he exclaimed, as if in a soliloquy:

"And dis all cum ob de goole-bug! de putty goole-bug! the poor little goole-bug, what I boosed in dat sabage kind ob style! Ain't you shamed ob yourself, nigger? —answer me dat!"

It became necessary, at last, that I should arouse both master and valet to the expediency of removing the treasure. It was growing late, and it behooved us to make exertion, that we might get everything housed before daylight. It was difficult to say what should be done, and much time was spent in deliberation—so confused were the ideas of all. We, finally, lightened the box by removing two thirds of its contents, when we were enabled, with some trouble, to raise it from the hole. The articles taken out were deposited among the brambles, and the dog left to guard them, with strict orders from Jupiter neither, upon any pretense, to stir from the spot, nor to open his mouth until our return. We then hurriedly made for home with the chest; reaching the hut in safety, but after excessive toil, at one o'clock in the morning. Worn out as we were, it was not in human nature to do more immediately. We rested until two, and had supper; starting for the hills immediately afterwards, armed with three stout sacks, which, by good luck, were upon the premises. A little before four we arrived at the pit, divided the remainder of the booty, as equally as might be, among us, and, leaving the holes unfilled, again set out for the hut, at which, for the second time, we deposited our golden burthens, just as the first faint streaks of the dawn gleamed from over the tree-tops in the east.

We were now thoroughly broken down; but the intense excitement of the time denied us repose. After an unquiet slumber of some three or four hours' duration, we arose, as if by preconcert, to make examination of our treasure.

The chest had been full to the brim, and we spent the whole day, and the greater part of the next night, in a scrutiny of its contents. There had been nothing like order or arrangement. Every thing had been heaped in promiscuously. Having assorted all with care, we found ourselves possessed of even vaster wealth than we had at first supposed. In coin there was rather more than four hundred and fifty thousand dollars—estimating the value of the pieces, as accurately as we could, by the tables of the period. There was not a particle of silver. All was gold of antique date and of great variety—French, Spanish, and German money, with a few English guineas, and some counters, of which we had never seen specimens before. There were several very large and heavy coins, so worn that we could make nothing of their inscriptions. There was no American money. The value of the jewels we found more difficulty in estimating. There were diamonds—some of them exceedingly large and fine—a hundred and ten in all, and not one of them small; eighteen rubies of remarkable brilliancy;—three hundred and ten emeralds, all very beautiful; and twenty-one sapphires, with an opal. These stones had all been broken from their settings and thrown loose in the chest. The settings themselves, which we picked out from among the other gold, appeared to have been beaten up with hammers, as if to prevent identification. Besides all this, there was a vast quantity of solid gold ornaments: nearly two hundred massive finger- and ear-rings; rich chains—thirty of these, if I remember; eighty-three very large and heavy crucifixes; five gold censers of great value; a prodigious golden punch-bowl, ornamented with richly chased vine-leaves and Bacchanalian figures; with two sword handles exquisitely embossed, and many other smaller articles which I cannot recollect. The weight of these valuables exceeded three hundred and fifty pounds avoirdupois; and in this estimate I have not included one hundred and ninety-seven superb gold watches; three of the number being worth each five hundred dollars, if one. Many of them were very old, and as timekeepers, valueless; the works having suffered, more or less, from corrosion—but all were richly jeweled and in cases of great worth. We estimated the entire contents of the chest, that night, at a million and a half of dollars; and upon the subsequent disposal of the trinkets and jewels (a few being retained for our own use), it was found that we had greatly undervalued the treasure.

When, at length, we had concluded our examination, and the intense excitement of the time had, in some measure, subsided, Legrand, who saw that I was dying with impatience for a solution of this most extraordinary riddle, entered into a full detail of all the circumstances connected with it.

"You remember," said he, "the night when I handed you the rough sketch I had made of the *scarabaeus*. You recollect also, that I became quite vexed at you for insisting that my drawing resembled a death's-head. When you first made this assertion I thought you were jesting; but afterwards I called to mind the peculiar spots on the back of the insect, and admitted to myself that your remark had some little foundation in fact. Still, the sneer at my graphic powers irritated me—for I am considered a good artist—and, therefore, when you handed me the scrap of parchment, I was about to crumple it up and throw it angrily into the fire."

"The scrap of paper, you mean," said I.

"No; it had much of the appearance of paper, and at first I supposed it to be such, but when I came to draw upon it, I discovered it at once to be a piece of very thin parchment. It was quite dirty, you remember. Well, as I was in the very act of crumpling it up, my glance fell upon the sketch at which you had been looking, and you may imagine my astonishment when I perceived, in fact, the figure of a death's-head just where, it seemed to me, I had made the drawing of the beetle. For a moment I was too much amazed to think with accuracy. I knew that my design was very different in detail from this—although there was a certain similarity in general outline. Presently I took a candle, and seating myself at the other end of the room, proceeded to scrutinize the parchment more closely. Upon turning it over, I saw my own sketch upon the reverse, just as I had made it. My first idea, now, was mere surprise at the really remarkable similarity of outline—at the singular coincidence involved in the fact that, unknown to me, there should have been a skull upon the other side of the parchment, immediately beneath my figure of the *scarabaeus,* and that this skull, not only in outline, but in size, should so closely resemble my drawing. I say the singularity of this coincidence absolutely stupefied me for a time. This is the usual effect of such coincidences. The mind struggles to establish a connection—a sequence of cause and effect—and, being unable to do so, suffers a species of temporary paralysis. But, when I recovered from this stupor, there dawned upon me gradually a conviction which startled me even far more than the coincidence. I began distinctly, positively, to remember that there had been *no* drawing upon the parchment when I made my sketch of the *scarabaeus.* I became perfectly certain of this; for I recollected turning up first one side and then the other, in search of the cleanest spot. Had the skull been then there, of course I could not have failed to notice it. Here was indeed a mystery which I felt it impossible to explain; but, even at that early moment, there seemed to glimmer, faintly, within the most remote and secret chambers of my intellect, a glow-worm-like conception of that truth which last night's adventure brought to so magnificent a demonstration. I arose at once, and putting the parchment securely away, dismissed all further reflection until I should be alone.

"When you had gone, and when Jupiter was fast asleep, I betook myself to a more methodical investigation of the affair. In the first place I considered the manner in which the parchment had come into my possession. The spot where we discovered the *scarabaeus* was on the coast of the main-land, about a mile eastward of the island, and but a short distance above high-water mark. Upon my taking hold of it, it gave me a sharp bite, which caused me to let it drop. Jupiter, with his accustomed caution, before seizing the insect, which had flown toward him, looked about him for a leaf, or something of that nature, by which to take hold of it. It was at this moment that his eyes, and mine also, fell upon the scrap of parchment, which I then supposed to be a paper. It was lying half buried in the sand, a corner sticking up. Near the spot where we found it, I observed the remnants of the hull of what appeared to have been a ship's long-boat. The wreck seemed to have been there for a very great while; for the resemblance to boat timbers could scarcely be traced.

"Well, Jupiter picked up the parchment, wrapped the beetle in it, and gave it to me. Soon afterward we turned to go home, and on the way met Lieutenant G——. I showed him the insect, and he begged me to let him take it to the fort. Upon my consenting, he thrust it forthwith into his waistcoat pocket, without the parchment in which it had been wrapped, and which I had continued to hold in my hand during his inspection. Perhaps he dreaded my changing my mind, and thought it best to make sure of the prize at once—you know how enthusiastic he is on all subjects connected with Natural History. At the same time, without being conscious of it, I must have deposited the parchment in my own pocket.

"You remember that when I went to the table, for the purpose of making a sketch of the beetle, I found no paper where it was usually kept. I looked in the drawer, and found none there. I searched my pockets, hoping to find an old letter, when my hand fell upon the parchment. I thus detail the precise mode in which it came into my possession; for the circumstances impressed me with peculiar force.

"No doubt you will think me fanciful—but I had already established a kind of *connection*. I had put together two links of a great chain. There was a boat lying upon a sea-coast, and not far from the boat was a parchment—*not a paper*—with a skull depicted upon it.

You will, of course, ask 'where is the connection?' I reply that the skull, or death's-head, is the well-known emblem of the pirate. The flag of the death's-head is hoisted in all engagements.

"I have said that the scrap was parchment, and not paper. Parchment is durable — almost imperishable. Matters of little moment are rarely consigned to parchment; since, for the mere ordinary purposes of drawing or writing, it is not nearly so well adapted as paper. This reflection suggested some meaning — some relevancy — in the death's-head. I did not fail to observe, also, the *form* of the parchment. Although one of its corners had been, by some accident, destroyed, it could be seen that the original form was oblong. It was just such a slip, indeed, as might have been chosen for a memorandum — for a record of something to be long remembered and carefully preserved."

"But," I interposed, "you say that the skull was *not* upon the parchment when you made the drawing of the beetle. How then do you trace any connection between the boat and the skull — since this latter, according to your own admission, must have been designed (God only knows how or by whom) at some period subsequent to your sketching the *scarabaeus*?"

"Ah, hereupon turns the whole mystery; although the secret, at this point, I had comparatively little difficulty in solving. My steps were sure, and could afford but a single result. I reasoned, for example, thus: When I drew the *scarabaeus*, there was no skull apparent upon the parchment. When I had completed the drawing I gave it to you, and observed you narrowly until you returned it. *You*, therefore, did not design the skull, and no one else was present to do it. Then it was not done by human agency. And nevertheless it was done.

"At this stage of my reflections I endeavored to remember, and *did* remember, with entire distinctness, every incident which occurred about the period in question. The weather was chilly (oh, rare and happy accident!), and a fire was blazing upon the hearth.

I was heated with exercise and sat near the table. You, however, had drawn a chair close to the chimney. Just as I placed the parchment in your hand, and as you were in the act of inspecting it, Wolf, the Newfoundland, entered, and leaped upon your shoulders. With your left hand you caressed him and kept him off, while your right, holding the parchment, was permitted to fall listlessly between your knees, and in close proximity to the fire. At one moment I thought the blaze had caught it, and was about to caution you, but, before I could speak, you had withdrawn it, and were engaged in its examination. When I considered all these particulars, I doubted not for a moment that *heat* had been the agent in bringing to light, upon the parchment, the skull which I saw designed upon it. You are well aware that chemical preparations exist, and have existed time out of mind, by means of which it is possible to write upon either paper or vellum, so that the characters shall become visible only when subjected to the action of fire. Zaffre, digested in *aqua regia,* and diluted with four times its weight of water, is sometimes employed; a green tint results. The regulus of cobalt, dissolved in spirit of nitre, gives a red. These colors disappear at longer or shorter intervals after the material written upon cools, but again become apparent upon the re-application of heat.

"I now scrutinized the death's-head with care. Its outer edges— the edges of the drawing nearest the edge of the vellum—were far more *distinct* than the others. It was clear that the action of the caloric had been imperfect or unequal. I immediately kindled a fire, and subjected every portion of the parchment to a glowing heat. At first, the only effect was the strengthening of the faint lines in the skull; but, upon persevering in the experiment, there became visible, at the corner of the slip, diagonally opposite to the spot in which the death's-head was delineated, the figure of what I at first supposed to be a goat. A closer scrutiny, however, satisfied me that it was intended for a kid."

"Ha! ha!" said I, "to be sure I have no right to laugh at you—a million and a half of money is too serious a matter for mirth—but you are not about to establish a third link in your chain—you will not find any especial connection between your pirates and a goat—pirates, you know, have nothing to do with goats; they appertain to the farming interest."

"But I have just said that the figure was *not* that of a goat."

"Well, a kid, then—pretty much the same thing."

"Pretty much, but not altogether," said Legrand. "You may have heard of one *Captain* Kidd. I at once looked upon the figure of the animal as a kind of punning or hieroglyphical signature. I say signature; because its position upon the vellum suggested this idea. The death's-head at the corner diagonally opposite, had, in the same manner, the air of a stamp, or seal. But I was sorely put out by the absence of all else—of the body to my imagined instrument—of the text for my context."

"I presume you expected to find a letter between the stamp and the signature."

"Something of that kind. The fact is, I felt irresistibly impressed with a presentiment of some vast good fortune impending. I can scarcely say why. Perhaps, after all, it was rather a desire than an actual belief;—but do you know that Jupiter's silly words, about the bug being of solid gold, had a remarkable effect upon my fancy? And then the series of accidents and coincidences—these were so *very* extraordinary. Do you observe how mere an accident it was that these events should have occurred upon the *sole* day of all the year in which it has been, or may be sufficiently cool for fire, and that without the fire, or without the intervention of the dog at the precise moment in which he appeared, I should never have become aware of the death's-head, and so never the possessor of the treasure?"

"But proceed—I am all impatience."

"Well; you have heard, of course, the many stories current—the

thousand vague rumors afloat about money buried, somewhere upon the Atlantic coast, by Kidd and his associates. These rumors must
have had some foundation in fact. And that the rumors have existed
so long and so continuously, could have resulted, it appeared to me,
only from the circumstance of the buried treasures still *remaining* entombed. Had Kidd concealed his plunder for a time, and afterward
reclaimed it, the rumors would scarcely have reached us in their
present unvarying form. You will observe that the stories told are all
about money-seekers, not about money-finders. Had the pirate recovered his money, there the affair would have dropped. It seemed
to me that some accident—say the loss of a memorandum indicating
its locality—had deprived him of the means of recovering it, and that
this accident had become known to his followers, who otherwise
might never have heard that the treasure had been concealed at all,
and who, busying themselves in vain, because unguided, attempts
to regain it, had given first birth, and then universal currency, to
the reports which are now so common. Have you ever heard of any
important treasure being unearthed along the coast?"

"Never."

"But that Kidd's accumulations were immense, is well known. I
took it for granted, therefore, that the earth still held them; and you
will scarcely be surprised when I tell you that I felt a hope, nearly
amounting to certainty, that the parchment so strangely found involved a lost record of the place of deposit."

"But how did you proceed?"

"I held the vellum again to the fire, after increasing the heat, but
nothing appeared. I now thought it possible that the coating of dirt
might have something to do with the failure: so I carefully rinsed the
parchment by pouring warm water over it, and, having done this,
I placed it in a tin pan, with the skull downward, and put the pan
upon a furnace of lighted charcoal. In a few minutes, the pan having
become thoroughly heated, I removed the slip, and, to my inexpress-

ible joy, found it spotted, in several places, with what appeared to be figures arranged in lines. Again I placed it in the pan, and suffered it to remain another minute. Upon taking it off, the whole was just as you see it now."

Here Legrand, having reheated the parchment, submitted it to my inspection. The following characters were rudely traced, in a red tint, between the death's-head and the goat:

"53‡‡†305))6*;4826)4‡.)4‡) ;806*;48†8¶60))85;1‡(;:‡*8†
83(88)5*†;46(;88*96*?;8)*‡ (;485);5*†2:*‡(;4956*2 (5*—
4)8¶8* ;4069285);)6†8)4‡‡;1 (‡9;48081 ;8:8‡1 ;48†85;4) 485†
528806*81 (‡9;48;(88;4(‡?34;48)4‡;161;:188;‡?;"

"But," said I, returning him the slip, "I am as much in the dark as ever. Were all the jewels of Golconda awaiting me upon my solution of this enigma, I am quite sure that I should be unable to earn them."

"And yet," said Legrand, "the solution is by no means so difficult as you might be led to imagine from the first hasty inspection of the characters. These characters, as any one might readily guess, form a cipher—that is to say, they convey a meaning; but then from what is known of Kidd, I could not suppose him capable of constructing any of the more abstruse cryptographs. I made up my mind, at once, that this was of a simple species—such, however, as would appear, to the crude intellect of the sailor, absolutely insoluble without the key."

"And you really solved it?"

"Readily; I have solved others of an abstruseness ten thousand times greater. Circumstances, and a certain bias of mind, have led me to take interest in such riddles, and it may well be doubted whether human ingenuity can construct an enigma of the kind which human ingenuity may not, by proper application, resolve. In fact, having once established connected and legible characters, I scarcely gave a thought to the mere difficulty of developing their import.

"In the present case—indeed in all cases of secret writing—the first question regards the *language* of the cipher; for the principles of solution, so far, especially, as the more simple ciphers are concerned, depend upon, and are varied by, the genius of the particular idiom. In general, there is no alternative but experiment (directed by probabilities) of every tongue known to him who attempts the solution, until the true one be attained. But, with the cipher now before us all difficulty was removed by the signature. The pun upon the word 'Kidd' is appreciable in no other language than the English. But for this consideration I should have begun my attempts with the Spanish and French, as the tongues in which a secret of this kind would most naturally have been written by a pirate of the Spanish Main. As it was, I assumed the cryptograph to be English.

"You observe there are no divisions between the words. Had there been divisions the task would have been comparatively easy. In such cases I should have commenced with a collation and analysis of the shorter words, and, had a word of a single letter occurred, as is most likely, (*a* or *I*, for example), I should have considered the solution as assured. But, there being no division, my first step was to ascertain the predominant letters, as well as the least frequent. Counting all, I constructed a table thus:

Of the character 8 there are 33.

; " 26.

4 " 19.

‡) " 16.

* " 13.

5 " 12.

6 " 11.

† 1 " 8.

0 " 6.

Of the character 92 there are 5.

:3 " 4.

? " 3.

¶ " 2.

—. " 1.

"Now, in English, the letter which most frequently occurs is *e*. Afterward, the succession runs thus: *a o i d h n r s t u y c f g l m w b k p q x z.* *E* predominates so remarkably, that an individual sentence of any length is rarely seen, in which it is not the prevailing character.

"Here, then, we have, in the very beginning, the groundwork for something more than a mere guess. The general use which may be made of the table is obvious—but, in this particular cipher, we shall only very partially require its aid. As our predominant character is 8, we will commence by assuming it as the *e* of the natural alphabet. To verify the supposition, let us observe if the 8 be seen often in couples—for *e* is doubled with great frequency in English—in such words, for example, as 'meet,' 'fleet,' 'speed,' 'seen,' 'been,' 'agree,' etc. In the present instance we see it doubled no less than five times, although the cryptograph is brief. Let us assume 8, then, as *e*. Now, of all *words* in the language, 'the' is most usual; let us see, therefore, whether there are not repetitions of any three characters, in the same order of collocation, the last of them being 8. If we discover repetitions of such letters, so arranged, they will most probably represent the word 'the.' Upon inspection, we find no less than seven such arrangements, the characters being ;48. We may, therefore, assume that ; represents *t*, 4 represents *h*, and 8 represents *e*—the last being now well confirmed. Thus a great step has been taken.

"But, having established a single word, we are enabled to establish a vastly important point; that is to say, several commencements and terminations of other words. Let us refer, for example, to the last instance but one, in which the combination ;48 occurs—not far from the end of the cipher. We know that the ; immediately ensuing is the commencement of a word, and, of the six characters succeeding this 'the,' we are cognizant of no less than five. Let us set these characters down, thus, by the letters we know them to represent, leaving a space for the unknown—

t eeth

"Here we are enabled, at once, to discard the '*th*,' as forming no portion of the word commencing with the first *t;* since, by experiment of the entire alphabet for a letter adapted to the vacancy, we perceive that no word can be formed of which this *th* can be a part. We are thus narrowed into

t ee

and, going through the alphabet, if necessary, as before, we arrive at the word 'tree,' as the sole possible reading. We thus gain another letter, *r;* represented by (, with the words 'the tree' in juxtaposition.

"Looking beyond these words, for a short distance, we again see the combination ;48, and employ it by way of *termination* to what immediately precedes. We have thus this arrangement:

the tree ;4(‡?34 the,

or, substituting the natural letters, where known, it reads thus:

the tree thr‡?3h the.

"Now, if, in place of the unknown characters, we leave blank spaces, or substitute dots, we read thus:

the tree thr . . . h the,

when the word '*through*' makes itself evident at once. But this discovery gives us three new letters, *o, u,* and *g,* represented by +, ?,
and 3.

"Looking now, narrowly, through the cipher for combinations
of known characters, we find, not very far from the beginning, this
arrangement,

83(88, or egree,

which plainly, is the conclusion of the word 'degree,' and gives us
another letter, *∂,* represented by !.

"Four letters beyond the word 'degree,' we perceive the combination

;46(;88.

Translating the known characters, and representing the unknown
by dots, as before, we read thus:

th.rtee

an arrangement immediately suggestive of the word 'thirteen,' and
again furnishing us with two new characters, *i* and *n,* represented
by 6 and *.

"Referring, now, to the beginning of the cryptograph, we find
the combination,

53‡‡!.

Translating as before, we obtain

.good,

which assures us that the first letter is *A,* and that the first two words
are 'A good.'

"It is now time that we arrange our key, as far as discovered, in a
tabular form, to avoid confusion. It will stand thus:

5 represents a
† " d
8 " e
3 " g
4 " h
6 " i
* " n
‡ " o
(" r
; " t

"We have, therefore, no less than eleven of the most important
letters represented, and it will be unnecessary to proceed with the
details of the solution. I have said enough to convince you that ciphers of this nature are readily soluble, and to give you some insight into the *rationale* of their development. But be assured that the
specimen before us appertains to the very simplest species of cryptograph. It now only remains to give you the full translation of the
characters upon the parchment, as unriddled. Here it is:

A good glass in the bishop's hostel in the devil's seat forty-one
degrees and thirteen minutes northeast and by north main branch
seventh limb east side shoot from the left eye of the death's-head a
bee-line from the tree through the shot fifty feet out.

"But," said I, "the enigma seems still in as bad a condition as ever. How is it possible to extort a meaning from all this jargon about 'devil's seats,' 'death's-heads,' and 'bishop's hostels'?"

"I confess," replied Legrand, "that the matter still wears a serious aspect, when regarded with a casual glance. My first endeavor was to divide the sentence into the natural division intended by the cryptographist."

"You mean, to punctuate it?"

"Something of that kind."

"But how was it possible to effect this?"

"I reflected that it had been a *point* with the writer to run his words together without division, so as to increase the difficulty of solution. Now, a not over-acute man, in pursuing such an object, would be nearly certain to overdo the matter. When, in the course of his composition, he arrived at a break in his subject which would naturally require a pause, or a point, he would be exceedingly apt to run his characters, at this place, more than usually close together. If you will observe the MS., in the present instance, you will easily detect five such cases of unusual crowding. Acting upon this hint, I made the division thus:

A good glass in the bishop's hostel in the devil's seat—forty-one degrees and thirteen minutes—northeast and by north—main branch seventh limb east side—shoot from the left eye of the death's-head—a bee-line from the tree through the shot fifty feet out.

"Even this division," said I, "leaves me still in the dark."

"It left me also in the dark," replied Legrand, "for a few days; during which I made diligent inquiry, in the neighborhood of Sullivan's Island, for any building which went by the name of the 'Bishop's Hotel'; for, of course, I dropped the obsolete word 'hostel.' Gain-ing no information on the subject, I was on the point of extending my sphere of search, and proceeding in a more systematic manner, when, one morning, it entered into my head, quite suddenly, that this 'Bishop's Hostel' might have some reference to an old family, of the name of Bessop, which, time out of mind, had held possession of an ancient manor-house, about four miles to the northward of the island. I accordingly went over to the plantation, and re-instituted my inquiries among the older negroes of the place. At length one of the most aged of the women said that she had heard of such a place as *Bessop's Castle*, and thought that she could guide me to it, but that it was not a castle, nor a tavern, but a high rock.

"I offered to pay her well for her trouble, and, after some demur, she consented to accompany me to the spot. We found it without much difficulty, when, dismissing her, I proceeded to examine the place. The 'castle' consisted of an irregular assemblage of cliffs and rocks — one of the latter being quite remarkable for its height as well as for its insulated and artificial appearance. I clambered to its apex, and then felt much at a loss as to what should be next done.

"While I was busied in reflection, my eyes fell upon a narrow ledge in the eastern face of the rock, perhaps a yard below the summit upon which I stood. This ledge projected about eighteen inches, and was not more than a foot wide, while a niche in the cliff just above it gave it a rude resemblance to one of the hollow-backed chairs used by our ancestors. I made no doubt that here was the 'devil's-seat' alluded to in the MS., and now I seemed to grasp the full secret of the riddle.

"The 'good glass,' I knew, could have reference to nothing but a telescope; for the word 'glass' is rarely employed in any other sense by seamen. Now here, I at once saw, was a telescope to be used, and a definite point of view, *admitting no variation,* from which to use it. Nor did I hesitate to believe that the phrases, 'forty-one degrees and thirteen minutes,' and 'northeast and by north,' were intended as directions for the leveling of the glass. Greatly excited by these discoveries, I hurried home, procured a telescope, and returned to the rock.

"I let myself down to the ledge, and found that it was impossible to retain a seat upon it except in one particular position. This fact confirmed my preconceived idea. I proceeded to use the glass. Of course, the 'forty-one degrees and thirteen minutes' could allude to nothing but elevation above the visible horizon, since the horizontal direction was clearly indicated by the words, 'northeast and by north.' This latter direction I at once established by means of a pocket-compass; then, pointing the glass as nearly at an angle of forty-one degrees of elevation as I could do it by guess, I moved it cautiously up or down, until my attention was arrested by a circular rift or opening in the foliage of a large tree that overtopped its fellows in the distance. In the centre of this rift I perceived a white spot, but could not, at first, distinguish what it was. Adjusting the focus of the telescope, I again looked, and now made it out to be a human skull.

"Upon this discovery I was so sanguine as to consider the enigma solved; for the phrase 'main branch, seventh limb, east side,' could refer only to the position of the skull upon the tree, while 'shoot from the left eye of the death's-head' admitted, also, of but one interpretation, in regard to a search for buried treasure. I perceived that the design was to drop a bullet from the left eye of the skull, and that a bee-line, or, in other words, a straight line, drawn from the nearest point of the trunk through 'the shot' (or the spot where the bullet fell), and thence extended to a distance of fifty feet, would indicate a definite point—and beneath this point I thought it at least *possible* that a deposit of value lay concealed."

"All this," I said, "is exceedingly clear, and, although ingenious, still simple and explicit. When you left the Bishop's Hotel, what then?"

"Why, having carefully taken the bearings of the tree, I turned homeward. The instant that I left 'the devil's-seat,' however, the circular rift vanished; nor could I get a glimpse of it afterward, turn as I would. What seems to me the chief ingenuity in this whole business, is the fact (for repeated experiment has convinced me it *is* a fact) that the circular opening in question is visible from no other attainable point of view than that afforded by the narrow ledge upon the face of the rock.

"In this expedition to the 'Bishop's Hotel' I had been attended by Jupiter, who had, no doubt, observed, for some weeks past, the abstraction of my demeanor, and took especial care not to leave me alone. But, on the next day, getting up very early, I contrived to give him the slip, and went into the hills in search of the tree. After much toil I found it. When I came home at night my valet proposed to give me a flogging. With the rest of the adventure I believe you are as well acquainted as myself."

"I suppose," said I, "you missed the spot, in the first attempt at digging, through Jupiter's stupidity in letting the bug fall through the right instead of through the left eye of the skull."

"Precisely. This mistake made a difference of about two inches and a half in the 'shot'—that is to say, in the position of the peg nearest the tree; and had the treasure been *beneath* the 'shot,' the error would have been of little moment; but 'the shot,' together with the nearest point of the tree, were merely two points for the establishment of a line of direction; of course the error, however trivial in the beginning, increased as we proceeded with the line, and by the time we had gone fifty feet threw us quite off the scent. But for my deep-seated impressions that treasure was here somewhere actually buried, we might have had all our labor in vain."

"But your grandiloquence, and your conduct in swinging the beetle—how excessively odd! I was sure you were mad. And why did you insist upon letting fall the bug, instead of a bullet, from the skull?"

"Why, to be frank, I felt somewhat annoyed by your evident suspicions touching my sanity, and so resolved to punish you quietly, in my own way, by a little bit of sober mystification. For this reason I swung the beetle, and for this reason I let it fall from the tree. An observation of yours about its great weight suggested the latter idea."

"Yes, I perceive; and now there is only one point which puzzles me. What are we to make of the skeletons found in the hole?"

"That is a question I am no more able to answer than yourself. There seems, however, only one plausible way of accounting for them—and yet it is dreadful to believe in such atrocity as my suggestion would imply. It is clear that Kidd—if Kidd indeed secreted this treasure, which I doubt not—it is clear that he must have had assistance in the labor. But this labor concluded, he may have thought it expedient to remove all participants in his secret. Perhaps a couple of blows with a mattock were sufficient, while his coadjutors were busy in the pit; perhaps it required a dozen—who shall tell?"

Imagining Edgar Allan Poe

· · · · · ·

BY SARA PARETSKY

The terror of suffocation and death are everywhere in Poe: Fortunato, walled into a living tomb in "The Cask of Amontillado"; Pluto, the reincarnated black cat, walled up with the dead wife of the anonymous drunk in the "Black Cat"; the man in "The Pit and the Pendulum," watching helplessly as the walls of the Inquisition's prison close in on him; the heart pounding loudly beneath the floorboards where the narrator has buried his victim in "The Tell-Tale Heart."

But terror isn't all that lies in Poe's stories. There's the blood that drenches people, there's love and a heartbreaking sense of loss, especially in poems like "The Raven" or "Annabel Lee," and there's the analytical, critical mind at work in the Dupin stories, "The Gold-Bug," and the thoughtful literary essays. Such a varied sensibility, combined with Poe's turbulent biography, makes it understandable that artists as different as Toni Morrison and Dominick Argento have tried to come to grips with him.

Every reader has his or her own take on the poet, some colored by his stormy life, some by his work. Andrew Taylor's *The American Boy* shows an inquisitive boy, the Poe who excelled as a student at Stoke Newington, the English prep school where he studied for five years. For Taylor, Poe is a detective manqué, as if Dupin emerged from the writer's own experiences. Taylor's Poe is a quick-witted, attractive youth whose presence in the novel helps unravel its Gothic mysteries.

Louis Bayard presents us with an eccentric, mystic young man: *The Pale Blue Eye* is set during Poe's few months as a West Point cadet. Bayard's Poe is obsessed with death, and Bayard's poetic voice is shaped by an unfortunate love affair with the daughter of the Point's doctor. The madness of the doctor's whole family is macabre in the extreme, and the denouement in the Academy's icehouse is a staggering episode.

If Poe left the Point in disgrace, it wasn't too serious—cadets and officers pooled their money to subscribe to his second collection of poems. And he's still something of a romantic hero at West Point: the cadets love his poetry, and apocryphal tales of his exploits are popular, including the legend that he appeared on parade naked except for his sashes.

For Toni Morrison, it is the issue of color and race that matters in Poe. In *Playing in the Dark,* Morrison writes:

> *No early American writer is more important to the concept of American Africanism than Poe. And no image is more telling than [the one at the end of* The Narrative of Arthur Gordon Pym of Nantucket*]: the visualized but somehow . . . unknowable white form that rises from the mists. . . . The images of the white curtain and the "shrouded human figure" with skin "the perfect whiteness of the snow" occur after the narrative has encountered blackness. . . . Both are figurations of impenetrable whiteness that surface in American literature whenever*

an Africanist presence is engaged. . . . These images of impenetrable
whiteness . . . appear almost always . . . with representations of black or
Africanist people who are dead [or] impotent.[1]

Poe lived a chunk of his life in the slaveholding South; at one
point, although he wasn't wealthy, he was in a position to sell a slave.
I might read the images of whiteness somewhat differently than
Morrison, but not the difficult, demeaning treatment of darkness. I
cannot bear to read Poe's depictions of Negroes, who always speak
in the stereotypic language of the obsequious slave and who feel fulfilled in their service of the white master—as Jupiter does in "The
Gold-Bug." Despite his manumission, Jupiter could not be induced
by "threats nor promises, to abandon what he considered his right of
attendance upon the footsteps of his young 'Massa Will.'"

Of all the literary and critical responses to Poe—including the
critiques of his substance abuse—the one I find most compelling is
Argento's *Voyage of Edgar Allan Poe*. This opera, composed for the U.S.
bicentennial, is an emotional account of Poe's voyage from Philadelphia to Baltimore, where he died in the kind of mystery that invites
conspiracy theories. Argento has a sort of psychological courtroom
battle over Poe, with Dupin conducting the defense and Poe's nemesis, the critic Griswold, attacking Poe for using the events of his
own turbulent life as the basis for his creative work. The staging,
with its insistent themes of blood, the intertwining of "The Masque
of the Red Death," which alludes to the deaths of Poe's mother, foster
mother, and bride from consumption, is shocking and compelling.

1. Toni Morrison, *Playing in the Dark*, quoted in Richard Delgado and Jean Ste-
fancic, eds., *Critical White Studies: Looking Behind the Mirror* (Philadelphia: Temple
University Press, 1997), pp. 79–80, passim.

The blood-drenched Poe, the racially charged Poe, the analytic, the poetic—all are aspects of this complicated writer; none explains him fully. When I read Poe, what makes his stories terrifying is a sense of helplessness. I imagine him suffocating—almost literally, in the alcohol he consumed and the blood he saw his consumptive mother cough up—as well as figuratively. His father abandoned him, his foster father never accepted him and ultimately cast him off, his mother died when he was two.

Most children blame themselves for abandonments like these, and in Poe's fiction it's the narrator who is almost always the perpetrator when evil deeds are done: "The Black Cat," "The Education of William Wilson," "The Tell-Tale Heart," "The Cask of Amontillado"—all have a narrator who is a knave or a madman. In "The Black Cat," the narrator goes out of his way to explain how vile he is, torturing the animals who have loved him, degrading himself with drink, beating his wife, and finally driving an ax into her brain.

Of course, my response is as partial as Bayard's or Argento's. I can't imagine trying to make such a difficult figure the subject of a novel or a story. In general, I'm uneasy with using real figures as players in a novel—highlighting one facet means overlooking others. Still, with Poe, I can understand the temptation to do so. The opium, the alcohol, the love affairs; the slave owner, the gambler, the writer—not even the masterful Stephen King could have invented such a complex character.

Edgar Allan Poe's father's name was David; Sara Paretsky's father's name was David. Both their last names begin with the letter "P." Poe's and Paretsky's mothers were both accomplished actresses. Poe died in Baltimore. Paretsky gave birth to Sisters in Crime in Baltimore. Baltimore is in Maryland, abbreviated "MD." Paretsky's grandfather was an MD. Poe created

Dupin, the earliest male private investigator; Paretsky created V. I. War-shawski, one of the earliest female PIs. Poe was not a drug addict; neither is Paretsky. Coincidence? Hard to believe. Paretsky is clearly a reincarnation of the master of noir. Or perhaps his great-great-great-granddaughter. Or an imposter.

The Raven

Once upon a midnight dreary, while I pondered, weak
  and weary,
Over many a quaint and curious volume of forgotten lore—
While I nodded, nearly napping, suddenly there came a
  tapping,
As of some one gently rapping, rapping at my chamber
  door.
" 'Tis some visitor," I muttered, "tapping at my chamber
  door—
      Only this and nothing more."

Ah, distinctly I remember it was in the bleak December;
And each separate dying ember wrought its ghost upon
  the floor.
Eagerly I wished the morrow;—vainly I had sought to
  borrow
From my books surcease of sorrow—sorrow for the lost
  Lenore—

For the rare and radiant maiden whom the angels name Lenore—
    Nameless *here* for evermore.

And the silken, sad, uncertain rustling of each purple curtain
Thrilled me—filled me with fantastic terrors never felt before;
So that now, to still the beating of my heart, I stood repeating,
" 'Tis some visitor entreating entrance at my chamber door—
Some late visitor entreating entrance at my chamber door;—
    This it is and nothing more."

Presently my soul grew stronger; hesitating then no longer,
"Sir," said I, "or Madam, truly your forgiveness I implore;
But the fact is I was napping, and so gently you came rapping,
And so faintly you came tapping, tapping at my chamber door,
That I scarce was sure I heard you"—here I opened wide the
    door;—
    Darkness there and nothing more.

Deep into that darkness peering, long I stood there wondering,
    fearing,
Doubting, dreaming dreams no mortals ever dared to dream
    before;
But the silence was unbroken, and the stillness gave no token,
And the only word there spoken was the whispered word,
    "Lenore?"
This I whispered, and an echo murmured back the word,
    "Lenore!"
    Merely this and nothing more.

Back into the chamber turning, all my soul within me burning,
Soon again I heard a tapping something louder than before.
"Surely," said I, "surely that is something at my window lattice;

Let me see, then, what thereat is, and this mystery explore—
Let my heart be still a moment and this mystery explore;—
　'Tis the wind and nothing more!"

Open here I flung the shutter, when, with many a flirt and flutter,
In there stepped a stately Raven of the saintly days of yore;
Not the least obeisance made he; not a minute stopped or stayed he;
But, with mien of lord or lady, perched above my chamber door—
Perched upon a bust of Pallas just above my chamber door—
　Perched, and sat, and nothing more.

Then the ebony bird beguiling my sad fancy into smiling,
By the grave and stern decorum of the countenance it wore,
"Though thy crest be shorn and shaven, thou," I said, "art sure no
　craven,
Ghastly grim and ancient Raven wandering from the Nightly
　shore—
Tell me what thy lordly name is on the Night's Plutonian shore!"
　Quoth the Raven, "Nevermore."

Much I marvelled this ungainly fowl to hear discourse so plainly,
Though its answer little meaning—little relevancy bore;
For we cannot help agreeing that no living human being
Ever yet was blessed with seeing bird above his chamber door—
Bird or beast upon the sculptured bust above his chamber door,
　With such name as "Nevermore."

But the Raven, sitting lonely on that placid bust, spoke only
That one word, as if its soul in that one word he did outpour.
Nothing farther then he uttered—not a feather then he fluttered—
Till I scarcely more than muttered: "Other friends have flown
　before—

On the morrow *he* will leave me, as my Hopes have flown before."
    Then the bird said "Nevermore."

Startled at the stillness broken by reply so aptly spoken,
"Doubtless," said I, "what it utters is its only stock and store
Caught from some unhappy master whom unmerciful Disaster
Followed fast and followed faster till his songs one burden bore—
Till the dirges of his Hope that melancholy burden bore
    Of 'Never—nevermore.'"

But the Raven still beguiling my sad fancy into smiling,
Straight I wheeled a cushioned seat in front of bird and bust and
    door;
Then, upon the velvet sinking, I betook myself to linking
Fancy unto fancy, thinking what this ominous bird of yore—
What this grim, ungainly, ghastly, gaunt, and ominous bird of yore
    Meant in croaking "Nevermore."

This I sat engaged in guessing, but no syllable expressing
To the fowl whose fiery eyes now burned into my bosom's core;
This and more I sat divining, with my head at ease reclining
On the cushion's velvet lining that the lamp-light gloated o'er,
But whose velvet-violet lining with the lamp-light gloating o'er
    She shall press, ah, nevermore!

Then, methought, the air grew denser, perfumed from an unseen
    censer
Swung by seraphim whose foot-falls tinkled on the tufted floor.
"Wretch," I cried, "thy God hath lent thee—by these angels he
    hath sent thee
Respite—respite and nepenthe from thy memories of Lenore;

Quaff, oh, quaff this kind nepenthe and forget this lost Lenore!"
　　Quoth the Raven, "Nevermore."

"Prophet!" said I, "thing of evil!—prophet still, if bird or devil!—
Whether Tempter sent, or whether tempest tossed thee here
　　ashore,
Desolate yet all undaunted, on this desert land enchanted—
On this home by Horror haunted—tell me truly, I implore—
Is there—*is* there balm in Gilead?—tell me—tell me, I implore!"
　　Quoth the Raven, "Nevermore."

"Prophet!" said I, "thing of evil!—prophet still, if bird or devil!
By that Heaven that bends above us—by that God we both
　　adore—
Tell this soul with sorrow laden if, within the distant Aidenn,
It shall clasp a sainted maiden whom the angels name Lenore—
Clasp a rare and radiant maiden whom the angels name Lenore."
　　Quoth the Raven, "Nevermore."

"Be that word our sign of parting, bird or fiend!" I shrieked,
　　upstarting—
"Get thee back into the tempest and the Night's Plutonian
　　shore!
Leave no black plume as a token of that lie thy soul hath spoken!
Leave my loneliness unbroken!—quit the bust above my door!
Take thy beak from out my heart, and take thy form from off my
　　door!"
　　Quoth the Raven, "Nevermore."

And the Raven, never flitting, still is sitting, *still* is sitting
On the pallid bust of Pallas just above my chamber door;

And his eyes have all the seeming of a demon's that is dreaming,
And the lamp-light o'er him streaming throws his shadows on the
   floor;
And my soul from out that shadow that lies floating on the floor
Shall be lifted—nevermore!

Rantin' and Ravin'

......

BY JOSEPH WAMBAUGH

Once upon a twilight teary, while I mourned so blitzed and bleary,
O'er my script which got demolished by a showbiz bloody bore,
Suddenly there came a dinging—"You've got mail!"—an e-mail
   singing,
Much annoyed with ears a-ringing, I decided to ignore,
And swilled another mug of suds, permeating every pore.
"'Tis only spam," I muttered then. This and nothing more.

Presently with breath a-reeking, I chose to do some e-mail peeking,
Which rained on me a host of doubts that pierced me to the core.
For Michael wanted "ruminations," and that filled me with
   trepidation,
He wished for thoughts about a scribe from golden days of yore.
A testimonial to this titan? But I had demons I was fightin'.
At least two hundred words, he urged. This and nothing more.

Now I felt my stomach burning, the hops and malts inside me
   churning,

As I remembered childhood learning, and volumes I'd explored.
Then my guilt it overtook me, Mike's insistent plea, it shook me,
The e-mail I should have deleted could now not be ignored.
I thought somehow I must comply, for Poe who's on a throne so
    high,
Deserves much thanks from such as I, and others gone before.

Thus I set off plodding, spurred by Michael's "gentle prodding,"
Hoping I could yet discover sentiments that soar.
I imagined many noble words, and thought I glimpsed a great
    black bird,
Whose unforgiving glower drove me to an icy shower,
To find within the power and draw temperance to the fore.
Alas, the water only froze me and made my bald spot sore.

This I say to Michael C., I ask that you envision me,
A forlorn wretch no longer musing, in his cups from all the
    boozing,
Who shall soon be mute and snoozing upon the study floor.
Before that swoon I swear to you, I'll quaff another brew or two,
In honor of courageous Poe, who threw open every door.
But I won't open "gentle" e-mails. Not now, and NEVERMORE!

Joseph Wambaugh, a former LAPD detective sergeant, is the New York
Times *best-selling author of* The Onion Field, The Blooding, The
Choirboys, *and many other fiction and nonfiction works. He has won a
number of awards, including the Edgar Award and the Rodolfo Walsh Prize
for investigative journalism. He lives with his wife in California.*

A Little Thought on Poe

••••••

BY THOMAS H. COOK

I was once asked what one-word description of a book would most likely cause me to read it. Without a blink, I answered, "Haunting." Why? Because I have found to my surprise that although people will often describe a book as "great," they will, upon further questioning, be wholly unable to recall a single line or scene or even the basic plot of a book that, though evidently "great," proved to be not in the least memorable. It is just the opposite with Poe, whose greatness, it seems to me, resides in the fact that his readers actually remember him. In poem after poem and story after story, we remember Poe. We remember that "when I was a child and she was a child," these two children lived "in a kingdom by the sea." We remember the Raven's bleak warning that in the end everything dissolves into the oblivion of "Nevermore." We remember the beating of a tell-tale heart and "the moaning and the groaning" of the bells. To remember a writer in this way is to be haunted by him, to have his words and scenes and characters forever alive in your mind. That is what true literary greatness is, and it is a greatness that was Poe's.

Thomas H. Cook is arguably America's shortest male crime writer. Utterly lacking in tough-guy characteristics, he remains the mystery world's most consistent no-show at sporting events, car races, horse races, and urban marathons. He has never painted his face in anticipation of the Super Bowl and is allergic to beer. His only experience with law enforcement was being pulled over for speeding, at which time he was given only a warning. As a boy, he wanted to be a great writer; then he read some great writers and decided he was nowhere near that good. Since then, he has churned out more than twenty novels and a smattering of nonfiction. He likes writing short stories because they're short, and he does not like writing long books because they're long. He has never read Remembrance of Things Past, *though on the street he is often mistaken for Marcel Proust.*

The Bells

I

Hear the sledges with the bells —
Silver bells!
What a world of merriment their melody foretells!
How they tinkle, tinkle, tinkle,
In the icy air of night!
While the stars that oversprinkle
All the heavens, seem to twinkle
With a crystalline delight;
Keeping time, time, time,
In a sort of Runic rhyme,
To the tintinnabulation that so musically wells
From the bells, bells, bells, bells,
Bells, bells, bells —
From the jingling and the tinkling of the bells.

II

Hear the mellow wedding bells —
Golden bells!
What a world of happiness their harmony foretells!
Through the balmy air of night
How they ring out their delight! —
From the molten-golden notes,
And all in tune,
What a liquid ditty floats
To the turtle-dove that listens, while she gloats
On the moon!
Oh, from out the sounding cells
What a gush of euphony voluminously wells!
How it swells!
How it dwells
On the Future! — how it tells
Of the rapture that impels
To the swinging and the ringing
Of the bells, bells, bells —
Of the bells, bells, bells, bells,
Bells, bells, bells —
To the rhyming and the chiming of the bells!

III

Hear the loud alarum bells —
Brazen bells!
What a tale of terror, now, their turbulency tells!
In the startled ear of night

How they scream out their affright!
Too much horrified to speak,
They can only shriek, shriek,
Out of tune,
In a clamorous appealing to the mercy of the fire,
In a mad expostulation with the deaf and frantic fire,
Leaping higher, higher, higher,
With a desperate desire,
And a resolute endeavor
Now — now to sit, or never,
By the side of the pale-faced moon.
Oh, the bells, bells, bells!
What a tale their terror tells
Of Despair!
How they clang, and clash, and roar!
What a horror they outpour
On the bosom of the palpitating air!
Yet the ear, it fully knows,
By the twanging
And the clanging,
How the danger ebbs and flows;
Yet the ear distinctly tells,
In the jangling
And the wrangling,
How the danger sinks and swells,
By the sinking or the swelling in the anger of the bells —
Of the bells, —
Of the bells, bells, bells, bells,
Bells, bells, bells —
In the clamor and the clangor of the bells!

IV

Hear the tolling of the bells —
Iron bells!
What a world of solemn thought their monody compels!
In the silence of the night,
How we shiver with affright
At the melancholy menace of their tone!
For every sound that floats
From the rust within their throats
Is a groan.
And the people — ah, the people —
They that dwell up in the steeple,
All alone,
And who tolling, tolling, tolling,
In that muffled monotone,
Feel a glory in so rolling
On the human heart a stone —
They are neither man nor woman —
They are neither brute nor human —
They are Ghouls: —
And their king it is who tolls: —
And he rolls, rolls, rolls,
Rolls
A paean from the bells!
And his merry bosom swells
With the paean of the bells!
And he dances, and he yells;
Keeping time, time, time,
In a sort of Runic rhyme,
To the paean of the bells —
Of the bells: —

Keeping time, time, time,
In a sort of Runic rhyme,
To the throbbing of the bells —
Of the bells, bells, bells —
To the sobbing of the bells;
Keeping time, time, time,
As he knells, knells, knells,
In a happy Runic rhyme,
To the rolling of the bells,
Of the bells, bells, bells: —
To the tolling of the bells —
Of the bells, bells, bells, bells,
Bells, bells, bells —
To the moaning and the groaning of the bells.

Poe in G Minor

. . . . . .

BY JEFFERY DEAVER

The year is 1971. I'm sitting on a stool on a low stage, two spotlights shining in my face. I clutch my dreadnought-size guitar. (Think Bob Dylan's Gibson Hummingbird on the cover of *Nashville Skyline,* but without the hummingbird.)

The venue is called the Chez, which I've recently learned means "The house of . . ." in French. (Not usually talented at languages, I pay attention in that particular class because I have a breathless crush on my professor, a cross between Linda Ronstadt and Claudine Longet, who, yes, shot that skier, but I don't care.)

The Chez is a coffeehouse in Columbia, Missouri, where I'm a junior in the university's Journalism School. I come here to perform folk songs in the evenings once or twice a week. The admission is free, the frothy pre-Starbucks concoctions are cheap, and owing to its location in a church, the place is alcohol-free. All of which means the audiences are sober, attentive, and—fortunately for me—forgiving.

Though I'm at school to become the next Walter Cronkite, singing and songwriting are my passions, and if I'd been able to make a living on the stage I'd have signed up in an instant—no insurance plan or 401(k) needed—even if the devil himself was the head of the record label's A&R department.

This Friday night I begin fingerpicking a melody that's not of my composition. It was written by Phil Ochs, a young singer-songwriter central to the folk music scene of the sixties and early seventies. He wrote a number of songs that embodied the psyche of that era, like "Draft Dodger Rag" and "I Ain't Marching Anymore," but the song that I'm performing this Friday is not social or political. It's a lyrical ballad—one that I love and with which I often open my sets.

Ochs generally wrote both the music and words for his songs, but for this tune he created the melody only; the lyrics were from Edgar Allan Poe's poem "The Bells." The poem features four stanzas, each describing bells' tolling for different occasions: a happy social outing, a marriage, a tragedy, and finally a funeral. The first stanza concludes:

Keeping time, time, time,
In a sort of Runic rhyme,
To the tintinnabulation that so musically wells
From the bells, bells, bells, bells,
Bells, bells, bells—
From the jingling and the tinkling of the bells.

Is "The Bells" Poe's best poem? No. It's a bit of a trifle, lacking the insight and brooding power he was capable of. But is it a pure pleasure to read aloud or perform? Absolutely. By the final verse my audiences were invariably singing along.

I have always loved Poe's prose fiction, and it has been a major influence, both informing the macabre tone of my writing and inspiring my plot twists and surprise endings. But I was a poet and songwriter before I was a novelist, and his lyrical works attracted me first. I believe that, in writing, less is more and that poetry, when well crafted, is the most emotionally direct form of written communication. Richard Wilbur, the former poet laureate of America, offered this metaphor about poetry (I'm paraphrasing): the confinement of the bottle is what gives the genie his strength. His meaning is that conciseness and controlled rhythm, rhyme, and figure of speech create a more powerful expression than unleashed outpourings.

In Poe's work the combination of this control and his preferred themes—crime, passion, death, the dark side of the mind—make pure magic.

Blend those two ingredients with music . . . well, culture don't get any better than that.

Phil Ochs was moved to adapt a poem, but Poe's prose works too have found second lives as musical compositions. Indeed, there aren't many authors—Shakespeare aside—whose body of work has provided seeds for so much melodic inspiration.

Claude Debussy, composer of *Clair de Lune* and *Prelude to the Afternoon of a Faun*, cited Poe as one of his major influences. He began two Poe-inspired operas, one based on "The Fall of the House of Usher" and one on "The Devil in the Belfry." Neither was completed by the composer, though a version of "Usher" was reconstructed in the 1970s and performed. Philip Glass, the minimalist composer, also wrote a successful opera based on "Usher," as did Peter Hammill, the British singer-songwriter.

Presently the British theater company Punchdrunk is staging its version of "The Masque of Red Death" at the Battersea Arts Center in London. The show—a "site-specific," interactive piece (the latest trend in theater, I hear)—features otherworldly choreography, classical music, and masked audience members roaming the elaborate, candle-lit performing space, mingling with the actors. Though not praised by all critics, the play is one of the hottest tickets in English theater, and the buzz is that it's headed for New York.

Sergei Rachmaninoff turned a Russian translation of "The Bells" into a choral symphony. The twentieth-century British composer and conductor Joseph Holbrooke wrote several Poe adaptations, including the symphonic works *The Raven* and *The Bells*, and he composed the music for a ballet based on "Masque." New York City choreographer David Fernandez wrote a short ballet based on "The Raven."

Lou Reed, a longtime admirer of Poe, produced a two-CD set entitled *The Raven*—his first release in some years—featuring exclusively work influenced by Poe. The material was performed by Reed and, among others, David Bowie, Ornette Coleman, Steve Buscemi, and Willem Dafoe.

Joan Baez, Judy Collins, and Stevie Nicks have all performed folk versions of "Annabel Lee," and the brilliant British art-rock group the Alan Parsons Project released *Tales of Mystery and Imagination*, an album filled entirely with Poe-inspired material. At least one track, I believe, actually made it into the Top 40. There have been many other performers, from Dylan to Marilyn Manson to Iron Maiden, who claimed inspiration by Poe or worked references from his work into theirs.

Oh, okay, I'll mention one other adaptation: my own musical version of Poe's "A Dream Within a Dream," which I composed when I was in my twenties and determined to slap the wrist of a self-delusional society. (Inexplicably, my adaptation did *not* make any Top 40 lists, so don't bother searching for downloads on iTunes—or even LimeWire.)

Looking at this recitation of adaptations, you can't help but wonder why Poe appeals to so many musicians, and ones of such vastly differing styles and forms (I mean, Debussy and *Lou Reed*?).

I think the answer is that Poe's work is inherently musical.

His storytelling is the stuff of opera, which has classic beginning, middle, and end structures, revels in crime, violence, the gothic, passion, and death, and is often over the top and borders on melodrama, sure, but, hey, we don't go to the opera for subtlety.

As for his poems—they uniformly display a lyricism and craft that the best, most emotionally engaging songs possess. Whether or not it's been set to music, Poe's writing is hummable.

After all, name another popular writer who could, with such intoxicating meter and imagery, write a poem embracing nothing less than love, tragedy, and death, that would find its way into concert halls and recording studios one hundred years later . . . *and* that coins and seamlessly fits in a six-syllable jawbreaker like "tintinnabulation."

Got you beat there, Will Shakespeare.

About Jeffrey Deaver

Once upon a morning bright, waking from too short a night,
The author wandered from his bed, nagged by some looming task,
    he knows.
Ah, yes, he's done his piece on Poe but has a bit more yet to go
Because his bio, it's now clear, just cannot be writ in prose.
It must be a poem, never prose.

Some fifty-seven years ago, he was born in Chicago.
He studied writing very young and practiced as a journalist
And then a lawyer in New York town but, truth be told, it got him down.
And so in 1989, he told his boss, "I call it quits."
The day job's dead. He called it quits.

Since then he's been writing thrillers, about folks fleeing hired killers
And detectives trying to track down psychos sick as the fiend Lecter.
The novels number twenty-four, short stories more or less two score.

Two movies sprouted from his books: Dead Silence *and* The Bone
    Collector.
Yes, Angelina and Denzel — The Bone Collector.

His books, known specially for their twists, hit worldwide
    best-seller lists.
Translated into thirty tongues, they're sold in many, many nations.
He's won top prizes overseas, and here at home three Ellery
    Queens.
He hasn't got an Edgar yet, but has received six nominations.
Poe, help him out — six nominations!

His latest tale, if you get the chance, is a series premiering Kathryn
    Dance,
Called The Sleeping Doll. *And due this summer, June or July,*
We'll see the author's popular hero, Lincoln Rhyme,
    in The Broken Window.
(Sorry, but it would take an Edgar Poe to make that last line fly.
He did his best; it just won't fly.)

EXCERPT FROM

The Narrative of Arthur Gordon Pym of Nantucket

Preface

Upon my return to the United States a few months ago, after the extraordinary series of adventures in the South Seas and elsewhere, of which an account is given in the following pages, accident threw me into the society of several gentlemen in Richmond, Va., who felt deep interest in all matters relating to the regions I had visited, and who were constantly urging it upon me, as a duty, to give my narrative to the public. I had several reasons, however, for declining to do so, some of which were of a nature altogether private, and concern no person but myself; others not so much so. One consideration which deterred me was, that, having kept no journal during a greater portion of the time in which I was absent, I feared I should not be able to write, from mere memory, a statement so minute and connected as to have the *appearance* of that truth it would really possess, barring only the natural and unavoidable exaggeration to which all of us are prone when detailing events which have had a powerful influence in exciting the imaginative faculties. Another reason was, that the incidents to be narrated were of a nature so positively marvellous, that, unsupported as my assertions must necessarily be (except by the evidence of a single individual, and he a half-breed Indian), I could only hope for belief among my family, and those of my friends who have had reason, through life, to put faith in my veracity—the probability being that the public at large would regard what I should put forth as merely an impudent and ingenious fiction. A distrust in my own abilities as a writer was, nevertheless, one of the principal causes which prevented me from complying with the suggestion of my advisers.

Among those gentlemen in Virginia who expressed the greatest interest in my statement, more particularly in regard to that portion of it which related to the Antarctic Ocean, was Mr. Poe, lately editor of the *Southern Literary Messenger,* a monthly magazine, published by Mr. Thomas W. White, in the city of Richmond. He strongly advised me, among others, to prepare at once a full account of what I had seen and undergone, and trust to the shrewdness and common sense of the public—insisting, with great plausibility, that however roughly, as regards mere authorship, my book should be got up, its very uncouthness, if there were any, would give it all the better chance of being received as truth.

Notwithstanding this representation, I did not make up my mind to do as he suggested. He afterward proposed (finding that I would not stir in the matter) that I should allow him to draw up, in his own words, a narrative of the earlier portion of my adventures, from facts afforded by myself, publishing it in the *Southern Messenger under the garb of fiction*. To this, perceiving no objection, I consented, stipulating only that my real name should be retained. Two numbers of the pretended fiction appeared, consequently, in the *Messenger* for January and February, (1837), and, in order that it might certainly be regarded as fiction, the name of Mr. Poe was affixed to the articles in the table of contents of the magazine.

The manner in which this ruse was received has induced me at length to undertake a regular compilation and publication of the adventures in question; for I found that, in spite of the air of fable which had been so ingeniously thrown around that portion of my statement which appeared in the *Messenger* (without altering or distorting a single fact), the public were still not at all disposed to receive it as fable, and several letters were sent to Mr. P.'s address, distinctly expressing a conviction to the contrary. I thence concluded that the facts of my narrative would prove of such a nature as to carry with them sufficient evidence of their own authenticity, and that I had consequently little to fear on the score of popular incredulity.

This *exposé* being made, it will be seen at once how much of what follows I claim to be my own writing; and it will also be understood that no fact is misrepresented in the first few pages which were written by Mr. Poe. Even to those readers who have not seen the *Messenger*, it will be unnecessary to point out where his portion ends and my own commences; the difference in point of style will be readily perceived.

A. G. PYM.
New-York, July, 1838.

Chapter X

Shortly afterward an incident occurred which I am induced to look upon as more intensely productive of emotion, as far more replete with the extremes first of delight and then of horror, than even any of the thousand chances which afterward befell me in nine long years, crowded with events of the most startling and, in many cases, of the most unconceived and unconceivable character. We were lying on the deck near the companion-way, and debating the possibility of yet making our way into the storeroom, when, looking toward Augustus, who lay fronting myself, I perceived that he had become all at once deadly pale, and that his lips were quivering in the most singular and unaccountable manner. Greatly alarmed, I spoke to him, but he made me no reply, and I was beginning to think that he was suddenly taken ill, when I took notice of his eyes, which were glaring apparently at some object behind me. I turned my head, and shall never forget the ecstatic joy which thrilled through every particle of my frame, when I perceived a large brig bearing down upon us, and not more than a couple of miles off. I sprung to my feet as if a musket bullet had suddenly struck me to the heart; and, stretching out my arms in the direction of the vessel, stood in this manner, motionless, and unable to articulate a syllable. Peters and Parker were equally affected, although in different ways. The former danced about the deck like a madman, uttering the most extravagant rhodomontades, intermingled with howls and imprecations, while the latter burst into tears, and continued for many minutes weeping like a child.

The vessel in sight was a large hermaphrodite brig, of a Dutch build, and painted black, with a tawdry gilt figure-head. She had evidently seen a good deal of rough weather, and, we supposed, had suffered much in the gale which had proved so disastrous to ourselves; for her foretopmast was gone, and some of her starboard bulwarks. When we first saw her, she was, as I have already said, about two miles off and to windward, bearing down upon us. The breeze was very gentle, and what astonished us chiefly was, that she had no other sails set than her foremast and mainsail, with a flying jib—of course she came down but slowly, and our impatience amounted nearly to phrensy. The awkward manner in which she steered, too, was remarked by all of us, even excited as we were. She yawed about so considerably, that once or twice we thought it impossible she could see us, or imagined that, having seen us, and discovered no person on board, she was about to tack and make off in another direction. Upon each of these occasions we screamed and shouted at the top of our voices, when the stranger would appear to change for a moment her intention, and again hold on toward us—this singular conduct being repeated two or three times, so that at last we could think of no other manner of accounting for it than by supposing the helmsman to be in liquor.

No person was seen upon her decks until she arrived within about a quarter of a mile of us. We then saw three seamen, whom by their dress we took to be Hollanders. Two of these were lying on some old sails near the forecastle, and the third, who appeared to be looking at us with great curiosity, was leaning over the starboard bow near the bowsprit. This last was a stout and tall man, with a very dark skin. He seemed by his manner to be encouraging us to have patience, nodding to us in a cheerful although rather odd way, and smiling constantly, so as to display a set of the most brilliantly white teeth. As his vessel drew nearer, we saw a red flannel cap which he had on fall from his head into the water; but of this he took little or no notice, continuing his odd smiles and gesticulations. I relate these things and circumstances minutely, and I relate them, it must be understood, precisely as they *appeared* to us.

The brig came on slowly, and now more steadily than before, and—I cannot speak calmly of this event—our hearts leaped up wildly within us, and we poured out our whole souls in shouts and thanksgiving to God for the complete, unexpected, and glorious deliverance that was so palpably at hand. Of a sudden, and all at once, there came wafted over the ocean from the strange vessel (which was now close upon us) a smell, a stench, such as the whole world has no name for—no conception of—hellish—utterly suffocating—insufferable, inconceivable. I gasped for breath, and turning to my companions, perceived that they were paler than marble. But we had now no time left for question or surmise—the brig was within fifty feet of us, and it seemed to be her intention to run under our counter, that we might board her without putting out a boat. We rushed aft, when, suddenly, a wide yaw threw her off full five or six points from the course she had been running, and, as she passed under our stern at the distance of about twenty feet, we had a full view of her decks. Shall I ever forget the triple horror of that spectacle? Twenty-five or thirty human bodies, among whom were several females, lay scattered about between the counter and the galley in the last and most loathsome state of putrefaction. We plainly saw that not a soul lived in that fated vessel! Yet we could not help shouting to the dead for help! Yes, long and loudly did we beg, in the agony of the moment, that those silent and disgusting images would stay for us, would not abandon us to become like them, would receive us among their goodly company! We were raving with horror and despair—thoroughly mad through the anguish of our grievous disappointment.

As our first loud yell of terror broke forth, it was replied to by something, from near the bowsprit of the stranger, so closely resembling the scream of a human voice that the nicest ear might have been startled and deceived. At this instant another sudden yaw brought the region of the forecastle for a moment into view, and we beheld at once the origin of the sound. We saw the tall stout figure still leaning on the bulwark, and still nodding his head to and fro, but his face was now turned from us so that we could not behold it. His arms were extended over the rail, and the palms of his hands fell outward. His knees were lodged upon a stout rope, tightly stretched, and reaching from the heel of the bowsprit to a cathead. On his back, from which a portion of the shirt had been torn, leaving it bare, there sat a huge sea-gull, busily gorging itself with the horrible flesh, its bill and talons deep buried, and its white plumage spattered all over with blood. As the brig moved farther round so as to bring us close in view, the bird, with much apparent difficulty, drew out its crimsoned head, and, after eyeing us for a moment as if stupefied, arose lazily from the body upon which it had been feasting, and, flying directly above our deck, hovered there a while with a portion of clotted and liver-like substance in its beak. The horrid morsel dropped at length with a sullen splash immediately at the feet of Parker. May God forgive me, but now, for the first time, there flashed through my mind a thought, a thought which I will not mention, and I felt myself making a step toward the ensanguined spot. I looked upward, and the eyes of Augustus met my own with a degree of intense and eager meaning which immediately brought me to my senses. I sprang forward quickly, and, with a deep shudder, threw the frightful thing into the sea.

The body from which it had been taken, resting as it did upon the rope, had been easily swayed to and fro by the exertions of the carnivorous bird, and it was this motion which had at first impressed us with the belief of its being alive. As the gull relieved it of its weight, it swung round and fell partially over, so that the face was fully discovered. Never, surely, was any object so terribly full of awe! The eyes were gone, and the whole flesh around the mouth, leaving the teeth utterly naked. This, then, was the smile which had cheered us on to hope! this the—but I forbear. The brig, as I have already told, passed under our stern, and made its way slowly but steadily to leeward. With her and with her terrible crew went all our gay visions of deliverance and joy. Deliberately as she went by, we might possibly

have found means of boarding her, had not our sudden disappointment, and the appalling nature of the discovery which accompanied
it, laid entirely prostrate every active faculty of mind and body. We
had seen and felt, but we could neither think nor act, until, alas! too
late. How much our intellects had been weakened by this incident
may be estimated by the fact, that when the vessel had proceeded
so far that we could perceive no more than the half of her hull, the
proposition was seriously entertained of attempting to overtake her
by swimming!

I have, since this period, vainly endeavoured to obtain some clew
to the hideous uncertainty which enveloped the fate of the stranger.
Her build and general appearance, as I have before stated, led us
to the belief that she was a Dutch trader, and the dresses of the
crew also sustained this opinion. We might have easily seen the
name upon her stern, and, indeed, taken other observations, which
would have guided us in making out her character; but the intense
excitement of the moment blinded us to every thing of that nature.
From the saffron-like hue of such of the corpses as were not entirely decayed, we concluded that the whole of her company had
perished by the yellow fever, or some other virulent disease of the
same fearful kind. If such were the case (and I know not what else to
imagine), death, to judge from the positions of the bodies, must have
come upon them in a manner awfully sudden and overwhelming, in
a way totally distinct from that which generally characterizes even
the most deadly pestilences with which mankind are acquainted. It
is possible, indeed, that poison, accidentally introduced into some
of their sea-stores, may have brought about the disaster; or that the
eating of some unknown venomous species of fish, or other marine
animal, or oceanic bird, might have induced it, — but it is utterly useless to form conjectures where all is involved, and will, no doubt,
remain for ever involved, in the most appalling and unfathomable
mystery.

Chapter XI

We spent the remainder of the day in a condition of stupid lethargy, gazing after the retreating vessel until the darkness, hiding her from our sight, recalled us in some measure to our senses. The pangs of hunger and thirst then returned, absorbing all other cares and considerations. Nothing, however, could be done until the morning, and, securing ourselves as well as possible, we endeavoured to snatch a little repose. In this I succeeded beyond my expectations, sleeping until my companions, who had not been so fortunate, aroused me at daybreak to renew our attempts at getting up provisions from the hull.

It was now a dead calm, with the sea as smooth as I have ever known it,—the weather warm and pleasant. The brig was out of sight. We commenced our operations by wrenching off, with some trouble, another of the forechains; and having fastened both to Peters' feet, he again made an endeavour to reach the door of the storeroom, thinking it possible that he might be able to force it open, provided he could get at it in sufficient time; and this he hoped to do, as the hulk lay much more steadily than before.

He succeeded very quickly in reaching the door, when, loosening one of the chains from his ankle, he made every exertion to force the passage with it, but in vain, the framework of the room being far stronger than was anticipated. He was quite exhausted with his long stay under water, and it became absolutely necessary that some other one of us should take his place. For this service Parker immediately volunteered; but, after making three ineffectual efforts, found that he could never even succeed in getting near the door. The condition of Augustus's wounded arm rendered it useless for him to attempt going down, as he would be unable to force the room open should he reach it, and it accordingly now devolved upon me to exert myself for our common deliverance.

Peters had left one of the chains in the passage, and I found, upon plunging in, that I had not sufficient balance to keep me firmly down. I determined, therefore, to attempt no more, in my first effort, than merely to recover the other chain. In groping along the floor of the passage for this, I felt a hard substance, which I immediately grasped, not having time to ascertain what it was, but returning and ascending instantly to the surface. The prize proved to be a bottle, and our joy may be conceived when I say that it was found to be full of port wine. Giving thanks to God for this timely and cheering assistance, we immediately drew the cork with my penknife, and, each taking a moderate sup, felt the most indescribable comfort from the warmth, strength, and spirits with which it inspired us. We then carefully recorked the bottle, and, by means of a handkerchief, swung it in such a manner that there was no possibility of its getting broken.

Having rested a while after this fortunate discovery, I again descended, and now recovered the chain, with which I instantly came up. I then fastened it on and went down for the third time, when I became fully satisfied that no exertions whatever, in that situation, would enable me to force open the door of the storeroom. I therefore returned in despair.

There seemed now to be no longer any room for hope, and I could perceive in the countenances of my companions that they had made up their minds to perish. The wine had evidently produced in them a species of delirium, which, perhaps, I had been prevented from feeling by the immersion I had undergone since drinking it. They talked incoherently, and about matters unconnected with our condition, Peters repeatedly asking me questions about Nantucket. Augustus, too, I remember, approached me with a serious air, and requested me to lend him a pocket-comb, as his hair was full of fish-scales, and he wished to get them out before going on shore. Parker appeared somewhat less affected, and urged me to dive at random into the cabin, and bring up any article which might come to hand. To this I consented, and, in the first attempt, after staying under a full minute, brought up a small leather trunk belonging to Captain Barnard. This was immediately opened in the faint hope that it might contain something to eat or drink. We found nothing, however, except a box of razors and two linen shirts. I now went down again, and returned without any success. As my head came above water I heard a crash on deck, and, upon getting up, saw that my companions had ungratefully taken advantage of my absence to drink the remainder of the wine, having let the bottle fall in the endeavour to replace it before I saw them. I remonstrated with them on the heartlessness of their conduct, when Augustus burst into tears. The other two endeavoured to laugh the matter off as a joke, but I hope never again to behold laughter of such a species: the distortion of countenance was absolutely frightful. Indeed, it was apparent that the stimulus, in the empty state of their stomachs, had taken instant and violent effect, and that they were all exceedingly intoxicated. With great difficulty I prevailed upon them to lie down, when they fell very soon into a heavy slumber, accompanied with loud stertorous breathing. I now found myself, as it were, alone in the brig, and my reflections, to be sure, were of the most fearful and gloomy nature. No prospect offered itself to my view but a lingering death by famine, or, at the best, by being overwhelmed in the first gale which should spring up, for in our present exhausted condition we could have no hope of living through another.

The gnawing hunger which I now experienced was nearly insupportable, and I felt myself capable of going to any lengths in order to appease it. With my knife I cut off a small portion of the leather trunk, and endeavoured to eat it, but found it utterly impossible to swallow a single morsel, although I fancied that some little alleviation of my suffering was obtained by chewing small pieces of it and spitting them out. Toward night my companions awoke, one by one, each in an indescribable state of weakness and horror, brought on by the wine, whose fumes had now evaporated. They shook as if with a violent ague, and uttered the most lamentable cries for water. Their condition affected me in the most lively degree, at the same time causing me to rejoice in the fortunate train of circumstances which had prevented me from indulging in the wine, and consequently from sharing their melancholy and most distressing sensations. Their conduct, however, gave me great uneasiness and alarm; for it was evident that, unless some favourable change took place, they could afford me no assistance in providing for our common safety. I had not yet abandoned all idea of being able to get up something from below; but the attempt could not possibly be resumed until some one of them was sufficiently master of himself to aid me by holding the end of the rope while I went down. Parker appeared to be somewhat more in possession of his senses than the others, and I endeavoured, by every means in my power, to rouse him. Thinking that a plunge in the sea-water might have a beneficial effect, I contrived to fasten the end of a rope around his body, and then, leading him to the companion-way (he remaining quite passive all the while), pushed him in, and immediately drew him out. I had good reason to congratulate myself upon having made this experiment; for he appeared much revived and invigorated, and, upon getting out, asked me, in a rational manner, why I had so served him. Having explained my object, he expressed himself indebted to me, and said that he felt greatly better from the immersion, afterward conversing sensibly upon our situation. We then resolved to treat Augustus and Peters in the same way, which we immediately did, when they both experienced much benefit from the shock. This idea of sudden immersion had been suggested to me by reading in some medical work the good effect of the shower-bath in a case where the patient was suffering from *mania a potu.*

Finding that I could now trust my companions to hold the end of the rope, I again made three or four plunges into the cabin, although it was now quite dark, and a gentle but long swell from the northward rendered the hulk somewhat unsteady. In the course of these attempts I succeeded in bringing up two case-knives, a three-gallon jug, empty, and a blanket, but nothing which could serve us for food. I continued my efforts, after getting these articles, until I was completely exhausted, but brought up nothing else. During the night Parker and Peters occupied themselves by turns in the same manner; but nothing coming to hand, we now gave up this attempt in despair, concluding that we were exhausting ourselves in vain.

We passed the remainder of this night in a state of the most intense mental and bodily anguish that can possibly be imagined. The morning of the sixteenth at length dawned, and we looked eagerly around the horizon for relief, but to no purpose. The sea was still smooth, with only a long swell from the northward, as on yesterday. This was the sixth day since we had tasted either food or drink, with the exception of the bottle of port wine, and it was clear that we could hold out but a very little while longer unless something could be obtained. I never saw before, nor wish to see again, human beings so utterly emaciated as Peters and Augustus. Had I met them on shore in their present condition I should not have had the slightest suspicion that I had ever beheld them. Their countenances were totally changed in character, so that I could not bring myself to believe them really the same individuals with whom I had been in company but a few days before. Parker, although sadly reduced, and so feeble that he could not raise his head from his bosom, was not so far gone as the other two. He suffered with great patience, making no complaint, and endeavouring to inspire us with hope in every manner he could devise. For myself, although at the commencement of the voyage I had been in bad health, and was at all times of a delicate constitution, I suffered less than any of us, being much less reduced in frame, and retaining my powers of mind in a surprising degree, while the rest were completely prostrated in intellect, and seemed to be brought to a species of second childhood, generally simpering in their expressions, with idiotic smiles, and uttering the most absurd platitudes. At intervals, however, they would appear to revive suddenly, as if inspired all at once with a consciousness of their condition, when they would spring upon their feet in a momentary flash of vigour, and speak, for a short period, of their prospects, in a manner altogether rational, although full of the most intense despair. It is possible, however, that my companions may have entertained the same opinion of their own condition as I did of mine, and that I may have unwittingly been guilty of the same extravagances and imbecilities as themselves—this is a matter which cannot be determined.

About noon Parker declared that he saw land off the larboard quarter, and it was with the utmost difficulty I could restrain him from plunging into the sea with the view of swimming toward it. Peters and Augustus took little notice of what he said, being apparently wrapped up in moody contemplation. Upon looking in the direction pointed out, I could not perceive the faintest appearance of the shore—indeed, I was too well aware that we were far from any land to indulge in a hope of that nature. It was a long time, nevertheless, before I could convince Parker of his mistake. He then burst into a flood of tears, weeping like a child, with loud cries and sobs, for two or three hours, when becoming exhausted, he fell asleep.

Peters and Augustus now made several ineffectual efforts to swallow portions of the leather. I advised them to chew it and spit it out; but they were too excessively debilitated to be able to follow my advice. I continued to chew pieces of it at intervals, and found some relief from so doing; my chief distress was for water, and I was only prevented from taking a draught from the sea by remembering the horrible consequences which thus have resulted to others who were similarly situated with ourselves.

The day wore on in this manner, when I suddenly discovered

a sail to the eastward, and on our larboard bow. She appeared to be a large ship, and was coming nearly athwart us, being probably twelve or fifteen miles distant. None of my companions had as yet discovered her, and I forbore to tell them of her for the present, lest we might again be disappointed of relief. At length upon her getting nearer, I saw distinctly that she was heading immediately for us, with her light sails filled. I could now contain myself no longer, and pointed her out to my fellow-sufferers. They immediately sprang to their feet, again indulging in the most extravagant demonstrations of joy, weeping, laughing in an idiotic manner, jumping, stamping upon the deck, tearing their hair, and praying and cursing by turns. I was so affected by their conduct, as well as by what I considered a sure prospect of deliverance, that I could not refrain from joining in with their madness, and gave way to the impulses of my gratitude and ecstasy by lying and rolling on the deck, clapping my hands, shouting, and other similar acts, until I was suddenly called to my recollection, and once more to the extreme human misery and despair, by perceiving the ship all at once with her stern fully presented toward us, and steering in a direction nearly opposite to that in which I had at first perceived her.

It was some time before I could induce my poor companions to believe that this sad reverse in our prospects had actually taken place. They replied to all my assertions with a stare and a gesture implying that they were not to be deceived by such misrepresentations. The conduct of Augustus most sensibly affected me. In spite of all I could say or do to the contrary, he persisted in saying that the ship was rapidly nearing us, and in making preparations to go on board of her. Some seaweed floating by the brig, he maintained that it was the ship's boat, and endeavoured to throw himself upon it, howling and shrieking in the most heartrending manner, when I forcibly restrained him from thus casting himself into the sea.

Having become in some degree pacified, we continued to watch the ship until we finally lost sight of her, the weather becoming hazy, with a light breeze springing up. As soon as she was entirely gone, Parker turned suddenly toward me with an expression of countenance which made me shudder. There was about him an air of self-possession which I had not noticed in him until now, and before he opened his lips my heart told me what he would say. He proposed, in a few words, that one of us should die to preserve the existence of the others.

Chapter XII

I had for some time past, dwelt upon the prospect of our being reduced to this last horrible extremity, and had secretly made up my mind to suffer death in any shape or under any circumstances rather than resort to such a course. Nor was this resolution in any degree weakened by the present intensity of hunger under which I laboured. The proposition had not been heard by either Peters or Augustus. I therefore took Parker aside; and mentally praying to God for power to dissuade him from the horrible purpose he entertained, I expostulated with him for a long time, and in the most supplicating manner, begging him in the name of every thing which he held sacred, and urging him by every species of argument which the extremity of the case suggested, to abandon the idea, and not to mention it to either of the other two.

He heard all I said without attempting to controvert any of my arguments, and I had begun to hope that he would be prevailed upon to do as I desired. But when I had ceased speaking, he said that he knew very well all I had said was true, and that to resort to such a course was the most horrible alternative which could enter into the mind of man; but that he had now held out as long as human nature could be sustained; that it was unnecessary for all to perish, when, by the death of one, it was possible, and even probable, that the rest might be finally preserved; adding that I might save myself the trouble of trying to turn him from his purpose, his mind having been thoroughly made up on the subject even before the appearance of the ship, and that only her heaving in sight had prevented him from mentioning his intention at an earlier period.

I now begged him, if he would not be prevailed upon to abandon his design, at least to defer it for another day, when some vessel might come to our relief; again reiterating every argument I could devise, and which I thought likely to have influence with one of his rough nature. He said, in reply, that he had not spoken until the very last possible moment, that he could exist no longer without sustenance of some kind, and that therefore in another day his suggestion would be too late, as regarded himself at least.

Finding that he was not to be moved by anything I could say in a mild tone, I now assumed a different demeanor, and told him that he must be aware I had suffered less than any of us from our calamities; that my health and strength, consequently, were at that moment far better than his own, or than that either of Peters or Augustus; in short, that I was in a condition to have my own way by force if I found it necessary; and that if he attempted in any manner to acquaint the others with his bloody and cannibal designs, I would not hesitate to throw him into the sea. Upon this he immediately seized me by the throat, and drawing a knife, made several ineffectual efforts to stab me in the stomach; an atrocity which his excessive debility alone prevented him from accomplishing. In the meantime, being roused to a high pitch of anger, I forced him to the vessel's side, with the full intention of throwing him overboard. He was saved from his fate, however, by the interference of Peters, who now approached and separated us, asking the cause of the disturbance. This Parker told before I could find means in any manner to prevent him.

The effect of his words was even more terrible than what I had anticipated. Both Augustus and Peters, who, it seems, had long secretly entertained the same fearful idea which Parker had been merely the first to broach, joined with him in his design and insisted upon its immediately being carried into effect. I had calculated that one at least of the two former would be found still possessed of sufficient strength of mind to side with myself in resisting any attempt to execute so dreadful a purpose; and, with the aid of either one of them, I had no fear of being able to prevent its accomplishment. Being disappointed in this expectation, it became absolutely necessary that I should attend to my own safety, as a further resistance on my part might possibly be considered by men in their frightful condition a sufficient excuse for refusing me fair play in the tragedy that I knew would speedily be enacted.

I now told them I was willing to submit to the proposal, merely requesting a delay of about one hour, in order that the fog which had gathered around us might have an opportunity of lifting, when it was possible that the ship we had seen might be again in sight. After great difficulty I obtained from them a promise to wait thus long; and, as I had anticipated (a breeze rapidly coming in), the fog lifted before the hour had expired, when, no vessel appearing in sight, we prepared to draw lots.

It is with extreme reluctance that I dwell upon the appalling scene which ensued; a scene which, with its minutest details, no after events have been able to efface in the slightest degree from my memory, and whose stern recollection will embitter every future moment of my existence. Let me run over this portion of my narrative with as much haste as the nature of the events to be spoken of will permit. The only method we could devise for the terrific lottery, in which we were to take each a chance, was that of drawing straws. Small splinters of wood were made to answer our purpose, and it was agreed that I should be the holder. I retired to one end of the hulk, while my poor companions silently took up their station in the other with their backs turned toward me. The bitterest anxiety which I endured at any period of this fearful drama was while I occupied myself in the arrangement of the lots. There are few conditions into which man can possibly fall where he will not feel a deep interest in the preservation of his existence; an interest momentarily increasing with the frailness of the tenure by which that existence may be held. But now that the silent, definite, and stern nature of the business in which I was engaged (so different from the tumultuous dangers of the storm or the gradually approaching horrors of famine) allowed me to reflect on the few chances I had of escaping the most appalling of deaths—a death for the most appalling of purposes—every particle of that energy which had so long buoyed me up departed like feathers before the wind, leaving me a helpless prey to the most abject and pitiable terror. I could not, at first, even summon up sufficient strength to tear and fit together the small splinters of wood, my fingers absolutely refusing their office, and my knees knocking violently against each other. My mind ran over rapidly a thousand absurd projects by which to avoid becoming a partner in the awful speculation. I thought of falling on my knees to my companions, and entreating them to let me escape this necessity; of suddenly rushing upon them, and, by putting one of them to death, of rendering the decision by lot useless—in short, of every thing but of going through with the matter I had in hand. At last, after wasting a long time in this imbecile conduct, I was recalled to my senses by the voice of Parker, who urged me to relieve them at once from the terrible anxiety they were enduring. Even then I could not bring myself to arrange the splinters upon the spot, but thought over every species of finesse by which I could trick some one of my fellow-sufferers to draw the short straw, as it had been agreed that whoever drew the shortest of four splinters from my hand was to die for the preservation of the rest. Before any one condemn me for this apparent heartlessness, let him be placed in a situation precisely similar to my own.

At length delay was no longer possible, and, with a heart almost bursting from my bosom, I advanced to the region of the forecastle, where my companions were awaiting me. I held out my hand with the splinters, and Peters immediately drew. He was free—*his*, at least, was not the shortest; and there was now another chance against my escape. I summoned up all my strength, and passed the lots to Augustus. He also drew immediately, and he also was free; and now, whether I should live or die, the chances were no more than precisely even. At this moment all the fierceness of the tiger possessed my bosom, and I felt toward my poor fellow-creature, Parker, the most intense, the most diabolical hatred. But the feeling did not last; and, at length, with a convulsive shudder and closed eyes, I held out the two remaining splinters toward him. It was fully five minutes before he could summon resolution to draw, during which period of heartrending suspense I never once opened my eyes. Presently one of the two lots was quickly drawn from my hand. The decision was then over, yet I knew not whether it was for me or against me. No one spoke, and still I dared not satisfy myself by looking at the splinter I held. Peters at length took me by the hand, and I forced myself to look up, when I immediately saw by the countenance of Parker that I was safe, and that he it was who had been doomed to suffer. Gasping for breath, I fell senseless to the deck.

I recovered from my swoon in time to behold the consummation of the tragedy in the death of him who had been chiefly instrumental in bringing it about. He made no resistance whatever, and was stabbed in the back by Peters, when he fell instantly dead. I must not dwell upon the fearful repast which immediately ensued. Such things may be imagined, but words have no power to impress the mind with the exquisite horror of their reality. Let it suffice to say that, having in some measure appeased the raging thirst which consumed us by the blood of the victim, and having by common consent taken off the hands, feet, and head, throwing them together with the entrails, into the sea, we devoured the rest of the body, piecemeal, during the four ever memorable days of the seventeenth, eighteenth, nineteenth, and twentieth of the month.

On the nineteenth, there coming on a smart shower which lasted fifteen or twenty minutes, we contrived to catch some water by means of a sheet which had been fished up from the cabin by our drag just after the gale. The quantity we took in all did not amount to more than half a gallon; but even this scanty allowance supplied us with comparative strength and hope.

On the twenty-first we were again reduced to the last necessity. The weather still remained warm and pleasant, with occasional fogs and light breezes, most usually from N. to W.

On the twenty-second, as we were sitting close huddled together, gloomily revolving over our lamentable condition, there flashed through my mind all at once an idea which inspired me with a bright gleam of hope. I remembered that, when the foremast had been cut away, Peters, being in the windward chains, passed one of the axes into my hand, requesting me to put it, if possible, in a place of security, and that a few minutes before the last heavy sea struck the brig and filled her I had taken this axe into the forecastle and laid it in one of the larboard berths. I now thought it possible that, by getting at this axe, we might cut through the deck over the storeroom, and thus readily supply ourselves with provisions.

When I communicated this object to my companions, they uttered a feeble shout of joy, and we all proceeded forthwith to the forecastle. The difficulty of descending here was greater than that of going down in the cabin, the opening being much smaller, for it will be remembered that the whole framework about the cabin companion-hatch had been carried away, whereas the forecastle-way, being a simple hatch of only about three feet square, had remained uninjured. I did not hesitate, however, to attempt the descent; and a rope being fastened round my body as before, I plunged boldly in, feet foremost, made my way quickly to the berth, and at the first attempt brought up the axe. It was hailed with the most ecstatic joy and triumph, and the ease with which it had been obtained was regarded as an omen of our ultimate preservation.

We now commenced cutting at the deck with all the energy of rekindled hope, Peters and myself taking the axe by turns, Augustus's wounded arm not permitting him to aid us in any degree. As we were still so feeble as to be scarcely able to stand unsupported, and could consequently work but a minute or two without resting, it soon became evident that many long hours would be necessary to accomplish our task—that is, to cut an opening sufficiently large to admit of a free access to the storeroom. This consideration, however, did not discourage us; and, working all night by the light of the moon, we succeeded in effecting our purpose by daybreak on the morning of the twenty-third.

Peters now volunteered to go down; and, having made all arrangements as before, he descended, and soon returned bringing up with him a small jar, which, to our great joy, proved to be full of olives. Having shared these among us, and devoured them with the greatest avidity, we proceeded to let him down again. This time he succeeded beyond our utmost expectations, returning instantly with a large ham and a bottle of Madeira wine. Of the latter we each took a moderate sup, having learned by experience the pernicious consequences of indulging too freely. The ham, except about two pounds near the bone, was not in a condition to be eaten, having been entirely spoiled by the salt water. The sound part was divided among us. Peters and Augustus, not being able to restrain their appetite, swallowed theirs upon the instant; but I was more cautious, and ate but a small portion of mine, dreading the thirst which I knew would ensue. We now rested a while from our labors, which had been intolerably severe.

By noon, feeling somewhat strengthened and refreshed, we

again renewed our attempt at getting up provisions, Peters and myself going down alternately, and always with more or less success, until sundown. During this interval we had the good fortune to bring up, altogether, four more small jars of olives, another ham, a carboy containing nearly three gallons of excellent Cape Madeira wine, and, what gave us still more delight, a small tortoise of the Gallipago breed, several of which had been taken on board by Captain Barnard, as the Grampus was leaving port, from the schooner Mary Pitts, just returned from a sealing voyage in the Pacific.

In a subsequent portion of this narrative I shall have frequent occasion to mention this species of tortoise. It is found principally, as most of my readers may know, in the group of islands called the Gallipagos, which, indeed, derive their name from the animal—the Spanish word Gallipago meaning a fresh-water terrapin. From the peculiarity of their shape and action they have been sometimes called the elephant tortoise. They are frequently found of an enormous size. I have myself seen several which would weigh from twelve to fifteen hundred pounds, although I do not remember that any navigator speaks of having seen them weighing more than eight hundred. Their appearance is singular, and even disgusting. Their steps are very slow, measured, and heavy, their bodies being carried about a foot from the ground. Their neck is long, and exceedingly slender; from eighteen inches to two feet is a very common length, and I killed one, where the distance from the shoulder to the extremity of the head was no less than three feet ten inches. The head has a striking resemblance to that of a serpent. They can exist without food for an almost incredible length of time, instances having been known where they have been thrown into the hold of a vessel and lain two years without nourishment of any kind—being as fat, and, in every respect, in as good order at the expiration of the time as when they were first put in. In one particular these extraordinary animals bear a resemblance to the dromedary, or camel of the desert. In a bag at the root of the neck they carry with them a constant supply of water. In some instances, upon killing them after a full year's deprivation of all nourishment, as much as three gallons of perfectly sweet and fresh water have been found in their bags. Their food is chiefly wild parsley and celery, with purslain, sea-kelp, and prickly pears, upon which latter vegetable they thrive wonderfully, a great quantity of it being usually found on the hillsides near the shore wherever the animal itself is discovered. They are excellent and highly nutritious food, and have, no doubt, been the means of preserving the lives of thousands of seamen employed in the whale-fishery and other pursuits in the Pacific.

The one which we had the good fortune to bring up from the storeroom was not of a large size, weighing probably sixty-five or seventy pounds. It was a female, and in excellent condition, being exceedingly fat, and having more than a quart of limpid and sweet water in its bag. This was indeed a treasure; and, falling on our knees with one accord, we returned fervent thanks to God for so seasonable a relief.

We had great difficulty in getting the animal up through the opening, as its struggles were fierce and its strength prodigious. It was upon the point of making its escape from Peter's grasp, and slipping back into the water, when Augustus, throwing a rope with a slipknot around its throat, held it up in this manner until I jumped into the hole by the side of Peters, and assisted him in lifting it out.

The water we drew carefully from the bag into the jug; which, it will be remembered, had been brought up before from the cabin. Having done this, we broke off the neck of a bottle so as to form, with the cork, a kind of glass, holding not quite half a gill. We then each drank one of these measures full, and resolved to limit ourselves to this quantity per day as long as it should hold out.

During the last two or three days, the weather having been dry and pleasant, the bedding we had obtained from the cabin, as well as our clothing, had become thoroughly dry, so that we passed this night (that of the twenty-third) in comparative comfort, enjoying a tranquil repose, after having supped plentifully on olives and ham, with a small allowance of the wine. Being afraid of losing some of our stores overboard during the night, in the event of a breeze springing up, we secured them as well as possible with cordage to the fragments of the windlass. Our tortoise, which we were anxious to preserve alive as long as we could, we threw on its back, and otherwise carefully fastened.

How I Became an Edgar Allan Poe Convert

. . . . . .

BY SUE GRAFTON

I hadn't had occasion to read Edgar Allan Poe since high school, so when Michael Connelly asked me to contribute a few laudatory words to this anthology commemorating Poe's two hundredth birthday, I said I'd consider his request. Please note: I didn't actually *commit* myself, but I did experience a mild surge of interest and told Michael Connelly I'd do what I could. After all, why not? This was late October 2007, and my comments wouldn't be due until the end of February 2008—a lead time of three months during which I might very well be killed.

Aside from the fact that I seldom agree to write anything "off-grid," my reservations were twofold:

1. I'm not a scholar by any stretch, and I generally refuse to hold forth on any subject except, possibly, cats.
2. I'd recently started work on *"U" Is for . . .* , and I knew I needed to focus on the task at hand.

Nonetheless, being a fan of Michael Connelly's (especially since, heretofore, he'd never asked me for anything), I bought a paperback edition of *Great Tales and Poems of Edgar Allan Poe* to refresh my memory. I sailed through the introduction and the section called "Chronology of Edgar Allan Poe's Life and Work." So far, so good. I did question the wisdom of his marrying his thirteen-year-old tubercular cousin, but boys will be boys, and poor Poe was known as a falling-down drunk.

In rapid succession, I read "The Pit and the Pendulum," "The Purloined Letter," "Manuscript Found in a Bottle," and "The Murders in the Rue Morgue." Oh, dear. That "Ourang-Outang" business really didn't fly as far as I was concerned. Let's not even talk about "The Gold-Bug," which left me cranky and out of sorts. I found Poe profligate with his exclamation points, and his overheated prose was larded with inexplicable French phrases. Not only that, he was much too fond of adverbs, and his dialogue fairly cried out for the stern admonitions of a good editor. Mon Dieu!! These are all writerly habits of which I thoroughly disapprove!!! Further reading of his work did nothing to soften my views. What was I to do? I had nothing nice to say about the man and no hope of faking it.

I wrote to Michael Connelly, begging to be relieved of my responsibilities. He wrote back and most graciously excused me. *Quel joie!!* I returned to *"U . . ."* and thought no more about the Poe anthology. Then, two months later, just when my guilt was beginning to subside, Michael wrote again on "the long shot of all long shots" that I might relent. In the unlikely event that I'd say yes, he cautioned that my term paper would be due, not the middle of February as originally thought, but closer to February 1.

I felt myself waver and wondered if there was any way I might be of help. I decided to renew my efforts before closing the door on him once and for all. Given the accelerated deadline, I took the only sensible action that crossed my mind. I turned to the Internet and Googled Edgar Allan Poe in hopes of cribbing an academic paper I could pass off as my own.

In the course of this random research, I came across a reference to a Poe story called *The Narrative of Arthur Gordon Pym of Nantucket,* which wasn't included in the collected works I'd bought. What caught my attention were comments I unearthed from the archives of Cornell University: *The Works of the Late Edgar Allan Poe; with a Memoir by Rufus Wilmot Griswold, and Notices of His Life and Genius by N. P. Willis and J. R Lowell,* 4 vols. (New York: Redfield, 1856). On page 434 of one of these volumes (alas, I know not which), either Mr. Griswold, N. P. Willis, or J. R. Lowell wrote the following: "Had this 'Narrative' been brought to a conclusion satisfactory, or even plausible, 'Arthur Gordon Pym' would have been the most perfect specimen of [Poe's] imaginative and constructive powers."

Well, *that* was curious.

Fifty key strokes later, I found the lengthy story online and reproduced as much of it as printer paper would allow. I'd read no more than a few paragraphs when I found myself transfixed. The prose was clear and accessible, with nary a !!! in sight. But what intrigued me was the challenge Poe had set for himself. *The Narrative ...* purports to be an account of an extraordinary (and entirely invented) journey across the Antarctic Ocean, as told by one Arthur Gordon Pym at a gentlemen's club in Richmond, Virginia, in the latter months of 1836. Those who hear of his remarkable adventures urge Pym to make the matter public. Pym declines, explaining that he kept no written journal during this protracted period and that he questions his ability to write, "from mere memory, a statement so minute and connected as to have the *appearance* of that truth it would really possess." The incidents, he says, are of a nature so marvelous that he doubts the public would regard his comments as anything other than "an impudent and ingenious fiction."

As luck would have it, among those present at the gathering is our very own Edgar Allan Poe, lately editor of the *Southern Literary Messenger,* who strongly advises Pym to prepare a thorough rendering of the affair and who further proposes to publish this chronicle in the *Southern Literary Messenger* as a work of fiction under his (Poe's) name. This ruse, says Poe, will allow Pym to fully air his tale without inciting the public's incredulity.

In January and February 1837, twenty-five chapters of this narrative appear in the *Messenger*, meticulously detailing a voyage to the South Pacific, which results in the alleged discovery of a new land, complete with the specifics of climate, atmosphere, water, novel plants, and strange animals, capped by a description of the inhabitants, who differ from all other races of men.

The response is unexpected.

As convincing as the author (Poe) has hoped to be in persuading the public that the tale is mere fable, letters are sent to Mr. Poe's address "distinctly expressing a conviction to the contrary." Far from viewing these exploits as fiction, the public believes them to be true. Edgar Allan Poe is forced to confess that the tale is not his, but is an unexpurgated and completely factual account of actual events that happened to Arthur Gordon Pym. Arthur Gordon Pym, in turn, is finally convinced to step forward and acknowledge the reportage as his own. He then proceeds to dictate his experiences in such an authoritative tone that the whole of it is accepted as gospel. So much so that a publishing house in London commences arrangements to reprint the work as a bona fide history.

Having established this dazzling turnabout premise, Poe now faces the tricky issue of how to bring the tale to a conclusion without leaving himself open to the very scientific scrutiny he's hoping to avoid. In order to sustain the authenticity of his deception—posing as Pym and limning a supposed fiction whose outing as truth motivates Pym to affirm his role as author and participant (whew!!) — Poe must find a means of completing the yarn without tipping his hand.

For a few moments, I put myself in Poe's shoes and pondered the possibilities. My temptation would have been to chuck the whole scheme as a rebellion of plot and character now desperately in need of quashing.

His solution was to make the following announcement:

> *The circumstances connected with the late sudden and distressing death of Mr. Pym are already well known to the public through the medium of the daily press. It is feared that the few remaining chapters which were to have completed his narrative, and which were retained by him . . . for the purpose of revision, have been irrecoverably lost through the accident by which he perished himself. This, however, may prove not to be the case, and the papers, if ultimately found, will be given to the public. The loss of two or three final chapters . . . is the more deeply to be regretted, as it can not be doubted they contained matter relative to the Pole itself, or at least to regions in its very near proximity; and as, too, the statements of the author in relation to these regions may shortly be verified or contradicted by means of the governmental expedition now preparing for the Southern Ocean.*

In support of this, Poe attaches a number of footnotes in which he clarifies and annotates the veracity of Pym's assertions in all of their particulars.

The elaborate and ingenious conceit of this story (which is, by the way, executed with unfaltering confidence) was finally sufficient to arouse my admiration and elevate my prior opinion of Edgar Allan Poe . . . at least in terms of this one stunning testimonial to his skills. I'm delighted to recommend *The Narrative of Arthur Gordon Pym of Nantucket* as exemplary of Poe's powers of invention. I do this with a clear conscience and in sincere support of this anthology honoring his work. Personal integrity aside, there is one more important point to be made: now Michael Connelly owes me.

Sue Grafton entered the mystery field in 1982 with the publication of "A" Is for Alibi, which introduced female hard-boiled private investigator Kinsey Millhone, who operates out of the fictional town of Santa Teresa (a.k.a. Santa Barbara), California. "B" Is for Burglar followed in 1985, and since then she has added eighteen novels to the series now referred to as "the alphabet mysteries." At the rate she's going, she'll reach "Z" Is for Zero in the year 2020, give or take a decade. She will be much much older than she is now.

Copyright Information

· · · · · ·

Copyright Information

DWIGHT HOWARD

Union Public Library
1980 Morris Avenue
Union, N.J. 07083

GIFTED AND GIVING BASKETBALL STAR

by Ryan Basen

E **Enslow Publishers, Inc.**
40 Industrial Road
Box 398
Berkeley Heights, NJ 07922
USA
http://www.enslow.com

Library of Congress Cataloging-in-Publication Data
Basen, Ryan.
  Dwight Howard : gifted and giving basketball star / Ryan Basen.
      p. cm. — (Sports stars who give back)
  Includes bibliographical references and index.
  Summary: "A biography of American basketball player Dwight Howard, focusing on his philanthropic activities off the court"–Provided by publisher.
  ISBN 978-0-7660-3586-7
  1. Howard, Dwight—Juvenile literature. 2. Basketball players—United States—Biography—Juvenile literature. 3. African American philanthropists—Biography—Juvenile literature. 4. Orlando Magic (Basketball team)–Juvenile literature. I. Title.
  GV884.H68B37 2010
  796.323092–dc22
  [B]
                                          2009026182

Printed in the United States of America

102009 Lake Book Manufacturing, Inc., Melrose Park, IL

10 9 8 7 6 5 4 3 2 1

To Our Readers: We have done our best to make sure all Internet addresses in this book were active and appropriate when we went to press. However, the author and the publisher have no control over and assume no liability for the material available on those Internet sites or on other Web sites they may link to. Any comments or suggestions can be sent by e-mail to comments@enslow.com or to the address on the back cover.

♻ Enslow Publishers, Inc. is committed to printing our books on recycled paper. The paper in every book contains between 10% to 30% post-consumer waste (PCW). The cover board on the outside of each book contains 100% PCW. Our goal is to do our part to help young people and the environment too!

CONTENTS

THE RISE OF A SUPERSTAR

As the horn sounded to signal the end of a National Basketball Association playoff game at Amway Arena in Orlando, Florida, Dwight Howard could not hide his glee. He smiled wide and lifted his arms in triumph while holding back tears of joy.

It was late on the night of April 28, 2008. Howard had just led the Orlando Magic to a five-game series victory over the Toronto Raptors in the first round of the NBA Playoffs. He had been a dominant player in the series. Howard, a twenty-two-year-old center in his fourth NBA season, scored 21

Howard, right, dunks the ball against the Toronto Raptors in the 2008 playoffs.

DWIGHT HOWARD FACTS

Birthday: **December 8, 1985**
Hometown: **Atlanta, Georgia**

points and pulled down 21 rebounds in the 102–92 win over Toronto. This marked the third time in the short series that the six-foot-eleven, 265-pound Howard tallied at least 20 points and 20 rebounds in the same game. He was the first NBA player to have done so three times in a playoff series in more than thirty years.

"It's an amazing thing for Dwight," Magic coach Stan Van Gundy said after the game. "He put a lot of effort into the series to be a force at both ends of the floor."[1]

Howard's performance helped Orlando, the third seed in the Eastern Conference, beat number six seed Toronto four games to one. It was the first time he had won a playoff series in his career and the first time the Magic had won a playoff series since 1996.

After the decisive Game Five, more than 17,000 fans inside the arena cheered. Magic executives and other employees were overjoyed. Players and coaches hugged and saluted the fans. Howard was ecstatic. "I was just so very happy. We put in a lot of work in the

**Howard (right) with NBA Commissioner David
Stern at the 2004 NBA Draft**

offseason to get where we're standing today,"
Howard said. "It hasn't hit me yet that we're moving
past the first round. We did something that hasn't
been done here in a long while. . . . To finish out a
series makes us feel really good."[2]

The victory over Toronto marked the first great
team accomplishment in Howard's NBA career—
a career that has just begun to take off. Howard had

DID YOU KNOW?

Howard loves to bowl. He owns six bowling balls and is one of the best bowlers among NBA players, according to New Orleans Hornets point guard Chris Paul.

entered the NBA just four years earlier—straight out of his Atlanta, Georgia, high school, no less—as the first pick in the 2004 NBA Draft by Orlando.

Howard has matured and improved his play every year since he was drafted. In his short career, he has already earned a selection to the NBA All-Rookie team, led Orlando back to the playoffs after a four-year absence, become a team captain at age twenty-one, won the Slam Dunk Contest, and been named a first-team All-NBA player.

After leading the Magic past the Raptors in the 2008 NBA Playoffs, Howard then helped Team USA win a gold medal in basketball at the 2008 Olympics in Beijing, China, a few months later. He has become a bona fide elite player.

"The hardest jump for a player is the one from very good to great, and Howard has made it," Ian Thomsen wrote in *Sports Illustrated* in 2008.[3]

In just four seasons, Howard replaced Shaquille O'Neal as the most dominant, popular big man in the NBA. Using supreme athleticism, strength, and hard work, he has established himself as one of the top rebounders and shot-blockers in the league, and his offensive game continues to develop. "He's a total freak of nature," an NBA Western Conference scout said. "He has a feel for the ball beyond his years."[4]

Howard has become a top player while also maintaining a promise he made while in high school: to be a good citizen and help grow the game of pro basketball. He often volunteers in the community, and he has his own foundation and runs a youth camp in Orlando. Howard has held on to the values and religious beliefs he learned as the son of two hard-working, strict parents in Atlanta. He is also a laid-back person, which endears him to teammates.

> **"He's a total freak of nature. He has a feel for the ball beyond his years."**
>
> *—NBA Western Conference Scout*

"Maybe the best thing about Howard is that he still has the same infectious joy he had when he came into the league as an eighteen-year-old," Jack McCallum wrote in *Sports Illustrated* during the 2007–08 season.[5]

MATURING AS HE GOES

Magic general manager Otis Smith once called Howard "the silliest player on the league's silliest team."[6] Howard has been criticized for not being serious enough during games. But nobody ripped him during the Toronto series in the spring of 2008. The Magic was only a slight favorite heading into the series, despite having won eleven more games than the Raptors during the regular season. Both teams were young and had made it to the postseason in 2007 for the first time in a while. Although both squads had lost the year before, the Raptors had won two games in their series, against the New Jersey Nets. The Magic, meanwhile, was swept 4–0 by the Detroit Pistons in 2007.

The Magic—and Howard—immediately took control of their 2008 series. The Magic won Game 1 in Orlando 114–100 as Howard tallied 25 points, 22 rebounds, and 5 blocked shots. Howard scored 29 points and grabbed 20 rebounds in Game 2, as the Magic edged the Raptors 104–103. After the Raptors won Game 3 at home easily, Howard had a huge impact on the most crucial game of the series.

The Raptors could have tied the series by winning Game 4. The Magic, however, would gain a crucial 3–1 cushion if it won the game. Howard finished the game with 19 points, 16 rebounds, and 8 blocks. The Magic rallied from a five-point halftime deficit to win 106–94.

DID YOU KNOW?

Men's Health magazine named Howard one of the twenty-five fittest people in the United States in 2008.

DWIGHT HOWARD FACTS

NBA players voted Howard as one of the players they would most like to play with in a 2008 poll conducted by *Sports Illustrated*.

The series returned to Orlando two nights later. The Magic built a double-digit lead in the second quarter and still held a big lead in the fourth quarter. Toronto rallied to pull within two points, but the Magic made a few late three-pointers to pull away with the ten-point victory.

Howard averaged 22.6 points and 18.2 rebounds in the series. After Game 5, coaches, teammates, opponents, media members—everybody, it seemed—was praising Howard.

"He's a phenom; he's the best center in the league," said Chris Bosh, Toronto's All-Star power forward. "He's probably the strongest guy in the league, and he knows how to use his body. It doesn't surprise me at all. I've seen him play this whole series, I've seen him play this season."[7]

Van Gundy noticed Howard was playing even better in the playoffs than he had during the regular season, when the league named him an All-NBA First Team player. "There was a different demeanor from him," Van Gundy said. "Dwight is a fun-loving guy and he likes to fool around. There are a lot of times during the year, not bad, but a lot of times during the year where I've got to try to bring him back to being serious when we're preparing. I did not have to say one word, from the start of preparation for this series all the way through."[8]

Howard appreciated the praise and respect, then he quickly went back to work. The Magic had to prepare to play the Detroit Pistons in the second round.

The series against Detroit was not as enjoyable or successful for Howard and the Magic. The veteran-laden Pistons were playing in the second round for the seventh straight season. The Magic had just two players who had appeared in a second-round series. Detroit played like the savvier, more experienced team it was, beating the Magic in five games. Howard struggled in the series, but he had a big game in the Magic's lone win in Game 3.

Despite the series loss against Detroit, Howard and his teammates were still excited about the future after a breakout regular season and the series win over Toronto. Orlando's projected starting lineup featured all five players under the age of thirty, and Howard and other key players were signed for several years. The Magic hoped the 2008–09 season would be the first of many when they would seriously contend for an NBA title.

Howard dunks for Team USA at the 2008 Beijing Olympics.

The spring and summer of 2008 continued to be great for Howard. After the playoff win, he joined some of the NBA's best players on the U.S. Olympic team. He averaged double figures in points and earned nearly 20 minutes per game on Team USA, as the elite squad went undefeated and cruised to the gold medal. Howard was ecstatic. He immediately said he wanted to play in the Olympics again when they are held in London, England, in 2012. But first he had a lot of work to do back in the United States. He and the Magic would soon start training camp to begin chasing an NBA title. "I am happy with what I've done so far," Howard said. "[But] where I want to be is nowhere near where I am now."[9]

YOUNG DWIGHT

Sheryl Howard and Dwight Howard Sr. tried several times to have children during the 1970s and early 1980s. But after seven miscarriages, the couple began to wonder if their dream of having children would ever come true. "We lost two sets of twins," Dwight Sr. said. "I would question God all the time, 'Why does this have to happen?'"[1]

The Howards eventually had three children, with Dwight Howard II born second. He was born on December 9, 1985, into a family that had tremendous faith, worked hard, and loved basketball.

Dwight Sr. and Sheryl played high school basketball while growing up in Swainsboro, a small town in Georgia. Sheryl also played basketball at Robert

Morris College. Dwight II's older sister, TaShanda, played college basketball at both Fort Valley State in Georgia and at Alcorn State in Mississippi. His younger brother Jahaziel joined the basketball team at the University of Central Florida in Orlando in 2008.

Dwight II was always athletic, and he was a star baseball and basketball player growing up. He began playing basketball at an early age, but at first he was not very big. In fact, when Dwight was in elementary school, older kids would not let him play in games with them because he was too short. But when Dwight was in fourth grade, the eighth- and ninth-graders started letting him play with them.

"They were a lot smarter and stronger, so I learned," he recalled. "They pushed me around a lot to see where my head was and see if I would back down."[2] But young Dwight never did.

Dwight was enrolled at Southwest Atlanta Christian Academy. He attended the small private

SOUTHWEST ATLANTA CHRISTIAN ACADEMY

Location: **Atlanta, Georgia**

Famous alumni: **Dwight Howard and Javaris Crittenton (point guard who has played for the NBA's Los Angeles Lakers, Memphis Grizzlies, and Washington Wizards)**

school from kindergarten all the way through high school. Dwight's mother taught physical education at the school. His father worked full-time as a Georgia state trooper, and he volunteered to be in charge of the school's athletics programs. Having his parents so involved in his daily life helped keep the family close.

Attending Southwest Christian taught Dwight to value his faith. He often participated in Bible study sessions at the school, which taught him about the teachings of Christianity. Dwight had a strict up-bringing. He was not allowed to trick-or-treat for Halloween because his parents felt the holiday contradicted their Christian beliefs. His family tried to focus on the true meaning of Christmas, so they did not celebrate the holiday with a tree or presents. Those lessons, along with the examples his parents set as hard workers, made Dwight humble.

A SUDDEN GROWTH SPURT

When Dwight was in middle school, he excelled as a point guard on his basketball teams. He was a quick, athletic player who understood the game. When he broke his left wrist, for example, he learned how to use his right hand to pass and shoot.

Dwight worked hard to prepare for his freshman year of high school. He worked out almost every day before the season. He broke his leg at the end of that freshman season, though, and had to sit out

Dwight in the gym at Southwest Atlanta Christian Academy in Atlanta, Georgia, in 2004

basketball tournaments in the summer. Nobody knew what to expect when he came back healthy for his sophomore year.

By then, Dwight had grown a lot. In fact, Dwight had grown five inches, shooting up to six feet nine inches tall. Despite growing so much so fast, Dwight maintained his coordination and athleticism. As a result, he became a standout high school big man. Quick opponents had trouble guarding him because they were not big enough, while big opponents could not guard him because he was too quick.

"Dwight's always had a high basketball IQ," said Courtney Brooks, Dwight's high school coach. "Now he's grown into his body. Or you could say his body has caught up with his game. In his ninth-grade year, he was so awkward and tall without being physically mature that he was basically sort of goofy. Now you see him out there and it's like poetry. He'll pick your defense apart. He can beat you scoring, passing, rebounding or blocking shots. He can do it every which way."[3]

> **" Dwight's always had a high basketball IQ. Now he's grown into his body. Or you could say his body caught up with his game. "**
>
> —*Courtney Brooks*

Dwight wrote a list of his life goals and hung it up in his bedroom. At the top of the list: Play in the NBA. His parents supported his goal, but they always assumed he would play in college before going to the NBA. Few high school players were good and mature enough to jump straight to the NBA. But suddenly Dwight looked like maybe he could do it.

BECOMING AN ELITE PLAYER

Dwight established a reputation in the Atlanta area as a top high school basketball player. As a sophomore, he helped the Southwest Christian Warriors advance to the state playoffs, then he scored a team-high 19 points in a playoff win. In that game, he scored 5 points in overtime, which included the go-ahead free throw made with less than twenty seconds to play. Southwest Christian won the game, 63–60.

He played well enough over the next summer in travel basketball tournaments to earn recognition from *Sports Illustrated*. Dwight led Southwest Christian back to the state playoffs in his junior year, but the Warriors lost to Whitefield Academy in the state final. Still, Dwight had become an elite player for his age. He was a quick big man who could bang inside and run the floor.

JOSH SMITH FILE

Team: **Atlanta Hawks**

Position: **Forward**

Size: **Six feet nine inches; 235 pounds**

Notable: **Won 2007 NBA Slam Dunk contest**

WHO ARE THE ATLANTA CELTICS?

The Celtics are an Amateur Athletic Union basketball organization that takes teams of young players to compete in tournaments around the United States. Besides Howard, Randolph Morris, and Josh Smith, Atlanta Celtics alumni include Dion Glover, who played guard in the NBA from 1999 to 2004.

Dwight Jr. (right) and Dwight Sr., before Dwight announces he will enter the 2004 NBA Draft

That summer Dwight played with the Atlanta Celtics in the Amateur Athletic Union (AAU). It was a squad of standout Atlanta players that traveled to tournaments and faced elite competition.

One of his teammates was Josh Smith, who later became a forward for the NBA's Atlanta Hawks.

DID YOU KNOW?

Josh Smith was born four days before Howard and attended the same preschool.

RANDOLPH MORRIS FILE

Team: **Atlanta Hawks**

Position: **Center**

Size: **Six feet eleven inches; 260 pounds**

College: **Kentucky**

Notable: **Made his NBA debut with the New York Knicks during the 2007–08 season**

Another teammate was Randolph Morris, a center who also later joined the Hawks.

The Celtics planned a two-month trip to play in tournaments around the United States. NBA scouts and basketball observers had heard of the Celtics before the trip, but few knew who Howard was. Although he was well known in Atlanta, he was not regarded as one of the top players in his high school class nationally. That was about to change.

THE LAST AMATEUR SEASON

By the end of his junior year of high school, Dwight Howard was a well-known high school player among Atlanta basketball fans and observers. But despite his rare combination of size, athleticism, and basketball knowledge, Howard was not yet considered one of the top high school players in the nation.

In 2003, Dwight joined Randolph Morris and Josh Smith on the Atlanta Celtics for a summer full of basketball. They would be playing sixty-five games in eight different tournaments over seventy days. The team hit the road for their first tournament, from May 23–25 in North Carolina.

The Celtics immediately attracted national attention. Led by their three impressive frontcourt players, they ended up winning several tournaments. "Playing together brings out the best in me and Josh and Randolph," Dwight said. "We're on the court competing for everybody's attention."[1] NBA scouts, college scouts, reporters, and representatives of shoe companies were in awe.

Dwight also attended the NBA Players Association camp in June. He was named the camp's most promising prospect. But by the time the summer was coming to an end, Dwight was exhausted.

When he finally returned to Atlanta in early August, his life was about to change. Dwight was suddenly the elite player in his class nationally. People wondered if he would skip college and declare for the NBA Draft after his senior year of high school.

"Dwight Howard, an ambidextrous power forward with the court sense of a point guard, turned out to be the revelation of the summer," Mike Tierney wrote in the *Atlanta Journal-Constitution*. "He's an early favorite to be the number one pick if he elects to bypass college and declare for next June's NBA draft."[2]

Dwight was unsure what to do. His goal had always been to play in the NBA, but he was not certain he was prepared yet. Skipping college for the NBA was a consideration, though. Dwight was big enough and athletic enough to do so.

Dwight also proved that he was mature enough. During one of his high school games, for example, an opposing player tried to fight him after they tangled under the basket. Dwight's father raged in the stands. But Dwight ignored the players' bait and walked over to calm down his father.

Dwight and his supporters had some doubts about whether he should skip college ball. "Physically, he knows he can compete," coach Courtney Brooks said. But "it is a big jump both physically and mentally."[3]

"We're just leaving our options open right now," his father said. "Dwight is just enjoying his life right now. He doesn't have to make a decision right now; it's unnecessary."[4]

> "Dwight Howard, an ambidextrous power forward with the court sense of a point guard, turned out to be the revelation of the summer."
>
> —Mike Tierney

THE FINAL SCHOOL DAYS

Dwight's senior year at Southwest Christian shaped up to be an interesting one. The TV network ESPN2 followed him around to produce a show. A reporter with the *Atlanta Journal-Constitution* newspaper also trailed him to write a series of articles.

A few months earlier, the Cleveland Cavaliers had picked high school player LeBron James with the top selection in the NBA Draft. James was only the second high school player ever taken with the top pick in the draft. People wondered who would be the third. Would it be Dwight?

Dwight was becoming so popular that he often signed autographs for adults before and after games on the road. One of his games even attracted fifteen NBA scouts. He played very well that year, displaying the myriad skills that had made him stand out among the top high school players in the country. He did so even though he was playing on a much higher level than some of his teammates.

Dwight tried to enjoy the year, tried to be a normal kid. He sang in his school's choir, organized a volunteer security team for his church, and tried to tune out his dreams of playing in the NBA. But those dreams were hard to ignore. "It's tough," he said. "I'm so close to all this stuff. Thinking about what team I'm going to play for, my shoe [deal]. I'm just

LEBRON JAMES FILE

Size: **Six feet eight inches; 250 pounds**
High School: **St. Vincent-St. Mary (Akron, Ohio)**
Team: **Cleveland Cavaliers**
Career Highlights: **Led Cavaliers to NBA Finals (2007); five-time NBA All-Star (2005–2009); selected with top pick of 2003 NBA Draft**

trying to play hard, have fun with my team and win a state championship. It's getting harder and harder because everywhere I go people are asking me what I'm going to do."[5]

Dwight was able to tune out those distractions well enough to be his usual dominant self on the basketball court. He led the Warriors to a 30–1 record and a trip back to the state playoffs. Then he played with a sense of desperation in the single-elimination postseason. "I don't want my senior season to end early," he said. "I'll never play here again. . . . I understand that I'm only going to have a chance to be right here, eighteen and in my senior year, just once. All of this is a blessing."[6]

In the state championship game, Dwight tallied a triple-double—26 points, 23 rebounds, and 10 blocks. Southwest Christian avenged their loss to Whitefield a year earlier and won 63–45. After the game, Dwight was ecstatic. After the previous year's loss to Whitefield, he had vowed to not let it happen again. Now he had delivered on that promise.

Dwight finished his senior year with an average of 25 points, 18 rebounds, and 8 blocks per game. Later that spring he was invited to play in prestigious all-star games such as the McDonald's All-American game and the Jordan Capital Classic. He was named most valuable player at the Classic. He tallied 18 points, 15 rebounds, and 6 blocks. But that was not the highlight of his weekend.

Dwight drives to the basket at the 2004 Jordan Capital Classic.

Before the game, he got to meet NBA legend Michael Jordan. He posed for a picture with Jordan, shook his hand, and then thanked him for speaking to the young players. Jordan told him he had the potential to be a great player.

Dwight seemed to handle all the attention well. He still acted like a regular high school senior. He went to his classes, earned a 3.0 grade point average, and enjoyed time with his friends at school. Dwight also gave back to his school and community. He read to kindergartners and chaperoned field trips for younger students. "Being a role model to them is very important to me," he said. "I speak to them every day and I can see that they look up to me."[7]

It did not surprise those who knew the Howard family well that he would remain so humble. While things around him were changing rapidly, he and his family stuck to their principles, rules, and regular activities. "He still observed a curfew," Mike Tierney wrote in the *Orlando Sentinel*. "Still had household chores. Still attended church several times weekly. Still largely was unspoiled in this material world. For his eighteenth birthday, his parents got him . . . an alarm clock."[8]

GOING PRO

In April 2004, Dwight held a press conference at Southwest Christian. Colleges such as North Carolina, Georgia, and Georgia Tech had recruited him hard, but he was still considering skipping college basketball. As TV cameras rolled and reporters watched, Dwight announced he was going to declare for the NBA Draft. The news was hardly a surprise.

"It's time to take the journey to new heights," Dwight said. "I promise you that I'll be a ballplayer you will be proud to watch and a young man you will be proud to know."[9]

Most basketball observers agreed that Dwight had made the right choice to bypass college. Many players had turned pro out of high school and the decision had worked out well for them. That group included NBA All-Stars Kobe Bryant, Tracy McGrady, and Kevin Garnett.

Dwight was named Gatorade's High School Player of the Year in 2003–2004.

But many players who went from high school to the NBA struggled and had poor careers. Perhaps they could have benefited from growing up while they played college basketball, people thought. But few people thought Dwight needed to go to college.

"It looks like to me that he'll be a big impact player for a long time," Houston Rockets general manager Carroll Dawson said. "He's got good instincts. He's been given a lot of athletic ability and a lot of size. When he learns the NBA game, what it takes to play in this league, the work ethic, the things

that you don't know about now, his future is
unbelievably great."[10]

THE DRAFT

The NBA Draft was about two months away, and
most experts predicted Dwight would be one of
the first two picks. The other expected top-two pick
was Emeka Okafor, a center who had just led the
University of Connecticut to a National Collegiate
Athletic Association (NCAA) title.

As Dwight prepared for the draft, his family also
had to take care of distractions such as finding him
an agent. Fortunately for Howard, his father and
uncle—Paul Howard, a district attorney—handled
that. When they selected Aaron Goodwin as his
agent, Goodwin praised the negotiations he had with
Dwight's father and uncle.

Dwight got back to work training for NBA work-
outs and preparing for his rookie season. That spring
he rose every morning at five and worked out in the
Southwest Christian gym before school. "I want to
say at the end of my career that I was one of the
hardest workers," he said.[11]

In early June, he graduated from Southwest
Christian. During the graduation ceremony, he was
awarded the Founder's Cup. That recognized his
overall body of work as a high school student.
Looking back, Dwight remarked that his senior year
had gone by way too fast. But Dwight's life was about

to go into even higher gear. At the age of eighteen, he was about to become a professional basketball player. He was ready, but cautious.

The Orlando Magic had won the top pick in the NBA's annual draft lottery, which determines what team gets the first pick. Just before the draft, the Charlotte Bobcats traded up to the second pick. That meant Dwight would likely either go to Charlotte or Orlando. The rumor was the Magic would take Dwight because scouts thought he had more potential than Okafor.

Dwight was not sure what the Magic would do. Even as the draft started, he did not know. Just after eight o'clock on the night of June 24, 2004, NBA commissioner David Stern walked to the podium on a stage at Radio City Music Hall in New York City. Leaning into the microphone, he announced that the Magic had selected Dwight Howard.

Dwight and his family cheered. "I was surprised," he said. "The whole day, I couldn't sleep. I couldn't do anything. I was thinking about this moment right here. And it's here. I'm very happy with the way things have fallen for me, and I'm ready to go to work."[12]

Dwight was ecstatic. Still a few months shy of his nineteenth birthday, he prepared to become a pro basketball player. It had been his dream since he was in middle school.

ROOKIE YEAR

4

The crowd at Phillips Arena cheered. Orlando Magic coach Johnny Davis congratulated his top players. They then sat down to rest for the remainder of the game. Dwight Howard just smiled and smiled and smiled some more as the time ran out.

It was the night of November 26, 2004, in Atlanta. Howard had just helped the Magic defeat the host Atlanta Hawks 117–99. Howard scored 24 points and grabbed 9 rebounds. It was his first game back in Atlanta since he had been drafted into the NBA. He could not stop smiling about his success.

That smiling would be a common sight in Howard's rookie year with the Magic. Any time he was playing well, he smiled his big, wide, toothy grin. Sometimes when he was not playing well, he still smiled. Teammates called him "Kodak," because he always looked like he was smiling for the camera. He was overjoyed to be playing professional basketball.

"Hopefully, he'll keep that exuberance," Davis said. "He's so refreshing. He reminds me of Magic Johnson. You watch him play and you can just tell that he really enjoys being on the floor."[1]

"Laughing keeps me at peace," Howard said. "I don't want to worry too much. I'm just having fun."[2]

Howard's upbeat personality served him well during an inconsistent rookie year. It was a season that began well and then quickly soured.

PREPARING FOR THE NBA

Howard had joined his Magic teammates shortly after he was drafted in June 2004. He immediately displayed his ability. He scored more than 20 points in three straight games in the NBA Summer League that July.

The Magic took steps to help Howard improve and make it through the long NBA season. They had assistant Clifford Ray work one-on-one with him for hours. Ray was a former NBA center and longtime assistant coach.

Howard was already a solid rebounder. But other aspects of Howard's game needed a lot of attention if he was ever going to become a star. So his coaches forced him to practice and play hard. That was not always fun.

The Magic assigned Howard a locker between Grant Hill and DeShawn Stevenson. Hill was one of the team's leaders. Although the forward was often injured, the 2004–05 season was his eleventh in the NBA. He had made six All-Star teams when he played for the Detroit Pistons in the 1990s. Stevenson, like Howard, was drafted straight out of high school. The Fresno, California, native was picked by the Utah Jazz in the first round of the 2000 NBA Draft and joined the Magic in the 2003–04 season.

The Magic did not ask Howard to do too much right away. Many high draft choices join young, struggling teams. They have to play a lot of minutes and score a lot of points as rookies. Howard had the advantage of joining a veteran team that did not need him to score a lot to win.

Orlando started the season with a healthy Hill. Over the summer they traded superstar forward Tracy McGrady to Houston for guard Steve Francis. Francis, Hill, and other veterans gave the Magic a

GRANT HILL FILE

Size: Six feet eight inches; 225 pounds

Position: Forward

College: Duke

NBA teams: Detroit Pistons (1994–2000); Orlando Magic (2000–2007); Phoenix Suns (2007–2009)

Career notes: 1994–95 NBA Rookie of the Year; seven-time NBA All-Star; four-time All-NBA pick

Steve Francis jumps on Howard's back after the rookie scored a key basket in a game in 2004.

good group to build around. The team only asked Howard to play solid defense, rebound, and try to score inside a bit.

GAME ON

Howard started the season well. He became the first NBA rookie since the 1991–92 season to record at least 10 rebounds in each of the first nine games of his career. But he did not shoot the ball much. In fact, a few weeks into the season, he was averaging just 8 shots per game.

STEVE FRANCIS FILE

Size: **Six feet three inches; 210 pounds**

Position: **Guard**

College: **Maryland**

NBA teams: **Houston Rockets (1999–2004); Orlando Magic (2004–2006); New York Knicks (2006–07); Houston Rockets (2007–08); Memphis Grizzlies (2008–09)**

Career notes: **1999–2000 NBA Co-Rookie of the Year; three-time NBA All-Star**

Settling into that role was a hard adjustment for Howard to make. He was used to being the star player in high school. Even on his loaded AAU teams, he had been able to take a lot of shots. But Howard did not complain about his limited involvement in the offense. "I don't care if I'm the one scoring points. If my team needs me to rebound and block shots, that's what I'm going to do. . . . I understand I'm not the superstar I was in high school."[3]

Howard had other adjustments to make as an NBA rookie. He was the youngest player by far on the Magic. That meant that while teammates went out on the town, he often stayed back at home or at the team hotel. He killed time by playing video games or going to the mall or to the movies, and he tried to avoid doing anything that would get him in trouble.

"I don't want to put myself in any predicament of messing up the name that I've got for myself," he

> **66 The guys here already know that I'm not going to go out and party all night. 99**
>
> *—Dwight Howard*

said. "The guys here already know that I'm not going to go out and party all night. I want them to look at me as a regular person and say, 'Dwight's someone you can look up to.'"[4]

A QUICK START

Howard especially enjoyed his first few weeks in the NBA. The Magic were winning. They started the season 11–5. Howard played a big role in one win. He grabbed 20 rebounds in a game for the first time on December 1, 2004, in a 129–108 victory over the Toronto Raptors.

Another one of those eleven early wins came in the November 26 game in Atlanta. Howard was overjoyed to be back in Atlanta. Before the game, he visited his old school and supervised middle-school students during their physical education classes. He was thrilled to be back at Southwest Christian, which he really missed.

Being home seemed to rejuvenate Howard. For the first time in his brief career, he showed he had solid offensive moves that could work in the NBA. His teammates noticed and passed him the ball more. He took advantage of the additional touches. "He hasn't been in awe or intimidated by anyone we've played this season," Davis said. "He's not in the shallow end anymore. He's in the deep water with the big boys and he's making great progress."[5]

HOWARD VERSUS OKAFOR

Besides games in his hometown, during his rookie year Howard also got excited for games against the Charlotte Bobcats. The Bobcats had rookie center Emeka Okafor. A few months after the Draft, reporters and other basketball observers wondered if the Magic had made the right choice by choosing Howard over Okafor with the top pick. Howard wanted to prove the Magic had been right.

The first time they met, on November 7 in Charlotte, Okafor outplayed Howard. Okafor tallied 12 points and 14 rebounds while Howard had just 5 points and 12 rebounds. The Magic lost 111–100. Early in the game, a fan stood up in the crowd and heckled Howard. The fan yelled at Dwight that he was no longer playing high school basketball.

Fuming, Howard stared at the fan. This was just one sign that he was not in high school any more. He was so accustomed to being cheered and coddled, but now he would sometimes be jeered and be a target for opposing fans.

Howard settled down the next time he played against Okafor. In a twenty-point win over Charlotte on January 7, 2005, he tallied 10 points and 12 rebounds. When they played again on March 24 in

Howard shoots over rival Emeka Okafor (right) of the Charlotte Bobcats in 2006.

Orlando, Howard had 14 points and 15 rebounds. But Okafor tallied 23 points and 10 rebounds as the Bobcats won that game.

Okafor sometimes put up better numbers because he played on an expansion team. His teammates were not as good as Howard's teammates. So Okafor got more minutes than Howard and was more involved in his team's offense.

It was the beginning of a new rivalry of big men in the Southeast Division of the NBA's Eastern Conference. Okafor soon became the favorite for NBA Rookie of the Year, which he later won.

A TOUGH STRETCH

It soon looked, however, as if the Magic might not make the playoffs. The Magic continued to play well through the All-Star break. But then they began to slide. They fell to 28–27 with a 112–103 loss to the Miami Heat on February 27, 2005.

Howard, like many of his teammates, was struggling. During one midwinter stretch, he posted double figures in rebounds only three times in twelve games. Coaches suspected he was getting exhausted. Many first-year NBA players hit the so-called "rookie wall" midway through the season. They are used to playing only thirty to forty games in a season. Now they have to play eighty-two, so they become fatigued in the middle part of the season.

But Howard soon rebounded. He gave the Magic a needed boost with his play in early March 2005. First, Howard earned a double-double (tallying double figures in two categories, such as points and rebounds) in a single half of a game. Then he did it again the next game. He finished with 20 points and 16 rebounds against the Sacramento Kings on March 2. Then he had 20 points and 15 rebounds against the New York Knicks on March 4. The Magic won both games.

A week later he played against the Minnesota Timberwolves. They featured Kevin Garnett, one of Howard's childhood idols. Howard tallied 19 points and 19 rebounds. He also did not back down when

Garnett tried to intimidate him, and Howard drew a technical foul from a fired-up Garnett. Although the Magic lost the game, Howard's teammates and coaches were impressed.

Howard's performance had improved greatly since a January 12 game against Garnett and the Timberwolves. In that game, Howard had posted only 6 points and 9 rebounds. "The first time, I think Dwight was mesmerized, coming face-to-face with his idol," Davis said. "I thought Dwight really grew up (in the second meeting)."[6]

Garnett was also impressed. "He's ten times bigger than [I was] when I was eighteen," said Garnett, who had also been an eighteen-year-old NBA rookie. "He's a freak of nature. The sky's the limit for that kid."[7]

But Howard's big game and improved play could not stop the Magic's slide. They dropped seven games in a row to fall to 31–34 on March 18. Davis was fired. Playing for an interim coach only made things worse. The Magic ended up 36–46, losing nineteen of their final twenty-four games. They missed the playoffs.

Howard dunks against the Charlotte Bobcats in 2004.

A GOOD FIRST SEASON

With the exception of the Magic's late-season slide, Howard was pleased with how his rookie season had gone. The Magic coaches and management were also happy, but they hoped he would continue to improve.

Howard had started all eighty-two games during his rookie year. He averaged 32 minutes per game, posting 32 double-doubles. He grabbed 20 rebounds in three games. He was exhausted. "I just played three high school seasons in one year," he said. "My rookie year went by so fast. I have to go get my battery recharged."[8]

The Magic hoped he would come back refreshed. They also hoped he would change his personality a bit. The team's management actually wanted Howard to smile less and to take the game more seriously.

Howard knew that his work had just begun. The Magic had drafted him first overall because they hoped he would develop into a superstar, not just a solid rebounder and defender. A lot was on the line over the summer and the coming season.

"I had an OK year. I thought I learned a lot," he said. "I have a lot of stuff to work on. Sometimes I was upset the way I performed on the court. Sometimes the light switch wasn't on. I want my team to know they can count on me a little more. . . . The Magic drafted me for a reason. I don't want to let the organization down. I want to be a great player."[9]

YEAR TWO

On an early spring 2006 evening in Philadelphia, the 76ers hosted the Orlando Magic in a late-season NBA regular season game. It was not a significant game. Neither team was going to make the playoffs. Both were struggling. But Dwight Howard made it a memorable game. Howard tallied 28 points and 26 rebounds. He dominated on both ends of the floor. Howard made the play of the game. He rebounded his own missed free throw and scored to put the Magic up 96–95 with three minutes left. Orlando led for the rest of the game and won 102–97.

It was the best game of the second-year player's career. It was a peek at the type of player he was becoming. "He's getting better in every phase of the game," Magic coach Brian Hill said. "Defensively, offensively, he's improving. He's really giving us something special."[1]

The latter part of Howard's second season in the NBA was fun. For the first time, he proved he had the ability to be one of the top players in the league. Those flashes of potential had the Magic excited about the future. That optimism was refreshing. The Magic needed it, because Howard's second season was proving to be a trying one for him and the Magic.

Howard became more involved in the offense, but he missed the old coach. He scored more around the basket, but he was frustrated that he could not develop a jump shot. The Magic started 7–6, but by the second half of the season they had lost eighteen of twenty games. They started the season with two All-Stars on the floor, but ended it without any All-Stars and a 36–46 record. After being in the playoff race for most of the first half of the season, they missed the postseason again.

But the way the Magic and Howard ended the season offered hope. Howard played well, averaging

BRIAN HILL FILE

Coached: **Orlando Magic (1993–1997 and 2005–2007); Vancouver Grizzlies (1997–2000)**

Career record: **298–315**

Career notes: **Led Magic to NBA Finals in 1995**

16.4 points over his last twenty games. The Magic won sixteen of their final twenty-two games. "At worst, Howard looks like he'll be good for a dozen rebounds and a dozen points a night for the next fifteen years," *Orlando Sentinel* columnist David Whitley wrote. "Sometimes, Howard seems too good to be true. We're ready to anoint him the second coming of a higher basketball power like (San Antonio Spurs forward Tim) Duncan. But the best birthday gift he can get is for everyone to just let him become Dwight. Whatever that may be, it should be worth the wait."[2]

NO SOPHOMORE SLUMP

Howard had entered his second season optimistic. In the offseason he had put on twelve pounds (5.4 kg) of muscle and improved his conditioning. He thought the Magic could make the playoffs and expected to be a big reason why they would.

Howard had enjoyed a solid rookie season. That gave him the confidence to feel as if he could succeed in his second year. "Last year I didn't know what to expect, and I was almost running around blind out there," Howard said. "But I grew a lot. I learned how the NBA works, especially the business side with coaches getting fired and players getting traded. It made me realize that you have to take everything you do on the court seriously."[3]

Howard grabs a rebound against San Antonio in 2006.

After narrowly missing the playoffs in 2004–05,
the Magic turned to a new coach for the 2005–06
season. They hired Brian Hill. Hill had coached the
Magic from 1993–1997 and the Vancouver Grizzlies
for a few seasons. He led the Magic to the NBA
Finals in 1995. Their best player then was young
center Shaquille O'Neal, whom many people
compared to Howard.

Hill immediately tried to get to know Howard and increase his role on the team. He visited the player at a family barbecue over the summer and promised that he would run much of the offense through Howard. That would be a big change from the previous season, when the Magic ran their offense mostly through Grant Hill and Steve Francis. Now Howard, who had averaged only 8.2 shots per game as a rookie, would get more opportunities on offense. He was excited about that.

"My responsibility as a player will grow this season," he said. "I need to be more aggressive to get the ball. At the other end, I have to be more aggressive defensively, denying people the ball. I'll have to be more physical this season because people are going to be pushing, holding, grabbing me more than before."[4]

Although Howard welcomed Hill's new approach to the game, he and his family did not like all of Hill's decisions. The new coach did not invite assistant Clifford Ray back. Ray had spent a lot of time helping Howard develop as a rookie. Both Howard and his father were upset that Ray would not return. Without Ray around, Howard had to take more responsibility for improving himself. How he managed his own game would influence how the Magic did in 2005–06.

A DECENT START

The Magic got off to a decent start in 2005–06. By late November they were 7–6 and riding a four-game winning streak. Howard had some big games in November. He blocked a shot by Celtics forward Mark Blount in the final seconds of a November 28 game to seal a win at Boston.

On November 16, he tallied 21 points and 20 rebounds in an 85–77 win over the Charlotte Bobcats and rival center Emeka Okafor. At nineteen, he became the youngest player in NBA history to score 20 points and pull down 20 rebounds in a single game. Howard also tallied 21 points and 16 rebounds in a November loss to LeBron James and the Cleveland Cavaliers.

Howard also displayed his trademark class. Late in a blowout win over the Portland Trail Blazers, he launched a long three-point shot for fun. The shot missed, but that was not the point. It was not a necessary shot to take and thus disrespectful, he said. So he promised to apologize to the Blazers.

ANOTHER MID-SEASON SLIDE

Orlando's season, however, quickly turned sour. Forward Grant Hill, an All-Star the season before, suffered a sports hernia injury and missed sixty-one games. Guard Steve Francis often hogged the ball on offense. His presence took away minutes and scoring chances from second-year point guard Jameer Nelson.

The Magic could have coped with that if the team was winning. But it was not. Orlando was only 18–23 at the midpoint of the season. The Magic were hovering near the eighth and final playoff spot in the Eastern Conference.

Howard was often inconsistent on offense. And although he was evolving into a premier shot-blocker and rebounder, he needed to work on his other defensive skills.

After the All-Star break in February, Orlando's season got worse. The Magic lost eighteen of twenty games between January 26 and March 6, 2006. Magic officials decided to act. The team clearly was not going to the playoffs this season. It had young players such as Howard and Nelson to build around.

JAMEER NELSON FILE

Size: **Six feet; 190 pounds**
Position: **Guard**
College: **St. Joseph's**
NBA teams: **Orlando Magic (since 2004)**
Career notes: **Averaged career-high 5.6 assists per game for Magic in 2007–08; named 2003–04 National NCAA Player of the Year**

Francis was holding those young players back, they thought. So they decided it was the right time to put the Magic in the hands of its young players. The franchise would sacrifice winning games now in an attempt to build a championship-caliber team later.

In late February 2006, the Magic traded Francis to the New York Knicks. All they got in return was two veteran players they did not plan to put in the lineup. The point, however, was to get rid of the veteran Francis and his high salary so that the Magic would have money to sign new players as free agents later.

"The things we've done might look frantic, but they are calculated moves," Otis Smith said. "What this does is magnify [Howard's role] a little bit more. It will allow him to be more vocal than in the past, allow him to say, 'This is mine, and I'm going to take it.'"[5]

AN EXCELLENT FINISH

The Magic did not expect their trades to pay off during the 2005–06 season. But they did. Orlando sat at 20–40 in late March and went 16–6 after that. Nelson, the other player Orlando had chosen in the first round of the 2004 draft, played well. He had averaged 8.7 points and 3 assists per game as a rookie coming off the bench. He almost doubled those averages in his first twenty-one games as a starter in 2006, after the Francis trade.

Howard (left) fights for the ball with Cleveland's LeBron James during a 2007 exhibition game.

Howard was also a big reason why the Magic went on the late-season tear. He posted double-doubles in sixteen of Orlando's final twenty games. He finished as the Eastern Conference's leader in rebounding, averaging 12.5 per game. Only Kevin

Garnett had more rebounds per game in the NBA (12.7).

Despite the good finish, Howard still had plenty of work to do in his quest to become an elite player. But the solid ending to the 2005–06 season gave Howard and the Magic hope for the future. Shortly before the season ended, the team extended the contracts of Howard and Nelson through the 2007–08 season.

In June, Howard attended the NBA Finals to watch the Miami Heat play the Dallas Mavericks. He enjoyed the loud crowds, high level of play, and theatrics. The whole atmosphere motivated him. Orlando had finished only four games out of a playoff spot. But Francis was gone, and Grant Hill was past his prime and often hurt. So the Magic's chances of qualifying for the postseason the next year were up to their youngest players.

Howard was not only OK with that, he relished the pressure. And he was ready to put it work to improve his skills. Despite showing glimpses of being one of the top young players in the NBA, he was not satisfied with how he had played during his second season.

> **"I want to get this organization back to where it was when Shaq and Penny [Hardaway] were here . . ."**
>
> —*Dwight Howard*

PENNY HARDAWAY FILE

Size: Six feet seven inches; 195 pounds

Position: Guard

College: Memphis State

NBA teams: Orlando Magic (1993–1999); Phoenix Suns (1999–2003); Toronto Raptors (2003–04); New York Knicks (2003–2006); Miami Heat (2007–08)

Career notes: Named to NBA's All-Rookie team with the Magic in 1993–94; named All-NBA in 1994–95 and 1995–96; four-time NBA All-Star; played for 1996 United States Olympic team that won the gold medal

"I just don't think I've been as good as I should be," Howard said. "Offensively, I haven't been as aggressive as I want to be."[6]

It was time for Howard to assert himself as a team leader, he knew. In his third season he would have to be even better if he wanted to reach his goal of being the Magic's franchise cornerstone. "I see myself playing the rest of my career here in Orlando," Howard said. "I want to be part of the foundation of this team. I want to get this organization back to what it was when Shaq and Penny [Hardaway] were here, where every game was full and people were excited to go watch the Magic."[7]

6

PLAYOFF TIME

Dwight Howard stood on the free throw line inside Amway Arena. It was a Sunday afternoon in Orlando, April 15, 2007. The Orlando Magic led the visiting Boston Celtics only 87–86 with just 4.6 seconds left to play. Howard bent his knees, lifted the ball, and fired it toward the rim. It went in.

Howard's free throw extended the Magic's lead to two points. They did not allow Boston to score again. Orlando won the game 88–86. More importantly, the Magic clinched a playoff berth for the first time in four years. Howard finished the game with 10 points and 14 rebounds. He would now get to play in the NBA's postseason for the first time. "It seemed like a long time," Howard said. "But we finally made it. Now it's a new season."[1]

Howard and the Magic secured a playoff spot in 2007 with a win against the Celtics.

Making the NBA Playoffs was a good way to cap Howard's third NBA season. It began just after he had played with elite players on the U.S. national team over the summer. It ended with Howard playing against other elite players, in a first-round playoff series against the Detroit Pistons.

In between those events, Howard continued to improve his game. He started to show real signs of a potential that would make him one of the top players in the NBA one day.

USA BASKETBALL

During his second NBA season, Howard had been selected to join the U.S. national basketball team for the next two years. He was invited to try out for the national team that would play in the 2006 World Championships. He could also play in the 2007 Olympic qualifying tournament and 2008 Olympics. He was thrilled. "I'm just thankful USA Basketball has picked me," Howard said.[2]

The national team picked Howard because coaches thought he would grow into a top inside player. They thought he could help the team a lot in the 2007 and 2008 tournaments. The team did not expect much from Howard in the 2006 tournament. With the pressure off him, he was able to head to the International Basketball Federation (FIBA) World Championships in Japan and play freely and enjoy himself. The U.S. only needed Howard to do what he did best: rebound and block shots.

Howard also found another role: team jester. On the team bus after a win in the tournament, for example, he picked up a microphone and did an imitation of Shaquille O'Neal. His teammates loved it.

The World Championships was a great experience. Howard came off the bench at power forward and center. He earned about fourteen minutes per game in the forty-minute contests (which were shorter than the forty-eight-minute NBA games).

Howard drives for Team USA against the Virgin Islands during the 2007 FIBA Americas Championship.

THE 2006 BASKETBALL WORLD CHAMPIONSHIPS

Champion: **Spain**

Runner-up: **Greece**

Third place: **United States**

He averaged 7.3 points, 4.6 rebounds, and 1.3 blocks in nine games.

Howard helped Team USA win its division in the preliminary round with a 5–0 record. Team USA advanced to the tournament semifinals against Greece but lost 101–95. The U.S. then bounced back to beat Argentina 96–81 to take third place.

Howard benefited from the experience. Being around top NBA players such as LeBron James, Carmelo Anthony, and Dwayne Wade showed Howard how the star players approached the game. "I had a great experience, being the youngest player," Howard said. "I was able to see how the veterans

TEAM USA AT THE 2006 WORLD CHAMPIONSHIPS

Dwight Howard (Orlando Magic)

Carmelo Anthony (Denver Nuggets)

LeBron James (Cleveland Cavaliers)

Joe Johnson (Atlanta Hawks)

Kirk Hinrich (Chicago Bulls)

Antawn Jamison (Washington Wizards)

Shane Battier (Memphis Grizzlies)

Dwayne Wade (Miami Heat)

Chris Paul (New Orleans/Oklahoma City Hornets)

Chris Bosh (Toronto Raptors)

Brad Miller (Sacramento Kings)

Elton Brand (Los Angeles Clippers)

control their teams and [see myself] being one of the leaders for the Magic—how I need to step up and be a leader."[3]

That was an important lesson for Howard, Magic officials said.

BACK TO ORLANDO

Howard took that experience with him when he returned to the Magic to start the 2006–07 season. He had high goals. He expected to display a better all-around offensive game, grab more rebounds, and play tougher defense in the paint. "What leads you to believe he's going to be a great one, if not one of the best, is his work ethic and his attitude," said Mike D'Antoni, a Team USA assistant coach. "His Achilles' heel right now is his shooting, but he's practicing hard on it every day and getting better at it."[4]

The Magic had not made the playoffs since 2003. Howard thought they could in 2006–07. Not only that, he figured they could contend for an NBA title. He said so just before the season.

Howard's prediction drew snickers from around the league. Orlando had not won a single postseason series since 1996, let alone the four it would need to take to capture a championship.

The Magic team that went 36–46 in 2005–06 returned with few changes. The team lost starting guard DeShawn Stevenson to the Washington

DESHAWN STEVENSON FILE

Size: Six feet five inches; 218 pounds

Position: Guard

NBA teams: Utah Jazz (2000–2004); Orlando Magic (2004–2006); Washington Wizards (2006–2009)

Career notes: Averaged career-high 14 points per game in 2007–08; averaged 11 points per game for the Magic in 2005–06

Wizards. It added only guard Keith Bogans in free agency and drafted guard J. J. Redick out of Duke. Howard pointed to the Magic's 16–6 finish to 2005–06. He thought that solid play would carry over to the start of 2006–07.

It did. Orlando started 13–4. Brian Hill was named Eastern Conference Coach of the Month for November. Forward Darko Milicic played well and forward Grant Hill was finally healthy and leading the team. But Howard was the biggest reason why the Magic played so well early on. He averaged an NBA-high 13.6 rebounds per game and contributed 17.1 points in November. He posted double-doubles in seven straight games. That play earned him Eastern Conference Player of the Month honors.

He was drawing so much attention under the basket that teammates got open looks to shoot on the perimeter. That helped the Magic shoot 38 percent from the three-point range through their first fifteen games, making them fourth-best in the NBA.

While Howard was still developing an offensive skill set, by early in his third season he was already one of the NBA's top rebounders. He was becoming a special NBA player, and people noticed. "It is the rare emerging young A-lister who not only claims to be more concerned with his rebounding than his scoring, but then backs it up with his play," L. Jon Wertheim wrote on *SI.com*.[5]

Howard also displayed an improved game on offense. He had developed consistent jump hook and drop step moves. He scored at least 20 points to go along with 20 rebounds in a game four times in the first few weeks of the season. "He could be one of those guys who totally changes how a team plays defense against somebody in the post because he can be such a threat in so many different ways," said Magic radio analyst Will Perdue, who played center in the NBA for thirteen seasons. "They're going to have to put out a defense just for him. A lot of guys, when they get bigger, they lose their quickness. He's just as quick."[6]

Howard attributed his improvement to the work he put in over his first two seasons, especially his rookie year when he rarely got the ball inside. "It was good for me because I had to find other ways to score," he said. "Now I know how to get [the ball] off the glass and post up for the ball."[7]

Howard's standout play earned him a spot on the Eastern Conference All-Star team for the first time.

He would come off the bench at center, behind Shaquille O'Neal. He had been upset when he was not selected during his second season, so he was thrilled to be chosen this time. "I think just being able to play with the best players in the game today will build my confidence," he said.[8]

At the All-Star Weekend in Las Vegas, Howard competed in the Slam Dunk Contest but lost. In the All-Star game he scored 20 points and pulled down 11 rebounds.

MIDSEASON SLUMP, TAKE THREE

The Magic had started 2006–07 so well, but in midseason they began to fade. They lost twenty-six of thirty-eight games to fall toward the bottom of the East. Howard began to struggle, which was one reason for the team slump.

Howard had become a better player, but his offensive skills were still not above average. Teams did not have to double-team Howard down low. Opponents began sagging off of him and focused on stopping his teammates on the perimeter. Even though he was still just twenty-one, Howard was criticized by NBA players and observers.

"We're going to see now just what type of player Dwight wants to be, and where he sees himself in this league," Kevin Garnett said. "He's going to have to do his homework. He's going to have to evolve his game."[9]

Just when the Magic needed him most, though, Howard improved his play. During a five-game stretch in February, he made 52 of 64 shots (more than eighty percent) from the floor to help the Magic get back to a .500 record.

Howard helped the Magic close the season strong. The Magic was only 34–40 in early April, and it did not look like they would make the playoffs. But they won six of their final eight games to sneak in and grab the eighth—and final—spot in the East.

> 66 **We're going to see now what type of player Dwight wants to be, and where he sees himself in this league.** 99
>
> *—Kevin Garnett*

Howard's play, especially down the stretch, drew raves from around the league. He was named to the All-NBA third team, meaning he was considered to be one of the top fifteen players in the league.

PLAYOFFS!

Postseason NBA basketball is much different from the regular season. The game slows down, and half-court offense and defense is emphasized. Stars often draw foul calls at the end of close games, while young, unproven players such as Howard do not.

So it was no surprise that the 2007 NBA playoffs would not be kind to Howard and the Magic. They faced the top-seeded Detroit Pistons, who had won

64 games during the regular season and had been to four straight conference finals. Detroit swept the series, winning all four games. Howard did not play his best, averaging 15.3 points and 14.8 rebounds per game, and the Magic were never close to winning the series.

DISAPPOINTMENT RUBS OFF

Although they had lost the playoff series, Howard and the Magic were not too upset about the 2006–07 season. The Magic had finally returned to the playoffs. Howard made his first All-Star game. He had become a top NBA rebounder and began to make moves more consistently on offense. For the second straight season, his scoring average increased over the previous year. Many people thought he was just scratching his potential.

Howard also continued to be one of the most popular players in the NBA. He signed autographs for hours, smiled his big smile, and often volunteered in the community. "The advice I give him is simple," said Joel Glass, a Magic employee. "'Dwight, don't change.'"[10]

As the 2006–07 season came to a close, many around the league believed that Howard had evolved into a solid person and excellent defender, but he still was not the offensive threat the Magic needed to be serious contenders. The question was: Would he ever become that threat?

BREAKTHROUGH SEASON

It was a mid-February night in New Orleans, Louisiana. Thousands of fans packed into the city's arena and eagerly awaited what Dwight Howard was going to do next. Howard was one of four contestants in the 2008 NBA Slam Dunk Contest. Already he had sent the crowd, including celebrity judges such as former Chicago Bulls guard Michael Jordan, into a frenzy with his dunks.

Now he had more great dunks to show off. As Howard prepared for his turn midway through the competition, he yanked his jersey off. He displayed the Superman shirt he was wearing underneath. He then added a cape. Fans cheered. Judges leaned forward in anticipation.

Wearing a Superman costume, Howard soars toward the basket in the 2008 NBA Slam Dunk Contest.

Howard leapt so high off the ground that he dunked the ball while his body was still a couple feet short of the hoop. The "Superman Dunk" was a hit. Howard used it as a springboard to winning the Slam Dunk Contest that night. The next day, everyone was talking about his move. "Dwight Howard was unbelievable," said David Thompson, a former pro basketball player who competed in the first Slam Dunk Contest in the 1970s.[1]

The Slam Dunk Contest was just one of many great moments in a breakthrough 2007–08 season for Howard. Howard was named a first-team All-NBA player and became the youngest player in NBA history to lead the league in rebounding. In addition, his Orlando Magic won its first playoff series in twelve years and captured the Southeast Division.

ANOTHER SUMMER WITH TEAM USA

The 2007–08 season essentially began for Howard in the summer of 2007. After the Magic lost to the Pistons in the playoffs in spring 2007, Howard joined the national team to compete in a qualifying tournament for the 2008 Summer Olympics.

Howard was much better for Team USA than he had been during the 2006 World Championships. He made nine starts in ten games at the tournament in Las Vegas, Nevada, earning 16.5 minutes per game (Games were again forty minutes long, as opposed to forty-eight in the NBA). He led Team USA in rebounding (**5.3** per game) and averaged 10 points (sixth on the team).

In a 127–100 preliminary round win over Mexico in late August, Howard made 9 of 10 field goal attempts and scored 19 points. Howard then led the team in rebounding in two straight single-elimination games. He pulled down 9 rebounds in a 91–76 win over Argentina in the quarterfinals and 6 in a 135–91 semifinal victory over Puerto Rico.

Howard split time at center with Amare Stoudemire. Their defense, size, and athleticism set the tone for Team USA. They were the dominant team in the qualifying tournament, winning every game by at least fifteen points. The United States qualified for the Olympics, which would be in Beijing, China, the following summer.

MAGIC TIME

Howard was excited for the Olympics, but that could wait. When he returned from Las Vegas, he concentrated on helping the Magic prepare for the

2007 AMERICAS OLYMPIC QUALIFYING STANDINGS

Champion: **United States**
Runner-up: **Argentina**
Third place: **Puerto Rico**
Fourth place: **Brazil**

upcoming NBA season. Howard was very optimistic. Since qualifying for the playoffs for the first time in four years, the Magic had made big moves in the offseason. Grant Hill's huge contract expired, which gave the Magic a lot of money to spend in free agency.

The club chose to sign Rashard Lewis, a twenty-seven-year-old forward who had been an All-Star with the Seattle Sonics. Lewis was a tall, athletic player known for his excellent shooting range. The Magic figured his outside touch would complement Howard's inside game. Lewis signed an enormous deal: $118 million over six years.

Howard was excited about the move to sign Lewis. "I feel like we have the team here to someday win a championship," Howard said. "And I really feel that way now that we've added Rashard. We just have to grow together."[2]

The Magic also signed Howard to an extension for $85 million over five years. Early in the season

RASHARD LEWIS FILE

Size: **Six feet ten inches; 230 pounds**

Position: **Forward**

NBA teams: **Seattle Sonics (1998–2007); Orlando Magic (2007–2009)**

Career notes: **Averaged 18.2 points per game for the Magic in 2007–08; named to Western Conference All-Star team in 2005 and Eastern Conference All-Star team in 2009.**

STAN VAN GUNDY FILE

Coached Miami Heat (2003–2005) and Orlando Magic (2007–2009)

Career record: **223–126**

Career notes: **Led the Magic to NBA Finals in 2008–09**

they traded for guard Maurice Evans. They let Hill go to the Phoenix Suns, while forward Darko Milicic signed with the Memphis Grizzlies.

The club was not done there. Also, in the offseason, management fired coach Brian Hill and replaced him with Stan Van Gundy. Van Gundy had led the Miami Heat to the Eastern Conference Finals in 2005 and had coached another dominant big man similar to Howard: Shaquille O'Neal.

The Magic added four new assistants to Van Gundy's staff, including Patrick Ewing, a former NBA All-Star center with the New York Knicks. Ewing was charged with helping Howard reach his potential at center. "In his progression of his game and career, Dwight has to develop a jump shot, a turnaround jump shot, a face-the-basket jump shot," Ewing said. "He's not going to be able to just overpower people. It's my job to help him develop that part of his game."[3]

Ewing and Howard immediately bonded. "He's the perfect guy. He can post, he can shoot and he had to deal with double teams," Howard said. "I have my own little style. I don't play like Patrick Ewing, but the stuff he does I can put it into my game."[4]

While the club around him changed, so did Howard. He really wanted to get better at shooting. So he worked privately with shooting coach Charles Richardson to extend his range. Opponents noticed right away. "Dwight's gotten much better as a player over the summer," Atlanta Hawks coach Mike Woodson said. "He's making free throws, and he's got that little face-up jump shot that he's making that we didn't see last year."[5]

In the preseason, Howard also worked hard at his passing, especially passing out of double-teams in the post.

Van Gundy was excited for the season to start. He had never coached a player quite like Howard before. He was pleased with how Howard looked

PATRICK EWING FILE

Size: **Seven feet; 240 pounds**

Position: **Center**

NBA teams: **New York Knicks (1985–2000); Seattle Sonics (2000–01); Orlando Magic (2001–02)**

Career notes: **Led Knicks to 1994 NBA Finals; 11-time NBA All-Star; 1985–86 NBA Rookie of the Year; named to 1989–90 All-NBA team** during training camp. He planned to take advantage of Howard's skills and the Magic's acquisition of Lewis by playing at a faster pace.

As the regular season began in late October, everything was set for the Magic to have a breakthrough season.

WASTING NO TIME

The Magic started the season on fire. They won sixteen of their first twenty games, despite playing twelve of those twenty contests on the road. They marched to a commanding early lead in the Southeast Division. They reminded some people of the Magic team in 1994–95 that played in the NBA Finals.

"There is so much of a resemblance," said Nick Anderson, a guard on the 1994–95 team. "I really think this team could become like our team of '94–'95. There are lots of similarities, starting with Dwight and Shaq."[6]

Howard was a big reason for the Magic's good start. In December, he averaged 21.7 points and 16.1 rebounds per game. He posted 14 double-doubles in 15 games. He tallied 21 rebounds and 4 blocks in a win over the Charlotte Bobcats, holding rival Emeka Okafor to only 4 points. He was named Eastern Conference Player of the Month.

Howard had good chemistry with his teammates. Hedo Turkoglu took advantage of open space created by opponents' focusing on Howard inside. Turkoglu would average career highs in points (19.5), rebounds (5.7), and assists (5) per game for the season. He would be named the NBA's Most Improved Player.

Howard also blended well with his new coach. Van Gundy pushed him and he responded. "Even as well as he's playing, we're asking him to do more," Van Gundy said. "I've pushed him hard and demanded a lot. He has accepted that. He understands that as the best player more is always going to be expected and we're probably never going to be satisfied."[7]

Howard also responded to another Van Gundy challenge: The coach made Howard and guard Jameer Nelson, also in his fourth season, the team captains for the season.

Howard again could draw from his experience on the national team for leadership skills. He had admired how players such as LeBron James, New Jersey Nets guard Jason Kidd, and Los Angeles Lakers guard Kobe Bryant sacrificed their games to help the team. "For us to come together and fall into different roles showed a lot of leadership," Howard said. "Instead of worrying about, 'I need to get a certain amount of minutes,' they did their job and did it well."[8]

SHOWING TRUE CHARACTER

The 2007–08 season was not all smooth for Howard. He did have one problem with his new coach. But the way he overcame that obstacle showed his true character.

During a close midseason game against the Cleveland Cavaliers, Howard complained about not getting the ball enough in the fourth quarter. Van Gundy benched him for a couple minutes. After the game, Van Gundy blasted Howard. He said Howard was concentrating too much on scoring and not enough on defense and rebounding.

Howard responded to the benching and Van Gundy's comments by listening to the coach. "I got frustrated a little bit," he said. "I got to do what's right for my team. They need me to be focused on what I can do. . . . If I don't do those things we're going to be a mediocre team."[9]

Two nights later, in the Magic's next game, Howard proved he was over the incident. Against the

Denver Nuggets he pulled down a career-high 24 rebounds, scored 23 points, and blocked 2 shots. The Magic won 109–98. "Coach said what he had to say. He felt I wasn't focused in the right areas," Howard said. "So I just came back and played as hard as I could. . . . He will never have to question my effort again."[10]

It was the Magic's last game before the All-Star break. They were 33–21, first in the division. Howard for the first time was named a starter in the All-Star game. "It's very big," he said. "We have some great centers in this league, Shaquille O'Neal being one of them, and to have the possibility to be able to start over him, it's an honor."[11]

After winning the slam dunk contest, the next day Howard played a game-high 30 minutes in the All-Star Game. He tallied 16 points and 9 rebounds to help the East win 134–128.

> "Coach . . . felt I wasn't focused in the right areas. So I just came back and played as hard as I could. . . . He will never have to question my effort again.
>
> —Dwight Howard

STRETCH RUN

Howard and the Magic did not suffer any letdown after the All-Star break. Orlando won eleven of thirteen games during one crucial stretch in February and March. The Magic clinched the Southeast Division when the second-place Washington Wizards lost a March 31 game to the Utah Jazz.

Howard was thrilled. It was the Magic's first division title since 1999. The club would have home court in the first round of an NBA playoff series for the first time since that year, when they had lost a series to the Philadelphia 76ers.

Howard was a big reason why the Magic had won the division. He averaged a team-high 20.7 points and 14.2 rebounds. He became the youngest player in NBA history to win the league rebounding title. He was named first-team All-NBA. Van Gundy was so impressed, he compared Howard to Shaq. He said Howard should be considered for the Most Valuable Player award.

"As good as his numbers are, they aren't really what indicates how good he is," Van Gundy said. "I think he definitely deserves to be in the conversation (for MVP). . . . To me, the two criteria are great individual season and team success. Dwight's had a heck of an individual year and the team's having success."[12]

Howard, already one of the NBA's top rebounders, was now a consistent scorer. He still lacked a dependable jump shot, but his athleticism, height, and improving knowledge of the NBA game made him lethal. "Dwight Howard is a supremely tough match-up because he's one of the fastest big men in

2008 NBA REGULAR SEASON REBOUNDING LEADERS

1. Dwight Howard (Orlando Magic): 1,161
2. Marcus Camby (Denver Nuggets): 1,037
3. Tyson Chandler (New Orleans Hornets): 928
4. Al Jefferson (Minnesota Timberwolves): 915
5. Tim Duncan (San Antonio Spurs): 881

the NBA," said Brendan Haywood, a center for the Washington Wizards. "He's one of the strongest, and he's one of the most athletic when it comes to jumping. He makes it tough on you because you can't take any possessions off. He's a highlight waiting to happen."[13]

BACK IN THE PLAYOFFS

The Magic drew the Toronto Raptors in the first round of the playoffs. Howard needed to play near his best for the Magic to win the series. Game 1 was April 20 in Orlando. Howard posted a game-high 25 points and 22 rebounds as Orlando built an early twenty-point lead. The Magic cruised to a 114–100 win.

The Magic jumped out to a 35–18 lead after one quarter in Game 2, but Toronto rallied. The game came down to the end. Twice in the final minute, Howard made key defensive plays. First he blocked a shot by Toronto All-Star forward Chris Bosh.

Later Toronto had the ball trailing by one point with seconds to play. The Raptors drew up a play for forward Chris Bosh. The All-Star forward got the ball and thought about driving. But he saw Howard in the paint, blocking his path. Howard held his ground. So Bosh settled for a jump shot. His attempt missed, and Orlando escaped with a 104–103 win. Howard was again dominant. He'd tallied a game-high 29 points and 20 rebounds.

Toronto won Game 3 108–94, but the Magic responded with a 106–94 win in Game 4. Howard had a game-high 16 rebounds and 8 blocks and added 19 points in the victory.

The win allowed the Magic to return to Orlando for Game 5 with a 3–1 lead in the series. They needed only to win that game to take the series. They did. Howard tallied a game-high 21 points and 21 rebounds as the Magic won 102–92.

ROUND TWO

The Magic faced a much larger challenge in the second round: the Detroit Pistons. Detroit had

2008 ALL-NBA TEAM

Dwight Howard (Orlando Magic center)

LeBron James (Cleveland Cavaliers)

Kobe Bryant (Los Angeles Lakers)

Kevin Garnett (Boston Celtics)

Chris Paul (New Orleans Hornets)

played in five straight Eastern Conference Finals. It was a poised, confident, deep team. The Magic were also confident but lacked Detroit's experience.

Detroit won the first two games at home. After the Magic won a blowout in Game 3, the Pistons won the next two games to take the series. Detroit won the two close games in the series, including a one-point win in Game 4 when Turkoglu missed a shot just before the final buzzer. In that game, Howard scored only 8 points. He only got one touch on offense in the final three minutes. He blamed himself for the loss.

The Magic were frustrated with the series loss. At times, they looked to be much more talented than the Pistons. Howard was so distraught he did not sleep the night after Game 5. "No doubt, we are as good as Detroit," Howard said. "But things didn't happen the way we planned it. It came down to a lot of mental mistakes that we made. We could have as easily won the series as we just lost it."[14]

HAPPY WITH PROGRESS

Despite losing to the Pistons in the playoffs for the second straight season, the Magic were satisfied with the 2007–08 season. It had been a year of break-throughs. The team's core of players was still young and improving. They were confident for the future.

"I think we have a great chance to win a champi-onship within this span of our contracts—not only

Magic assistant Patrick Ewing (left) talks with Howard before a 2009 playoff game.

one, but two," Lewis said. "It's most definitely the start of something special here."[15]

Howard, now one of the top players in the NBA, was especially young. He was only twenty-two when the season ended. Howard was not yet peaking. That was the amazing thing. He was already one of the elite players in the NBA, in only his fourth season out of high school. But he could still improve.

"I just want to see him being the dominant player of his generation," Van Gundy said. "He's still got a long way to go in his development, which is scary— if you're another team."[16]

A REAL ROLE MODEL

Throughout his career Dwight Howard has been known as one of the most generous, outgoing players in the NBA. Howard has his own charity, often volunteers in the community, and hosts his own basketball camps to help kids improve at the game.

Howard's foundation is called the Dwight D. Howard Foundation. He founded it in 2004 when he started playing in the NBA. Howard, along with his parents, Dwight Sr. and Sheryl, run the foundation. Their goal, according to the foundation Web site, is: "To empower young people to reach their highest potential by initiating and supporting

WHAT IS THE DWIGHT D. HOWARD FOUNDATION?

The foundation is Dwight Howard's charity, which raises money with camps and a prayer breakfast to help kids in Atlanta and Orlando. It was founded in 2004.

community-based programs that promote the education and to strengthen family relationships of all of America's children."[1]

With the money the foundation raises, it has awarded scholarships for students to attend Southwest Atlanta Christian Academy—where Howard went to school—and Lovell Elementary School and Memorial Middle School in Orlando, Florida. Key fund-raising events for the charity include the camps and a prayer breakfast. The first camp took place in the summer of 2004, just after Howard had graduated from high school. It hosted 162 kids for five days of basketball and educational sessions.

A FREQUENT VOLUNTEER

Howard has also helped in the community in other ways. After Hurricane Katrina devastated the Gulf Coast in the southeastern United States, Howard donated money to help people there recover. In 2008, Howard joined Orlando Magic teammates, Orlando's mayor, and other community leaders to help build a playground at Orlando's Santa Barbara Apartments.

"If the playground brings a smile to the faces of all the kids here, that's better than any dunk, winning any slam-dunk contest, could be," he said. "It's good for everyone."[2]

For his efforts in the community, Howard earned the Rich & Helen DeVos Community Enrichment Award in 2005. The award, which is named in honor of the Magic owners, recognizes a Magic player who has dedicated his efforts off the court for the purpose of enhancing others' lives, according to a report from the DeVos charity. Howard was nominated for the award again

> **"If the playground brings a smile to the faces of all the kids here, that's better than . . . winning any slam-dunk contest, could be."**
>
> *—Dwight Howard*

WHAT IS THE RICH & HELEN DEVOS COMMUNITY ENRICHMENT AWARD?

It is an annual award given to an Orlando Magic player who helps others in the community. It is named to honor Magic owner Rich DeVos and his wife.

Howard claps hands with children on the Great Wall of China in 2006.

the next year, but teammate Bo Outlaw won it that year. The DeVos charity officials spoke highly of Howard when it announced that Outlaw had won in 2006.

"[Howard's] love for children didn't go unnoticed as he volunteered much of his time to the youth in Central Florida and his hometown of Atlanta.

87

Howard plays with a boy during the 2007 Special Olympics basketball clinic in Macau.

He advised youngsters that hard work and faith will bring you to the top. He continues his community outreach touching a variety of groups," the DeVos charity wrote in 2006.[3]

Howard hosted another youth camp in August 2008, just days after he returned from the Olympics in China. He could have been at home resting and recovering from his jet lag, but he preferred to spend time with local kids. "It's great being around the kids and just getting to come back to the States," Howard said. "I just missed it so much and you just appreciate life, being in China."[4]

Howard mentored some older kids earlier that summer. He also took part in several events for the NBA's Read to Achieve events, encouraging kids to read. Howard and NBA players Bobby Simmons and Charlie Bell also attended the NBA Players Association Camp and answered questions from high school players. Even though he has been in the NBA for only a few seasons, he has already made a big mark on communities with his foundation and generosity.

WHAT IS READ TO ACHIEVE?

Read to Achieve is an NBA community program that encourages kids to read. Many NBA players volunteer to visit schools and read to kids for the program.

9

OLYMPIC GOLD

About a dozen American basketball players stood near center court inside the Olympic basketball arena in Beijing, China. Wearing matching navy blue jerseys with red trim and white letters, they raised their hands high in the air and saluted a cheering crowd.

A few minutes later, these players on the U.S. men's team received the ultimate honor: Each bent his head while an Olympic gold medal was placed around his neck. The players were rewarded for winning the tournament at the 2008 Olympics. They had just defeated Spain on a late August evening in the championship game.

Dwight Howard was one of the players receiving a gold medal that day. In the medal ceremony,

2008 OLYMPICS MEN'S BASKETBALL TOURNAMENT

Champion: **United States**
Runner-up: **Spain**
Third place: **Argentina**

he stood next to teammates Chris Bosh and Kobe Bryant, grinning as his medal hung around his neck. He held a bouquet of flowers.

Howard was part of a crucial victory for USA Basketball. The win restored the United States as the top basketball power in the world for the first time in eight years. Team USA had lost international tournaments in 2002, 2004, and 2006 after winning every international competition but one since 1972.

Howard was a big reason behind the national team's success in 2008. He started at center in the Olympic tournament. Along with Bosh, he controlled the paint on defense, pulled down rebounds, and offered inside scoring. The 2008 Olympics was a coronation of Howard's effort in international basketball. It marked the third straight summer Howard played for Team USA and the second straight summer that he had helped the United States win a key tournament.

From left, Chris Bosh, Howard, LeBron James, and
Carlos Boozer show off their Olympic gold medals.

GETTING TO CHINA

Team USA had easily won the 2007 Olympic qualifying tournament, but the Olympic Games were
something else. Team USA had begun preparing for
the 2008 Olympics a few years earlier. After Team
USA was embarrassed by finishing sixth at the 2002
World Championships and third at the 2004
Olympics, USA Basketball hired former Phoenix Suns
general manager Jerry Colangelo to find the right
players to get the United States back on top.

Colangelo, along with head coach Mike Krzyzewski and assistants Nate McMillan and Mike D'Antoni, wanted talented players who had high character and would work hard. Howard fit that mold. In early 2006, he was one of twenty-four players selected to try out for the team.

Many people criticized Howard's selection. At the time he was only in his second NBA season. He was not yet an All-Star. He was a raw player with limited offensive skills playing for a lousy NBA team. Yet Colangelo expected Howard to improve. He thought by the time the 2008 Olympics rolled around, Howard would be a great player.

Colangelo was right. Howard was an All-Star Game starter and All-NBA player in the 2007–08 season. By the summer of 2008, he was one of the top big men in the game, which made him a legitimate threat on the 2008 U.S. Olympic team.

Howard was excited about playing in the Olympics. After the 2007–08 NBA season ended, he got a couple months off and then joined the U.S.

JERRY COLANGELO FILE

- Managing director of the U.S. men's national team; elected chairman of USA Basketball's Board of Directors for 2009–2012
- Held various roles for Phoenix Suns, including general manager, coach, and president
- Career notes: Named NBA Executive of the Year in 1976, 1981, 1989, 1993

> **❝It's the Olympics. I represent something bigger and better than myself.❞**
>
> —*Dwight Howard*

team for training camp. The team headed to China in early August.

"It's the Olympics. I represent something bigger and better than myself. It's a chance to do something incredible," Howard said. "I just want to represent my country. I never had a chance to do it before. This is my chance to do something good for my country."[1]

GOING FOR THE GOLD

Howard was the first player to touch the ball for the Team USA in the Olympics. He tipped off in the opening game against Yao Ming, the center for host China who also played for the Houston Rockets. Many observers thought China would have an edge in the post because it had the seven-foot, six-inch Yao and seven-foot center Yi Jianlian. Howard, at six feet eleven inches, was Team USA's tallest player.

MIKE KRZYZEWSKI FILE

- Coach: Duke (since 1980)
- Career notes: Led Duke to NCAA titles in 1991, 1992 and 2001; led Team USA to title in 2008 Summer Olympics

But Howard held his own against the Chinese giants. Team USA started the tournament well. It beat China 101–70. Then it defeated Angola 97–76, Greece 92–69, Spain 119–82, and Germany 106–57 in its other preliminary-round games. Team USA won its division in the preliminary round with a perfect 5–0 record.

Howard scored 13 points against China, 14 against Angola, and 10 against Spain. He pulled down a team-high 6 rebounds against Greece. His best game came against Germany, when he tallied a team-high 22 points and 10 rebounds.

In the single-elimination round, Team USA beat Australia 116–85 in the quarterfinals and Argentina 101–81 in the semifinals. Howard had 8 points and 7 rebounds against Australia and 10 points and 9 rebounds against Argentina.

The championship game was set for August 24 against Spain. Team USA had crushed Spain earlier, but the Spanish played much better with the gold medal on the line. The game was tight in the fourth quarter, but Kobe Bryant made late clutch shots. Team USA survived a furious Spanish rally and held on to win 118–107. The U.S. players were ecstatic, including Howard. He had 8 points and 5 rebounds in the win.

Howard was one of the dominant big men of the tournament. He performed well against standout forwards and centers such as Yao and Yi of China,

Howard, right, embraces Kobe Bryant after winning the gold medal at the 2008 Olympics.

Chris Kaman of Germany, and Pau and Marc Gasol of Spain. Howard averaged 10.9 points and 5.8 rebounds in 8 games. Only Bosh had more rebounds for Team USA.

2008 OLYMPICS

Team USA leaders after all eight games:
- Rebounding: Chris Bosh (49); Dwight Howard (46)
- Scoring: Dwayne Wade (128); LeBron James (124); Kobe Bryant (120); Carmelo Anthony (92); Dwight Howard (87)

Overall it was a great experience for Howard. He spent a few weeks in China. He joined his superstar Team USA teammates in playing cards and watching other Olympic events such as boxing, swimming, and the U.S. women's basketball team's games. "They treated us like the Beatles over there," he said. "It was ridiculous. Everywhere you went was just a crowd of people. And the people there are so great. They're disciplined, they work really hard and they love taking pictures. Everybody's got a camera, so all they did was take a lot of pictures."[2]

After the tournament Howard was so excited that he immediately said he would like to stay with the national team and play in the 2012 Olympics, which will be in London, England. "I would love to be back," he said.[3]

CONFERENCE CHAMPIONS

Dwight Howard stood at the free throw line inside Orlando's Amway Arena on a late spring Saturday night. The Magic was hosting the Cleveland Cavaliers in Game 6 of the 2009 Eastern Conference Finals in front of an excited, sellout crowd. Orlando led the series 3–2. It only had to win this game to become Eastern Conference champions.

As the crowd chanted "M-V-P" late in the fourth quarter, Howard sank both free throws to give the Magic a nineteen-point lead. The crowd roared. Cleveland made a slight rally, but with just over two minutes left, Howard threw down a vicious dunk to

Howard, right, shoots over Cleveland's Zydrunas Ilgauskas in the 2009 playoffs.

extend the lead to seventeen points. The crowd went crazy.

Orlando won 103–90. The Magic clinched the series and advanced to the NBA Finals for the first time since 1995. Howard, in his fifth season, would already be playing in his first NBA Finals.

STUPENDOUS SEASON

Howard's performance in Game 6 culminated another excellent season. He scored 40 points and pulled down 14 rebounds. It marked his seventeenth double-double in eighteen playoff games.

During the regular season he was an All-NBA player for the second straight year. He again led Orlando to the Southeast Division title. He again was a dominant defender. Howard also took new steps in 2008–09. He flashed improved offensive moves, was a better free-throw shooter, and led the Magic two rounds further in the playoffs than they had gone in 2008.

BECOMING A COMPLETE PLAYER

After Howard helped the U.S. Olympic team win a gold medal in August 2008, he returned home anxious to start the NBA season. He listed high goals. He wanted to be named NBA Defensive Player of the Year and to lead the NBA in blocks for the first time. He also wanted to win an NBA title. Overall, he had a more serious approach to his career. Of his first couple seasons, Howard said, "for me, the biggest thing was being on ESPN highlights. Now it's seeing my team win."[1]

The Magic returned nearly every player from the breakthrough 2007–08 team. They added rookie guard Courtney Lee and free-agent guard Mickael Pietrus. The team was loaded.

2008–09 ALL-NBA TEAM

LeBron James (Cleveland)

Dwight Howard (Orlando)

Kobe Bryant (L.A. Lakers)

Dirk Nowitzki (Dallas)

Dwayne Wade (Miami)

The Magic got off to a great start. By the mid-point of the season they were 33–8. In January they swept the three Western Conference division leaders—San Antonio Spurs, Los Angeles Lakers, and Denver Nuggets—on the road.

Howard was again named a starter in the All-Star game. He unveiled a more consistent offensive game, which included a jump hook with both hands. He continued to block shots, grab boards, and shut down opposing centers. He was playing like one of the top players in the league and showing signs of

DID YOU KNOW?

When he was selected by fans to start the 2009 All-Star game, Howard became the first player in NBA history to earn more than 3 million votes.

DID YOU KNOW?

Anchored by Defensive Player of the Year Howard, the Magic as a team in 2008–09 finished No. 1 in defensive rebounding, No. 2 in three-point defense, and No. 3 in field goal defense in the NBA.

leadership. "He's come back a lot more mature and he is holding us all to a standard now," Magic point guard Jameer Nelson said.[2]

The Magic clinched the Southeast Division title in April and finished with a 59–23 record. It was the franchise's best mark since 1995–96, when it went 60–22. Orlando finished third in the East, just behind Cleveland (66–16) and the Boston Celtics (62–20).

Howard averaged 20.6 points and 13.8 rebounds in the regular season. He was named to the All-NBA and All-Defensive teams. He tallied 20 points and 20 rebounds in seven different games. No other NBA player got that many points and rebounds in a game more than once. And, just like he had hoped, he was named Defensive Player of the Year and led the NBA in blocks. He also led the league in rebounds for a second straight year. "It's like he can guard two guys at once, which is almost impossible to do," said 76ers forward Andre Iguodala. "He's just a freak of nature."[3]

THE 2009 POSTSEASON

Despite the Magic's improvement, the team was considered a long shot in the Eastern Conference playoffs. Cleveland, with forward LeBron James, was the heavy favorite. The defending NBA champion Boston Celtics were a close second. But as the playoffs started, Celtics All-Star forward Kevin Garnett was ruled out with an injury. Orlando's chances improved a bit.

The Magic lost the opening game of their first-round series against the Philadelphia 76ers, blowing an eighteen-point lead. But Orlando responded. The teams split Games 2 and 3. Howard then tallied 18 points and 18 rebounds as the Magic won Game 4. Howard took over in Game 5. He scored 24 points and grabbed 24 rebounds as the Magic won 91–78. "He really played the game at a high, high energy level," Magic coach Stan Van Gundy said.[4]

66 **It's like he can guard two guys at once, which is almost impossible to do. He's just a freak of nature.** 99

—Andre Iguodala

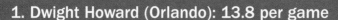

2008–09 NBA REBOUNDING LEADERS

1. Dwight Howard (Orlando): 13.8 per game
2. Troy Murphy (Indiana): 11.8
3. David Lee (New York): 11.7

Howard was such a force that he got carried away a bit. In the first quarter he accidentally hit teammate Courtney Lee in the face with his elbow. Lee had to leave the game and missed three games with a fractured sinus. He would have to wear a mask to protect the injury for the rest of the season. Later, Howard grabbed a rebound, threw out his elbows, and drilled 76ers forward Samuel Dalembert. The 76ers claimed Howard hit Dalembert on purpose, but Howard said it was accidental. The NBA suspended Howard for Game 6. Howard would learn from that mistake. The Magic won Game 6 without Howard and advanced to face Boston in the second round.

They split the first two games in Boston. In Game 3, Howard avoided a confrontation with Celtics center Kendrick Perkins. In the third quarter, Perkins committed a hard foul on Howard and then stared at him. But Howard ignored Perkins, seeking to avoid another suspension. He stayed in the game and dominated. He tallied 17 points, 14 rebounds, and 5 blocks as the Magic won to take a 2–1 series lead.

The Magic blew late leads and lost both of the next two games. Howard was frustrated. He had taken only 10 shots in the Game 5 loss. That marked the fourth time in ten postseason games that he had attempted fewer than a dozen field goals. "You've got a dominant player. Let him be dominant," he said in a news conference after the game. "I have to get the ball."[5]

Writers and analysts said Howard was being self-ish. Van Gundy and Magic general manager Otis Smith were upset that Howard took his complaints to the media instead of coming directly to them. Critics predicted the Magic would fall apart, lose Game 6, and exit the playoffs.

But Howard's outburst actually benefitted the team. The Magic listened and got the ball more to him in Game 6. He responded, tallying 23 points and 22 rebounds. He attempted 16 shots. The Magic trailed by one point late in the fourth quarter, but a Howard basket helped them rally to win 83–75. "Howard's criticism of his coach in the heat of the playoffs seemed to be an omen of impending doom," Ian Thomsen wrote in *Sports Illustrated*. "In fact, the outburst was a sign of hope. It was the long-awaited signal that Howard was ready to lead."[6]

Howard's strong play carried over to Game 7. He tallied 6 points and 5 rebounds in the first quarter as the Magic built a ten-point lead. They cruised past

2008–09 NBA BLOCKS LEADERS

1. Dwight Howard (Orlando): 2.9 per game
2. Chris Andersen (Denver): 2.5
3. Marcus Camby (L.A. Clippers): 2.1
4. Ronny Turiaf (Golden State): 2.1

2008–09 NBA ALL-DEFENSIVE TEAM

Dwight Howard (Orlando)

Kobe Bryant (L.A. Lakers)

LeBron James (Cleveland)

Chris Paul (New Orleans)

Kevin Garnett (Boston)

the Celtics 101–82. Howard had 12 points and 16 rebounds for the game. The Magic was going to the Eastern Conference Finals for the first time since 1996.

MAGIC UPSET

Orlando's opponent in the conference finals was Cleveland. The Cavaliers had the regular season MVP, LeBron James, and finished with the NBA's best regular-season record. They had swept both of their first two playoff series against the Detroit Pistons and Atlanta Hawks. They had home-court advantage. They were expected to win the series against the Magic and advance to the NBA Finals. There, most experts thought, the Cavaliers would face the Los Angeles Lakers. Then James and Kobe Bryant, thought to be the two best basketball players in the world, could square off. But Howard wanted to prove he was one of the world's elite players, too, and the Magic wanted to spoil the James-Bryant finals.

Cleveland led Game 1 by fifteen at halftime. Then the Magic took over. Howard dunked the ball so hard in one possession that he broke a shot clock. He finished with 30 points and 13 rebounds, making 14 of 20 field goals. Teammate Rashard Lewis hit a three-pointer with fifteen seconds left to give Orlando a one-point lead. When Cleveland guard Mo Williams missed a jumper at the buzzer, the Magic had a 107–106 win.

After Cleveland won Game 2 at home, the Magic won both of the next two games in Orlando. Howard made 14 of 19 free throws in Game 3 and had one of the most clutch performances of his career in Game 4. James forced overtime with two free throws in the final second. Then Howard took over. He made the first three baskets of overtime and sank two free throws to extend the Magic lead with twenty-one seconds left. He finished with 27 points and 14 rebounds as Orlando won 116–114 to take a 3–1 series lead. "Dwight showed why he's the most dominant player in the league," Magic forward Hedo Turkoglu said. "He was huge in overtime."[7]

Cleveland won Game 5, and Howard's performance in Game 6 was one of the highlights of the NBA season. Not only did he score 40 points and pull down 14 rebounds, he also made 12 of 16 free throws. His performance reminded observers of how far the twenty-three-year-old had come in only five

seasons since he was drafted out of high school. So did this statistic: In the eight games since Howard demanded the ball, he had averaged 23.8 points and led the Magic to a 6–2 mark against the top two teams in the Eastern Conference.

ON TO THE FINALS

The Magic were again heavy underdogs against the Lakers in the NBA Finals. This time they struggled. The Lakers cruised in Game 1 and won Game 2 in overtime. Howard was largely ineffective in the first two games, but he responded in Game 3. Howard scored 21 points and grabbed 14 rebounds. The Magic led 104–102 in the closing seconds, but Bryant had the ball. He drove inside. Howard stepped up and knocked the ball out of his hands. Teammate Pietrus fell on the ball and was fouled. Pietrus made both free throws, and the Magic held on to win 108–104.

But the victory only prolonged the series by a bit. Despite being in the NBA Finals, the Magic were a young, inexperienced team. Key players Howard, Turkoglu, Lewis, Lee, Nelson, and Pietrus were all thirty or younger. None had ever played in an NBA Finals. Van Gundy had not coached in one.

Dwight Howard and the Magic beat Cleveland to clinch the Eastern Conference title.

The Lakers had advanced to the Finals the year before, when the Celtics beat them. Bryant, teammate Derek Fisher, and coach Phil Jackson had won three titles together from 2000–2002.

It was only a matter of time until the Magic's inexperience hurt them. That happened in Game 4. Orlando led by twelve at halftime, but the Lakers outscored the Magic 30–14 in the third quarter to take the lead.

The Magic responded. Howard threw down consecutive dunks late in the fourth quarter as Orlando took a five-point lead and possession of the ball in the final minute. The Lakers cut the lead to three and fouled Howard with 11.1 seconds left. Howard only needed to make one of two free throws to give the Magic a likely victory. But he missed both.

The Lakers took advantage. Fisher made a three-pointer to force overtime, and the Lakers won again. The loss crushed the Magic. They were still rattled in Game 5. They fell behind by double digits at halftime and lost 99–86. Howard especially struggled. He finished with just

> 66 **What I told Jameer is just look at it, just see how they're celebrating, and it should motivate us to want to get in the gym and get better.** 99
>
> —*Dwight Howard*

11 points and 10 rebounds. He sat on the bench for much of the game in foul trouble.

As the Lakers celebrated, most of the Magic players went to the locker room. Howard and Nelson stayed seated on the bench. They watched for several minutes as the Lakers received the championship trophy and were congratulated by NBA officials. "What I told Jameer is just look at it, just see how they're celebrating, and it should motivate us to want to get in the gym and get better," Howard said. "Our goal was within reach. We were three games away from having the NBA title. So I told him next year we've got to be even hungrier to be champions."[8]

Regardless of how the Magic would fare the next season, 2008–09 had been an excellent campaign for Howard. At only twenty-three years old, he emerged as one of the NBA's top players and proved he could carry a team deep in the playoffs. As Rod Thorn, the general manager for the New Jersey Nets, put it: "Who knows how good this kid can be?"[9]

CAREER ACHIEVEMENTS

- Led Southwest Atlanta Christian Academy to a Georgia state title in 2004

- Selected first overall in NBA Draft

- Led NBA's Eastern Conference in rebounding (12.5 per game) in 2005–06

- Selected to play for United States national team in World Championships and Olympics

- Named Eastern Conference All-Star for first time in 2007

- Named to All-NBA third team in 2007

- Named starter in All-Star Game for first time in 2008

- Won NBA Slam Dunk Contest in 2008

- Led Magic to two Southeast Division titles

- Led Magic to first playoff series win since 1996 in 2008

- Started for U.S. team that won gold medal in 2008 Olympics

- Named NBA Defensive Player of the Year in 2008–09

- Led Magic to the NBA Finals in 2009

CAREER STATISTICS

Year	Games	Points	Rebounds	Blocks	Assists	Steals
2004–05	82	981	823	136	75	77
2005–06	82	1,292	1,022	115	125	65
2006–07	82	1,443	1,008	156	158	70
2007–08	82	1,695	1,161	176	110	74
2008–09	79	1,624	1,093	231	112	77

FOR MORE INFORMATION

FURTHER READING

Phelps, Digger, with John Walters and Tim Bourret. *Basketball for Dummies*. Foster City, CA: IDG Books Worldwide, 2000.

Woods, Mark. *Basketball Legends*. St. Catherines, Ont: Crabtree, 2009.

WEB LINKS

Dwight D. Howard Foundation
http://www.dwight-howard.com/
foundationwhatwedo.html

Howard's profile on NBA.com
http://www.nba.com/playerfile/dwight_howard

Orlando Magic official site
http://www.nba.com/magic

CHAPTER NOTES

CHAPTER 1. THE RISE OF A SUPERSTAR

1. John Denton, "Magic celebrate series win," *Florida Today*, April 30, 2008, p. 1D.

2. John Denton, "That's a rap!," *Florida Today*, April 29, 2008, p. 1D.

3. Ian Thomsen, "NBA Midseason Report," *Sports Illustrated*, February 18, 2008, Vol. 108 No. 7, p. 37.

4. Chris Ballard, 'Class of the Glass," *Sports Illustrated*, January 23, 2006, Vol. 104 No. 3, p. 48.

5. Jack McCallum, "Growth Spurt," *Sports Illustrated*, December 10, 2007, Vol. 107 No. 23, p. 84.

6. Ibid.

7. Ken Hornack, "Little doubt he's 'The Man,'" *Daytona Beach News-Journal*, April 29, 2008, p. 6B

8. "Howard's 21 points, 21 boards power Magic to second round," *The Associated Press*, April 28, 2008, <http://scores.espn.go.com/nba/recap?gameId=280428019> (August 31, 2008).

9. Mike Tierney, "Next big thing still has room to improve," *New York Times*, Feb. 27, 2008, Sports, p.4.

CHAPTER 2. YOUNG DWIGHT

1. Ian Thomsen, "Higher Calling," *Sports Illustrated*, June 21, 2004, p. 56.

2. Ray Glier, "A well-grounded star," *USA Today*, November 13, 2003, p. 11C.

3. Sekou Smith, "College or NBA? That's his choice," *The Indianapolis Star*, January 20, 2004, p. 1C.

CHAPTER 3. THE LAST AMATEUR SEASON

1. Alexander Wolff, "They Got Next," *Sports Illustrated*, August 18, 2003, p. 60.

2. Mike Tierney, "The last days of youth," *Atlanta Journal-Constitution*, January 25, 2004, p. 1C.

3. Sekou Smith, "College or NBA? That's his choice," *The Indianapolis Star*, January 20, 2004, p. 1C.

4. Marc J. Spears, "Grounded for life," *Denver Post*, December 21, 2003, p. C-01.

5. Smith, January 20, 2004.

6. Spears, December 21, 2003.

7. Curtis Bunn, "Howard sets out on right path," *Atlanta Journal-Constitution*, April 15, 2004, p. 2F.

8. Mike Tierney, "Wonder Years," *Orlando Sentinel*, July 18, 2004, p. C1.

9. Chris Broussard, "6-11 Prep Star May be No. 1 in NBA Draft," *New York Times*, March 24, 2004, Sports, p. 5.

10. Roscoe Nance, "Howard counts his blessings," *USA Today*, June 24, 2004, p. 1C.

11. Ian Thomsen, "Higher Calling," *Sports Illustrated*, June 21, 2004, p. 56.

12. Eric Prisbell, "Magic Makes Howard No. 1," *Washington Post*, June 25, 2004, p. D01.

CHAPTER NOTES

CHAPTER 4. ROOKIE YEAR

1. Mike Bianchi, "Please, Dwight, Don't Lose That Winning Smile," *Orlando Sentinel*, November 16, 2004, p. D1.

2. Ibid.

3. Noel Neff, "Game On!" *Weekly Reader*, December 10, 2004, Vol. 38 No. 6, p. 12.

4. Chris Broussard, "6-11 Prep Star May be No. 1 in NBA Draft," *New York Times*, March 24, 2004, Sports, p. 5.

5. Tim Povtak, "Return Home Is Sweet For Howard," *Orlando Sentinel*, Nov. 27, 2004, p. D1.

6. Brian Schmitz, "Howard Growing Up Quickly," *Orlando Sentinel*, March 13, 2005, p. D4.

7. Ibid.

8. Brian Schmitz, "Breakthrough Performance," *Orlando Sentinel*, April 24, 2005, p. C8.

9. Ibid.

CHAPTER 5. YEAR TWO

1. Tim Povtak, "Howard rises to occasion," *Orlando Sentinel*, April 16, 2006, p. C7.

2. David Whitley, "Just wait until Howard's game grows up, too," *Orlando Sentinel*, December 8, 2005, p. D1.

3. Brian Schmitz, "Growing By Leaps and Bounds," *Orlando Sentinel*, October 9, 2005, p. D1.

4. Ibid.

5. Brian Schmitz, "Magic lock up future," *Orlando Sentinel*, March 28, 2006, p. D1.

6. Tim Povtak, "Summer To-Do List Includes New Wall," *Orlando Sentinel*, April 20, 2006, p. D9.

7. Brian Schmitz, "Howard learning from watching," *Orlando Sentinel*, June 16, 2006, p. D5.

CHAPTER 6. PLAYOFF TIME

1. Ken Hornack, "Laborious Berth," *Daytona Beach News-Journal*, April 16, 2007, 1B.

2. David DuPree, "The youth experiment," *USA Today*, July 24, 2006, p. 10C.

3. Brian Schmitz, "Howard predicts NBA title," *Orlando Sentinel*, September 27, 2006, p. C3.

4. DuPree, July 24, 2006.

5. L. Jon Wertheim, "Part man, part child," *SI.com*, March 2, 2007, <http://sportsillustrated.cnn.com/2007/writers/the_bonus/03/01/dhoward/> (August 31, 2008).

6. Roscoe Nance, "Howard makes Magic in paint," *USA Today*, November 29, 2006, p. 1C.

7. Ibid.

8. Brian Schmitz, "Howard earns first all-star nod," *Orlando Sentinel*, February 2, 2007, p. D4.

9. Tim Povtak, "When will Howard be the guy?" *Orlando Sentinel*, April 3, 2007, p. D3.

10. Wertheim, March 2, 2007.

CHAPTER NOTES

CHAPTER 7. BREAKTHROUGH SEASON

1. Oscar Dixon, "Theatrics revive dunk contest," *USA Today*, February 18, 2008, p. 7C.

2. Tim Povtak, "1-2 Punch," *Orlando Sentinel*, July 13, 2007, p. D1.

3. Brian Schmitz, "Howard schooled by NBA legend," *Orlando Sentinel*, October 7, 2007, p. C3.

4. Ibid.

5. Brian Schmitz, "Howard gets a lot of help with shot," *Orlando Sentinel*, October 10, 2007, p. D1.

6. Brian Schmitz, "Sizzlin'," *Orlando Sentinel*, December 5, 2007, p. D1.

7. Roscoe Nance, "Main Magic act at center," *USA Today*, November 28, 2007, p. 1C.

8. Ibid.

9. Brian Schmitz, "Family Feud," *Orlando Sentinel*, February 12, 2008, p. D1.

10. Brian Schmitz, "Answering the call," *Orlando Sentinel*, February 14, 2008, p. D1.

11. Brian Schmitz, "Howard honored by start," *Orlando Sentinel*, January 25, 2008, p. D1.

12. John Denton, "Howard: By leaps and bounds," *Florida Today*, April 4, 2008, p. 1D.

13. Roscoe Nance, "Main Magic act at center," *USA Today*, November 28, 2007, p. 1C.

14. Brian Schmitz, "Picking up the pieces," *Orlando Sentinel*, May 15, 2008, p. D1.

15. John Denton, "Magic's top goal: Improve," *Florida Today*, May 15, 2008, p. 1D.

16. Brian Schmitz, "Magic season in review," *Orlando Sentinel*, May 14, 2008, p. D4.

CHAPTER 8. A REAL ROLE MODEL

1. "What We Do." <http://www.dwight-howard.com/foundationwhatwedo.html> (July 30, 2009).

2. Tim Povtak, "Team makes time for children," *Orlando Sentinel*, March 8, 2008, p. D3.

3. "Outlaw Named 2006 Winner of Rich and Helen DeVos Community Enrichment Award," *NBA.com,* April 1, 2006, <http://www.nba.com/magic/community/Outlaw_Named_2006_Winner_of_Ri-174392-803.html> (September 24, 2009).

4. Kyle Hightower, "Howard a Bigger Man," *Orlando Sentinel*, August 31, 2008, p. C3.

CHAPTER NOTES

CHAPTER 9. OLYMPIC GOLD

1. Brian Schmitz, "Greater Glory," *Orlando Sentinel*, August 6, 2008, p. B1.

2. Kyle Hightower, "Howard a Bigger Man," *Orlando Sentinel*, August 31, 2008, p. C3.

3. Dwight Howard, "Two Wins From Gold," *NBA.com*, August 21, 2008, <www.nba.com/news/inside_presence .html#080821_01#080821_01> (August 31, 2008).

CHAPTER 10. CONFERENCE CHAMPIONS

1. Brian Schmitz, "Howard expanding list of superpowers," *Orlando Sentinel*, October 1, 2008, p. B1.

2. John Schuhmann, "Magic's Howard now setting his sights on NBA gold," *NBA.com*, December 23, 2008, <http://www.nba.com/2008/news/features/john_schuhmann/ 12/23/howard1223/index.html> (June 5, 2009).

3. Brian Schmitz, "Howard wins top defender," *Orlando Sentinel*, April 22, 2009, p. C1.

4. David Whitley, "Superman fells both friends, foes," *Orlando Sentinel*, April 29, 2009, p. C4.

5. Ian Thomsen, "Magic Show," *Sports Illustrated*, June 8, 2009, Vol. 110 No. 23, p. 42.

6. Ibid.

7. Mike Bianchi, "Howard: NBA's Dwightmare," *Orlando Sentinel*, May 27, 2009, p. C1.

8. Howard Beck, "Loss Tough for Howard, Yet He Can't Look Away," *New York Times*, June 15, 2009, p. D3.

9. Chris Ballard, "The Happy Dunker," *Sports Illustrated*, April 20, 2009, Vol. 110 No. 16, p. 36.

GLOSSARY

assist—A pass that leads to a basket.

center—The position on a basketball team responsible for controlling the area closest to the basket, often relied on for rebounding.

charity—An organization that gives to the needy.

contract—A written agreement between a player and a team stating how much the player will be paid and for how long he will play for the team.

draft—A process in which professional sports teams choose players in order.

field goal—A basket made while the clock is running in basketball; any shot other than a free throw.

free throw—Also known as a foul shot, an attempt given to teams after a foul or technical foul has been called.

forward—The position on a basketball team that is relied on for close-range shots and rebounding. Forwards are often taller than guards but shorter than centers.

Olympics—A sporting competition pitting teams from different countries against one another in multiple sports.

playoffs—A series of games between two teams to eliminate the losing team and send the winning team on to another round until just one team remains as the champion.

point guard—The position on a basketball team responsible for running the offense, usually passing to teammates and shooting when necessary.

rebound—To gain possession of the basketball after a missed shot.

rookie—A first-year professional.

shooting guard—The position on a basketball team usually responsible for shooting long-range shots.

INDEX

INDEX

T

Team USA, 57–58, 70, 76,
91, 93, 97. *See also*
Olympic Games; World
Championships

V

Van Gundy, Stan, 6, 11,
73–74, 76–77, 79, 83,
103, 105, 109

W

World Championships,
58–61, 70, 92